Ask The Right Question

By noon the wounded had been dealt with, the enemy dead stripped, bodies over the wall. Neither Harald nor Rorik thought the Wolves would try again that day, but Yosef posted two guards on sentry and the rest ate in armor.

The day dragged on. Harald saw Elaina in the doorway, beckoning, followed her up to the guestroom. Kara was folding tunics, packing saddlebags.

"We have to leave. Tonight, out the postern. Before we get Yosef and everyone killed. Help us persuade him."

"You aren't asking the right question."

Elaina looked at him, puzzled.

"Big wolfpack outside, three decades, maybe more. Some of them hunting you a month or more. You—two Ladies of no special rank or station. Yet they're storming a castle, risking war with a provincial lord to get at you. Why *you*?"

There was a long silence. It was Kara who broke it. "Your mother, Elaina."

Elaina looked up. "We agreed to leave."

"If we can't trust our friends, slit our throats now and save the folk outside the trouble."

"I should have changed the name."

Harald looked straight at her. "Want to keep that secret, child, you'd need a new face too. Think; it's a useful habit. Why do they want to take your mother's daughter?"

Comprehension. Harald spoke.

"Can't put pressure on a corpse, child. Your mother's alive. Best news I've had the past year."

Harald

David D. Friedman

HARALD

A Baen Book

Baen Publishing Enterprises
P.O. Box 1403
Riverdale, NY 10471
www.baen.com

ISBN 10: 1-4165-5537-4
ISBN 13: 978-1-4165-5537-7

Cover art by Kurt Miller
Map by Chris Porter

First Baen paperback printing, April 2008

Distributed by Simon & Schuster
1230 Avenue of the Americas
New York, NY 10020

Library of Congress Cataloging-in-Publication Data: 2005035549

Printed in the United States of America

10 9 8 7 6 5 4 3 2 1

Dedicated to

CJC

who does it better

Donald Engels

who taught me about logistics

and

Nicholas Taylor

"A good gentle man,

our world dark by his loss"

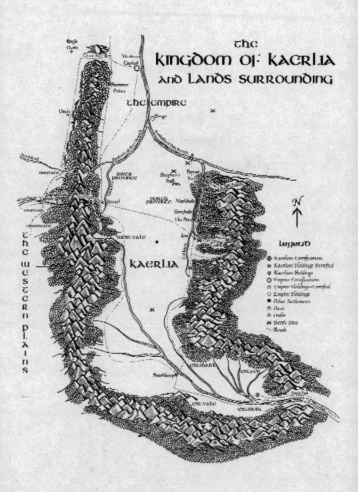

The
KINGDOM OF KAERLIA
and Lands Surrounding

THE EMPIRE

THE WESTERN PLAINS

KAERLIA

N

Legend

Kaerlian Fortifications
Kaerlian Holdings Fortified
Kaerlian Holdings
Empire Fortifications
Empire Holdings-Fortified
Empire Holdings
Other Settlements
Oasis
Under
Battle Sites
Roads

Prologue:
Wolf, Cat and Lady

Aliana could see tents going down, pack mules being rounded up and loaded. In the yard before the hostel two men were saddling horses. Uphill, wardens with staves were gathering by the entry posts to the road that led up to the Northgate. The high pass was open.

She wriggled backwards, untied hammock and cover, kicked apart the circle of stones that had guarded her tiny fire. A few more minutes to unroll the mail hauberk, pull it on, repack, carry everything farther into the woods where her mare was tethered. Habit won out over hurry and sense; she led the horse a few hundred yards parallel to the forest edge before coming out of cover and mounting. By the time she reached the gateposts the other riders were waiting, behind them the pack trains beginning to form up.

One of the two men was wearing a black cloak with the royal wolf's head scarlet on the breast. Aliana noted graying hair and beard, the quality of the black horse, but still kept her distance, moving to keep the other man between her and the Wolf.

Lamellar coat, worn and dusty, bow one side the saddle, quiver the other, helmet off, eyes wide and alert in a young face under dark hair. A Northvales cataphract, headed home. The cat glanced at Aliana, gave a friendly nod, said nothing. Her tension—she had no doubt that if she had been carrying her lance the blade would have been shaking like a leaf—eased a little.

The senior warden lifted the crossbar, motioned the Wolf ahead. The other man looked at Aliana, hesitated a moment, then followed; his pack horse followed him. Aliana waited until the warden gave her an impatient glance then urged her horse forward through the gateposts and onto the upward leading path towards the forest fringe.

Once out of sight of watchers below she stopped, sat listening a moment, slid off her horse, uncased and strung her bow, took cover behind a tree and waited, unmoving, watching the path uphill of her. Only when the sound of voices warned that the first of the pack trains was near did she remount and follow the other riders. The path wound steadily upwards. As the day passed the trees became smaller, faded to brush. The ground dipped, then rose steadily. Beyond, perhaps a mile ahead, dark horse and rider, some distance behind him the other. Neither looked back.

By the time the light began to go she had let the gap open wider. She tethered her horse in a patch of grass well to the left of the path, spread bedding on the ground behind a low boulder on the other side, made a meal of biscuit, dried meat and dried fruit, and fell asleep to the noise of insects.

The second day, trail descending, forested vales between foothills and the main range. The sun set early behind peaks to the west, the sky still bright. She reined the mare to a stop, one hand on her neck.

Woodsmoke. Ahead, in forest shadows, a red spark.

"Welcome to my fire, Lady."

Unlikely enemy. And if he was, she thought with a sudden shiver, she was dead already, sitting a horse in plain sight, bow unstrung and cased. She slid from the mare's back, led towards voice and fire. The cat was alone, sitting with his back to a tree. The strung bow in its saddle sheath rested against the tree to his left; his hands were empty.

Mixed with the smoke was the smell of cooking meat; as she came nearer she could see two sticks over the fire and a round pan balanced on rocks just above the coals. Moving slowly he picked up a flat stick, leaned over the fire, used the stick to transfer something from the pan to a wide leaf in his other hand and held it out to her—an oat cake, only slightly scorched. He passed her a small dish of salt. As she took it he reached in, took a little, sprinkled it over the cake, leaned back against the tree. She took a small bite—sweetness of oats, salt tang, safety.

The mare stopped searching out patches of grass, lifted her head, sniffed.

"She smells the creek, maybe my horses." He nodded in the direction the mare was looking. "Time you get back the rabbits will be done."

They were. The two sat by the fire sharing the meat, more oatcakes, dried apple slices from Aliana's supplies.

"Your first trip over Northgate?"

She nodded.

"Mine too, this direction. Father says to fill up with water tomorrow just after we leave the tree line—spring is off to the right and marked. After that a long day dry. Fill up again at Cloud's Eye, then most of a day up and over the high pass. Half a day down and we pick up Silverthread, follow it into Mainvale. I'm home; you've another two hours to your hold. Big oak tree where the path turns off; you can't miss it. They'll be glad of news from east of the mountains."

"Not mine."

"Better than none."

They fell into a comfortable silence. At length she roused herself, carried hammock and bedding into the forest, fell asleep almost at once.

Next morning, horses saddled and waterbags filled, firewood gathered and bundled on the packhorse, they set off together.

"Stay a little back; I may get us dinner."

She looked curiously at him—the path was more than wide enough for two—but let her mare fall back. As soon as she was well behind he had bow out, arrow to the string. A few minutes later he drew and loosed; there was a wild fluttering in the woods ahead, then silence. He angled off into the woods, leaning down from the saddle. A moment later back on the path, freeing the arrow, lifting up the bird's body for her to see. By the time they stopped for lunch he had added a second bird and a rabbit.

"One good thing about being first through the gate— game isn't shy yet."

"Your father told you that too?"

He thought a moment.

"My sister, last spring. The bad thing is the snow at the top of the pass. She said it took two hours in the hot spring before she finished thawing out."

Above the tree line he put away the bow; she let her horse draw even with his. He pointed upslope to the moving dot of the third rider.

"Faster horse, no armor, pushing hard. Most of a day ahead by Mainvale."

"The farther the better. I don't like Wolves."

"Klari's from the old king's day—messenger, not hired sword. Besides, he's out of King's territory now."

He saw that she looked puzzled.

"Someone attacks you here it's the King's concern, not ours; the Law doesn't run outside our borders. Where he is now, your sisters could call him to law, demand blood money."

"How can you tell where the border is?"

"This side of the ridge, see where the path climbs up through a knife cut, steep slopes both sides?"

She looked and nodded.

"That's Raven Stream—last choke point east."

"I thought there weren't any streams here."

"A hundred years ago, back when the Kingdom still thought we belonged to them, an army three thousand strong tried to force the pass. A thousand cats, two hundred Westkin, held them. After three days they gave up and went home. It wasn't water the ravens drank. Above Raven Stream is ours."

Camped that night by the shore of Cloud's Eye, they let

the horses drink full. Sunset rimmed the twin horns, outlined the narrow cut between; the path wound back and
forth, always up, to vanish into the cleft. The fire was
welcome. She looked up from it.

"What will the Vales do?"

Niall looked at her in silence, waited. After a moment
she spoke again.

"The royal pets are good enough at murder, but that's
over now. Southplains, a big wolfpack, six decades, sixty
men, ran into a tatave under Lady Caralla. Even odds. She
sent the last two back to tell their friends it wasn't a game.
There aren't enough bullies and cutpurses in Eston town—
in the Kingdom—to face our host in the open. The King
has to know that by now. Either he calls out the provincial
levies—whichever ones he trusts to fight us—or he gets
help somewhere else. Vales and Kingdom, allies thirty years
and more. That has to be why there's a King's messenger
ahead of us. If he claims the alliance, asks the Vales to send
their host against us, the way they did against the Empire?"

"The Vales aren't a person; you can't ask them things.
The King can hire just like anyone else. Will he get cats to
fight the Order? Not many."

"If he asks the Senior Paramount to bring his army
east? He was the old king's general."

"The Senior Paramount doesn't have an army. West of
the mountains nobody owes allegiance to anyone. The
host fought because we didn't want the Empire on two
sides of us, followed Harald because he was the best general we had. Besides, if he could he wouldn't. You'll see
the sun rising out of the western plains before Harald
makes war on the Order."

"You're sure?"

"Ask your sisters in Valholt, day after tomorrow. They know their neighbors."

The next morning was the climb to the pass, on foot to spare the horses. As they rounded the shoulder of the mountain the slopes on the left drew close; they were climbing with cliffs on either hand.

Niall halted a moment, looking up the slope, then raised his hand. Aliana, leaning against her horse for warmth while she tried to catch her breath in the thin air, thought something moved on a ledge ahead to the right. A few minutes later she saw a figure scrambling down the rocks—a young man, unarmed save for a dagger. He reached the path, glanced at Aliana, looked up at Niall, spoke.

"The King's messenger came by yesterday afternoon in an awful hurry; he'll be through the pass by now. What's the news?"

"The King has announced that his cousin is Lady Commander of the Order, Leonora having appointed her and resigned without telling anyone but him. Leonora hasn't been seen since and the Council isn't inclined to take it on his word. It's a bloody mess, the Emperor is doubtless celebrating, and Father will not be pleased. If you want the rest of the story, come home. Your friends can guard the pass without you; nothing's coming through but trade."

The youth was looking curiously at Aliana.

"Liana, my nephew Asbjorn. Having hunted everything else in the vales, he's decided to come up here and hunt rocks. 'Bjorn, this is the Lady Aliana, bound for Valholt."

Asbjorn gave Aliana a long look.

"Speaking of hunting, Uncle mine . . ."

Niall glared at him. Asbjorn stepped backwards, tripped over a rock, did a tidy backwards roll and scurried off up the slope.

At the top of the pass the snow had been trampled down by wardens and Wolf, but blowing wind had spread it again. They went through mounted, save one drift that had to be cleared by main force. By the time they were through and going down, the green breadth of the valley below them and the brown plains beyond, both were wet, Aliana shivering despite wool tunic and cloak. Niall spoke over the noise of the wind.

"Another half hour to shelter."

The shelter when they came to it was a corner in the rock just off the path, two walls, a roof of wood and turf. Niall helped Aliana off the mare, led her into the angle, crowded in all three horses to make a living wall against wind and cold. He held her against him until body heat from men and beasts had warmed the space a little, then freed a blanket from the roll behind his saddle, wrapped it around her body, secured it with leather thongs. They ate a cold dinner, spent the night huddled together for warmth wrapped in all the bedding they had.

The next morning, clear and cold, they started down, leading the horses. By noon there was a stream running beside the path; they stopped, let the horses drink a little, went on. The air grew warmer. Bushes and short grass covered the slope; they stopped again to let the horses graze while Niall kindled a fire of brushwood, heated water in his one pan, added a thick syrup of honey and herbs from a leather bottle, poured the hot sweet drink into a cup, tasted it and passed it to Aliana. The pan rinsed in the stream, he put it back over the fire; while it dried he mixed water and meal on a flat stone. They ate the oat cakes hot from the pan.

The sun was most of the way down the sky when they reached the tree line, passing a flock of sheep tended by a child who waved at them. Niall waved back and called out something. A little way into the forest a side path led off to the right. Niall stopped.

"This is home. You can stay the night if you like; Mother's always glad of guests."

She hesitated a moment.

"How far to Valholt?"

"Two hours, easy going. Safe enough; we don't have bandits this side of the mountains. Watch for the oak tree by the turnoff—big branch missing on one side. You'll be there before dark."

"I'd best go then."

"Come visit when the sisters are done talking you dry."

Niall watched her out of sight then turned down the path. As he came into the clearing he saw a black horse cropping the grass in the home field. A child weeding the lower garden saw him, dropped what she was doing, started to yell.

"Niall's home. Niall's home."

He slid off his horse. Someone took the reins from his fingers. He climbed the stairs to the wide porch that ran around the hall. The door opened; Gerda was there, her face calm as always. He caught his mother in his arms.

Over her shoulder he saw his father, plainly dressed, rising from the table where the King's messenger sat.

Niall Haraldsson was home.

BOOK I:
How Harald Haraldsson Visited the King and Returned Home

Quietly

Who travels widely needs his wits about him

Haraldholt had been buzzing for days. The King's messenger had brought, along with the royal version of the winter's events, an invitation. His Majesty was holding council in his great castle south of Eston and the presence of the Senior Paramount of the Northvales, his father's ally and general, was greatly desired.

Gerda's first response, once the messenger was out of sight and her youngest son had finished his account of the King's quarrel with the Order, was that her husband should send back a courteous no. The Lady Commander was probably dead. A king mad enough to attack one of his father's allies should not be trusted with the other. It took Harald a day and a half to talk her around; the rest of the household had only guesses as to how.

That settled, there were a thousand things to do—armor to relace, clothes to mend or make, messages to send. Most of them got done. Five days after the King's message arrived, two cats rode east from Haraldholt.

Hrolf and Harald spent the first night in the shelter below the high pass, by good luck empty, the next between Cloud's Eye and the forest. The end of the third put them on the western slope of the foothills. Before dark of the fourth day they had made camp off the trail, a mile above the warden's hostel and the entry posts.

An hour after full dark they broke camp, led the horses down the path and along the forest edge. A mile south of the hostel and its campgrounds they came out of the woods, mounted, rode east. By midnight they reached the west bank of the Tamaron, a sleepy stream swollen with spring melt, forded it. Dawn found them well out in the central plain, hidden in a dip of the land. Most of the day was spent resting, one sleeping while the other stood guard. In late afternoon they mounted again, heading south and east.

For the next three days they rode across the plains. Several times they passed flocks of sheep; the shepherds seemed inclined to keep their distance. Once they passed a burnt out farmstead. Twice too they saw groups of riders. One followed for a while at a trot, but having closed half the distance sheared off.

Harald turned to Hrolf.

"Prudent."

Late in the third day Hrolf stopped his horse, pointed.

"What's that?"

"Village here three years back. Someone put a wall around it."

They rode forward, stopped just outside arrowshot. The high timber wall was pierced by a gate, over the gate a walled walkway. Heads moving on it.

The gate opened. One man came through, on foot,

unarmored. Halfway to the two cats he stopped. Harald glanced at Hrolf, slid from his horse. Hrolf leaned down, caught the bridle, held it while Harald walked forward, empty hand raised.

"We come in peace."

"In peace welcome then." Middle-aged, graying hair, wide shoulders—by dress and speech a farmer. Harald hesitated a moment, signed to Hrolf, whistled. The mare trotted over, followed by the packhorse; he led them through the gate. Hrolf rode. Inside the wall the usual scatter of houses and huts, eight or ten new cottages and a surprising number of people. The wall had a walkway along the inside, almost a man's height below the top. A sentry over the gate, another near the middle of each wall. At one side of the gate, next to the stairs leading up, an orderly stack of spears.

"Will you join us for dinner? The boys will take your horses."

Hrolf looked at Harald, Harald nodded. Their host led them into one of the largest of the houses.

"Rest a minute; I'll get you something to drink."

He went through the door at the back; there was a sound of voices. In a few minutes he was back with a clay pitcher of beer.

"You'll be dry from the ride. Dinner soon."

He ate with his guests at the small table—wheat bread, a thick stew of lentils and root vegetables. They shifted to benches by the fire while the rest of the family replaced them at table.

"Long ride?"

Harald nodded.

"Four days over Northgate, three after."

"Welcome to rest here a few days."

"Kind of you. Stay the night, with your leave. On our way in the morning."

"We could use a couple of trained men."

"Done all right for yourselves. Wall looks solid. People hereabouts can use bows. Unless you're expecting a legion at your front door."

"Bandits. Some say they're King's men, some don't. Not much difference that we've seen. Lord's hold is way up in the mountains. We lost a few folk, more cattle, decided to take care of ourselves. We've got spears, bows."

"Good luck to you. Should be home by summer— could pass the word. If two or three of our lads come across, help guard and train, can you feed them through the winter?"

"No problem. A couple of men, with armor, who knew what they were doing would help a lot."

"You could make armor for your men."

"From what?"

"Westkin mostly use hardened leather—not as hard as iron, but light. We use it too, mostly for the horses."

They spent the evening discussing leather hardening and showing their host how to lay out and lace a lamellar coat, the night in their host's bed, at his insistence. After a breakfast of bread and porridge, they fetched the horses. Harald and Hrolf mounted; their host's wife passed up a sack—bread, hard-baked to keep, and sausage.

"Food for your ride."

"And many thanks. You or yours have cause to come west, we're the first holding over the pass."

Their host gave him a long look. Harald nodded; they rode out of the village.

Cat's Claws

**Early shall he rise who has designs
On another's land or life**

Two more days brought them to where plains turned to
forest, running up in hills and valleys into the eastern
range. They forded the Caldbeck, turned south on the
road that paralleled the forest edge. Before sunset they
were rubbing down their horses in the stable of a small inn
where the main road met the road running up the valley
to Eston and the King's castle. A clatter of hooves in the
courtyard and a loud voice:

"Beer and food. Tell them to take care of the horses.
We'll see you inside."

Footsteps went off. Another voice yelled for the stableboy. After a long wait he appeared, was cursed for a lazy
fool, started to bring the horses in one by one, muttering
under his breath. He saw the two cats, stopped with a
start. Harald spoke first.

"Not friendly folk."

The boy looked at them.

"Do you need your horses taken care of too?"

"Grateful for some hay in the manger, grain if you've got it. We can pay. Other than that they should be all right. No hurry."

The boy nodded, led the horse into a stall, went out for another.

Harald reached up to where he had hung his saddle, pulled the saddle mace free, stuck it in his belt, untied the rain cloak, wrapped it about him. His companion spoke in a low voice.

"The horses?"

"Not all night, but they should do for an hour; two safer than one."

Hrolf nodded, armed and cloaked himself and followed Harald into the courtyard.

The inn was a big dining room, kitchen built on at the end, stairs to sleeping rooms above. Most of the party of riders were at the one big table; their leader was arguing with the owner.

"King's men, King's road. You want to be paid for two lousy rooms, send the bill up to the castle."

He turned on his heel, went to join the rest. One of them was yelling for beer. They got it.

The owner saw Hrolf and Harald in the door, motioned them in.

"You see how it is. You're welcome to benches in the hall, but gods know when you'll get to sleep."

"By your leave, we'll eat here, sleep over our horses. Hay's softer than wood."

"Suit yourself—how many horses?"

"Four."

"A silver penny'll feed you and them, buy space for both."

Harald gave him a long look.

"High, but times are hard. I'll throw in breakfast in the morning, bread and sausage to take with you for lunch. Bound up Eston way?"

Harald nodded, paid, found a bench in one corner of the room. After some time the one serving maid got free of the big table long enough to bring mugs of ale, bowls of thick soup, a flat loaf of dark bread. They ate in silence. Aside from the riders, there were only a handful of men and no women.

The big man was talking, his voice only a little slurred.

"I say tomorrow. Bitches aren't expecting us."

"Peaceful, like the lordling said?"

"By the time we're done, peacefullest hold in the damn kingdom. Leave at dawn, lunch in their hall."

He fell silent, glanced around the room. Harald was slumped on the bench, head down on the table, Hrolf draining the last few drops from his mug. Two others were stretched out on benches by the big fireplace, wrapped in cloaks.

Bedded down in the hayloft over the horses, they took quiet counsel.

"Dawn to noon, say a six-hour ride. What holds that close?"

Hrolf thought a moment.

"Big one up the valley?"

"Too close to the castle. If it's still there the King has it—or his cousin's friends in the Order. Besides, I only counted twelve; they wouldn't try that one without more.

It'll be some little place, four or six Ladies, a few helpers. No guessing where. Have to follow."

The next morning they heard voices and the noise of horses below, lay still until the stable was empty. Twenty minutes later, packed and saddled, they followed, fresh hoof prints clear on the road south. At the top of the rise they slowed. The road ahead, visible for a mile or more to the next rise, was empty. Harald crossed the flat, took the long downslope at a gallop; Hrolf followed.

Two hours south the road forked—the main south, the tracks east. The eastern road ran up a small valley into the mountains, thinning to little more than a path. Ahead shouts and a heavy thudding noise. Coming over the next low rise in the path they could see the whole tiny battle spread out before them.

To the left of the road the hold, little more than a fortified house. In the stone courtyard a body, mail over the gold-brown robe of the Order. The door shut, three men with a tree trunk trying to open it. Up on the roof two archers shooting down into the courtyard where one attacker lay while another, weapon arm limp at his side, crouched behind his shield. Four more crowded the courtyard, shields up to protect the men with the ram. On the other side of the road two more men, with bows, shooting from behind trees. One of the archers on the roof fell back.

Harald's bow was out, arrow on the string, two more held by the fingers of his bow hand. He nodded right, drew and loosed. The first missed, the second caught the archer high in the back. The man turned, looked uphill with an astonished expression. The third arrow took him in the throat. Harald gave a glance to Hrolf's man, down as well, and rode for the courtyard.

The wounded man at the rear of the attack heard the hooves, turned, died. The ram swung again, the noise echoing through the courtyard; the door split, revealing a slight figure with shield and sword behind it. The ram swung back, fell to the ground; the last of the three carrying it looked with astonishment at the arrow point emerging from his chest, went to his knees, collapsed. There was sudden silence.

The Lady in the doorway stepped forward, shield up. Harald sheathed his bow with his left hand, raised his right palm out and empty, slid down.

"Where are the horses?"

She looked at him, confused.

"They came on horses. Left somewhere, probably with a man to watch them."

"I don't know. Pounding on the door. Mara went. I have to see if she's . . ."

Harald looked up at Hrolf. "The horseholder. Then our horses."

Hrolf rode out of the courtyard; Harald helped the Lady lift the body. The sword the fallen Lady had been holding clattered on the stones. Although he had no doubt, he still felt for a pulse.

"I'm sorry."

"She can't be. So quick. Took the second one's sword arm before he had the shield up. But there were so many. She told me to close the door. I did."

"She was right. She won. They lost."

He caught the Lady with an arm around her shoulder,

held her against him until she stopped shaking. Together they carried the body into the hall, laid it on the table.

"Back in a minute."

He spent it walking around the courtyard making sure there were no mistakes.

When he came back, the Lady had been joined by two more. She was young, they younger—by age and dress not yet full members of the Order. One, with a pale face, was holding a cloth tightly to her shoulder, blood oozing between her fingers and around the arrow shaft. He turned to the oldest:

"Heat water to clean her wound; I'll get my kit."

He went to the door, whistled; when his horse came he reached into the right-hand saddlebag, pulled out a wrapped bundle. Back inside he found the wounded girl seated, the other holding her hand with one hand, the bandage over the wound with the other.

"Arrow out, clean the wound, sew it up. Not fun but you should live—I did. Can you hold still?"

She nodded.

By the time the arrow had been broken off and the barbed head carefully drawn, the Lady was back with a basin of hot water. Harald cleaned the wound. From his bundle he got a small flask, pried free the wax seal.

"This will hurt. Sorry."

He carefully poured some of the contents onto the wound. The girl drew a hard breath. He reached into the bundle again, drew out a long strand of sinew, needle already threaded. In a few minutes it was over. He looked at her face; her eyes were still open.

"If you can put up with my surgery you can survive any-thing. Live."

She closed her eyes, drew a deep breath. He looked around, spoke to the Lady.

"She should be lying down. Do you have a pallet you can bring in?"

She nodded, left. There was a noise of hooves on stone. The unwounded girl looked up, startled.

"It's all right."

Hrolf came in.

"There was only one. I left their horses—too many to deal with by myself. Ours are all in the courtyard."

The Lady came back with a pallet. Harald helped her arrange it by the fireplace, picked up the wounded girl, laid her gently on it, kneeled there a moment. Stood up.

The Lady looked at him, suddenly shy. "I'm sorry. I should have thanked you. We, the sisters . . . We're in your debt."

"An old account, both ways; figuring the balance is past my powers."

She looked curiously at him; he fell silent a moment, then spoke. "The question is what you do next."

"What can we do?"

"You could complain to court of murder by His Majesty's Wolves, but from what I've heard of matters I don't recommend it."

"Or?"

"You can abandon the hold, flee to your sisters some-where safer. You'll know more than I where that would be, but you could go north; Stephen's a fine man for failing when it suits him and I can't see him hunting you with any enthusiasm. I'm told Caralla is somewhere in the south plains with an adequate number of sisters, but finding her may not be easy; she isn't one to sit."

"Or?"

"We clean up this mess, get rid of the bodies, get someone to fix your door, sell the horses somewhere they won't tie to you, supposing anyone recognizes one, which isn't likely. Wolves—you never saw any Wolves. Sit tight, be very careful, ready to run if they try again. Far as their commander knows they've vanished off the map—maybe run, maybe dead. One more thing for their friends to worry about."

"Which would you do?"

"The last, at least for a while. You have one sister who shouldn't be moved just now if you can help it. Besides, it leaves your enemies with a puzzle. That's worth doing."

"And you?"

"Find someone can guide us north over the hills and keep quiet about it. We drop down into the valley, east road for Eston—what we would have been doing if none of this had happened. Who'll know we got there the long way?"

A Cautious Guest

**A guest should be courteous when he comes to the table,
And sit in wary silence.**

Two days later they reached the fork in the east road—left to Eston, right to the King's castle. Harald took the right fork alone, a shallow ford, then three miles through the woods to where the land lifted in a bare hill crowned with stone walls. Beyond the moat the gate was open but guarded.

"What's your errand to the King's castle?"

"To the King."

"He isn't hiring foreigners, last I heard. You think different, wait off the road; guard captain will be by in an hour or two."

Harald took the opportunity to look over the castle and its surroundings. Brush had grown back even farther since his last visit, cover for archers in easy bowshot of the walls. Position them at night, seize the gate with any of two or three tricks . . . it would take a fair force if the castle was properly garrisoned, and it probably was, but not impossible.

His thoughts were interrupted by a clatter of hooves behind him. Turning, he saw a cluster of horsemen; one in the front carried a staff with the banner of North Province, beside him Lord Stephen deep in conversation with his captain. Harald looked down. After the first ranks passed he looked up again, raised his hand to one of the rearmost riders as the company came to a halt.

"By the gods. What are you doing cooling your heels outside the gate?"

"Gate guard thinks nobody matters less he arrives with a young army. Didn't feel like arguing; it's been a long ride. Besides, looks as though Stephen thinks the same. Isn't it safe to ride around the Kingdom nowadays?"

"Maybe. Maybe not. Hard times."

Harald joined the rear rank of Stephen's guard, with them rode through the gate to the stable where grooms were finding stalls for the new arrivals. He stayed to unsaddle one horse, unload the other, rub both down, see them supplied with water and hay. His armor, rolled up, went with pack bags, saddle and gear on a high shelf at the far end of the stall, bedding in a separate bundle, saddle blanket and armor padding spread out over the rest and hanging down. His warhorse butted her head against it a few times curiously, then settled down to the serious business of eating.

In the stable yard a small crowd by the tank where men, stripped to drawers, were splashing water on themselves, washing off the dust of travel. Harald joined them, stood dripping and shivering a few minutes more, dried himself with what he had been wearing, pulled on a clean tunic, went back in to fetch his bedding, then crossed the castle yard and plunged into the chaos of the great hall. He drifted over to a convenient corner, half behind a pillar, slid his bedding under a bench, sat down, back against the stone wall.

Talk among the men, castle garrison and guards of half a dozen provincial lords, was as always mostly food and women, save one cluster in a corner leaning over their dice with grim concentration. The handful of Wolves for the most part kept together. One tried to join a group of guards; they ignored him and after a few minutes he backed away. Four women in the dress of the Order, all strangers to him, stood at the far end of the hall, talking to nobody; one was wearing a plain circlet of gold set with a green stone. If there was talk in the hall about current troubles it was not in a voice meant for strangers.

Word came to clear the hall; men drifted out into the yard while servants set up the long tables. A tall stranger eyed Harald curiously.

"Come a long way?"

"Too long; getting old."

"Vales?"

"Mainvale."

"I thought I recognized the accent. Had a friend from one of the smaller vales south of you. Half the time I couldn't tell what he was saying. You're easier."

"Too much time this side of the mountains."

"Who are you with?"

"Nobody yet—just me."

The man gave him a longer look. "I know someone who might be hiring."

The doors of the great hall opened again, this time to a

blast of trumpets, somewhat out of tune. Harald found a seat at one end of the length of table claimed by Stephen's guard, a friend one side, stranger the other. Stephen himself was at the south end of the hall, with the King and the other provincial lords at a raised table. A lady came in, sat by the King, dress particolored green and silver, red hair, graceful form, too far away to make out the face. On the King's other side a noble Harald did not recognize, a big man. Beside him a man in black, scarlet wolf's head plain on his chest.

Stephen was looking about the hall curiously; his gaze passed over the group of his own men, returned, shifted to the goblet in front of him. The doors to the kitchen opened. There was another fanfare, this time in tune. Servants in the royal colors brought platters to high table, a larger number, more plainly dressed, to the hall. Harald turned to his companion.

"His Majesty seems pleasantly occupied."

"Lady Anne, daughter to Estfen Province. Above my station. You might try your luck, but not this month."

"I'll leave that to youngsters like His Majesty. The other side?"

"That's Andrew, King's cousin—his mother's kin. Big man in the southern provinces."

"And his friend?"

"Wide fellow, gray streak? That, gods preserve us, is old Mark's successor. Mord. Turned the Wolves from what they were under the old king to . . ." He fell silent.

As platters and pitchers emptied, more were brought. At the end of the third course servants set out bowls of nuts and dried fruit, basins of water. Looking up the hall,

Harald saw the King rising, saying something to his table companions. The provincial lords and the King's cousin rose, the rest remained. Stephen looked down the hall straight at Harald, turned, followed the King out the door at the back of the hall.

Harald took the outside stair; as he expected they were meeting in the room above the south end of the hall. There were two guards at the door; one stepped in front of him, spear held crosswise.

"Sorry friend. Royal business, visitors not welcome. The King's holding Council."

"Why I've come."

Harald reached into his pouch, drew out the scroll, unrolled it, handed it to the guard. He looked at it, handed it to the other. As he read it his eyes widened. He gave Harald a long look.

"Let him in."

"Orders are to let in Their Excellencies. If he's a provincial lord I'm Lady Commander of the Order."

The other one looked down at the scroll, read aloud:

"To Harald Haraldsson, Senior Paramount of the North Vales, His Majesty James, King of Kaerlia, Protector of Eston, Lord Warden of the Northern Marches, sends cordial greetings."

The guard with the spear stepped back. The other opened the door. Harald went through it.

A long table, the King at one end. At his side his cousin, his chair a little back. Along the table lords of ten of the twelve provinces, Stephen near the far end.

The King looked up. Stephen spoke, "Your Majesty will remember the Senior Paramount."

The King's expression remained puzzled.

"How did you get here?"

"I rode, Your Majesty."

"Alone? There was supposed to be an escort."

"Was there, Your Majesty? I do not commonly require an armed guard to ride in your Kingdom. Has the Empire invaded?"

"I am sorry. For some reason I was not informed that you were here. I hope my servants have taken care of your needs."

"Your Majesty's servants have provided space for horses and gear in your stable, dinner for me in your feast hall. I have no complaints as to your hospitality."

"We will try to do better than that." The King motioned to a servant standing silent by the wall, spoke to him briefly. The man went out. Harald seated himself. The King rose.

"My lords. I have invited you here for advice concerning affairs of the kingdom, assistance in dealing with them. Before we are done each will be free to raise such concerns as trouble his province. For tonight, the most pressing matter is the rebellion of parts of the Order against their Lady Commander. We offered her assistance in enforcing her authority. Our efforts have been defied with force, loyal men killed. In three provinces, it may be more, the rebels are up in arms. What is your counsel?"

There was a long silence. Finally Harald spoke. "If I understand the account your messenger brought me, Your Majesty, the trouble arose in a transfer of the office of Lady Commander from the Lady Leonora to your cousin the Lady Alicia, a transfer that the Council of the Order has not as yet accepted."

The King nodded, waited for Harald to continue.

"By the Order's custom, the Lady Commander can propose a successor but not appoint one; the candidate must be approved by the Council. If the Lady Leonora has resigned the office and the Lady Alicia not yet been approved, then there is no Lady Commander whose orders Your Majesty's servants might enforce."

"The Order cannot be allowed to fall into chaos. These matters occurred in my Kingdom, it is for me to resolve the dispute. I have ruled in favor of the claim of the Lady Alicia."

Andrew leaned forward, spoke: "Your Excellency will remember the dispute concerning control over Order lands in Estvale. The matter was put to His Majesty's father and his decision accepted."

Harald shook his head.

"That matter was submitted to His Majesty by the parties. In this case, as I understand it, the Council has neither requested his present Majesty's judgment nor accepted it. But in any case, surely there is an easier answer, one that costs blood of neither His Majesty's servants nor the Ladies."

The King looked down the table at him.

"Name it."

"As I understand Your Majesty's account, the Lady Leonora chose the Lady Alicia for her successor. She does not appear to have told her sisters in Council of that choice."

"I told them."

"Your Majesty's voice in Your Majesty's Council; her voice in hers. Let the Lady Leonora speak to her sisters.

She persuades them to her choice or they persuade her to change it. In either case no more killing."

"That would indeed be an excellent solution, were it possible. The Lady Leonora has chosen seclusion. We cannot ask her to abandon her cell."

"To save the blood of her sisters? Her cell. For that she would leave her grave, gods permitting."

"Enough. Are there other matters you would bring before us?"

Harald paused a moment, then spoke again. "Another that grows from this: the Empire."

"What has it to do with a quarrel in my Kingdom?"

"Your Majesty knows that four times in the past twenty years the Empire has invaded the Kingdom's land, seeking to bring it under their rule."

"And four times we sent them home with their tails between their legs."

Harald remained silent, looking at the King, for a long moment. The King started to speak, stopped, looked round the table. Harald broke the silence.

" 'We' included the host of the Order—two thousand of the best light cavalry this side the western plains. If the Empire invades tomorrow, how many?"

"The Empire is not going to invade tomorrow. Not this year. Not next year."

Andrew spoke. "The Empire is tied down in Belkhan, a hundred miles and more north and east of the Borderflood, besieging a castle that has not fallen in a hundred years. One war is enough for them. They may settle the revolt in two years, in three. By then our troubles are dealt with, the Order more safely ours than before."

"I fear, my lord, that your information is out of date. A month ago, Cliff Keep fell to the second and twenty-third legions under Commander Artos. With the Inner Lands open, the rest of the rebels made terms or fled. If His Imperial Majesty wishes to turn his attention south the legions—more important, the Commander—are free."

Harald stopped. The room was silent. The King looked at his cousin. Andrew shook his head.

"I have heard no such news. Rumor. Perhaps a story spread by the Imperials to discourage other provinces from rebellion."

The King turned to Harald. "Your Excellency?"

"My neighbor's son was with the rebels."

"One mercenary. Even if he is honest, he might have been fooled by rumor—especially if he was looking for an excuse to come home." Andrew fell silent.

Harald looked straight back at him. "He brought Gryfydd an Gwyllian with him; we had the Count to dinner two nights before I left Haraldholt. The revolt's done."

Andrew said something quietly to the King, rose, left the room. Nobody spoke. At last the King broke the silence.

"My thanks for your news. This indeed means that we must settle the rebels quickly."

"Peacefully, Your Majesty. Corpses cannot fight. Every Lady your Wolves kill is one less bow beside us when next we face the legions."

"I will remember that, Excellency. But we have talked too long; my throat at least is dry."

The King clapped his hands. A moment later the door opened, admitting servants with wine, beer, trays of sweetmeats. As they put them out the King rose, walked to the door, turned.

"Refresh yourselves, Excellencies. I will be back shortly."

Stephen turned to Harald. "Things were very peaceful."

"In this room perhaps. What do your watchers on the Borderflood see?"

"Nothing coming across the fords but a few pack trains."

Harald turned to the lord across the table, younger than Stephen, broken nose, a long scar from cheek to chin.

"And the western fords?"

"More than a few—most of them heading over Northgate to your doorstep. The usual guards, some of them your people. No armies."

"I passed some of them coming east. My womenfolk are doubtless overjoyed."

The King came back into the room, took his place at the head of the table. Two of the lords refilled their goblets; the room grew silent.

"His Excellency has pointed out that we must settle the rebellion quickly with as little bloodshed as can be, lest the Empire find opportunity in our troubles. I had hoped to succeed without calling on your levies by expanding the royal messengers into a force sufficient for the purpose. Their chief asks more money to recruit more men. Your judgment."

Gray hair, gray beard, the lord of Estmark rose to his feet.

"Your Majesty, I'll speak plain. I don't know how many of the bandits in the plains are Wolves and how many only say they are, but my people, farmers, are arming, building walls, asking troops from my guard to protect them. We need fewer, not more."

A southern lord stood.

"I've had no trouble with Wolves, Majesty. But anyone can see what they are—men with swords, not soldiers. Hire two thousand, open field against the host, you'd have a lot of graves to dig. Make peace or make war."

He sat down; the King waited a moment, but no one else spoke.

"So we are agreed. To deal with the Order we call out the provincial levies—enough of them to outmatch the rebels."

The room was silent. The southern lord spoke first.

"Spring planting's mostly done. I can raise a half levy without hardship. Two hundred men."

The man next to him, younger, stood.

"Three hundred."

The King looked around the room.

"Lord Stephen?"

"We plant later. And Harald's news means men on watch the length of Borderflood, more behind. I could send a hundred perhaps—but not soon or far."

"Brand?"

The scarred man spoke. "Like Stephen. I can send men if Your Majesty commands it, but that strips the border."

The count went on, southern lords more willing than northern. The King turned at last to Harald.

"Two thousand men—more with two lords not yet to Council. A half levy of my own lands makes another thousand. The levy of the Vales is, I think, two thousand.

Bring half. Facing four thousand the rebels must yield; our troubles are done with no more killing."

Harald looked up.

"I fear your Majesty has been misinformed."

"You did not bring twenty cacades of cataphracts to my father's last war with the Empire?"

"Indeed I did, Your Majesty. But the Northvales, as your father in his wisdom recognized, are no more a province of the Kingdom than the Kingdom is a province of the Empire. I brought an army across the Northgate to the support of my allies, not a levy in service to my king."

"I care little what you call it, so long as you bring it."

"Your Majesty is less than prudent. Thirty years the Empire has been held off by an alliance of three parts— Kingdom, Vales, Order. You tell me now that one of my allies makes war on the other, and ask me to join the fray. If I bring the host of the Northvales across the mountains, how sure are you which side it chooses? Better we stay home. Better yet you make peace with the Order."

Harald sat down. The room fell silent until at last the King spoke.

"The hour is late; tired men quarrel. We discuss these matters, the two of us, tomorrow day, call Council tomorrow even. With fortune Estfen and Estmount will be here by then."

Words

**Courteous greeting
Then courteous silence
That the stranger's tale be told.**

He woke in a bed, sheets, a rough blanket. It took most of
a minute to work out why it wasn't a bedroll under a tree.
He pulled the shutters open. His own bedroll was in the
corner; he remembered retrieving it from under a bench
in the great hall. There was a basin and a ewer of water on
the table—luxury indeed. Harald washed hands and face,
unbarred the door, crossed the castle yard to the stable.

Both horses had fresh water, clean feed. He pulled
down saddle blankets and armor padding, checked that
they were dry, folded them, put them back on the shelf,
apologized for having neglected to bring apples. One set
of saddlebags went over his shoulders back to his room,
where he changed into fresh clothes and set off for the
great hall in search of breakfast.

Sitting by himself, Harald broke a chunk off a convenient
loaf, ate it with sausage, cheese, bites from a withered

apple out of the winter's store. When he finished he looked around. At one table Stephen, Brand, and a random collection of both men's guard were finishing breakfast. Stephen caught his eye, got up, headed for the door. Harald waited until he was through it before rising to follow.

The two ended on an empty stretch of the west ramparts, looking out over slope and forest to the central plains and the west range beyond, peaks blurring white against a clear sky. Stephen spoke first.

"With eyes twenty years younger you could almost see home."

"Through rock? Never that good."

They fell silent, Harald waiting. Finally Stephen spoke.

"I said we hadn't seen anything but trade crossing the fords. Truth, as far as it goes. Hoofprints. Groups of five or ten riders, not an army. Odd prints."

The stone they were leaning on, hollowed by the wind, had collected a thin layer of dust. Harald drew a shape in it with his finger, a rough U barbed at both ends. Stephen nodded.

"Not raiding, not guesting. Plains not woods. Ride at night, rest at day, through as quick as they can and south, that's my guess."

Harald's turn.

"Last night before feast, talking with a stranger, tall fellow, blond. Asked who I was with, said someone was hiring. Maybe not just cats."

Stephen gave him a worried look.

On his way to the stable, wallet full of apples lifted from store while their guardian carefully looked the other way, a royal servant found him.

"His Majesty would be glad of your company for the noon meal."

Harald nodded his assent.

"The terrace above great hall, a half hour past the noon bell. Shall I fetch you then?"

"I can find it."

His errand to the stable done, Harald found his way to the old orchard at the south end of the castle. Most of the stones were overgrown with moss. He sat looking at the one that was not until the noon bell roused him.

When he got to the terrace the King was waiting, the lady Anne seated at his side. Harald saw no reason to question the King's taste then, less by the end of the meal.

"They say your valleys are cold; is that why the wool is so good?"

"Upper end of the valleys for wool, lower end, out on the plains for mutton."

"The people on the plains. Nobody could tell me. How do they live? Who are they?"

"Westkin. Our word, not theirs; half the vales have relatives west. Wife's brother married a girl out of Fox clan. They call themselves Illash—People. Nomads mostly, herd sheep, horses, cattle. A little farming, places there's enough water—most of the plains pretty dry. Herd cattle for food, steal 'em from each other for fun. Pleasant life."

"There are a lot of them, aren't there?"

"Big plains. Kingdom, Vales—fit all of us in with room to spare."

"And fierce. What keeps them from coming over the pass, attacking, conquering us? Are they afraid of you?"

Harald laughed.

"We came over the pass, two hundred-odd years back. The vales were empty. Westkin like flat land. Wouldn't mind your plains, but a lot of mountain between them and everywhere else they want to be. Clans raid each other. A few wild ones up into the lower vales, sometimes. With us over Northgate to raid the Kingdom, fifty years back. Ended when Henry, king that was, settled matters, thanks be."

He stopped. Looked down. When he looked up her eyes were on him, the King's on her. She watched Harald's face a moment, then went on.

"Is that why it's the Empire, not the plains, you've had to fight all these years?"

Harald waited for her to continue.

"I mean, they're farmers, like us. They want the same land. Your Westkin don't."

He looked her full in the face.

"His Majesty wants wisdom, hasn't far to look."

"But since the lady Anne is fair as well as wise and we have matters of moment to discuss, best we continue without the distraction of her beauty. Lady mine?"

Anne rose, nodded to both men, departed. They sat silent a while. At last the King spoke.

"Your Excellency took me to task last even for speaking of the Vales as though part of the Kingdom. Yet in law and justice they are; the first settlers were in allegiance to my ancestor. My father let the claim lapse. That does not mean I must."

"Law and Justice. Your Majesty's lands owe armed men, a month's service, so many from this province, so many from that. What get they in return?"

"Protection from their enemies. Justice to settle their quarrels."

"Your Majesty's grandfather, his father, his, back two hundred years. Half the year, the high pass closed, could not protect us if they would. Other half they didn't. Defended ourselves, settled our own quarrels. Still do. Your word runs this side the mountains. Our side, the Law."

"That was then. If we can reach a settlement, we two, that's now. You want your law, you keep it—with my strength to settle matters if needed. My strength to protect you from your enemies."

"You purpose to send a few thousand heavy horse over Northgate, case one of the clans gets unfriendly, Empire pushes south our side the mountains?"

"Of course not—that's your part. We protect this side of the mountains."

"Your land, not ours. With our help. We protect our borders, help protect yours, counts as you protecting us. Sure you don't think you should be a province of ours?"

"That's the Empire's idea—both of us their province. You're juggling words. Fighting them on our land protects you too; that's why you send cats to help. Why you came yourself to fight for my father."

"One reason. Rather you other side Northgate than Empire, true enough. Still your war not ours. Empire crosses Borderflood, beats you, no Kingdom. We can hold Northgate till the mountains fall down. Doubt the Empire lasts that long."

He stopped. The King was silent, searching for words. Finally he spoke.

"I've heard of the legions; you've faced them. Maybe you're right, maybe you can hold the high pass without us. Maybe the Empire would trade with you, instead of closing the pass and the roads north until you made terms.

"But you're better off, we're better off, together. You were my father's ally. He didn't live forever; you won't. What comes next, who knows? You swear yourself my man. I swear to maintain you as lord of the Northvales. The Empire knows we stand together, not just you and me but our sons and theirs. They go look for land somewhere else."

"Your Majesty can't maintain me as lord of the Northvales. I'm not. Isn't a lord of the Vales, never was."

"It's not what you call yourself, but you're the one the cats fight for. You spoke of sending troops over the pass. I can't afford an army. But a hundred, two hundred, good men, take orders, deal with problems without asking your people to fight their own kin. Maybe there isn't a lord of the Northvales. There could be."

The King fell silent, watching Harald.

"Your Majesty has interesting ideas. Two problems. First, I don't want to be lord of the Northvales; paramount suits fine. Second, I couldn't get it. I go where cats want, they follow. Try to make myself lord of the Northvales, be at the wrong end of a lot of arrows."

"You understate your own power. Take time to consider my proposal. You gave two problems. Let me give two answers, and then let the matter be for now.

"You say the cats follow because you are going where they want. My men follow me from loyalty—they know they are mine to command. It could be that way for you. I could help make it that way.

"Second, consider the consequences—not now, but in time. I need troops I can trust, not a host that fights for me if it's in a good mood, goes home if it isn't. In a year, two years, when my present troubles are solved and the Empire, gods willing, off fighting someone else. Your host is two thousand. Mine is ten. My father was content with your terms. I may not be."

"Your Majesty speaks frankly. Some day the road to the high pass, show you something along the way."

The King looked at him curiously.

"Valley. Downhill from where your grandfather tried to force the pass, year I was born. Full of bones. Two thousand I brought east to help Henry. Didn't empty the vales. Second time, while 'Nora and I played hide and seek with the Emperor's generals up and down the plains, wife's brother and his friends were busy west of the mountains. A legion and ten cacades of cavalry the Empire sent south. Not many came home again across the low pass. Hold the Gate with two thousand cats—need more, they're there."

Harald rose, stretched legs stiff with sitting, nodded to the silent King, left.

Later that afternoon, returning to the orchard, he found it no longer empty. The lady looked up at him startled, rubbing her eyes—a little older than Anne, a little less well dressed, a great deal less happy. He looked away, sat down on the tombstone of some king whose name could no longer be read in the worn letters, looked back at her. She was rising.

"Would have a tale, damsel, to while the time?"

"No. Yes." Voice as uncertain as the words.

"Time yet to dinner. A sad place to sit alone." He looked

around at the trees, the stone paving, the stone he was sitting on.

When he looked up again she was sitting on the paving, looking down at the hands in her lap, still.

"Yes."

"The Vales, my grandfather's father's time. The full tale of Saemund Heavyhand is long; I tell only of the vengeance for his oathbrother Cuhal's slaying, and that one killing in which Saemund had no hand at all.

"Now Cuhal was out of the west, a man of Otter clan, but long living among our people for love of Saemund's sister, and she the fairest of all that kindred."

The tale wound on, two killers, one kin to Saemund and so untouched by the vengeance he took for his friend's death, the trick by which Cuhal's sons, though not yet of age, paid out their father's killer. Harald paused, then gave the ending.

"The younger stopped a moment, and answered.

" 'I do not know the cause of that yelling downhill, but it may be they are asking if Cuhal had only daughters, or sons too,' then turned and ran up the mountainside after his brother."

"A good story indeed and brave boys. Are there many such tales in your land?"

"Many and many, damsel. Winters are long in Northvales."

"You sit here often?"

"From time to time. A quiet place to think, the company peaceful."

She gave him a shy smile, gestured to the King's stone.

"I knew him, a little, when I was younger; we all did. When I am sad I sit here. It doesn't change things, but somehow . . ."

"A good and gentle man, our world dark by his loss. I too visit with him."

Their eyes met. Above them a deep note.

"Dinner. I must to my lady." She dropped him a quick curtsey, was off.

During the dinner one of the royal servants brought Harald, eating with friends at the far end of the hall, word that the Council had been postponed to the next day, two lords being still absent.

The next morning he again met the lady Elen in the orchard, this time accompanied by two younger ladies, and entertained them with Fox clan tales, clever tricks of their name beast.

"The story yesterday was from your own vales. How is it you know so many of these?"

"Fox clan? Parts of two years with them, learning horse, bow and lance. There are no riders like the Westkin."

"They welcome foreigners who come to learn the arts of war of them? It seems hardly prudent." That was the youngest and best dressed of the three.

"I helped them steal cattle, horses once, from their neighbors. Saved my oathbrother from a most shameful capture too. Vales, plains, we're all cousins west of the mountains."

"And between stealing horses and saving brothers, had you time for sisters too? What are the ladies of the plains folk like?"

Silence fell. At last Harald spoke slowly.

"Very fair, some of them. I was otherwise engaged at the time."

The youngest looked ready to ask another question. He spoke first.

"Have I told you what council the fox gave the raven, and how the snake died?"

Afterwards he excused himself to see how his horses were being cared for. The ladies remained behind. Looking back he saw the three of them, their heads together. One looked up at him, then away.

The lord of Estmount had come in during the afternoon, with apologies for his tardiness and his neighbor's absence. If the lady Anne felt neglected for lack of a father she showed no sign of it. Council was held, but dealt mostly with a tangled dispute over water and grazing rights in the southern provinces. At last it was agreed that the King's cousin would look into the matter and advise the King.

The next afternoon the three ladies came again, accompanied by Anne.

"Here my lady."

For a moment her mouth was half open, then she caught up her usual composure.

"It is good of Your Excellency to entertain my ladies. My sister too."

The three were frozen, staring at Harald.

"Rather they me, lady. I seldom see flowers here so early in the year. Will it then please you to sit and hear a tale?"

"It would." She gathered up her skirt, sat down on one of the flagstones. "Your own deeds. Surely the hero of half the battles of the past thirty years has one or two suited to our ears."

"As you will, lady. Will you have my first battle? It is a good tale, though I am not the hero of it."

She nodded, settled back against a tree trunk.

"You know that King Henry in his wisdom made peace with the Vales, abandoning his father's claim to lordship. It made him friends among the wiser of our people. Young men are not always wise, nor fond of peace; some had been dreaming of brave deeds, rich plunder, east of the mountains. But the next year was drought on the western slopes and beyond. The Westkin declared water peace on the clans, moved the herds west for grass. We had fields, houses.

"His Majesty, peace on him, sent herds of sheep, mules loaded with grain, all he could spare over the pass. Young men are no happier to starve to death than old.

"A gift for a gift, we say. We had our chance the next spring. Trouble on the Borderflood for years, getting worse. His Majesty had settled his western border. He called out the levies, every lance he could raise, marched north against the Empire. Five hundred of us came over the high pass to help him.

"Imperial cavalry from all over, some good—they hire Westkin off the plains when they can—some not. That year mostly mediums from the northwest provinces, heavies out of the client kingdoms east of here. Brave, but they'd never fought cats before. While His Majesty was keeping an eye on the main army, we had our own battle. Westkin tactics. They ran out of men before we ran out of arrows. First blood, light losses. We thought we were winning.

"So did His Majesty. He brought the Imperial army to battle. Four legions, as many more lights. He tried to break them with a cavalry charge."

Harald stopped a moment, his eyes blind to the orchard around him.

"Imperial heavies, the legions, best infantry in the world. We were out of it, watching, waiting to be sent in after the lines broke. The Order too; even then Henry had enough sense not to throw light lancers at legions. It was all his own people, heavies—six thousand men.

"The javelins brought down half the front rank, then the long spears came down. Horses don't like running into a hedge of steel. I wouldn't either. It was a bloody mess.

"We did our best to cover the retreat, we and the Order. The Third Prince—he's Emperor now—sent his lights to finish the business, while the legions dealt with what hadn't gotten away.

"Aiming one way while riding another looks very fine. Broken ground, low hills, big boulders, bad for cavalry, even ours—but it was my first war. I rolled when I hit, was lucky not to break anything.

"And there I was, light archer's shield, sword at my belt, five or six wild men with swords and shields coming my way, one with a two-hander taller than he was, and he a big man. Not a friendly face in sight. Backed up between bank and a big boulder, where they couldn't all come at me at once, hoped to have one or two for company.

"The first was careless. I was fighting the second, wondering how long my shield would last, when he suddenly got the most surprised look I've ever seen on a man's face and dropped. Hand-to-hand is a muddle—given the choice I do my killing at range—but I was sure I hadn't touched him, too busy staying alive."

The orchard was still, the four ladies hardly breathing.

"Looked behind for the next one. He was lying on his face. Head of a line of corpses. Then I saw her.

"Rock on her left, bush on her right, picked them off, starting at the back, till she ran out. If anyone had seen her—you don't fight sword and shield with a longbow, not at close quarters. Order aren't trained to shoot from the saddle. Longbows not much use on horseback anyway.

"She called her horse; it came. Carried both of us till we got to camp, my remount."

He fell silent. At last Anne spoke.

"And afterwards? What happened to the brave Lady? Did you see her again?"

"As to the fate of the Lady Leonora, you must put that question to His Majesty. He has seen the Lady Commander more recently than I."

Anne's face went white. Harald stood up, stumbled a little on stiff legs, and in the silence walked out of the orchard.

Bird On the Wing

A small hut of one's own is better,
A man is his master at home.

The next morning he woke late and heavy headed, both due to a late evening of drink and gossip in the guard barracks. While helping himself to what was left of breakfast in the great hall, he heard the King's voice and looked up.

"Your Excellency. Today my lords and I hunt in the woods and meadows south of here. Will you join us? I have heard tales of your skill with the bow."

"What does Your Majesty hunt?"

"Deer."

"Hard to miss; rabbits are a better test. But I'll come."

Returned to his room he considered the matter, stripped to his under tunic, pulled on the mail shirt he commonly wore under his war coat, a second tunic over that. In the stable he saddled his mare, slid bowcase and quiver over their hooks and tied them down, pulled sword and belt from the middle of one long bundle, wrapped the belt around his waist—despite some days of the King's hospitality it still fit—drew the blade out a few inches, slid it back, and rode out to join the gathering company. With the lords were several ladies also mounted, Anne not among them, and a small crowd of servants.

Two miles south the woods were open, the land mostly level. The King planted his banner in a meadow; the servants set to putting up tables, building fires, while lords and ladies went in search of game. Some followed the dogs and their keepers, others, Harald among them, in other directions.

He was sitting his horse in solitude, watching the bushes for movement, when a stag came out of the woods at a full run. It vanished into the woods ahead. Harald reached for his bow, urged his horse ahead with voice and knees, leaned forward.

He was out of the saddle, the world spinning around him, hit the ground rolling, a sharp pain in his right arm, up again, back to a tree. Out of the corner of his eye, movement. He put his right hand on his sword hilt, ignoring the pain, turned. A man was coming out of the woods, a long staff in his hand, a second man behind him.

"My damn horse threw me and ran. A silver penny if you find him for me."

The man looked at him, hesitated, turned, spoke to his companion. The two turned and disappeared back into the woods.

He put two fingers of his left hand in his mouth, whistled. Again. A moment later the horse came out of the trees, reins trailing; Harald saw that she was favoring her left forefoot. He steadied himself against the horse, looked down. Six inches above the hoof a red line, sharp as if drawn by a ruler. He reached down with his good hand, felt the leg; no break. At least one of them had been lucky. He mounted.

In the middle of the clearing was a dead pine tree. Harald walked the horse over, reached up, broke off a short length of branch with his left hand. Right arm across his lap, he laid the stick along it, reached under the saddle skirt for a leather thong.

It took ten uncomfortable minutes to roughly splint the broken arm with lengths of branch. He reached behind him, drew out the dagger that rested crossways in the small of his back, cut a long strip from the lower edge of his tunic. He wrapped it around sticks and arm, drew it tight, cut a slit in the front of his tunic, slid in the right arm, tied it to his body with another thong, using hand and teeth to make the knot. Gerda would be unhappy at the state of his clothing, but that was nothing new. More unhappy if he didn't come back to her.

The world faded in and out on the way out of the wood, back down the road to the castle. It didn't seem to bother the horse.

Approaching the stable, he saw a familiar form.

"Henry."

"Harald. I heard you were here."

"Hurt myself riding; need your help."

The guard captain took in the bound arm, the color of Harald's face, reached up. Harald swung his right foot up and over the saddle, slid into his arms.

"I'll get a groom for the horse."

"Better deal with it yourself."

Henry gave him a puzzled look, followed Harald's glance down at the horse's forefoot.

"Yes. I'll get one of my men to help you back. Where have they put you?"

"Karl's old room, against the wall by the New Tower."

The arm resplinted with help of another friend from the barracks, Harald rested, trying to ignore the pain. Outside the unbarred door he heard Henry's voice. Another. He relaxed, called out: "Come in."

The lady Elen came through the door, eyes wide.

"I heard you were hurt, Excellency."

"Most folk call me Harald."

"My lady always . . ."

"Lady Anne calls me 'Excellency' because His Majesty does. His Majesty uses the title in hopes I'll forget who I am and where I come from, decide the North Vales are really a province of his kingdom and I'm their lord. His father got most things right, that included, not all."

"Can I get you anything?"

"You can get me a pitcher of beer and two mugs, then sit here and let me tell you the rest of Saemund's tale, help me forget what my arm feels like. If you would, leave word for the King I won't be at Council tonight and why."

When she returned, with pitcher, mugs, and a servant carrying a stool, he was asleep.

The next morning he was still light-headed and the arm had swollen. Elen having brought him breakfast, he let her help him retie the splints, then told her the first part of Saemund's tale. Later Stephen arrived with news of the previous evening's Council meeting. The King had again proposed calling out a part levy to deal with the Order.

Stephen, backed by Brand, had pointed out that the more
men were called to their month's service now, the fewer
would be available later, when and if Imperial troops
crossed the Borderflood into their provinces. He proposed
instead that Harald, with friends in both camps, be asked
to try to negotiate a settlement with the Order. The meeting
had broken up with no decisions made. Harald gave
Stephen a complete account of the previous day and sent
him off to collect rumors.

It was most of a week before Harald felt well enough to
consider the trip back over the mountains. He spent most
of it in bed, gossiping with friends, entertaining a surprising diversity of visitors with stories from the Vales and
beyond. The day he decided it was time to be up and
about, the King came to visit.

"I hope my people have been taking good care of you."

"Concerning the hospitality in your castle I have no
complaints, Majesty. I hope not to impose on it much
longer."

"What do you mean? You can't leave now."

Harald looked at him curiously.

"I still need your counsel. Besides, you can't cross the
width of the Kingdom and the high pass until your arm is
healed."

"Your Majesty can have my counsel now; it is simple
enough. So far as the Order, your choice is war or peace.
War, lose or win. Lose, the matter is ended, at least for
you. If a half levy suffices to win, you then have the
Empire to deal with—no allies, half the provincial levy
spent. Two thousand of your own men, fewer after dealings
with the host. Three thousand from the provinces. Your

lady cousin and fifteen of her ladies. Again, that ends the game for you. I invite such of my friends as can to come over the pass and help settle Newvale, garrison Northgate, learn to live with the Empire east as well as north.

"Peace is simpler still. Give back the holdings your men have seized. Pay the Order blood money for Ladies killed. Turn loose the Lady Commander—she can see over the Borderflood as well as I can. If Leonora is dead, put the matter to the Council of the Order, abide their judgment— and don't visit my side the mountains any year soon. Or after."

"I will consider your words. But you stay my guest until I decide you are well enough to travel. When you go home, it is with an escort of my men. I will not have it said that I sent you out alone to be killed by bandits between here and the pass."

"Your Majesty has odd ideas of hospitality."

The King made no answer, turned, walked out of the room.

Harald considered the matter for a long hour before he rose, found his cloak, set out for the kitchen and storerooms behind and then, somewhat burdened, to the stable. Having apologized suitably for neglecting the two horses he returned to his room carrying a smaller bundle. An hour's rest preceded a visit to the barracks to chat with friends. Not surprisingly, two planned to ride over to the city later that day. Harald entrusted one with a list of gifts for various of the castle ladies—his one-handed state making the ride imprudent—money to pay for them, a message for a friend. He left, ignoring diverse comments centering on good fortune, a busy convalescence and things a broken arm did not bar. Back in his room he rested for another hour before making his preparations.

His bundle included a dagger blade, a mail coif, two short lengths of ash, a long strip of woolen cloth, another of linen. He resplinted the arm, taking the opportunity to feel out the break, only partly healed. The wool wrapped over the bandage. Over that the dagger blade lying flat along the back of his forearm, the wooden pieces at either side. He wrapped the whole forearm in the mail coif, over that the linen. The arm being now bulkier as well as heavier, he retied his sling, taking care with the knot.

After another hour's rest a servant arrived with food for his dinner. Harald thanked the man, sent him off with a message for the King. The answer came as he finished eating.

Half an hour later he gave a last look around the room, pulled on his cloak, went out into the fading light. Up the steps to the ramparts, along them to the door of the north tower. Men had been working on repairing a worn part of the wall. With his left hand he clumsily lifted a block of stone, heaved it up to the top of the wall, steadied it.

The guard at the door opened it for him; Harald went in. The King was waiting.

"You said you required speech with me here. On what matter?"

"Whether I am your guest or your prisoner. I purpose to leave. Will you let me?"

"I cannot."

"I am not your man to command. Would you be at war with both your father's allies together?"

"It is just that I do not wish. If you leave and do not reach home, I will be blamed. If you leave and reach home angry as you now are, you may come back with an army. You have spoken bluntly; I do so now. I grant that holding you is poor hospitality, but I have no choice. You do not have my leave to go, and I have given orders to the guards at the gate. You will not have my leave until your arm is healed and our dispute settled—peace with the Order or war, as I choose. It may be I will take your counsel, it may be not."

"If you hold me here, do you think that gets you peace? I am not the only man in the Vales. When my kin come in force to fetch me home, what then?"

"Why should they? They do not know why you remain here or for how long."

Harald looked at him in frank astonishment.

"Your Majesty's castle is an hour ride from a town full of busy tongues. What happens here is told there, and much that does not as well."

"Rumor. Your friends are two weeks ride west of here. Will they come over the mountain and across the plain, sift out the truth, ride home, collect an army, return? By then the matter is settled between us. They know you came here, that is all they know. If need be I can close the pass westbound—the traders will be mostly through by now. I do not think it will come to that."

"As to my broken arm, how I came by it, Your Majesty's policy and my judgment thereon—save Your Majesty has falcons enough to kill every pigeon in Eston, that news reached Haraldholt three days ago. Today's is already on the wing, and nothing on four legs will catch it. This time tomorrow half Mainvale knows I am held here."

The King was silent, staring at Harald.

"When the Empire crossed the border six years back, do you think I waited two weeks for a rider to reach me before calling out the host? His Imperial Majesty would be sitting here, not you. We trained the first birds twenty years ago."

The King spoke slowly.

"It seems all choices go ill. If I must have war with the Vales, better you here than leading the host."

"Have I Your Majesty's leave to depart?"

"No."

"Then I go without it." Harald stepped towards the door, his left hand pulling at the knot in the sling.

"Stop him."

The guard stepped from the doorway into the room, his spear held crosswise to block. Harald caught the spear in his left hand, pulled. His right forearm, freed from its sling, swung like a mace, wrapping around to strike the back of the guard's head.

The King stepped forward, reaching for his dagger, mouth open. Harald, his left hand holding the spear by its middle, rested his right arm against the shaft and pushed. The swinging butt caught the King just over his left ear; he crumpled to the ground.

Harald bent over him; the King was still breathing. He walked over to the guard, dropped the spear by him, stood a moment catching his breath. Then he stepped out the door and yelled.

"Help! Assassin! To the King!"

With his left hand he shoved the block of stone off the wall; it fell into the moat with a loud splash. When the first guard reached him he was looking over the wall.

"He went into the moat. Call out the guard. After him!"

Men shouting, horns blowing. Harald ran through the dark for the stable, reached it in a crowd of men. He pulled a panicked groom out of the pack, got his help saddling the mare, bowcase, quiver, saddlebags, a thick bundle behind the saddle.

The bridge down, the gate open, men streaming out. Harald joined them. Once over the moat and into the dark he brought the mare to a gallop, trusting her footing, found the turn to the west road, took it.

With no hoofbeats behind he slowed to a walk, retied the sling for his aching arm. Two hours west, where a stream flowed across the road to join the river running down the valley, he stopped, dismounted, led his mare up a path to the right. A short way in he stopped, broke off a pine bough. Leaving the horse he went back and did what he could, one-handed by moonlight, to wipe out the prints of her passage.

Somehow he made it back onto the horse. The path left the stream, climbing along the side of a little valley. Again the stream on his right, now broad and shallow. Where it was bordered by rocks he swung the mare into the water, followed the stream uphill, away from the path. Dawn found him among trees, the stream to his left, the path well out of sight beyond it. Past the brush to his right he found a small meadow. With the last of his strength he unsaddled the mare, rubbed her down with handfuls of dry grass. The grass was soft, cloak warm, the bundle of bedding . . .

It was past noon before the sun shifted far enough to come out from behind the oak tree and shine into his eyes. He kept them closed while he followed step by step what he could remember of the night's journey, opened them at last to the feel of a velvet muzzle against his cheek.

"You've had your breakfast, heart's delight, and yes I'm sorry we had to leave him behind. Now I've to find mine. And more." He fed the mare handfuls of grass, walking around the meadow's edge while she nuzzled at his shoulder, stopped where an old tree had fallen a little back into the woods, one end supported by a massive boulder. An hour's work dragging dead branches and the shelter, not yet weatherproof, was at least sight proof. Saddle, saddlebags, useless bow and quiver went into it. Over the pile his rain cloak.

The next step was pine branches cut a safe way off to thatch the shelter, or snares, or . . . He found himself lying in the piled pine needles by his shelter, the sun a considerable way down the sky, considering that perhaps, at his age, a broken arm deserved more respect than he was giving it.

Sanctuary

**With half a loaf and an empty cup
I found myself a friend**

Over the next few days, working with long breaks, Harald succeeded in thatching his shelter, locating a small swamp well supplied with cattails, and snaring one rabbit. He also spent several frustrating hours discovering his inability to tickle trout left-handed—the fish kept escaping at the last moment just as he was about to flip it onto the bank—and fell back, with better success, on hook and line.

That morning he was fishing, back to a rock, trying not to think about cattail roots. A bundle of string in wet starch. But letting his arm heal and the hunt die down would take longer than his supplies were going to last; best save the remaining travel food for travel. He resolutely turned his mind to the more entertaining topic of his recent host, with aching head, trying to explain what had become of his guest and why.

"Hullo."

Harald looked up. The boy was standing on the other side of the creek, barefoot. He called across.

"Any luck? The big pool downstream is better."

Harald reached down, held up the largest of his catch. The stranger appearing unlikely to act on his advice at once, the boy walked a little downstream, waded across, came back up the bank. Harald looked up at him.

"Hungry? Should be enough for two."

The boy was staring down at Harald's splinted right arm, eyes wide. He stepped back.

"You're the one they're hunting for."

Harald gave him an enquiring look.

"Two men. Staying at our farm, eating our food. Scaring Mother. There's enough for the two of us, but they eat more. Now they want us to slaughter something for them. This time of year!"

Harald, a farmer himself most of the time, gave a sympathetic nod.

"They said a rider with one arm broken. Where's your horse?"

Harald gestured towards the line of brush.

"The little meadow? We sometimes use it for fall pasture. Can I see?"

"After lunch. I like my fish fresh."

Fire from the buried coals took a few minutes blowing; dry branches gave only a little smoke, dispersed in the thick leaves above. Jon helped Harald clean the trout, a messy job with only one hand. By the time they were done the flames were mostly burned down. The boy helped him arrange a rough grill of peeled green sticks over the coals, spread out the fish.

"Tell me about the men looking for me."

"Say they're from the King, say they need to find you,

money to pay for news. Went looking yesterday. Mail shirts. Swords. Both together. Up and down the path, brush around it. Not likely to come this far—we're most of a mile from home. Hear them coming."

"How close are your neighbors? If there's trouble with the men, will they help?"

"Downstream there's nobody till you get to the main road, valley people, strangers. Upstream old Olaf and his boy a good hour's walk. More people further up. Ragnar went for a soldier, fought in the big war six years ago. Has a sword. But there are two of them."

Harald thought a moment. Got up.

"Come see my horse."

The mare trotted across the meadow to them. Jon stood frozen, his mouth open.

"She's beautiful."

"Smart too." Harald pulled a wrinkled apple from somewhere, fed it to the horse. She lowered her head, sniffed for more. Gave up in disgust, walked over to Jon.

"I'm sorry. I could find some white roots, bring them tomorrow?" He shyly stroked the big head.

They sat for a while on the bank, feeding her handfuls of green grass.

"Will they notice you're gone?"

"Not till they want something. They'll expect the horses rubbed down this evening in the stable. Turned out the cow to make room. Took our bed, too."

"Do you want me to kill them?"

Jon looked up at him, startled. Hesitated a moment.

"Can you?" He glanced down at the broken arm.

"Probably. With your help. Not today."

"Yes. I'll come tomorrow."

"Better not to tell your mother. Easier to hide things you don't know."

Jon nodded. After he had gone Harald got out his bow, a handful of arrows, a length of leather thong. Stringing the recurve was tricky, but he had one hand, two legs and forty years of practice. That done he went looking for a convenient bank of earth. It had been a long time.

Late the next day Erik, the older of the two Wolves, saw the widow's boy coming out of the stable.

"Got 'em rubbed down proper, fed, watered?"

"Yes sir."

"Grain, not just hay?"

The boy hesitated, looked away.

"Yes sir."

"I'll come see. Don't go off."

The stable was dark. Erik was still blinking when the first arrow hit him. He looked down in astonishment at the feathered shaft sprouting from his belly, a hand's breadth above the belt, looked up, started to yell. Harald, sitting in the half loft above the stall, back to a post, bare feet against the bow, loosed the second arrow.

The door opened. Jon peered in, saw the crumpled body, stepped back, yelled.

"Come quick. Your friend's hurt."

Harald nocked a third arrow, drew it back.

By the time Harald had freed the bow from his feet, made his way to the ground, made sure both men were dead, Jon had joined his mother on the porch. She listened to him a moment, looked up. Harald faced her.

"My counsel, they left yesterday. The boy and I can deal with the bodies."

"The horses?"

"See if they're marked. Some way to sell them, no questions? Need be, I could take one when I go."

She thought a moment.

"I think I know someone who could sell them for me."

Harald whistled, waited. The mare came out of the woods, walked past Harald to Jon. Jon bent down, pulled something from the ground, gave it to her. His mother looked at the horse, smiled. Harald put on his best frown.

It took the rest of the evening to strip the bodies of the Wolves, load one onto the mare, the other on one of the geldings, and dump them a considerable distance off in the woods for their namesakes to deal with. The gelding was unhappy at the smell of blood, but Jon gentled him. By the time they got back, Jon himself was looking white. His mother hugged him, led him inside, came out again.

"I'll be back in the morning."

"Sleep here. I'll find blankets, make up a bed in the hay. You'll want dinner too."

He hesitated a moment, nodded, took the mare into the stable, himself to the well to wash off the worst of it.

Harald spent almost two months with them while the broken arm healed, paying for his board with fish, snared rabbits and, towards the end when he could again use a bow, two deer. Most of his time was spent in the woods out of sight, much of it with Jon. The boy, used to animals, took to riding like a Westkin child. The bow was too stiff for him to draw; Harald shaped one from a branch of ash, taught him to shoot from horseback.

"Come over the mountains some day, we'll get you a proper bow."

"What's wrong with this one? I like it."

"Longbow's fine on foot. Too clumsy on horseback. Aiming left, see an enemy right, what do you do?"

The boy tried to swing the bow across. The lower limb caught on the mare's neck; he dropped the bow. The mare looked up at him curiously.

"Horn bow that wouldn't happen."

"Is it really made of horn?"

"Belly horn, back sinew, a little wood to hold them together. Takes a year to make, lasts a lifetime. More if you're careful. Or careless. We learned them from the Westkin."

When Harald finally set off again on the mare, Jon walked him the first few miles up the trail into the mountains.

"Will I see you again?"

"Likely. Heading home over the pass, but I'll be back. Things to deal with near here. May take a while."

The boy stroked the horse's neck, his face buried in her mane.

"Expect she'll be back too."

"Promise?"

"Can't bind the world. Try."

He dismounted, gave Jon a long hug.

"Take care of your mother. When it's all over, come visit, meet my boys."

Jon nodded, said nothing.

Enemies and friends

A wayfarer should not walk unarmed

It took Harald two days to make it up the valley and over, much of the time leading the mare, and work his way down the far side of the ridge to the head of the next valley north. Then west, following the stream that flowed down to the plains. Beyond plains the high pass, home.

That evening he heard voices, smelt a breath of smoke, turned the mare off the path and into the woods. A wide circle was cleared of trees, its center a mound, two men watching. A wisp of smoke came out; one of them put a clod over it. Harald quietly unstrung his bow, wrapped bow and quiver into the bundled bedding behind his saddle, rode out of the trees.

He spent the night with the charcoal burners, traded smoked meat for bread only two days from the oven. In the morning they sat watching the mound, sharing their cheese and bread, his sausage and dried apples.

"Come a long ways?"

"Fair. In the hills trapping, guesting, widow woman."

Harald gave them a sidelong glance. The younger of the two grinned at him. Harald spoke again.

"I've got furs. Traders down valley, on the road?"

"Maybe at the inn. The path comes out of the hills, goes on a bit, crosses the road north. Big building, stable, picture of the sun on the sign. Pack trains come by with salt, pretty things from the city. Going back to your widow lady, maybe?"

"Maybe."

Stopping for lunch, a walnut tree caught his eye. A brief search unearthed half a dozen of last year's nuts, still in their dry hulls. A few stones, a coal from its bed of moss in his clay firebox, threads of bark, twigs, branches. His pan, filled with water from the stream, went over the small fire; he patiently shredded the walnut hulls into it.

Hair, beard and face. The creek provided a pool to rinse in, a still shallow for a mirror. More dye for patches of gray. He dumped out what was left, rinsed the pan, scrubbed it with sand. Fresh coals into the fire box, more moss. Water on the fire.

It was almost dark before he reached the inn, its yard crowded with pack mules being unloaded. A small coin persuaded the stableboy—a stall, hay, a little grain. When he had finished rubbing down the mare, Harald shoved saddle, saddlebags, rolled war coat onto the shelf at the end of the stall, the horse blanket over all, gave the mare a final pat and strict instructions, went off to the inn.

The big room was crowded, a fire at one end. Near the door a knot of Imperials, the chief trader, his assistants, two or three smaller traders traveling with him. One table was packed with the group's guards, still in armor, another had half a dozen of what looked like local farmers, one of the faces vaguely familiar. Harald slid through the crowd to the fire, put out his hands to warm them, stood looking at the flames, listening.

The Imperials were speaking Tengu, the Emperor's tongue if not quite to the Emperor's standards. The roads were muddy, bandits a nuisance, but the Kingdom's little court was buying, the weavers in the city were selling, and matters could, on the whole, be worse. The guards were talking what he suspected was Bashkazi, which might have been useful if he had grown up a few hundred miles farther east. The farmers were mostly complaining about the weather.

Harald spotted the innkeeper coming down the stairs from the upper rooms, drifted over to him, spoke in the nearest he could manage to the traders' dialect.

"The small room at the end—it is free?"

The innkeeper looked him over curiously.

"My master wishes me to arrange."

"Two silver pennies." The man held up two fingers.

Harald didn't blink.

"Moment."

He went past the crowd of traders, nodding familiarly at one, out the door. Back with a bundle on his shoulder.

"Arrange." He handed the innkeeper the coins, climbed the stairs. The room had a bed, a bar for the door, a window looking over the porch roof to the stable. Dinner a risk he could do without. With luck he could buy bread and sausage in the morning. With such a crowd, the innkeeper was unlikely to keep track of who slept where.

He woke before dawn, chasing a memory through

dreams. A face. Blond hair. A farmer's tunic—no. He came suddenly awake. One of the farmers. The man who knew someone who was hiring mercenaries.

Nobody was up in the yard yet, but he thought he saw movement in the stable door. He pulled on the mail shirt, over that his cloak, gave one regretful glance at his blankets, swung the shutters wide, stepped out onto the porch roof, a short drop to the yard, two steps to the stable.

The boy looked up at him, startled.

"Help me with my horse; I have to get on the road early today, ahead of the others."

"I. I need to . . ."

Harald blocked the doorway.

"Help me with the horse. An extra coin for you."

The boy, nervous, saddled the horse, strapped saddle-bags behind, Harald watching. He reached up for the bundle on the high shelf, tossed it to Harald, bolted for the door.

Seconds were a price that had to be paid. The hardened leather chest piece—all he had of the mare's barding. He pulled out bowcase and quiver, hooked them to the saddle, shrugged into the lamellar coat. Over that the cloak, for whatever good it did. Into the saddle. Harald burst out of the stable, headed for the north road, brought the mare to a full gallop.

Nobody in sight yet. He lashed down bow case and quiver, pulled out the bow, strung it. Hoofbeats, a horn. Three men at least coming out of the trees behind the inn, perhaps more. The light archer's shield to the outside of his bow arm; he checked the saddle mace, butt up in its pocket at the side of the bowcase.

Trees, more trees. The forest spread down the hills, out onto the plain; the North Road ran through it for miles. In the open, with a full quiver, he could deal with riders behind him, but . . .

The first arrow glanced off the flap guarding his thigh; he never saw the archer. Two more glancing, then a sharp pain in his calf; the mare broke stride a moment, was back in her gallop.

"Brave lady." He pulled the leg up, snapped off the projecting point; there was no time for more.

An archer rose from beside a tree, almost in front of him. In one smooth motion Harald drew and loosed. Yells behind. He saw an arrow coming from in front, knocked it aside with the shield, missed another—it caught in the cloak, stopped by the armor. He thought he heard the higher twang of a crossbow, felt something in his back.

The road broke out into a long clearing. Turning in the saddle, Harald put two arrows into the nearest pursuer. The man fell back, his hands still clutching the reins; the horse swung to one side, went crashing through the trees. His third caught the next rider in the throat, tumbled him out of his saddle. More behind, and men with bows coming out of the woods. Harald glanced ahead.

The clearing ended against a steep bank; the road swung left across its face. The archers were too close. He brought the mare to a sliding stop where the road turned, wheeled, back to the bank, face to the enemy.

Two riders died, the third reached him. He caught the sword on his shield's rawhide edge, felt it cut and catch, struck back with the saddle mace, felt the blow go home. The bow into its scabbard. The mare reared under him, turned, struck out with forehooves; the attacker on that side clutched his reins as his horse shied aside, tried to bolt. Harald jammed his shield into the man's face, struck once to cripple the shoulder, a second time to kill, felt a heavy blow on his helm.

For a moment the world turned black. Somehow he stayed in the saddle as the mare backed him free of the tangle. Then block and blow as the mounted Wolves swarmed around him. At least no arrows. A line of fire across his right shoulder, another over his ribs. He struck back, felt the strength draining from his arm. The world swung around him, the mace loose in his fingers.

"Back or die, dogs."

The voice was above and behind him. The mare was still backing, he was again for a moment clear. The remaining Wolves, still between him and their own archers, were looking not at him but up.

"We are here on the King's business, Lady." The face of the leading rider blurred, but he knew the voice.

"Too much of the King's business here. Back. Your archers down their bows or die. We're in cover; they aren't."

One of the archers must have tried to draw or run. He heard the bowstrings behind him, thought he heard the arrows thud home, the man grunt.

"Next?"

The familiar voice spoke.

"Bows down, men back into the woods, meet at the inn. We'll settle this later."

The riders were backing away, turning. Harald watched, what remained of his shield raised. He heard voices, noise behind him, held steady. It was dark early. He would have to . . .

The ground came up, struck him.

He woke first to a stab of pain, held himself still. He was flat on his face; someone was examining his back with a sharp knife.

"Not deep, but the bastards' bolts are barbed." He considered telling her about the little flask in his kit. Considered it again.

The next time he was on his back, lying on something soft, what felt like a rolled up cloak under his head. He was light-headed and most of him hurt, but so far as he could tell by cautious twitches there were no arrows actually sticking in him. Progress. Voices.

"I don't know who but I know what, and I saw him kill four Wolves while you were stringing your bow. That's more than we've done all month."

"I'm sorry. I was nervous. Everything was so fast."

"Fighting's like that. You'll learn. Or not."

"It was . . ."

"I've never seen better. The horse as good as the man. But now they're our problem. We can't leave him. We can't take him with us; he'd be dead in a day. We can't stay here—eventually that Wolf captain will decide he has a big enough pack and come looking."

Harald spoke:

"My horse."

"She's in better shape than you are. Nothing broken, nothing that won't heal."

He closed his eyes, breathed slowly, let the world fade back.

Hoofbeats in front, behind. He felt his body swaying. A horse litter. Gods grant neither beast bolted.

"No you can't. 'Thora, stop the beast."

"You stop her."

The hoofbeats stopped, the litter stopped swaying. Something cold and wet against his shoulder. He reached up, stroked the mare's muzzle.

He was lying in a bed. Too hot. Dull aches, none of which seemed to matter. Someone was trying to talk to him.

"Old Gudmund and Anna will take care of you. We have to go. They'll send word when they can. You're their nephew Karl. A falling tree hurt you."

It was a struggle to open his eyes, to force his mind to think, his mouth to speak.

"Can you get a message to your hold, up the top of Mainvale?"

There was a long silence, voices whispering together.

"Yes. It will take time."

"No hurry. When someone goes. Lady Aliana. Nobody else. Niall. His father. Home next spring."

"We are to tell the Lady Aliana in Valholt at the top of Mainvale that Niall's father will be home next spring?"

Harald nodded, closed his eyes, was again asleep.

He slept for a long time, brief intervals for water, a little soup. The legions advanced, a wall of shields, unbreakable. He signaled; the trumpet sounded. The boulders rolled down. He saw the faces, horror, courage, surprise. Crushed bodies. Men moaning. The wind blew, the field faded like mist. Leonora pulling off corpses with a cold face, looking, finding. He forced his eyes to open. His leg hurt.

A wrinkled face leaned over him. Behind her a lifted curtain, beyond a small room, a fireplace. She was saying something. He strained to understand. His mouth was dry; he nodded. She held the cup to his lips.

After the fever broke the dreams changed for the better. Sometimes he was awake for hours, strong enough to lift a cup, spoon soup. Sliding away into sleep, he saw the Imperial left come down on the Order—heavy cavalry, Belkhani, twenty cacades, a forest of lances. The Ladies stood their ground, pouring arrows into the charging ranks. Watching from the hilltop, waiting for the center and right to move against him, he stopped breathing. At the last moment, impossibly late, the front ranks almost on them, up and away, fleeing for their lives. The Order's lights gradually drew away from the slower heavies; the charge ground to a halt. Two hundred yards beyond the milling lines the Ladies were again dismounted, too far for his eyes but he knew arrows were flying down the wind, Belkhani falling. A second time, a third, impossibly precise, perilously close, the line of Ladies shooting as the cavalry bore down on them, up and away before the lances closed.

He had seen the drill over and over. This was real. The fourth charge ground to a halt, the Belkhani ranks thinned, tired horses, tired men. Their lances swung up. At the left end of the Order's line a figure raised her hand. The line of riders, mail silver in the morning sun, wheeled, shifted weapons in an instant, lances down, heartbreaking grace, the silver wave swept down on the astonished cavalry, over it, on. Three legions in front of him still untouched, four thousand light infantry on their right, but she had won him his battle. Darkness. Light. Darkness again.

Again light. He rode the wind, the floor of the world in all directions to the sky. The stolen horses ahead. Hoofbeats behind would never catch them. He heard Conor yell.

The bay had stumbled over something, gone head over heels, her rider flying, rolling. Harl spun the black, charged their pursuers, faces over shields, both spears leveled at him. At the last moment he leaned down the side of his horse, ducking the points, back up, spear crosswise, leaning into it, knees locked to the horse's side.

It almost drove him from the saddle, but braced for the shock he rode it through, heard his spear snap, felt his horse driven back on its haunches. He spun the horse again, joy bubbling in his throat. Both ravens were out of the saddle, one running after his horse, the other doubled up—the spear butt must have knocked the breath out of him. Harl brought the black into a canter after the rider-less horse, heading it to the left. Conor ran alongside, caught the mane, up. The herd still ahead, still moving, six horses. As he drew even, Conor turned, waved, finger sign for seven. They rode on, both laughing.

Harald opened his eyes. The arm on the blanket was skeletal, muscles withered, skin wrinkled. A moment before he had been young, the wind in his hair, his oath-brother laughing beside him. He clenched his hand. The claw fingers moved.

His hand. His arm. The end of the bed. He tried to move his foot; the blanket stirred. A wood wall, mud chinked. Carefully, feeling down the years, Harald put the world back together. Conor was dead of the fever ten years ago, more. Harald had fostered one of his sons.

It was a week before he could walk, steadied by a stick. Once he could go more than a few steps he asked after the mare, stumbled out to the little stable. Gudmund showed him where his gear was hidden. A child's bow would have been more useful, but that would change. A week later, naked in the stream, he scrubbed himself clean for the first time in months. Wounds all healed, even the twisted dimple in his left calf. Thinner than he could remember, weak as a child, moving like an old man. Alive. An old man's face looked back at him out of the water, gaunt, hair and beard white. He shivered; the wind was cold. A dead leaf floated by. He looked west. Through trees, over the plain, through rock. Snow falling, snow banks head high in the pass. He dried himself off, pulled on a patched tunic, walked back to the cottage.

Harald lay in bed, eyes closed. Anna and Gudmund were by the fire on the other side of the room. He was a little deaf, so her side of the conversation could for the most part be understood.

"I left sign for the sisters, but it could be weeks. Here tomorrow, next day at best."

"They'll search the stable. The horse. You heard what happened to Katrine. We have to get him away. Maybe the woods?"

". . . cold . . ."

"I know. But if they find him. Not just him."

"We could sit tight. Nephew. Neighbors won't tell. . . . But . . ."

The conversation went on, voices rising and falling;

from time to time he could catch one or two of Gudmund's words.

When he was sure they were asleep he rolled out of bed, lowering himself quietly to the floor, feeling under the bed for clothing. It was his own, plain enough to suit. He dressed hastily, the warmest he could find. Not warm enough. One blanket from the bed went around him, a belt to hold it. He untied the purse, reached into it. The loose stone by the fireplace. He dropped a handful of gold coins on top of whatever it held, put the stone back. Two more blankets, the rest of his clothes. Boots. Cloak. A sausage from dinner, a hard roll. The clay fire box, coals.

The two oxen dreamed of green fields; the mare heard him, stamped, moved to her stall's door.

"Not long now, lady love. Cold for you, me too, but at least moving."

He lifted a square of floor, pulled out the saddle blanket, draped it over her. Saddle. Saddlebags. Handfuls of apples from the bin at the back of the stable. He leaned against the mare's side, breathing hard. She butted her head against his shoulder.

From the little farm in the eastern fringe of North Province where foothills ran up to the mountains his nearest friend was three days travel north and west. The sky was clear, the wind at his back. At first he walked, but the mare was in better shape than he was. From time to time he woke enough to be sure they were still going in the right direction. A little before dawn he found a windfall and a heap of leaves, mostly dry, near a clearing of brown grass. He left the mare to graze, curled up in the leaves, blankets wrapped around him.

The next day it started to snow. He went on for several hours, using wind and the lie of the land, felt himself slipping, caught himself, opened his eyes. The ground was covered with a thin white layer. He found shelter for both of them under an overhanging bank.

By morning the snow was deeper. He scraped clear as much grass as he could, fed the mare apples, himself from what was left of his traveling food. One more day's rest, then . . .

The next morning cold but clear. They set out, using the sun and the shape of the land. Downhill was mostly west. Downhill was good. By noon he was stumbling, holding on to the saddle, afraid to risk riding and falling. Shelter this time was a tall pine, branches weighed down by snow, space under almost clear. Dead branches made a fire; he melted snow, warm for the mare, hot for him, ate the last of his food.

They were in flat land now; he mounted. It began to snow. As it grew darker he searched for shelter. Nothing. He pulled the blanket tighter around him under his cloak.

The mare had stopped, was sniffing something. With an effort he dismounted. Hoofprints. Recent; the snow was still falling. Someone was going somewhere.

The mare stopped again, Harald holding on by one hand. He leaned against her for a moment, shivering, put out his hand. Stone. Wood. A gate. Looking up, he saw walls, a tower, faint against falling snow.

"Hullo."

Silence.

Cold fingers found the mace where he had tucked it

under the saddle flap. He pounded the butt against the wood with what strength he had left. Again.

Above him a voice.

"Who's there?"

"A traveler, lost. Followed hoofprints."

"Just a minute."

A small shutter opened in the door; he thought he saw something pale behind it. More noises. The gate swung open. He followed the mare into a small courtyard.

After that everything seemed to be happening at once. A boy spoke to the mare, stroked her head, led her off telling her what a brave horse she was. Someone closed the gate. A man with one arm around Harald's shoulders helped him up the stone stairway, a small hall, a chair by the fire. Someone was yelling at several other people, but he wasn't sure what about. The clay mug in his hand was warm, the wine hot and sweet.

Hospitality

**Alone on a long road,
I lost my way:
Rich when I found another;
Man rejoices in man.**

He woke in a bed, a small room, fire in the fireplace at one end. A lump by his feet, a rock wrapped in cloth by the feel; someone had said something about hot rocks, sometime, but he couldn't remember who or when. A face. A boy, the boy who had taken the mare, was looking curiously into the room.

"Hullo. You're awake. I'm Henry; everyone calls me Hen. Father's in the hall. He says if you're awake you can join him for noon meal, if you want. I didn't wake you?"

"No. And yes. I'll be a few minutes."

Someone had brought up his saddlebags, the heavy bundle that held his war coat, the lighter bundle of bedding wrapped around cased bow, quiver. Nothing had been opened; courteous folk. The floor was cold against his feet; he had to catch hold of the headboard to keep

85

from falling. After a moment the world steadied. His body was still slow to do his bidding. He limped over to the saddlebags, opened them, pulled out clean clothes.

The hall was as small as he remembered. By the wall straw pallets were piled, bedding neatly rolled up. The long trestle table, covered with a litter of plates, mugs, platters, filled two-thirds of the room. A woman was clearing things away. At one end a man was sitting. He rose as Harald came into the room.

"Welcome to Forest Keep. I'm Yosef, the castellan, hold from North Province. The snow's stopped, but it's no weather for a man your age to be out in alone. Or mine for that matter." He stopped, looking at Harald.

"Harl, from Northvales some time back. I wasn't alone, that's why I'm alive; mare spotted the tracks. That and your hospitality. I'm your debtor."

Yosef gestured to the table.

"My boy, the guards, have left a few crumbs. Sit, eat."

After the meal, Harald thanked his host, went back up the stairs for a wool overtunic and cloak, into the courtyard to explore the little castle. One corner was the old keep, its ground floor the stable, above that the old guard room, now the preserve of the castle women, top floor occupied by the guard captain and his wife. The next corner, the other side the main gate, was the new keep with the hall, guestroom and lord's chamber above. Ground floor of the new keep was storerooms, the kitchen a wooden structure built on, sharing one wall with the keep, one with the outer wall of the castle.

He ended in the kitchen, drawn by the smell of baking bread. One of the castle guardsmen, there getting in the way of the cook, was chased out, a roll steaming in his hand. Harald found a convenient corner, enjoyed the warmth of the small room.

"New face good to see—you last night's arrival?"

Harald nodded.

"Young men steal half the bread I bake. Only fair we old men get our share." The cook tossed Harald a roll; Harald caught it, bit into it while looking around the kitchen.

"Lend you a hand? Meat to be cut up, I've handled a blade."

The cook looked him up and down, nodded. Harald spent the next hour reducing a deer, brought in by two of the guardsmen the previous day, to pieces suitable for the pot.

At dinner Harald met Rorik, the guard captain; his wife and two younger women brought food up from the kitchen. Asked about news from outside, Harald confessed that he had spent the past months visiting with friends up in the hills, apologized, and offered a story instead. By the time the fire had burned to ash the little hall held every man, woman, and child in the place, save for the two guardsmen on sentry duty, including a six-month-old baby asleep in her mother's arms. Harald tied up the last thread of a feud that had occupied the folk of Greenvale for two generations, off and on, and fell silent. Hen was lying at his feet, eyes closed, a smile on his face, looking absurdly young. Yosef bent down, picked up his son, carried him off up the stairs.

The next morning, after breakfast, Yosef told Harald that, if he had no urgent need to be elsewhere, he was welcome to guest with them until spring brought better weather for traveling.

Three weeks later Harald was coming into the stable with a sleeve full of apples when an arrow whipped past his nose, thudded into the wall, stuck there quivering. He stepped back, slammed shut the door with his right hand, reached left-handed for his dagger.

"I'm sorry; are you all right?" It was Hen's voice. Harald carefully put the dagger away. He was gathering spilled apples when the door opened. Hen stood there, bow in one hand, arrow in the other, a worried expression on his face.

"I was just practicing; I didn't hurt you did I?"

"No. Better luck next time."

"They took down the butts by the postern when it got cold, and Father won't let me go out and shoot at snow banks. If I don't shoot all winter I'll be hopeless by spring. I finished my target last night."

Walking cautiously back into the stable, Harald saw that what the arrow had stuck in was not the stone wall of the stable but a thick mat of carefully braided straw almost two feet across, hung from a peg jammed between the stones.

"Perhaps you should shoot at the end that doesn't have a door in it?"

"I never thought of that."

Harald took down the target, handed it to Hen, pulled out the peg, walked to the other end of the building, hammered it into a crack with a convenient stone. Hen handed him the target; he hung it on the peg. The two of them dragged a bundle of straw to the end by the door for Hen to use as a ground quiver. Harald watched for a while, then went out, closing the door behind him.

The next day he went back to the stable with more apples, ended up sitting on a stool watching Hen shoot. The best that could be said for his aim was that all of the arrows ended up somewhere in the target. When finally one failed even to do that, the boy stopped, glared at his bow, muttered something under his breath.

"Your bow didn't aim that arrow; you did."

The boy glared at him.

"Unjust to the bow. Bad for the liver. Makes for bad shooting, too."

Hen looked as if he couldn't decide whether to laugh, cry, or throw something. He settled for a question. "Why do the arrows wobble through the air?"

"You're plucking the string. Here."

Harald took the bow in his left hand, drew back the string a few inches with his right, released to a loud twang.

"See how I plucked sideways as I let go?"

The boy nodded.

"Makes the arrow wobble sideways. Bad aim, less range. Don't pluck, just open, let the string go." This time the release was almost soundless. He handed Hen back the bow.

Over the next few weeks, Harald got in the habit of ending his visits to the mare by sitting for a while watching Hen shoot. The boy politely offered to give Harald a turn with his bow, Harald politely declined, restricting himself to advice when asked. Hen, without asking, explained that the reason he had to learn to shoot was not for hunting, although hunting was all very well, but because he was still too small to use a sword.

"Last summer, at Lord Stephen's, they let me practice

with a wooden blunt. He said I was pretty good—the lord did. I beat one boy two years older. But Father won't give me a real sword. He says I'd get killed."

"In a real fight you probably would. If a strong man— Rorik, say—swung at you as hard as he could, what would you do?"

"Block with my shield."

"Ever have someone that big hit your shield hard?"

"No. I could duck."

"Ducking a sword's easier to say than to do. Did you manage it with the blunts?"

"No. But if I had to . . ."

"Had to's a bad time to do your learning."

"He can't hit me with a sword if I'm up on the castle wall with a bow and he's down below trying to batter the door down."

Harald nodded approvingly.

"Killing safe as you can. Much to be said for it. Ever shot out of an arrow slit?"

The boy shook his head.

"Tomorrow."

The next day, Harald and one of the guards carried a bundle of hay out the main gate, left it on the ground five feet from the wall. Hen watched.

"Enemy with a battering ram. Where do you shoot him from?"

The boy ran up the stairway to the top of the wall, leaned far over trying to find a way of shooting down. The guard caught the back of his tunic, hauled him back in.

"I could have done it."

Harald answered, "Could be; some day show you how.

Way you were doing it, only question is if you fall out and break your neck before or after someone on the other side puts an arrow through you. They can shoot too. Think, boy. Don't want them breaking down the door, killing us all."

Hen thought; Harald and the guard watched. The boy got up, ran along the wall to the door into the tower of the old keep. Harald gave the guard a satisfied look, followed. Inside, he heard the voice of one of the women asking Hen what he was doing in their room. Hen said he was stopping someone from breaking down the front gate and killing them all.

While Harald explained, Hen carefully examined the arrow slits, ending up in one cut into the wall partway up the spiral stair to the chamber above. Harald looked through a lower slit; there was nobody near the hay. When Hen had shot his arrows, the two went back down together. Two were in the hay bundle. The boy collected all eight, went back to his arrow slit; Harald remained behind to be sure nobody went out the gate at the wrong time. After the fourth round, he heard a step behind him, turned.

It was Yosef. Harald held up a finger to his lips, pointed at the hay, waited. An arrow sprouted out of it. Another. Another. When the last went home there was a yell from the tower, Hen out the ground floor door and running for the gate. He stopped when he saw his father.

"Might be some use yet, boy, ever comes to it."

They went out together.

Harald's strength came back slowly, but it came. Alone at night he uncased his bow, warmed it by the fire, strung it, drew, held at full draw for long seconds before his arm began to shake. By the flickering light he checked over the lacing of his lamellar war coat, replaced frayed thongs more by touch than sight. He oiled the ring shirt, patched the padding under it. Spring was a month away, perhaps longer. It too would come.

Visitors

Safe to tell a secret to one,
Risky to two,
To tell it to three is folly.

"The trumpet blew, the King's men in the middle started rolling boulders over and down. Imperials weren't happy when they saw them coming."

"The rocks wiped out the legions?"

"No such luck. The rocks tore holes in the shield wall. The rest was up to us."

"You charged them? Didn't you tell me that was stupid?"

"Would have been. We poured in arrows from just outside javelin range. Cats on the left, Order on the right. They tried to reform, but it was too late, and the rocks kept coming. Legionaries are good, but they die just like other people."

"What about—"

They heard voices in the courtyard below. Hen was on his feet first. Harald paused to pull his cloak around him.

Yosef was there already, Rorik beside him. One of the guards was opening the gate. Two riders came into the courtyard through the falling snow. The smaller spoke:

"Elaina ni Leonor, my sister Kara ni Lain. We come in peace."

Yosef stepped forward.

"I am Yosef, castellan of Forest Keep for Stephen of North Province. In peace be welcome."

Harald saw her swaying in the saddle, stepped forward. The Lady swung one foot over, slid down; he caught her as she fell.

Yosef spoke. "The hall is warmest; can you manage her?"

Harald nodded. "Hardly weighs anything." It was true. Despite the mail hauberk, he had carried boys who weighed more.

The other Lady was off her horse but on her feet. At a glance from his father, Hen took both horses. Harald carried Elaina up the stairs, through the door Yosef opened. Kara followed.

Yosef pulled one of the straw pallets in front of the fire; Harald kneeled, put her down gently. In the fire light, the stump of an arrow stood out from her side. He heard a gasp behind him.

"She didn't tell me."

Footsteps. Hen answered his father's unspoken question.

"Old Jon has them, is rubbing them down."

Harald spoke. "In my room, the open saddlebag. A bundle, so long, tied with a red cord."

While he waited for the boy to come back with his kit, Harald looked over the wounded Lady, peeling back the wet cloak, careful not to disturb the arrow. Besides the rent in the hauberk where the arrow had gone through, there were three more, sword slashes by the look of them, two oozing blood. He looked at her pale face in the firelight. His breath caught in his throat.

When it was all over, Elaina was unconscious but bandaged and alive, wrapped in blankets in front of the fire, Kara sitting beside her. Harald washed the needle, the small knife, dried them, threaded another strand of sinew, assembled the kit, tied it, his mind elsewhere. Someone put a warm mug in his hand.

He looked up at Yosef.

"You'll want to leave them here tonight; it's too soon to move her. I'll get my things down from the guest room tomorrow morning; with luck it'll be safe to carry her up by then."

"I'm not leaving my sister."

"Of course. You'll want a pallet on the floor next to her; she might wake in the night."

Someone came in with a tray of food up from the kitchen. Harald's eyes met Yosef's. Yosef broke a piece of bread, sprinkled it with salt from the bowl, handed it to Kara. She took it, eyes still on the huddled body by the fire, tasted it, looked up startled.

"Thank you."

Yosef looked at her a moment, spoke.

"Are you wounded too?"

"I don't think so. Something here?"

She felt by her neck; her hand came away sticky with blood. The wound was shallow, a glancing arrow between cap and mail. While Harald was washing and bandaging it, Kara started to talk in a low voice.

"After the ambush, when they were chasing us. She said to let her do it, hold back with the bow. I usually do what she says. She didn't tell me she was wounded. Besides, she's better than I am at hand-to-hand. Better than anyone. Was."

"Will be." Harald spoke softly. "She's young, strong."

The Lady's face softened a little. She put her head down in her hands.

The next morning Harald separated his bedding and the saddlebag with his clothes, shoved everything else in a corner of the guest room, went downstairs to claim a space by the wall. Elaina was still sleeping, Kara watching her. Hen, silent for once, watched both while two of the guards ate quietly.

"You'll be going up to the guestroom on the next floor, soon as it's safe to move your sister. Want us to fetch your things up?"

Kara thought a moment, nodded.

Hen jumped up. "I'll go."

Harald took an absent-minded bite from a chunk of bread, leaned over the sleeping girl, put the back of his hand to her forehead. It was hot.

"Has she eaten, drunk anything?"

Kara shook her head. He put a little wine in a goblet, laid it near Elaina's head.

"Wakes while I'm gone, see if she'll take that. I'll try for broth up from the kitchen." He went out.

Elaina woke, slept, woke again; her sister spooned warm broth into her when she could. While she slept Harald checked over Kara's wound. He made her take some of the broth too, bread dipped in it. Before dinner he carried the sleeping girl carefully up the stairs in his arms, laid her on the bed. Hen brought the bowl of broth; Harald put it on the hearth, almost into the fireplace, spoke to Kara.

"She needs to stay warm too; that's why I moved the bed so close to the fire."

"I'll lie with her."

"Of course. Lie still if you can; she needs the sleep."

Kara got up to put another log on the fire, wincing a little, noticed Hen staring at the two longbows leaning up against the wall. She kneeled, warming her hands.

"Have you killed people?"

"Tried. Didn't stay around to see."

"I'll be in the next room, with Father. Anything you need, just call; I sleep light."

Kara nodded her thanks; they went out. Harald closed the door.

Two days later, Harald brought in a platter of food, Hen a pitcher of beer, both to the small table that someone had found and placed by the bed. Elaina spoke. "Harl, stay a minute please."

Hen hesitated, went out. Harald sat down on the hearth near the head of the bed, warming his hands at the coals.

"You've been very kind. Everyone has. I, we, hoped you could tell us things."

He waited.

"Yosef, your lord, he welcomed us, gave Kara bread and salt, that's three days. But he's the man of the North Province lord. North Province lord is the King's man."

Kara spoke. "King isn't exactly our friend, lately."

Harald let himself look up at the face above him for a moment. Not easily frightened or turned. The cheeks were unscarred, eyes clear, hair, washed clean by her sister the night before, dark. He forced his gaze away, turned to Kara, sitting at the other end of the hearth.

"Yosef is not my lord; I'm a guest here as well. A good and generous man, else I might have died in the snow three months back. He will not turn you over to your enemies, or send you out for them to hunt down, saving a direct order from his lord. Maybe not then; Stephen chooses his people well. And his hall is a long day's ride from here; Yosef has no reason to send there, or Stephen here. Not much safety in the world, this side the grave. More here than most places."

The two girls said nothing. He got to his feet slowly, went out.

The weather warmed towards spring, the snow melted. Harald took the opportunity to exercise the mare, riding in the woods near the castle. Once Elaina was on her feet again, she let Hen show her and Kara around Forest Keep, looked curiously at his archery range in the stable, fingered the target, gave Kara an inquiring glance. Kara looked at the target, shook her head. Hen looked at her, protested.

"It works fine."

"For you. At this range, our bows would shoot right through it. Stone walls aren't good for arrows."

"We have lots of hay."

Hen and Kara spent the afternoon rearranging some of the stored hay to make a head-high stack of tightly bound bundles at the far end of the stable, where Hen had his target. They were almost done when Harald came in, looked around, then at Hen.

"Haven't been practicing much lately, but you won't miss by that much."

"It's for the Ladies. Their bows would shoot right through my target."

"Ladies tried it yet?"

"I'll get our bows." That was Elaina.

"I'll get them; mine too." Hen went, Kara with him. While they were gone, Harald braided some of the loose straw into a palm sized circle, pinned it to the hay with a long splinter of wood, then rummaged around the corners of the stable looking for something; Elaina watched curiously. At last he came up with a chunk of broken spear shaft, a scrap of old leather.

When Kara and Hen came back with the bows and quivers, Elaina glanced at the haystack, the circle, her sister. Kara strung her bow; the others stood back. The first arrow went into the circle. The second. The third an inch outside. Hen watched in awe. Harald spoke.

"Good enough, if you find an enemy who stands still while you shoot at him. Hold up and we'll try something more interesting."

He stuck the wooden piece into the middle of the pile, well to the right, pinned the leather a foot lower on the left. Kara looked at him.

"You sound like my mother."

Harald looked straight at Elaina, did his best to look puzzled.

"Don't look much like her."

Hen looked from one to the other, a blank expression on his face. Elaina laughed.

"She's Kara ni Lain—Harl heard it when we came.

That's Kara daughter of Elaina. I'm named after her mother—she and my mother were friends. Like us. She died when Kara was twelve."

"You mean she isn't your daughter? I thought you looked a little young." Harald kept a straight face as long as he could. Hen figured it out, laughed.

"But you do sound like my mother—Elaina ni Liana not Elaina ni Leonor." Her sister gave her a worried glance, looked away.

"Yes. So I'll say what your mother would: stop talking, start shooting." Kara looked startled, nocked an arrow, stared at the piled hay.

"Wood. Straw. Leather. Leather. Straw."

At each word Kara drew, released. The worst was a hand's breadth from its target.

Kara waited a moment, lowered her bow.

"Straw."

Arrow to the string, bow up, arrow into the circle.

"You'll do. 'Laina?"

Shooting at the straw circle, Elaina did almost as well as her sister. But one of the shafts called for leather went to wood instead, another wild. She put the bow down, pale faced, breathing hard.

"She's still recovering; it isn't fair. She needs to rest."

Harald looked at Hen.

"Won't be fair if an enemy arrives tomorrow, either."

Elaina nodded.

"I'll rest now, after we eat shoot again, again tomorrow. Harl's right."

They had two more weeks. She used them.

⚜ ⚜ ⚜

A different story this time, a larger audience—Hen sitting with the two Ladies on their bed while Harald, on a cushion by the hearth, told how the quick wit of a Lady saved herself and a treasure. Her lover had just found the hidden bowstring, restrung his bow, when Elaina held up her hand. Harald stopped. In the silence he could hear voices in the courtyard.

A mounted man just inside the gate; looking down from the door at the top of the stairs, Harald could see the patch of red on the breast of his cloak. He stopped, Kara and Elaina behind him; Hen squeezed by to see better. Yosef and Rorik were in the middle of the courtyard. One of the guards was swinging the gate closed, two more hurrying up the stairs to the top of the wall. The stranger was speaking.

"They came here. They are here."

Yosef was calm. "Who guests with me is my affair."

"I speak in the King's name. They are rebels against their Order, to be handed over to us and delivered by us to their superiors."

"I am North Province's man. When Stephen of North Province commands me to deliver up guests to their enemies, I will consider the matter. For a voice out of the night, no."

The Wolf gave a long look around the little castle.

"Open the gate again, then. I must to my companions. I return in the morning; think on it before you set yourself against His Majesty's commands."

Yosef looked at Rorik, Rorik called up to one of the guards on the wall above the gate. The man looked out, turned back.

"Clear."

The gate open, the Wolf out, the gate closed again, barred. Yosef spoke with Rorik, then came up the steps into the hall, leaving the guard captain behind in the courtyard. Harald stepped forward.

"They may send to Stephen's Hall, but I think not. By my counsel we sleep armed."

"Rorik's as well. He does not think it will be at night, I have doubts they try us at all; Stephen is a bad enemy. But better safe. The guards watch while we arm, eat, then we watch while they take their turn."

Yosef's glance included the two Ladies. He turned back to Harald.

"You have been a soldier and know yourself best. Sentry duty at least—I can arm you from castle gear if you wish it."

"No need. I did not arrive at your gate stark naked."

He turned and went up the stairs to the guestroom. While the two Ladies got out mail hauberks, padding, helped each other into them, Harald pulled two bundles out of the stack in the far corner, unrolled them. The bow he laid carefully a little distance from the fire to warm, then drew on padding, mail, heavy war coat. Sword belt over all, quiver hooked on one side, bow scabbard the other. Kara turned, saw him, froze.

" 'Laina."

She turned as well. He nodded to both, picked up the bow, felt along its length a moment, sat down, strung it slowly, bending the recurve back across his thighs, working his way down the bow adjusting its curve, face intent. Satisfied he stood up, slid the bow into its scabbard, went out and down the stairs, leaving the two Ladies staring at each other.

Through the night they kept two men on guard, changing every few hours; the rest slept in armor in the hall. At dawn they were all up, breaking their fast on bread and soup. Then down into the courtyard. Harald turned to Yosef.

"Tree trunk at your door, ladder to the wall, likely the limit of their siege craft, archers in the woods. I'll take the slit covering the front gate from the old keep—it gives the best angle. Another archer in the new keep, the other side of the gate—your best man. Or Lady Kara."

Yosef looked at him doubtfully, hesitated, spoke. "I don't doubt your experience, but it's been a long time since you've used that bow."

Harald smiled, Hen spoke.

"Show them. My range in the stable. It'll give you a chance to practice, too."

Harald looked down at the bow in his hand, up at the boy. "Stone walls are hard on arrows." Hen's gaze fell. In one smooth flow Harald nocked, drew, released. Beating wings at the far side of the courtyard. He walked over, freed the arrow from the shed wall, the pigeon still moving weakly.

"I've been practicing."

Bow in one hand, bird in the other, he walked over to the kitchen door.

Two hours after dawn, a trumpet at the gate, a loud voice. Yosef answered from the wall above. The rider turned, rode back into the trees; as he reached them arrows flew. Yosef was already ducking for shelter; they missed.

The arrow slit gave Harald a view of the space in front of the door. Something moved into it, a crowd of men, some carrying a tree trunk, some a crude roof to shelter them from above, more at either side with big shields. The shields left their lower legs uncovered; he drew, shot, again, again. One of the shieldmen stumbled to his knees; Harald put two arrows through the gap before it closed.

There was a yell from above the gate, the sound of stone hitting wood, wood breaking. The cook and the castle women were pushing over the big rocks that someone, at some time in the past, had piled on the wall above the gate. The roof swayed, exposing men under it. Harald shot, again and again, as he found targets. A shield man had raised his shield to help hold up the wooden roof; before Harald could shift his aim the man was down. Someone else—probably from the slit below him. The ram down, the attack finished, men running for the woods; Harald dropped one of them. Yelling above, on the castle wall. He ran up the stairs to the roof.

While one group attacked the front gate, another had gotten a ladder up to the back wall of the castle, four men up it. One was fighting with a castle guard on the wall, two more behind him, one of them trying to get a spear past. The fourth, shield side to Harald, was partway down the wall, at the top of the stair Rorik was running up.

A tiny castle; everything close to everything. Harald's first shot dropped the fighting man. The spearman, suddenly unprotected, stepped back from the guard's advance, was blocked by his own man behind. A flurry of blows, Harald shot again, again. All three were down, the guard running for the ladder while Rorik, shield held high, traded blows with the fourth Wolf.

Harald took precious seconds to transfer two arrows from quiver to bow hand, nocked a third, waited. A face above the ladder, chest clear of the wall. Harald put three arrows into it in as many seconds, some part of his mind on Conor's father who taught him the trick. The man fell, the guard reached the ladder top, pushed it over. The Wolf fighting Rorik lowered his shield to block a chop at his leg; Harald shot him through the throat.

He took a long look around. The castle wall was clear of enemies. Rorik and the guardsman were on the back wall, bending over the body of another of the guards. On the front wall, sheltered by the rampart, Yosef and one of the guards were helping another, obviously hurt. Harald did a quick count, turned, went back down the keep stairs.

The archer at the lower slit was not Elaina but Hen; he looked up as Harald came down the stairs.

"I got one of them."

"One of them got you." Harald pointed at the spreading stain on the front of the boy's tunic. "Let me see."

Hen looked surprised. The arrow had sliced across the boy's chest; the wound was bleeding but not deep. Harald pulled a strip of cloth from under the skirt of his war coat, wrapped it around the boy's body over the wound.

"Good thing people are born with armor." Hen looked puzzled. "Breastbone. Want to kill someone, don't aim there. Next time, wear something."

In the courtyard, Yosef ran over to his son.

"I'm all right Father, just a scratch, I killed one of them."

Over his head the two men's eyes met. Harald nodded. "Yes and yes."

By noon the wounded had been dealt with, the enemy dead stripped, bodies over the wall. Hen delighted in a mail shirt, only slightly damaged; it reached well below his knees. Three of the defenders, Hen included, were injured, one badly. Neither Harald nor Rorik thought the Wolves would try again that day, but Yosef posted two of the remaining guards on sentry and the rest ate in armor.

The day dragged on. Harald sat by the wounded guard in the hall while one of the women fed him. He saw Elaina in the doorway, beckoning, followed her up to the guestroom. Kara was folding tunics, packing saddlebags.

"We have to leave. Tonight, out the postern. Before we get Yosef and everyone killed. Help us persuade him."

"You aren't asking the right question."

Elaina looked at him, puzzled.

"Big wolfpack outside, three decades, four, maybe more. Some of them hunting you a month or more. Two Ladies, no special rank or station. Storming a castle, risking war with a provincial lord. Why?"

There was a long silence. It was Kara who broke it.

"Your mother."

Elaina looked up. "We agreed."

"If we can't trust our friends, slit our throats now and save the folk outside the trouble."

"I should have changed the name."

Harald looked straight at her.

"Want to keep that secret, child, need a new face too."

She looked blankly at him, startled by the excitement in his voice.

"What is it?"

"Think; it's a useful habit. Why do they want to take your mother's daughter?"

Comprehension. Harald spoke.

"Can't put pressure on a corpse, child. She's alive. Best news I've had the past year."

Kara spoke, slowly. "If we can't leave, what do we do?"

"Send for help. Stephen's a day's ride away. Times like this he'll be feeding fifty swords in his hall, maybe more."

"Lord Stephen, the King's man. Can we trust him?"

Harald looked amused. "If the King trusts him to show up with an army when and where he's told, His Majesty's more of a fool than I think. Yosef trusts him. I trust him. His people trust him not to get them killed if he can help it. You'll be all right."

"I'll go."

It was Hen in the doorway, his father behind him.

"I know the paths, can get past them."

Harald shook his head.

"You don't know the way to Stephen's hold; you've been there twice in your life."

"Father can tell me."

"You're wounded, you can hide but you can't fight, and the guards at the gate might not believe you. I'll go."

Yosef, both hands on his son's shoulders, spoke over him. "Can you find your way?"

"Once I get to the north road. You'll have to tell me the first part."

"What if they chase you?" That was Hen again.

"Expect I have more arrows than they have men."

Harald gave Hen and his father a friendly nod, went past them, down the stairs, out to the stable.

Dark. The mare saddled, loaded, waiting by the postern gate. Harald in full armor. Hen, Yosef, the two Ladies. Elaina still arguing:

"A lot of them, it's a long way. I should . . ."

Harald tapped his quiver, gentled the mare. "I was breaking legions when you were at your mother's breast, child. Damn nuisance you were too." He led the mare out the postern into the night, Elaina staring after him.

Homeward

If you know a friend you can fully trust,
Go often to his house

Getting through the siege lines was easier than he had expected, since there weren't any. He saw several fires through the trees, heard voices of men around them. Only at the last minute, after he had mounted, was there a shout, footsteps running through the woods towards one of the fires. Harald moved off as quietly as he could. Several times he heard hooves, once someone yelling. Into the dark, through the forest, west and a little south by the stars. An hour later he heard the sound of hard packed dirt under the mare's hooves, stopped, looked right, left, the cleared road silent under the stars. He turned, rode north.

He rode all night and most of the morning, the last few hours through the plains as the tall hill grew closer, the timber walls at its top catching the sunlight. The gate was open, guarded. The gate guards looked up in surprise at a Northvales cat some considerable way from home, swaying in the saddle, the horse almost as tired as the man.

"Forest Keep is under siege; message for Lord Stephen."

The younger man stood frozen, his mouth open. The older gestured the rider forward.

"I'll take you. Arthur, Ragnar."

Two boys came running from the stable.

"Take the man's horse, rub her down, feed her."

Harald nodded his thanks, followed the guard between buildings towards the mass of the great hall.

It was a single enormous room, wood pillars along the sides, a long fire down the center, smoke rising, or not, through a hole in the roof. Near the far end its lord was sitting, talking with several of his men. He looked up, eyes widening. Harald spoke first.

"I bring a message from Yosef, castellan of Forest Keep. He is under siege and prays your aid."

Stephen looked at him, silent for a moment, then spoke to one of the men.

"Take Yosef's messenger to the south guest house. Food and drink." Then, to Harald, "I will join you there, hear more."

As Harald left, Stephen's voice faded behind him, other voices, hurrying footsteps. A man ran past, down the hall, out the other side door.

The guest house was a single room, newer than most of the hold, a fireplace at one end, a bed at the other, a table between. Harald pulled off his armor, did his best with the ewer and basin on the table. A servant came in, dumped a pail of burning coals onto the hearth, stacked wood above it. Another brought bread, cheese, sausage, a pitcher of beer. Harald was seated, eating slowly, when Stephen came in, closed the door, took the other chair, gave him a questioning look.

"Two Ladies, wounded, took refuge with Yosef a month back. I was guesting too, after some problems on the way home. One was Elaina, 'Nora's youngest.

"Day before yesterday, man at the gate, said he was a king's messenger. Demanded 'Laina, Kara. Yosef told him they were his guests, he was your man, not the King's. Yesterday they attacked, tried to storm the keep. Yosef, six guards, the Ladies, his boy Hen—not a bad shot, too brave for his own good." Harald fell silent a moment.

"And you."

"And me. Held them."

"How many?"

"I saw maybe fifteen, twenty, but there were more shooting from the woods. Three decades, four?"

Stephen sat thinking a while, then shoved his chair back, stood up.

"I'll have to send to the King. Thorvald to Forest Keep, three decades to keep him company, he's a careful man. I'll follow with more tomorrow. You'll want some rest. I'll have them send more food later. See you in the morning before I leave."

He looked straight at Harald for a moment. Harald looked back, nodded. Stephen went out.

By the time Harald woke it was almost dark. The table was spread with a cloth, on that a platter, on that an assortment of sausage, dried meat, dried fruit, cheese, bread— much of it hard baked biscuit. Dinner enough for three men. Harald ate some of the bread and cheese while he was putting on his armor, dumped the rest of the platter's contents onto the cloth. A minute later he was out of the room, the bundle of food concealed by his cloak.

In the stable he found the mare, rubbed down, fed and rested. He saddled her with the help of a curious stable boy.

"A little exercise before night time, good for both of us. Can you take a message to your lord?"

The boy looked up curiously.

"Lord Stephen is sending a messenger. I would like him to carry a brief message from me as well."

The boy waited expectantly.

"The message is that Harald regrets having had to depart in haste, and hopes to visit again shortly. Do you have that?"

"Harald regrets having had to depart in haste, hopes to visit again shortly."

"That's right. Tell Stephen you have to tell that to the messenger."

The boy ran off. Harald strapped on bedding and saddle-bags, stuffing the bundle of food into one of them, hooked on bowcase and quiver, led the horse out of the stable. Five minutes more took him through the gate, into the night.

Ten miles west, half the night gone, he made camp on the far slope of a ridge half a mile from the road. No doubt Stephen had several men who could succeed in not following him, but there was no reason to make things harder for them than necessary. He slept till dawn, climbed to the top of the ridge; the road was empty. He went back to sleep. Near noon he lunched on Stephen's bounty, removed the faint signs of his camp, mounted.

Stephen's hill to the base of Northgate he counted four days travel, more or less—a little more without a remount, a little less without an army. Late afternoon of the fourth found him ten miles north of the hostel, a little west of the road. He made camp in a wood running down from the foothills. Beyond loomed the mountains, their far side home. He wondered what his oldest grandson was up to. A year. No doubt Gerda had coped.

The road north was empty; Harald spent most of the remaining daylight searching the woods for food. It was still empty when he got back. When dark fell he built his fire in a hollow out of sight of the road, dined on fresh meat and wild greens with a little of his dwindling supply of biscuit.

The next day the road carried a few riders and a mule train south from the Empire—Belkhani guards. He remained hidden, foraged for food, let the mare graze her fill. Late the next day his luck changed. Mules, horses, even a few wagons. Traders, mule drivers, from the Imperial provinces in the far northwest by their dress. Guards in lamellar armor. Cats. They made camp less than half a mile from where he watched.

The guard commander was a cautious man; sentries ahead, behind, to both sides of his camp. The one on the hill side was a big man with a slight limp. Luck. Harald waited until dark, spent most of an hour moving quietly through the woods. 'Bjorn would have been there and back, probably with Gunnar's helmet under his arm; some advantages to being young.

"Gunnar."

The guard froze, turned, walked away from the voice.

Stood a minute. Walked back. Relieved himself against a tree, spoke softly.

"Who?"

"Harald Haraldsson." A long pause before Gunnar spoke again.

"Nice night for a walk; bit far from home."

"Guard captain?"

"Kari Egilsson, bottom of Greenvale."

"Tall, left eye missing. Hiring?"

"Left two with fever, Kolskegg saw a pretty face three days back, probably still there. Could be."

"I'll be by in the morning. I'm Connol Hrolfson, bottom of Mainvale. Pass the word."

Harald faded back into the night.

The mare was less than enthusiastic about walking when she should have been sleeping; it took ten minutes of talk and two apples to change her mind. Harald crossed the road, east then north, a wide loop around the traders' camp. By an hour past midnight he was half a mile north of them.

Dawn came too early. He packed, trimmed his beard, rode south. A sentry stopped him well short of the tents; Kari was earning his pay.

Kari himself rode up while the traders were breaking camp. The two men talked; the guard captain rode back to talk to the traders. In a little while he returned. Gunnar had assured the traders that his friend Connol, if inclined to be solitary, was a good man in a fight. Food and shelter over the pass, a chance of pay if all went well, but no promises.

Late that afternoon they made camp where there was still grass for the animals, well downhill from the hostel.

Another pack train was there already; a third came in before dark. Camp rumor said one from the south provinces, the other out of Eston. It also said the camp just below the gateposts, horses and men, wasn't traders. Harald considered a nighttime ride through the woods and up, decided against; not all Wolves were fools.

The chief trader spent most of the morning cursing the Wolves and their king in an interesting variety of languages. They appeared to be checking every man, beast and cart coming west from Eston and taking their time about it. It had never happened before; the air was full of rumors. Harald's favorite involved the King's cousin, his lady love, and a treasure in royal jewels. One of the traders, old in the ways of the world, offered a simpler explanation: the Wolves were holding things up until offered a suitable reward not to. The chief trader stopped cursing, thought a minute, and rode off to the hostel.

Whether due to his efforts or not, by the time they finally got to the gateposts things were moving faster. One of the Wolves questioned the chief trader and the guard captain. The members of the train, men and beasts, were sent through in single file, a Wolf watching from each side. Harald looked curiously from side to side as they went through; neither Wolf looked familiar. One of the other guards said something rude in a strong south vale accent; the guard captain turned in his saddle to glare at him. Then up the road and into the woods.

Late afternoon, a brush-covered hillside. Ahead on the right a small camp, a dozen Wolves. Harald spotted three more spread across the slope. Gunnar edged his horse right.

"Lost? The gateposts are that way."

The nearest Wolf glared at him, made no answer. Two hours farther on they stopped to camp.

One of the wagons was for food—convenient, at least until they reached the steep part of the pass. Harald filled a bowl with stew, a plate with bread, dried apples. He ate the stew standing by the mare, watching the fire where a sheep turned, tilted the plate to let its contents slide into the open saddlebag. Untidy, but he was tired of being hungry. He refilled the plate, collected a sizable chunk of mutton, noticed the chief trader's eyes on him.

After dinner, Harald walked over to the feed wagon, got a sack of oats, fed some of it to the mare, absentmindedly dumped the sack with the pile of his gear outside the tent pitched for him and three of the other guards. He moved the mare to the side of his tent away from the camp, told her not to wander, carried his gear into the empty tent. As night darkened, most of the cats gathered around a fire to trade lies. The mule drivers and camp servants had their own fire, the traders the biggest tent; Harald could see lantern light through the walls, hear voices. He spent a few minutes considering the pleasures of a good night's sleep, then went to the back of the tent, tested the stakes.

Kari's voice at the tent door. "Connol, you there?"

Harald grunted assent; the guard captain came into the tent where he was spreading out his bedding.

"Making an early night of it?"

"Early up yesterday, not so young as I was."

"Trader Boss wants to see you before you go to sleep. Not all traders are fools."

"Wagons over the high pass?"

"They come apart, go on the mules for the last bit."

Harald revised his opinion of the trader, his hopes for a night's rest. The guard captain went out. Harald rolled the bedding back up, pulled out a loose tent stake, slid his gear under the edge of the tent, followed it, replaced the stake. Twenty minutes later he was moving through the dark.

"Who's there?"

"Connol. Boss wants me to check ahead a bit. Crazy, but it's too early to sleep and the beer barrel went dry." He moved off into the dark, uphill, towards the pass.

By dawn he was on the downslope of the foothills, green forest in the distance, the main range beyond. He stopped briefly to let the tired mare graze, feed her oats, himself cold mutton. The road behind was empty. Traders might not like being tricked but they had little reason to do the King's work for him. Besides, anyone who had somehow worked out Harald's identity would surely have sense enough not to send cats after him.

There remained the problem of keeping man and horse alive over the pass; half a sack of oats would not do it. He reluctantly stood up, called the mare.

"Green grass down there, brave heart."

Harald set off down the road; the mare followed.

By nightfall things were looking a little better. Four hours in the shadow of the trees made up for at least part of the previous night. A supper of cold mutton and bread, then back to sleep.

He spent the early morning dealing with his half of the food problem while the mare dealt with hers. Two rabbits, a fat bird, only one broken arrow. He had hoped for a deer, but not enough to spend the rest of the day looking; the pack train would arrive eventually and he preferred to avoid complications.

He stopped early that day, spent the night at the west end of the wooded lowlands—the last good grazing east of the pass. In the morning, two hours in a field at the wood's edge, far enough from the trail to have been missed by the early caravans, provided a considerable bundle of grass. As he sat cleaning his sword, it occurred to him that it was the first use he had made of it on the trip. It was an old issue—on campaign, every pound mattered—but at least he had a new argument next time it came up.

Another easy day's ride brought him to Cloud's Eye. Of the grass that rimmed the high lake little was left.

Approaching the final narrow before the pass he stopped, fed the mare the last of the oats, brought out from a pocket of the saddlebags a folded piece of painted cloth. His lance was, presumably, still in the King's castle with the packhorse and most of the mare's barding. He tied the cloth to the end of a sapling, cut in the woods two days before, held it up. The wind took his pennon, spread it. He walked forward; the mare followed.

Suddenly the cliff walls to right and left were no longer empty. The first came at a run, jumping from one invisible foothold to another.

"Grandfather, you're back."

"And my son's idiot child is as usual doing his best to break his neck."

Harald caught up Asbjorn, pretended to try to throw him into the air, put him down again with a loud groan.

"Grow much more and you'll be carrying me."

The mare nuzzled the boy's shoulder. He fumbled in the saddlebag, came out with an apple.

"Not only does he buy the beast's loyalty, he does it with my apples."

"And whose gold did you fight the Emperor with?"

Harald tried to look angry, failed. The two walked together up the path, the mare between them, to where the cats guarding the pass stood waiting.

BOOK II:
Payment of Debts

A man should be loyal through life to friends,
And return gift for gift

Unfinished Business

It is always better to be alive.

Harald's first day back was spent getting clean, apologizing to his wife, making much of his grandchildren—Asbjorn was the oldest—and telling the tale of his adventures to a steadily growing audience of relatives, friends and neighbors. The second was a council of war, including Egil, Harald's eldest son, Hrolf, back the previous fall, the senior Lady from the nearby hold and several neighbors. Discussion continued the next day, now including the Greenvale paramount, who had been visiting kin halfway up Mainvale. Messages to Harald's friends—Harald had a lot of friends—went downvale on horseback, over the hills on foot. While waiting for replies, Harald sent two cats east with messages and found an excuse to visit the Order hold to see what his youngest son was looking so happy about. When he returned he discovered, not to his surprise, that Gerda had already satisfied herself on the matter.

Niall looked up at his father's step, back to brushing his horse.

"I visited Valholt yesterday."

Niall said nothing.

"Will she stay or go?"

He looked up, puzzled.

"Will she marry you—gods know Gerda could use another woman of sense about the place—or stay in the Order? She can't do both."

"She . . . We . . . I don't know."

"You know their customs. A Lady can take a lover, can bear him a child. But if she marries she is no longer a part of the Order. Sometimes the Order rears the child—most often daughters—sometimes father's or mother's kin. There's always room here; one more in the pack we'd hardly notice."

"I don't think she would leave the Order. Not now, at least. I've thought . . . It hasn't come to that yet. She's not . . ."

Niall was still looking at the horse, not his father. Harald didn't think he had ever seen his son blush before.

"You don't have to decide today, but you do have to decide. She is a brave lady, you love her, and she, for some odd reason, seems to love you. Get a chance, talk to your sister."

Harald gave his youngest son a brief hug, walked back to the hall.

During the next week the woods about Haraldholt filled with men; supplies poured up the vale on the backs of horses and mules. Twelve days after he came home, Harald was off again, east over the high pass with two cacades of cats, two hundred mounted archers, at his back.

HARALD   125

Like Harald and Hrolf a year earlier, the force reached
the forest above the campground in four days, made camp
at dark. Two hours before dawn the column, minus a
decade with the remounts, filed silently along the final
mile of trail to take up their positions hidden in the forest
edge uphill from the campgrounds. At first light they
began to move—two decades on the right of the line
heading south and east on a wide sweep to cut off escape,
the rest of the force coming down like a wave on the
Wolves' camp.

On the porch of the hostel a warden saw them and ran
into the building. Men came out, most in sleeping robes.
Voices, a stir in the pack train camped below. In the
Wolves' camp a sleepy sentry looked up, yelled, died.
The first man out of his tent, eyes blinking, clutching a
sword still in its bard, faced a ring of mounted cats, bows
ready. He considered the situation briefly, dropped his
sword. Not all were so prudent. A dozen Wolves together,
swords drawn, tried to break out of the ring. None made
it.

While the prisoners were being disarmed and bound,
Harald rode over to the hostel to apologize for the distur-
bance, down to the traders' camp, then back. One of the
cats had a fire going. The prisoners, arms bound behind
them, were crowded in the middle of the campground
while cats went through the tents making sure all were
empty. Harald rode out to them.

"The King's Messengers are dissolved. Some of you
may be of some use for something. You will be branded"—
he gestured to the fire—"with a cross on your forehead
so that I will know you again, dispersed unarmed about

the countryside. If I discover a man of you under arms, I hang him."

One of the bound men stepped forward: "We are the King's men."

Harald looked him up and down. "Murdering the King's friends is his concern. Murdering my friends is mine."

"I appeal to the King's justice."

"I will remember to mention the matter when next I see His Majesty."

"Now do you cut my throat?"

"If I judged plain speech so, I would have slit my own these many years past. Carry your complaint to the King if you will. But you go unarmed and on foot."

The first group of Wolves were given two days' food out of their own supplies, one day's water, directions to a spring a day's walk north and a village two days beyond that, and sent up the north road unbound, disarmed and on foot with two cats for escort. The next group went south. The cats took most of the remaining supplies to replace what they had used coming over the pass. Some of the captured horses were loaded with weapons and armor and sent out to villages in the plains and up into the western valleys; Harald did not think their lords would object. The remaining horses went back over the pass in care of a pack train boss from the vales.

Early afternoon they started east, the prisoners on foot. The next morning the remaining Wolves were sent north and south. The men would not starve; summer labor was always scarce.

Three days later the high hill. Harald camped his men

at the bottom, a long bowshot from the walls for courtesy's sake, sent a few into the town at the hill's bottom to see what could be bought. He was not surprised, half an hour later, to see a rider coming down the path from the hilltop.

"My lord asks what brings you into his province in arms?"

"When last I visited His Majesty, he expressed surprise that I traveled without escort. Having discovered his advice to be good, I have followed it."

Stephen's man looked slowly about the orderly lines of small tents, a lance with pennon flying at the end of each.

"I do not think you need fear bandits."

"We met some impeding trade over the pass and dispersed them. Now I travel to Forest Keep to thank the good Yosef for his hospitality, offer him aid if he has need."

"Lord Stephen visited Forest Keep some weeks ago. The attackers were gone. He left a few men. How long do you remain here?"

"We leave tomorrow." Harald gestured to where half a dozen cats were driving a small herd of sheep and several burdened pack horses. "We eat well tonight. If any wish to join us, I would gladly repay some part of the debt for past hospitality."

"I will tell my lord."

The messenger rode back up the hill; Harald walked back to where his decade was camped. Egil had their tent up. He unrolled his bedding and took a nap.

"Father, a guest."

Harald opened his eyes, stuck his head out of the tent, followed it. Sniffed.

"I smell dinner. Will you join us?"

Stephen nodded, accompanied Harald and Egil over to the small fire. One of their companions had brought a large pot of porridge, a leg of mutton balanced on top. The cats filled their plates and bowls and, at a glance from Harald, wandered off.

Late the next day the force neared Forest Keep. Harald left them a little distance off, rode up with only Egil. Yosef met him in the courtyard; the two embraced.

"Yosef, this is my son Egil. Egil, Yosef, castellan of Forest Keep."

A small figure came running out of the stable, wrapped itself around Harald.

"And his son Henry." Harald carefully detached Hen, peeled back his tunic neck, felt the arrow wound.

"You'll do."

He turned back to Yosef. "I've brought some friends."

"Your friends are welcome to my castle."

"Quite a lot of them. Travel having become so dangerous, I crossed the high pass with two cacades of cats. By your leave they camp outside your walls. My son and I will gladly accept your hospitality within."

"Told you."

Harald turned to look; it was Kara who had spoken. The two had come out of the stable after Hen and were standing there listening. He walked over to them, spoke to Elaina.

"Are you well enough to ride? To fight?"

She nodded.

"Can you two find your sisters? I was planning a hunt, and they may know where the game is."

Kara looked at him curiously; Elaina put it in words. "What do you hunt?"

"Wolves."

Kara nodded, turned, went back into the stable. Hen followed her, leading the mare.

At start of dinner they were missing both Kara, who had ridden off in search of friends, and Hen, who had last been seen heading out of the gate in the direction of the cats' camp. When they were half done, he came running into the hall to his father.

"Father, there are hundreds of them. Horses, lances, tents . . . It's an army."

He stopped, looked at Harald, back to his father.

"Father, Harl, he's . . ."

Harald spoke.

"Harl was what the Westkin named me, back when I was a little older than you are now. I think your father has figured out the rest of it."

Hen sat down by his father, continued watching Harald. Someone passed him a plate of food.

The next morning was a council of war—Harald, Egil, Yosef, Rorik, Elaina, Kara, and an older Lady that Kara had brought back with her. Hen sat looking into the fire pretending not to listen. The Lady spoke first.

"Up in the fir woods above Willow Creek. We don't know how many, but it's a lot—six decades at least, maybe more. We only have two 'taves, more coming in. But bows in the woods . . ."

Harald nodded. "Some of us might get hurt. Better to get them out."

The Lady produced a rough map; Yosef corrected

details. Harald leaned over it, looked back up at Yosef. "Willows along the creek, meadow up to fir woods?"

Yosef nodded. Harald pointed at the map.

"Along Willow Creek should be one way up to the east pass."

Yosef nodded again. "One way goes up Ashvale, south of here, the other along Willow Creek and over. Might be why they're there."

"Either way, a pack train, no guards . . ."

Harald fell silent; the two men's eyes met.

Harald sent out scouts, spent the rest of the day consulting on details. Hen divided his time between following Harald around, spoiling the mare, and exploring the cats' encampment; the remaining sheep had come in and were being butchered, cooked, and smoked. After dinner he went off with Elaina. In the morning Harald's force set off for Willow Creek, accompanied by Yosef, Rorik, his guards—Stephen's men were left to hold the keep—and twenty packhorses, heavily laden. An hour out they were joined by Elaina, Kara and three octaves of the Order. At noon they stopped, ate, made final plans. The Ladies, reinforced by three decades of cats, crossed the shallow creek, headed east and up into the woods that fringed its north shore. Egil, with one decade, went south and east, aiming for the back side of the pine woods uphill of the Wolves' camp. An hour later the pack train set off—Yosef and his men, armor hidden by their cloaks, leading the string of pack horses.

The meadow was silent. The pack train moved slowly, parallel to the creek on their left but avoiding the soft banks, half a dozen men cloaked against the cold breezes blowing down from the pine-covered slopes on their right, a score of loaded horses.

From the edge of the pines a mass of mounted men charged the pack train, yelling; behind them more on foot, some with bows.

Packhorses scattered, riders bolted for the stream, pursued by men and arrows; one fell. From the willows arrows came back at the mounted Wolves. Some tried to charge the hidden archers along the creek, others fell back towards the pine woods at the other side of the meadow.

Yells from the trees, cries of "fire, fire, the woods." Scent of woodsmoke down the air. More Wolves crowding out of the forest on foot, pouring across the meadow. Someone looked left, yelled.

The front line of cats stretched across the meadow from edge to edge. Charging, lances down, they hit the mixed mass of riders, men on foot, went through it. The second line stopped just short of what was left, poured in arrows.

From the edge of the creek someone came running into the chaos. A Wolf, somehow still mounted, rode at him. Arrows from the willows; the horse ran on, saddle empty. From down meadow came the gray mare. Hen looked up from his father. Harald gave the boy one startled look, dismounted, bent over Yosef.

"He's still breathing. I think it's all right. What are you doing here?"

Hen said nothing. Out of the woods came Elaina, Kara behind her. Harald looked at her, looked at the boy, bent over his wounded friend.

The battle done, chaos gradually settled into order. A

few Wolves were prisoners, the rest dead. Yosef and two horses from the pack train, two of the Ladies and one of the cats that had waited in ambush along the creek, had wounds, none, to Harald's eye, dangerous. Hen was his father's concern; if nearly getting him killed failed to persuade Elaina that the boy did not belong in a battle, nothing Harald could say was likely to do it. The girl needed a mother's hand.

Harald looked up from one of the wounded, saw Egil coming out of the woods. He rode over to his father, dismounted.

"Worked like a charm; Rorik was right about the winds downslope."

"All out?"

"Bonfires still going some. Left Flosi and his brother to watch them, make sure nothing caught."

"Couple decades, work back up, make sure there's no one left. Then see what's in their camp we can use." Egil went off. Harald returned to his work.

They made camp near the stream, west of the battle-field. The Wolves' camp provided dinner, supplies for a week or more. As it grew dark, Harald heard a horse's hooves. Voices. He looked up, startled. One of the younger cats, a tall figure behind him, mounted.

"Harald. A Lady. Looking for you."

Dark hair under steel cap, down to mailed shoulders. Strong face neither young nor old. She slid down into his raised arms. He squeezed, lifted her off her feet.

Her voice was a whisper. "I found her."

He froze, let go. Looked up; with both on their feet she was still taller than he was.

One glance from Harald cleared the nearest fire; he led
her over, sat down, looked around. Nobody.

"Where?"

"South Keep. The rest of my 'tave keeping an eye on it;
they're a family of hunters. One friend inside, servant
woman. Fair garrison, fifteen decades, twenty."

Harald thought a moment, the map of the Kingdom
clear in his head. Between Eston and the northern border
two royal holds, nestled up into the eastern range. Birds in
both, unless someone had changed things. South Keep
almost in the hills at the south end of the Kingdom. Long
ride. Royal garrisons, if there were any, east edge of the
plains. Along the west edge provincial lords with their
house guards, but not like the border provinces. He
turned back to Caralla.

"Make noise up north; I can do that with these. Then
south. How many tataves between here and South Keep?"

"Mine, another I can find for sure, maybe more."

They fell silent, thinking. Something else occurred to
him.

"Your sister's here; nearly got a boy killed, helped him
to a battle he'd no business in. Don't suppose you . . . ?"

"'Laina? Not a hope. We need a landmark. You don't
know the south?"

"Egil does; spent a month chasing that girl in Southvale.
Didn't catch her, either. Caught it from Asdis when he got
home, though, wouldn't speak to him for a week. Talk to
him in the morning; I'm for bed. You don't know about
Niall. Ask Egil."

Ghost War

**The tactful guest will take his leave
Early, not linger long**

"If you don't mind my asking, Harald, what are we doing?"

"Heading north to one of the King's castles. Going to siege it."

Knute looked skeptical. He was the youngest cat in Harald's decade, but Egil wouldn't have chosen a fool. Harald continued, his voice louder.

"Don't think twenty decades can siege a castle? I've done it with two."

Heads turned, men looked at each other, started drifting over from the other fires. Harald stayed silent until they had settled.

"The Prince, Emperor that is, smashed us at Iffin ford; you know the story. Forty miles wrong side the border, but it was Henry's first war. A thousand, fifteen hundred heavies. Most of the rest of us got away, headed home. Five hundred cats, a thousand Ladies, four thousand heavies and change—and some of them not in the best of shape.

"Didn't look too bad till a rider came in with news. Empire had Markholt, last castle north, our side the border."

He stopped, waited for the expected question.

"The Empire sieged a big castle while they were fighting a war forty miles the other side of the border? How'd they do that?"

"Not steel. Gold. We all make mistakes. Castellan marched his garrison out, some excuse or other. Empire marched in. One man got away, got to us."

The cats were silent, waiting.

"Coming home in a hurry, big garrison sitting in Markholt, line of march, supply line too, flying the wrong colors. Figured I'd best do something. Got some friends. Two decades—no, I lie. Olaf had a wounded Lady to take care of, couldn't come. Two decades scant one. Headed south, still had remounts, lot faster than the army.

"Markholt's head of a valley, against a cliff. Downhill cleared a good bowshot, then woods. They hadn't heard about the battle yet. All they knew, we could have beaten the Prince and been coming to deal with them, all eight thousand of us. Gate closed, ramparts manned, ready to hold to the last man. What our side should have done.

"Scouted it out by daylight, through the woods. Come night we were ready. Been collecting wood. Time we were finished, forty campfires in the woods, all along the edge. Who knows how many behind? They didn't. A thousand men, easy. Could be more.

"Didn't get much sleep; forty campfires eat a lot of wood. Kept them going three nights. That got the army past, wounded to the next keep south, still ours. We headed for home. Figure I woke up somewhere around Cloud's Eye."

That brought a laugh. The story ended, the men dispersed. Harald turned back to Knute.

"Heading for Markholt. Thirty years is a long time. Don't figure anyone'll remember."

Two miles down valley from the castle, two riders, staring at the column of cats, Harald's pennon at their head. A brief exchange, one of them at a gallop back up to the castle. The other sat his horse and waited.

Harald turned to Knute. "Ride off west, message to our main force. Two miles should do it. You'll find us sieging the castle when you get back."

Knute gave a brief puzzled look. His face cleared. He rode off grinning.

Harald rode up towards the rider.

"Can you take word to the castellan of Markholt?"

The man nodded.

"Tell him he is under siege. Your King has taken the Lady Commander of the Order, my friend these thirty years past, by treachery, holds her still, makes war on her sisters. When I guested with him, his people sought my life. When I departed, much against his will, they hunted me across the Kingdom. My patience is at an end."

The man gave one more long look at the massed column, turned, rode back to the castle.

Half an hour later the castellan watched as the column of cats came into sight around the final bend, flowed up the valley road to the wide clearing around the castle, turned left along the edge of the cleared area and into the woods. They rode in a narrow column of twos, but there were a lot of them. He watched until finally the flow stopped and the lights of campfires began to appear among the trees, then turned to the captain beside him.

"How many?"

"Five hundred easy, maybe a thousand. Half the damn host. It's real."

The castellan thought a moment before replying.

"If we have to fight cats, this is the place to do it. They can build stuff, but there's no siege train, nothing they can't carry on horseback."

"He won't try to storm us; Harald doesn't waste men. We aren't what he's here for."

The castellan looked curiously at the other man, waited.

"He wants the King. Not sure I . . ." He stopped, looked around. "Harald summons us to siege, we send word. The King comes to lift the siege. Not your problem or mine."

The castellan nodded agreement, took one more look at the fires—there were more now—then started down the tower staircase.

The next afternoon the cats were again on the move, out the beaten path through the woods to the road just out of sight of the castle—a route most of them had already ridden four or five times. They left behind stacks of gathered firewood and two octaves of the Order, with instructions to keep fires going until the castle ran out of patience or they ran out of wood. Harald reached the next royal castle south a day later and summoned it too to siege. The next day he left another small group behind to tend fires, with scouts south to warn them if a relief force approached, and rode west into the plain.

In camp that evening, sitting with Egil, Harald ran over the possibilities.

"If they had birds—and they should—His Majesty got word from Markholt three days ago, Grayholt yesterday. His people, Eston levies, central provinces. Messengers to Stephen, Brand. Might think he could get four thousand men up north. My guess he's on the way. Waits too long, looks weak, who knows who might come in?"

"If he thinks you have the whole host, part of the Order too?"

"Might sit. Either way, calls what he has north. South Keep, twenty decades, that's a lot. He'll pull half, easy. On the road now if he has a bird for them. Up the east edge while we're going down the west. Even that far south the plain's fifty miles across. Cara's scouts between us. A decade out on our left, just in case."

Egil thought a moment. "Province people? Have to see us coming south."

"Straight to their lord, considers his conscience, counts swords, repairs his walls. Nobody in the South is coming after a force this size—not without calling up levies first. Message to the King, but it has to catch him. Rider. Pigeons can't find an army."

The two fell silent.

With two horses for each man, the cats made good time. Nine days after they left Grayholt they pitched camp on a grassy hill at the south end of the plain. A day later Caralla joined them with two tataves and part of a third— a hundred and fifty Ladies. While horses grazed and their riders rested, Harald, Egil and Caralla made their plans. Caralla was the first to speak:

"She's still there; Mari saw her three days back."

"Garrison?"

"Six decades, maybe seven. Rest marched out nine, ten days ago."

Harald looked at Egil. "Birds. Both ways."

Egil thought a moment. "Where do you think he is?"

"Back home. Hot, tired, mad. Royal army too."

Caralla looked at him, put it in words: "Angry is stupid."

Harald nodded.

While the others rested, traded news and gossip, Harald rode south into the woods nearby to hunt mushrooms. When he found what he wanted—nightbells favored the damp underside of dead trees—he used a stick to break them off, as gently as he could, into a pan. The pan, with water, went over a small fire. While it heated Harald went off in search of game.

By the time he got back the fire was mostly out, the liquid cool. He tied the mare to a tree some distance away, took a leather water bottle from his saddlebag, propped it upright against a stump next to the fire. The liquid from the pan went, with care, into the water bottle, the remains of the mushrooms into a hole scraped in the soft dirt. He found a buried coal, used it to light a candle, dripped wax around the stopper for a better seal. Returned to camp, the sealed bottle went to Caralla. The next day the combined force moved out.

Noon meal, the great hall of the keep crowded with men. Fresh venison, bought from hunters working the woods outside the village. Bored soldiers. A new barrel of beer. Old rumors.

"And I say it's a revolt by the northerners. Why else pull a hundred men north fast as they can go? Next the levies, north against south like in the old stories."

Carl shook his head. "And the Emperor eats us for dinner. The lords aren't that stupid."

"It's the Order. His Majesty finally figured out you don't fight soldiers with trash, decided to do it right."

There was a crash. Looking up, Carl saw one of the men crumpled, another standing over him with a broken pitcher and an odd expression.

"A snake. It's crawling on him."

He knew Helgi was crazy, but not that crazy. Carl took another drink of beer. Somewhere behind him, at the other end of the hall, someone was saying something in a high voice. Things were finally getting interesting.

Outside, the gatehouse guards recognized the wagon, swung the gate wide. One of them called out to the driver: "Got much today? One deer don't go far."

On the wall above, a sentry clutched at an arrow, crumpled. The wagon lurched against the open gate, stopped; the two oxen pulling it, somehow free, set off for the castle yard on an unsuccessful search for grass. The wagon's driver raised a bow, put an arrow through one of the men at the gate. Caralla, clear of the cloth that had disguised her as a dead deer, came out of the back of the wagon at a run, hit one guard with her shoulder, spun past into the tower doorway; the little room was empty. A guard came after her, heading for the winch and the beam that would release the portcullis—at least one man in the castle who knew his job. She struck at his shield with all her strength—once inside the small room, her longer weapon was a fatal handicap. He stepped back instead of forward.

It was his last mistake. All other noise was drowned in thunder as the column of cats came in the gate, split right and left around the inside of the castle wall, shooting as they rode. The last of the guards on the rampart died. The second column of cats, Harald at their head, came through the gate, up the stone ramp, into the great hall.

The hall was chaos—guardsmen unconscious on the floor, guardsmen fighting each other, guardsmen dying under the arrows of the mounted cats crowded into one end of the hall, a few beginning to throw down their arms. At the far end a captain was trying and failing to hold a knot of guards together in front of the door, shields up against a rain of arrows. Tall, blond hair showing under the edge of a steel cap. Harald drew and released; the arrow slammed into the closing door. The man was gone.

Off his horse onto the bench, down the length of the table dodging plates and pitchers, shoulder to the door and through it, Caralla at his heels. Running footsteps echoing down the stone stairway. Harald let Caralla pass him on the second spiral, his breath burning in his throat. At the top of the third the door was open. A short hall, at the end a door. Two guards. The captain said something to them, went through. They spread out and moved to block Caralla.

Harald shot the halberd man through the throat. The other swung. Caralla glanced the blow, struck back, circled. He turned to face her. Harald put two arrows in his back and stepped past the falling body into the room, nocking a third.

A tall woman, gray haired, already on her feet, reaching down with her right hand to the chain that linked it to the floor. The captain, his sword out, swung at her. Harald drew, looking for a clear shot.

Leonora moved first. She sidestepped the rush, pulling tight a second chain that ran from ankle to floor; the captain went over it. The wrist chain, somehow freed from the ground, swung in a blurring circle. He moved once and was still.

Just to be sure, Harald shot him through the body.

"Castle ours, still fighting. Cara, the door."

Freeing a dagger from the dead captain's belt, Harald slid the blade under the iron staple that chained Leonora to the floor, driving it in with his mace. He grabbed the dagger's handle with both hands, looked up. Leaning down, she wrapped her joined hands around his. One heave and the staple came free. They joined Caralla at the door. The hallway was empty.

From the sounds up the stairway, the fighting was over. Harald led them up, not down the stairs. He was looking for something.

A considerable way north, most of a day later:

"Your Majesty. A bird just came in."

The King took the thin paper, read the message written in tiny letters. His face lit up. Twice Harald had used them against him; now it was his turn. The southern provinces were loyal, birds for Southdale and Goldfell in the tower. And . . .

He turned to Philip. "Would Harald know we have birds in South Keep?"

The old man thought a minute.

"Doubt it. Here to the Vales was his worry, the rest of it ours."

The King sent a boy running for his captain. With luck, this time . . .

And either way, at least it would be over.

A day's ride short of South Keep the royal army, swelled by hasty levies, met the first sign of an enemy. Off the road to the right, well out of arrowshot, a small cluster of mounted Ladies. Ahead, where the road ran along the woods, a smaller cluster of cats. The King spoke to the captain at his right side, the captain signaled. Gradually the army slowed to a halt. The King turned to his captain.

"Scouts? Catch them now, surprise later."

The captain nodded, stopped. Above the cats, the wind took the pennon on a lance point, blew it straight.

"That's Harald."

"What?"

"Next to his pennon man, gray horse."

"Gods." The King thought a moment, his face fierce.

The figure on the gray horse raised his bow, drew, shot. The King lifted his shield, saw no sign where the arrow had gone. Southdale, riding at his left, spoke.

"Not even Harald can pick us off at four hundred yards, Majesty."

The King turned to him.

"Take the levies, lift the siege of South Keep. You'll want the infantry from Eston; they're behind us on the road." The provincial lord nodded. The King turned to his captain.

"Send Mark and his men after them"—a gesture

right—"he has light cavalry to run them down, heavies to break them if they stand."

"He can't take on the whole Order, Majesty."

"The Order's a day south of here besieging South Keep. If he does run into trouble he can fall back on Southdale and the main force. We take the rest of your company and go after Harald."

"Harald has a lot of tricks, Majesty."

"He can't be very tricky with fifteen men. His army, what there is of it, is at South Keep. He's been fighting me with bluffs for a month. This is the last. Just remember— we want a prisoner, not a corpse."

An hour later the King had seen no reason to change his mind. The cats, charged by twenty times their numbers, had shot a few arrows, then fallen back into the trees. The King's captain spread his men to block any move back to the road and followed them. Occasional arrows through the trees were evidence that they were still there; the valley walls beginning to rise on either side of them would slow any attempt to break out of the trap.

The valley narrowed, the royal force thinned to a column moving through the trees and up. Ahead sunlight. They broke out of the woods, surged forward, stopped. Somewhere behind them something fell with an echoing crash.

The valley ahead was blocked by a wall of rocks and dirt a man's height and more. Above it massed spears, a line of archers. Right and left the steep slope of the valley wall was scattered with cats on foot, bows ready. At the King's left, horsemen surged forward, swords out, fell under a rain of arrows. The King turned in his saddle, arms spread.

"Hold."

A man on foot, forcing his way through the packed horses to the captain's side.

"It's blocked; they've brought down a big tree behind us, maybe more."

Looking up, the King saw Harald's pennon, Harald himself at the center of the wall, a tall Lady beside him. The King hesitated a moment, moved forward, yelled up at him.

"If I yield, will you let my men go?"

"Dismount, arms and armor on the horses. We take the horses down to the plain, let them go; when we are gone, your men follow on foot."

The King turned to his captain.

"Andrew is in the castle; tell him I'll make the best terms I am able, send word when I can."

He swung his horse sideways against the earth wall, drew his sword, held it hilt out. Harald leaned down, took it, thrust it into the earth beside him, reached a hand down. The King caught the hand, one foot on the saddle, the other against the earth wall, scrambled upwards.

At the top of the wall he stood, looked at Harald, the tall gray-haired woman beside him, froze. The blood left his face.

"You're dead. You've been dead for a year."

Harald broke the silence, took her hand.

"I can assure Your Majesty that the Lady Commander is with us in the flesh."

The King tore his eyes from Leonora's face, looked wildly around. Stopped. Looked back at her. Hesitated. Spoke slowly.

"My lady, I have wronged you past excuse. You have fair claim to my life."

Leonora nodded. Nobody spoke. Below them the horsemen had dismounted and begun, under the watchful eyes of their captain and the archers above, to take off their armor and pack it onto the horses.

An hour into the plain, the King riding with Harald, silent. A short column of riders crested a ridge. As they drew near he recognized the dress of the Order. Harald stopped his men, waited. The newcomers fell into line; their leader rode up to where Harald sat his horse, the King on one side, the Lady Commander behind them. Her eyes widened. Harald spoke first.

"No problems?"

"Like a charm. Over the ridge, sharp right. Then they were busy jumping ropes—or not. We kept going. Probably still chasing us south."

"Someone you should meet."

She moved forward; the mare turned, backed, leaving the Lady facing the King, Harald on one side of her, Leonora on the other.

"Your Majesty, may I introduce the Lady Caralla?"

The King looked up. A tall Lady, mail covered with dust.

"Our daughter."

The King drew a long breath.

Harald spoke again.

"Before beginning a feud, count kin."

An Education

Silence becomes the Son of a prince,
Brave in battle:
Merry and glad
Until the day of his death.

When they stopped for the night, it occurred to the King that he had no idea where he was to sleep or on or under what. He hesitantly put the question to Harald.

"Egil will pitch our tent; watch how he does it. I'm pairing you with Knute; his partner got hurt up north, staying with friends till he's safe to ride. Spare tent half, bedding, on my remount. Not exactly what you're used to."

Egil showed him how two squares of tightly woven wool, supported on three half-lances—the cats carried two-piece lances, ten feet of pole being a nuisance when not in use—went together to make a tiny tent, barely big enough for two people.

"What do you do if there's only one of you?"

"Hope it doesn't rain. Or make a half sized tent and knock it down every time you crawl in and out."

"We sleep on the ground?"

"Bedding under you. It's not so bad if you shape the ground to fit."

Caralla's voice behind them. "Cats like to wake up stiff and sore. It makes them fierce."

Egil didn't even look up. "Hammocks are fine in the woods. Out here, by the time you finish lashing the stand and staking and unlashing and unstaking, you've lost half the day."

By the time he had finished speaking, she was gone. He backed out of the tent, pointed to the shallow hollows he had scooped at hip height.

"Don't suppose you had an older sister?"

The King shook his head.

"Some folk have all the luck."

Around the fire with Harald's decade, the talk turned again to tents, the King conceding that the cats' version was considerably more portable than his.

"You think your pavilion is a pain to lug around, should have seen His Imperial Majesty's. Damn thing took its own pack train."

Faces turned to Harald. It was the King who asked the obvious question.

"How did you happen to get a look at the Emperor's pavilion?"

"He wasn't using it at the time."

The voice out of the dark was Caralla's.

"After the battle, Father talked one of the cacades into taking charge of it. Their remounts and the Emperor's pack mules lugged the thing over the pass. Took the whole family two days to get it set up in the back meadow."

"Just what every meadow needs." That was one of the cats; listeners, King included, responded appropriately.

"Don't laugh. Silk hangings, tent poles banded with gold. By the time the story spread a bit, every highborn in the Imperial army had gold tent poles and chests full of silver and jewels. Made it easy to raise troops the next time." Harald fell silent. Someone poked the fire.

The King's first chance to talk to Harald alone came the next day, when the column halted at noon to breathe the horses and feed the men. He took it.

"Why did Andrew's captain lie to him about the Lady Commander? There must have been a reason."

"How did he say she died?"

"He didn't." The King looked down. "I don't think I wanted to know."

"Close your eyes in a fight, might not open them."

"Everything was going wrong, sliding out of my hands. I might have swallowed my pride, taken your advice. But with her dead . . . You made it plain enough."

"Never in your hands. Emperor wasn't. I wasn't. Order wasn't. Your own lords aren't. Luck, things go right for a week. Life isn't a picture."

"I thought, if something went wrong, I could always put it back."

He looked down the long column of cats and Ladies, beginning to mount up, turned back to Harald.

"Last time, just before you showed me I didn't run the world, you said something about how you came by your broken arm. Afterwards . . . I wondered."

"Someone tried to kill me. I figured you for the most likely."

Harald whistled, the mare came, the King's horse followed. Both men mounted. The King spoke. "I was still hoping to put things back. Dead is dead."

He looked back at the column of Ladies.

"Mostly."

Five days later they drew rein; Harald pointed ahead.

"Fortified village. Sell us sheep, maybe oats. Want to come?"

The King gave a surprised look, nodded.

"Anyone asks, 'James.'"

The leader of the village welcomed Harald and his friend, pointed proudly to the sentry over the gate.

"Last fall, a big band came by, thought a wall meant something inside it. I figure the armor saved two, three lives. In your debt."

"You made it. We got a bed for the night, food—fair trade. Trouble since?"

"Wolf pack burned out two, three houses north of here. Not us."

When they left the village Harald was poorer by several gold pieces, richer by sacks of oats—some ground to meal—and a small flock of sheep. The next day was spent dealing with both. James—Knute had tired of addressing his tentmate as "Your Majesty" and the rest had followed his lead—was given brief instruction in converting oatmeal to oat cakes, spent much of the day at it while his companions handled the messier job.

James looked up from the fire to find Harald watching him, nibbling on a cake from the stack.

"Best warm."

"I think I've got it, but some of the ones I did first . . ."

"Always the horses."

There was a long pause, smells from the larger fires where meat was being prepared. James was the first to speak.

"Back home, they smoke meat for days, weeks sometime."

"Keep it for months, too. This'll be gone in a few days. Then beans if we can cook them, oat cakes, dried stuff while it lasts."

James hesitated a moment before speaking again:

"What should I have done? When I thought the Lady Commander was dead. It was wrong to hold you, but . . . you could come back with an army."

"Why didn't I?"

James looked over the busy scene, gave Harald a puzzled look.

"This isn't an army; could have brought ten times as many. Two thousand cats, near that many Ladies, good as anything you have, better than most. Me commanding. You can raise eight thousand—if everyone shows up. How long before some of your lords decide a king who tears the alliance apart, hires bandits to burn out their people, isn't what they want? Estfen, married to Estmount's sister, they move together. Or North Province, River. Once two go, balance swings, out of a job. Some might think they could do it better. Might be right. Way I saw it, you took my daughter's mother prisoner, maybe killed her, tried to kill me. Why didn't I come back with the host?"

James smelled something burning, turned three oatcakes, considered.

"Think, boy. Useful habit."

There was a long silence; finally James broke it.

"The Emperor."

"The Emperor. Doing his work for him. Told you back then. Every Lady you kill, every one of your people I kill, one less. Pretend war. South Keep, had to kill for real to get 'Nora out alive. Pulled some north, got a friend to spike a barrel of beer with nightbells, saved what I could. Next year, year after, I'll need them."

"It didn't work. Maybe it couldn't. But I'd talked with people from the wars. Heard stories. We needed cats, Ladies, you. How could I hold for a lifetime when the best third of my army could stay home if it felt like it?"

"Henry did it. Thirty years."

"Mother said . . ."

"Your mother had singers to sing pretty ballads about honor and glory to folk as hadn't seen a thousand lancers die on the legions' spears. Ballad, you just have to be brave. Seen a lot of brave men die. Killed some. War, do with what you have. Never did figure out how she thought he was going to hold the legions after he finished trying to conquer us. Sing ballads at 'em, maybe."

Harald turned, wandered off; James returned his attention to what he was doing. When he was done he sorted out the worst of the scorched cakes and went looking for horses.

The next morning they again headed north. A day south of the Borderflood they made camp. Harald sent out scouts, Leonora messengers. Two days later, one of them came back.

⌗ ⌗ ⌗

Early morning, a column of horsemen riding single file south, bows, quivers, leather armor. To their left, half a bowshot or less, the forest, right the plain, rolling in long waves to the western range dim in the distance. Two scouts ahead, one left near the forest edge, one right riding for the ridge top.

Out of the forest arrows, men and beasts falling, horses bolting for the plain, riders clinging to the side away from the attack. Over the ridge. On the far side, a hundred yards beyond, a line of cats. A storm of arrows.

Harald yelled out something in a language James had never heard before. Everything stopped. From behind a dead horse, one of the nomads stood up, bow in his left hand, right hand empty, yelled something back, turned, yelled something else to what was left of his force, most of them behind the bodies that provided such cover as there was on the flat plain. Those that could stood up; James noticed that the first had an arrow sticking out of the back of his right leg. The battle was over. Cats, dismounted, hurried over to do what they could for the wounded.

Later, while the cats were helping the few unwounded nomads deal with their dead and James, feeling useless, was watching, Harald brought over a pair of saddlebags.

"War leader had them, not Westkin work. Take a look."

The saddlebags were heavy. Each was half filled with leather bags. James opened one, spilled a handful into his palm, bright in the morning light. Most of the coins were new minted, the Emperor's face not yet blurred by wear.

When Harald returned, the gold was back in the saddlebag; James was looking at two scrolls, one still sealed. He unrolled the other; both bent over to read.

At the top, words, numbers:

LX toxo. XXX B prin, XXX ager, LX

At the bottom, in a different hand:

Moondark, three days after. Meadow east of Sunsign house. Turlogh knows. Password: Strayed horses. Counter: Dappled?

Harald spoke.

"Read Tengu?"

James nodded. "Sixty bows, thirty emperors before, thirty meadow, sixty. But the rest is in our speech."

"Some of the Westkin learn it, mostly from us, speak it, read it. Probably their war leader did."

"Sixty bows. Is that how many men they had?"

Harald nodded.

"Thirty emperors in advance, thirty when they reached the meadow, sixty sometime later?"

Harald nodded again. "The Emperor is getting generous in his old age—two gold pieces each."

James looked up: "Where were they going?"

Harald pointed at the rest of the writing, stood up, went off to help with the funeral.

The mound finished, a fire was kindled above it. Harald and two of the surviving nomads gave long speeches of what sounded like poetry in the Westkin tongue. The survivors were sent off to a nearby village, some in horse litters, a decade of cats for escort. Weapons and gear of the fallen—what had not gone into the mound with the dead men and horses—was loaded on the surviving horses along with most of the nomads' supplies. The next day James looked up from his thoughts, saw a hill in the distance crowned with walls. They camped near its bottom. Harald set off for the gate—accompanied by Leonora and a king unsure whether to feel surprised.

Eyes followed Leonora; nobody gave any sign of recognizing James until they were alone with Stephen in one of the smaller buildings near the hall, a guard outside the closed door. The North Province lord embraced the Lady Commander, then turned to the King.

"How may I serve Your Majesty?"

"Tell me what has been happening."

"Your cousin sent word to me, I suppose others, that you had been taken prisoner by the Senior Paramount, feared dead. Word of you or him to the castle, or to one of his men staying at the Sun in Splendor, an inn south of here. I am to be ready to call out my levies upon a day's notice."

The King turned to Harald. "By your leave, I would send Andrew word that I am well, the Lady Commander alive and in authority over the Order."

"Your Majesty is free to do as you desire. I have no claims over you."

Leonora spoke: "And I postpone mine until a time better suited to deal with them."

James thought a moment, spoke slowly. "As to your claims against me, I give you self judgment—name what I owe and I will pay it, to the limit of what I have. My lord Stephen, you are witness. Find me foresworn and you are released from any duty you owe me.

"Best I bring word how matters stand to my cousin myself. Can you provide men to guide me?"

Stephen nodded. "Thorvald and his brother know the roads from here to the castle. The inns too."

Harald spoke:

"To Stephen's borders I will escort you, with your leave. Farther south risks misunderstandings. The Sun is a day's ride beyond. From there the castle is two days' more. By my council go quietly, eyes open."

"I will not travel in such state as to attract attention. Once in my castle, I am safe with my cousin and my own men."

"Safety is scarce, in castle or out."

The King turned back to Stephen.

"Before I depart, one matter more. The royal messengers are from this hour dissolved and without authority. I trust you to deal with the matter in your province, word to Brand in his. I will speak with the others."

Stephen nodded.

Royal Homecoming

**Crooked and dark the road to a foe
though he on the highroad dwells**

The main room of the Sun was half full. James and Thorvald shared a table and a pitcher, thought about dinner while they waited for their companion to come in from the stable. Near the fire a family—elderly man, wife leaning on a staff, grown daughter, all wrapped in cloaks against the evening chill. A few more guests were scattered about the room. The door opened. A broad-shouldered man came in, three more behind him, all wearing swords. He threw back his hood, revealing dark hair, a gray streak running through it.

James spoke.

"Here's an unexpected friend."

He stood up, waved.

Mord saw him, turned, said something to one of the men behind him. With the other two he walked across the room, looked carefully at James, sat down.

"It appears Your Majesty has escaped your enemies."

159

"Enemies? I have been with friends."

"Harald and the Order accept the new Lady Commander?"

"The Lady Leonora commands the Order. The cause being ended, so is the quarrel."

"Before Your Majesty makes such decisions, it were well to take counsel with your advisors."

"The decisions are taken. One concerns you. You heard of Estmark's words at Council."

"If there are bandits in Estmark, they are not ours."

"I have seen villages with new walls."

"Rumors of trouble, fears of war."

"Charred timbers, the bodies of bandits wearing my badge. It will stop. The company of messengers is dissolved. We will find you other duties."

"Rather we will find you better counsel. Your Majesty believes his enemies against his friends."

Mord looked about the hall, hesitated a moment, spoke to Thorvald.

"We will take charge of his Majesty. Say nothing to anyone."

He rose to his feet. The King remained seated.

"Tell my cousin that I am well, at peace, and will return in my own time. What messengers you have, release. They have no longer leave to bear Our badge."

"Your Majesty goes now and with me."

"I will not."

"Whether you will or not."

Mord put one hand on his sword, looked about the hall. The men with him stepped forward. Thorvald stood up, reached for his dagger. From a bench by the wall a man took two steps forward, caught him about the waist, wrestled him down. The King spoke.

"It seems I do have enemies."

"And I friends; most in this room are mine. Your Majesty comes now with me, and quietly."

"Silence I can deny you. Traitors! Loyal men to their king!" He stood, backed, reaching for his dagger.

The sword came out, swung. One of the three by the fire stepped forward, a chair lifted in her hands. It caught the blow, twisted. Mord stepped back, staring at a broken blade.

The two others were on their feet, cloaks sliding off to reveal armor. Mord shouted, pointed. Two of the men on the benches were up, swords and daggers coming out. The gray-haired man batted a sword aside with his left arm, struck with the mace in his right. The Lady's staff licked out, back; a Wolf clutched at his stomach, blood running between his fingers.

Mord shouted, "Nae Halla. Kal."

Short bows, gray robes of the western plains, they poured through the door, took up positions left and right. The surviving Wolves stepped back, out of reach of Leonora's spear. Harald took one step back, right side to the fireplace, left arm with its archer's shield in front of him. Caralla froze, chair still raised between Mord and his king. Mord spoke:

"Last is best. Lay down your weapons."

The King looked around the room, spoke.

"I am James of Kaerlia and your king. Are you all traitors?"

Mord laughed. "Their king is some filthy savage out on

the plains. But they are as fond of gold as we are. There is much to be said for servants with their own tongue."

James spoke again. "I will come with you; let the rest go."

"All come with me. Or die."

Harald's voice was calm. "Last is best."

Mord saw where he was looking, turned. The men standing either side the door had their bows half drawn, arrows pointed at him.

Harald spoke again:

"Raven clan rode south into ambush. The men who met you in the meadow were mine."

Mord hesitated, leaped for the King. Caralla brought her chair down across his wrist; the dagger clattered to the floor. Bowstrings sung.

The remaining Wolves, more prudent than their commander, let weapons fall; two of them released Thorvald. Harald's men bound them. Harald sat down at the largest table, motioned James and Thorvald to join him. Leonora carefully wiped the blade of her spear on a dead Wolf's tunic, leaned it against the fireplace, went into the kitchen. Voices. She returned with a pitcher of beer in one hand, a loaf of bread in the other. The stew, when it arrived, had a distinctly scorched taste. They ate it anyway.

The next morning at breakfast, Harald asked James his plans.

"To the castle, quietly. If I recognize any more old friends I will pass them by. From there, reassure the lords, dissolve the messengers, seek to discover which of my people have been taking the Emperor's gold."

"The first evening I spent in your hall, Mord was sitting beside Andrew. It was Andrew who told you that Leonora was dead."

The King looked up, startled.

"My mother's sister's son—as near an older brother as I had, after Robert died. And for years before that Robert was always up north with Father. While I live, Andrew is my right hand. If I die, my uncle's boy inherits and Andrew goes back to being one more southern lord—with better birth than land. He has no reason to seek my life, much to guard it."

An hour later James and his two companions were on the road. A little past noon, nearing the turn to the long valley with Eston and the castle at its head, they heard hoofbeats, reined to one side. It was a single rider, cloaked and hooded. Passing, sunlight struck a glint of fire under the hood. The King shouted, "Anne."

The horse came to a sliding stop, wheeled. She threw back her hood.

"James. Gods be thanked. You're going the wrong direction."

"What do you mean?"

"Treason. I passed a pack of Wolves not a mile south. Your enemies, by now mounted and moving. North or into the woods."

"Can we get past and safe to the castle?"

"The least safe place in your kingdom; I'll tell you the whole tale when there is time. We must ride."

Thorvald spoke. "Your Majesty, I hear horses. Take the lady's counsel now, discuss it later."

The group turned. Around the far bend, horses. Anne

pulled her hood back up too late; the lead rider shouted, spurred to a gallop.

"Look to the lady, Majesty." Thorvald charged their pursuers, sword out, his brother beside him. The King hesitated a moment; Anne did not. He followed her.

Five miles north, the fresher horses were gaining. A long open stretch, the lead Wolves in sight, Anne and James almost abreast. A shout from the woods ahead.

"Right, for your lives."

Anne wheeled her horse, James followed. They crashed into the edge of the forest, through brush; the horses slowed. He looked back. A horse running free, a cluster of Wolves around a body, some off their horses with bows out.

"This way. On foot."

They followed, leading their horses up and over a series of low ridges, coming to a stop at last at the edge of a clearing where two horses were tethered to a tree. Their guide, when she stood still long enough for a clear look, was younger than Anne. Mail over golden brown tunic, bow. Order. They stood a moment, catching their breath, uncertain.

A voice behind them. "What have we?"

Startled, James turned. Wider, plainer of face, similarly garbed and armed.

"We should go first. I'm Elaina ni Leonor; my sister Kara ni Lain."

"The lady's name is Anne, mine James. You are sister to Caralla ni Leonor?"

"We have the same mother. Do you know Cara?"

"She saved my life not long ago; it seems to be a family habit."

"Kara spotted the Wolves this morning. They were coming this way, so we got ready for them. We don't like Wolves."

"All things considered, I cannot blame you. We are your debtors. Might you by chance increase the debt by directing me to where Harald Haraldsson and the Lady Commander are encamped?"

Anne spoke, surprise in her voice: "You are at peace with Harald?"

"With Harald and with the Lady Commander. In their debt. You were right; I was wrong."

She spoke gravely. "Then if your question has not changed, my answer has."

It was some time before they again noticed the two Ladies.

By Kara's advice they avoided the road; the woods were safer if slower. Before nightfall they made camp east and north of the inn. The two Ladies helped their guests construct a shelter, floor it with pine boughs, then vanished into the woods. James was the first to speak.

"You said you had a tale."

"Did you ever tell Andrew why we quarreled?"

"No."

"He took your room in the castle, left me in mine. I think he hoped . . . He didn't know about the sliding panel. I listened."

"And?"

"Heard him instruct Mord to have his Wolves find you, kill you, blame Harald. Heard him hint to two provincial lords that William was too young to rule, that if they supported him instead they would not lose by it.

Heard him instruct his people to have certain of the garrison imprisoned. He has brought in men loyal to him. There are mercenaries in the castle I have not seen before. Some will not speak in any language I know. I think Westkin. And there is more."

"Enough and too much. What else?"

"The Emperor's man in Eston paid a long visit. Too fast for me to follow, but I think they have an understanding."

"That first lunch. Harald was right."

"Usually, I think. What did he say?"

"That if I required wisdom, I hadn't far to look."

Kara, her head three feet from theirs, smiled. She came to her feet soundlessly, moved like a shadow through the woods to her hammock.

Three days later they reached Stephen's hill, Harald's force encamped below it. Elaina led them past the cats' encampment to where the Order's banner, green circle on gold, flew above lines of hammocks, cooking fires, tethered horses. Two women at a fire near the banner looked up, came to their feet. Elaina hesitated a moment, then slid off her horse, ran to her mother. Caralla walked over, nodded to the King, looked curiously at his companion. James was the first to speak.

"Anne, the Lady Caralla ni Leonor, Elaina's sister. Lady Caralla, Anne of Estfen, my betrothed."

Anne looked down, spoke: "I understand I have you to thank for my lord's life."

Caralla looked puzzled a moment, then her face cleared.

"I just followed orders. It was one of Father's set-piece battles—everything important settled five minutes before it starts."

This time it was Anne who looked blank. James explained.

"The Lady is daughter to Harald."

"Fortune indeed. Speaking of whom, it would be well to find him."

"Father's up hill with Stephen; we can take you."

She walked over to the other two, got their attention. Elaina remounted, Leonora and Caralla fetched their horses. Elaina rode by her mother; Caralla caught Kara's glance, fell back to join her. When they reached the gate it was open; Leonora led the party through it.

In Stephen's council chamber Harald looked up, saw Anne, smiled.

"All this way for stories? I'm flattered."

"It would be worth the ride, but I have one to tell first."

Leonora sent Elaina and Kara off, with instructions to stay out of trouble. The rest were silent as Anne repeated what she had seen and heard. When she was done, Harald spoke.

"The Westkin you saw. What were their tattoos?"

Anne thought a moment. "The one who seemed to be in charge of the others had a black bird on his forehead."

"Ravens. At least he has sense enough not to mix clans. Any idea how many?"

"They had half the west barracks."

"Fifty to a hundred. What else?"

"A company, thirty or forty, that seemed to be his people—accents from the hill country south of Estmont. Another company I think were mercenaries. The Wolves mostly lodged in Eston, but ten or twenty in the castle, maybe more."

James broke in. "What about my people?"

"He quarreled with the captain of your guard for losing you—and living. Sent them all off to Eston. Of the men you left behind, he sent some with messages. Two at least he locked up; I don't know if he gave any reason. Of the old garrison, maybe ten are left."

Leonora summed it up. "Fewer than two hundred, almost all loyal to Andrew." She looked at Harald; he nodded, spoke.

"Stephen, what can you raise fast?"

"Messengers out today? Two-fifty, maybe three hundred, five days from now. Five, six more days for the rest. We'd best assemble on my southern border, plains west of the road. Plenty of grass."

"What about Brand?"

"If he's home when the bird gets there, a hundred in five days—farther to come. Maybe more. Four hundred more in another week or so."

"'Nora?"

"Three tataves in camp, one in the hills east. Do we pull in our scouts, Stephen's, from the border?"

"No. Four tataves, my people, Brand and Stephen's. Leave James's folk in Eston out—too hard to get word to them without its getting to other people. Bring them in after. Taking the castle gets the birds, might get Andrew, might not. He'll have more people south. Snake clan, maybe. Mercenaries from over the eastern passes. Useful stuff, gold. Need a royal banner."

Harald, Leonora, and Stephen spent the rest of the afternoon working out details with occasional help from Caralla; James and Anne sat, hands linked, listened, answered an occasional question. When they were done, servants brought dinner.

Eight days later Harald reached the fork in the road where he had separated from Hrolf a year before—left to Eston, right to the castle. A Lady, dressed as a traveler, mounted, was waiting. He gave her an enquiring look; she spoke quietly.

"Caralla's watching the gate, the rest are scattered between here and there. Nothing that looks like a messenger the past two days."

"Stay; we don't want word going out, either. Not till we send it."

She nodded, backed her horse into the woods to let the columns pass. They made camp in the twilight, set sentries on all three roads. Well before dawn the Order broke camp, moved off into the woods toward the castle.

The sentry above the gate heard hoofbeats, looked up. Out of the forest edge, a bowshot and more from the gate, a rider came galloping. More. Dark cloaks, a red splotch on the breast of one—Wolves. A lot of Wolves. Something behind them. He yelled to the captain of the gate, the guards below. As the gate swung ponderously open—the bridge was already down—the castle courtyard filled with yells, running feet. Men ran past him; he reached down for the bow and quiver at his feet, rose again. Something struck him a sudden blow on the chest. He looked down—an arrow.

Anne watched, hidden at the forest edge, out of bowshot from the walls. From the brush ahead arrows poured at the castle. She turned to Elaina.

"Some of them are going high."

"At the far rampart, shooting blind. Arrows from behind make men nervous."

The lead force in their borrowed plumage were through the gate. Behind them the pursuers, a double column of cats at a gallop. The gate stayed open; they went through. After them the main body, banners of North and River, between them the royal banner. By the time James reached the castle courtyard the fighting was over, the ramparts swept clean, the courtyard spotted with bodies, men laying down their weapons. Harald, in the middle of the courtyard with his cats spread out behind him, was arguing with one of the nomads. He turned to the King.

"Wants supplies over Northgate; Emperor might not be too happy with them any more. I said parties of ten, my messenger first. He thinks I'm being rude. Can I invite him and senior kin to stay a week as guests while junior kin head home? Wounded to stay till they can travel. Useful folk to know."

James nodded.

Bets Won And Lost

The coward believes he will live forever
If he holds back in the battle,
But in old age he shall have no peace
Though spears have spared his limbs.

The chair in the King's council chamber was at least as comfortable as a saddle and Harald had slept in a lot of saddles. He came out of a half doze at a familiar voice, opened his eyes. The guard captain appeared to have survived his brief imprisonment without serious damage. Harald was the first to speak.

"Henry. You owe me a gold piece."

The King looked puzzled, the captain blank; neither spoke.

"I'm here, aren't I?"

The guard captain shook his head.

"It doesn't count; I was locked in the dungeon."

"When we made the bet, we didn't say anything about who I had to take the castle from. Besides, you weren't locked up for the past three years. Told you to keep the brush down."

"And I told His Majesty."

"And I had more urgent matters to deal with. Fortunate you didn't tell Andrew. I gather the two of you had a bet."

"Five years back. 'Nora?"

"Sober, and off settling a fight between two of my commanders who weren't. Never heard the terms."

"Stephen?"

"You said you could take the castle. Henry said you couldn't—not without a siege. One gold piece. To Harald if he did it, to Henry if he tried and failed."

The King reached into his purse, pulled out a gold piece; Henry caught it out of the air.

"Pay him. My fault."

Harald closed his eyes again, considered the situation. Andrew had left the castle with the contents of the treasury and most of his own people, probably on word of either Mord's failure or Anne's escape. The mercenaries and nomads had been left behind to hold the castle, the Wolves, Harald suspected, in the hope that the King might show up without an army.

They were talking about birds. Philip's voice. Harald opened his eyes again.

"Your Majesty's cousin commanded me to send birds to most of the provinces south of here; he did not tell me why or what messages they carried."

"What does that leave us?"

"Nothing for Estfen or Estmount; he sent the last three to each the day of his departure. Two birds still for Estmark. South one for the hills, one for the plains. Two for Westval. One other thing, Majesty."

James looked up.

"I sleep in the tower under the birds. This morning, bell woke me, yelling. Someone pounded on the door. No voice I knew. Didn't pull the bolt—figured it was worth waiting to know more. After a while he went away."

Harald turned to the King. "Majesty, Anne should be here."

The King gave him a puzzled look.

"If the southern provinces are in revolt—hills, plain, everything east—you'll need the other half of the kingdom to deal with them, full levies. If they are with Andrew because he told them you're dead, they're fighting me, you should move fast with what you have—and bring your banner. The lady is Estfen's daughter, Estmont's niece, nobody's fool."

The King looked around the room. "Henry, you know the lady Anne's apartments?"

He nodded.

"Take word that I would be glad of her counsel. While we wait I will send for refreshment."

The refreshment came, followed by the lady.

Harald put the question to her. She thought a moment before answering.

"Estmark is friendly to Andrew because he wants his word with His Majesty, next time he quarrels with us. Father hasn't forgiven Andrew for last time. Nobody likes him much. If he told any of the three he planned to seize the throne by force, they'd bring you his head, happy to do it. South plains, hills, I don't know."

Harald nodded to her, turned to the King. "By my counsel we leave a skeleton garrison here, under Henry. Call out the Eston levies, what they can mount of them.

Bird to Westval—they're close. Spend tomorrow getting ready, assembling supplies, sweeping the Eston taverns for what's missing of your guard. Next day west and south. Order out first as scouts, all the way across the plain in case they come up the west edge."

"Should we send birds to everyone else to tell them I'm alive and Andrew a traitor?"

"Messages can lie. It's your face we need. Pigeon can't carry that."

The next morning Harald, sleeping in a room at the base of the south tower, was awakened by voices nearby, thumping noises, someone singing off key. Dawn. Through the arrow slit he observed a team of men with axes, Henry among them, cutting brush. There being nothing handy to throw, he went back to bed.

A day and a half later, the army formed up outside the walls. Harald was feeding his mare a last handful of oats when he heard voices raised behind him.

"And I say, love of my life, that treasures are safest guarded by high walls. You are my treasure; you stay."

"A lot of men those walls guarded are feeding worms just now."

"Henry is a careful man. He'll have the rest of the Eston levies to help him."

"I'm safer with you. More useful, too."

"Harald will be there to tell me when I'm being stupid. All that leaves is to remind me what I want to stay alive for. You can do that from here. Enough."

Harald, moving to the head of the forming column: "Talk to you like that, heart's delight, be walking."

But only the mare heard.

Three days later a scout brought word. A sizable body
of cavalry flying the Westval oak tree, ahead and right.
Harald brought the army to a stop. James came up beside
him; Harald spoke.

"Any reason to think he wants you dead?"

The King shook his head, spoke to his captain. With
banner carrier and twenty of his guard, he rode forward
ahead of his army. The Westval contingent approached
cautiously, stopped well out of arrowshot. The King rode
towards the center of their line; the oak tree moved to
meet him. After a very long half hour James came back,
accompanied by the provincial lord and several of his
men. Another half hour was spent explaining the situation
before the combined force moved again south.

Two days later scouts came in with word of a force
moving up the center of the plain, screened by nomads.
Harald formed up his little army. Three provinces—seven
hundred heavy cavalry—with two hundred of the King's
guard and a hundred Eston crossbows, were the center.
The Order force, grown to over three hundred, was the
right, Harald's two hundred cats the left. They advanced
behind a thin screen of cats and Ladies. A little past noon
the opposing force came into sight. Harald positioned the
crossbowmen and Ladies at the top of a low ridge,
portable pavises for shelter, the cavalry a little down the
slope, and waited.

Banners blew in the breeze—the three eastern
provinces out in force, Estfen left, green hart on silver,
Estmark's boar on the right. In the center, with Estvale,
Andrew's bear, blue on gold, a body of heavy cavalry in
foreign armor. Nomads a screen in front of the army,

shooting at long range, falling back to their main body in the center.

Out of the Order forces on the right a single rider, straight for the Estfen banner. Steel cap off, hair streaming fire in the wind. Harald, riding at the center beside the King, drew a long breath.

"Good girl."

"Gods. Back at the castle. What is she . . ."

"Saving your neck. Her father's, too."

On the left, a rider out to meet Anne. The wind caught the King's banner, blew it out—he rode forward ahead of his guard, in plain sight, the banner beside him. At the opposing center, the bear banner surged forward, Andrew's mercenaries around it, the nomads ahead. Most of the rest of the center, the right, all of the left, held.

"Back, Majesty. They've seen you. That charge is for us."

The King wheeled, fell back into line with his guard. Harald was shooting steadily, aiming high for the charging mercenaries. A horse, hit by a nomad arrow at long range, went wild; the rider pulled it out of the line. The nomad force split left and right across the face of Harald's army shooting as they rode, opening a gap for the charging cavalry. Crossbows on the center, long bows on the right, shot back. On the left the cats, pivoting on the royal center, swung like a door to block the nomad column.

The King's captain swung down his arm, the royal standard dipped, the heavy cavalry moved forward, lances down. Faster. At a gallop the two masses of cavalry met, the King's longer line wrapping around the ends of the attackers.

From the front slope of the ridge Harald could see the

whole battle spread out below. In the center, where the two charges met, a tangled mass of men, most still mounted, fighting hand to hand. On the left the nomads, outnumbered by the more heavily armored cats, had avoided them as best they could, turned right again, aiming for the fringe of the battle, their path marked by a trail of bodies. On the right, part of the nomad force had ridden around the end of the Order's line. The rest had turned back and were shooting into the melee from the far side, out of range of the archers on the ridge. Beyond the battle, more than a bowshot from where Harald watched, twelve hundred men, the massed levy of three provinces, sat their horses while riders hurried up and down the line.

Now they were moving. The nomads, caught between the charging line of heavy cavalry and the central battle, scattered for their lives. A small body of horsemen broke from the melee, joined the fleeing nomads. Most of the mercenary heavies, already outnumbered and locked in battle with the King's center, were less lucky.

Harald, having spent the final minutes of the battle shooting at the men around Andrew's banner, sheathed his bow. The surviving mercenaries were laying down their weapons. The surviving nomads—along with a few of the Order's horses driven off from behind their line— were almost out of sight. The King was no longer on his horse but still on his feet.

A group of riders were forcing their way towards the King through the tangle of dead men and horses where the eastern provinces, taking the mercenaries in the rear, had finished the battle. One was Anne; the shield beside her showed a green hart on silver. Her father. Harald took a careful look around the battle field, walked his horse down to join them.

The King was standing over the body of his captain. Harald, off his horse, spoke from out of sword reach.

"James. Let me take a look at him."

The King looked around, lowered his sword, stepped back. Harald kneeled by the captain, pulled a long strip of cloth from under the skirt of his war coat, bound up the worst of the wounds. When he finally looked up the King was holding Anne tightly, listening to her father.

"Andrew claimed you were dead, Harald and the Order burning and looting, northern provinces maybe trying for the crown. Thought we might as well come see. Nomads got me wondering. They had to get here somehow. Only two passes west. Harald owns one, the Emperor owns the other. I wondered about gold to pay them, too."

Harald spoke from his knees: "I think he'll live. Two men, stretcher, to get him out of here, blankets to keep him warm."

He turned to Estfen. "Westkin came over the low pass, south quietly in dribs and drabs. His Imperial Majesty provided the gold. Anyone found Andrew yet?"

Estfen shook his head. "He broke off at the end with his escort, left the banner behind. His House Guard too."

"Damn. Anyone found the Maril commander?"

One of Estfen's guards spoke.

"Big man over there tangled up with the bay; don't think he's alive."

Several of the mercenaries were gathered around the body. Harald spoke to them slowly.

"Maril. Hfi sac Kaerl, Tengu?"

One of them looked up. "Speak tongue. Some."

"Who is in charge of your people?"

That produced a quick conference in their own language. One of them, right arm bound tight to his body, armor splotched with blood, came forward. The other pointed at him.

"Helf top still alive. Think."

The injured man called out something. A minute later, another Maril limped over from beyond the tangle of bodies around Andrew's fallen banner.

"I speak your language."

Harald looked up from helping two of the guards get their captain onto a stretcher.

"Your Majesty, this is Janos son of Kanos. Helped us run the Imperials out of River province back when all of us were younger. Janos, His Majesty of Kaerlia. Henry's boy. Fellow you and your friends just did your best to kill."

Janos exchanged a few words with Helf, turned to the King, gave a low bow.

"Your Majesty, I and my fellows are your prisoners. The terms are yours to set."

James thought a moment.

"You have two choices. Go home, on foot, we keep everything but supplies to get you there, horses enough to carry the wounded that can't walk.

"Or take service with me. You get your horses, arms and armor back. When I think you've earned them, we can talk about pay."

Janos bowed again to the King, turned to his fellows. The discussion was too fast for Harald to follow any of it. When it ended, Janos turned back to James.

"Provision for our wounded?"

"Same as ours. Nearest villages that can feed them."

"I accept. For myself, all here. Your men."

He dropped clumsily to one knee, wincing. The King took his hands between his own. When they were done, Harald spoke.

"Let me look at that leg."

"Only fair."

As he spoke, Janos pulled the feather end of a broken shaft from his belt, held it out. Harald looked, nodded, set to work.

Stephen came over, accompanied by a man in blue and gold who bowed to the King, spoke.

"Your Majesty. What's left of your cousin's guard asked me to tell you we didn't know."

The King gave him a long look. The guard captain met it.

"Bandage your wounded, bury your dead. Swear to me. What's left of you are with my guard till this is over."

The King waited until the wounded had been dealt with before ordering his pavilion pitched. Harald, last to arrive, found the King on a camp stool, six provincial lords standing, Leonora sitting in a corner. He found a travel sack filled with something soft, sat down next to her. The King spoke.

"Excellencies, Lady Commander, my lord Harald. My cousin is defeated but not taken. Before we plan for the morrow, let us count today's losses." He looked around.

Estfen spoke first. "Half a dozen wounded, one badly. Maril were already engaged; we took them in the rear."

"One company missed my signals, joined the charge. Eight dead, twelve wounded." That was Estvale.

"Five went; lost three of them."

The King's center had suffered more—of nine hundred cavalry, some seven hundred still fit to ride. Order, cross-bowmen, and cats, exchanging arrows with the nomads at long range, light losses. The Maril and Andrew's small guard had suffered most of all. Of four hundred heavy cavalry, a hundred and fifty without serious injury.

"Now what? Do we chase my cousin north and try to catch him or figure he's the Emperor's problem?"

Estfen spoke. "The first thing is to send riders to every-one who isn't here, tell them His Majesty is safe, at peace with Harald and the Order, Andrew an outlaw. How do we settle Wolves, Ladies, all that?"

"The Company of Royal Messengers is dissolved by my order. Any from my father's day are ordered back to my castle; I'll still need people to carry messages. The rest are dismissed. The Order is under the command of the Lady Commander. I owe her blood money for any Ladies killed by the Wolves. The fault is mine; I'll accept her count."

"What about land?"

The King looked puzzled.

"Wolves seized Order land, sold it."

"Any transfer not approved in writing by the Council is void. That's been law for two hundred years." That was Leonora.

"Be a lot of unhappy people down south."

The King shrugged. Nobody spoke.

A familiar voice outside the tent; the King looked up, startled.

"Would Your Majesty like to feed your guests?"

Anne came into the pavilion, followed by two men with

trays, one with pitchers. Conversation stopped. She offered mugs of beer to the King's guests, starting with Harald and Leonora; the men filled plates and passed them. After a few minutes, James spoke again.

"Before we were so pleasantly interrupted, I was asking advice on dealing with Andrew."

There was a long silence; Estfen broke it.

"Do I understand, Your Majesty, that Andrew was receiving troops and gold from the Empire?"

The King nodded.

"Then it isn't my advice you want." Heads turned, another long pause. At last Harald spoke.

"Your Majesty told me why you trusted your cousin. Close to you, not in the immediate line of succession, better off with you alive."

The King nodded. "I still don't understand. He had four hundred heavies, guard and Maril together, two hundred nomads. Double that, he still couldn't have come close to taking me on. If I was dead he might have persuaded one or two lords to back him against young William, but not enough. Something is missing."

"Ambushed Westkin south of Borderflood, showed you what the warleader was carrying. Lots of gold. Scrolls. You read the open one. I read the other. Didn't say who it was for, but I think we can guess. Little less than two weeks, legions cross the river."

Harald stopped speaking; the tent was silent.

Payment in Full

For the Warrior weapons
And wit.

The next morning messengers went out, from the King to call out the provincial levy, from the Lady Commander to assemble the host. Westval, having fought the battle in his own province, took charge of distributing the wounded among his villages while the rest of his levy assembled. The others moved north in three columns—the levies of North and River under their lords, accompanied by a tatave of the Order, up the middle of the plain, the eastern levies, with a second tatave, up the western edge, and the rest of the army, with Harald and the King, along the eastern edge, as they had come.

A little past noon James found Harald riding beside him and took the opportunity for questions.

"Do you think he'll try to double back south?"

"Doubt it."

"So why spread out? Scout screen the width of the plains. Do you think the Imperials might come early?"

"Doubt it."

The King looked curiously at Harald.

"Imperials could come early. Andrew could turn south. Enemies don't always do what I expect. Friends neither.

"Three thousand horses eat a lot of grass. Spread out, move slow, more grazing, more grain left when we need it. More villages to buy food from, too.

"Some Ladies to talk with. Be back."

Harald pulled his mare out of line, watched the double column move past. Saw a familiar face, fell in beside.

Elaina looked up. "Mad at me again?"

Harald said nothing. Kara shook her head. "He knew. Could have sent her back. Didn't."

"Think I can see through a steel cap?"

She shook her head. "You can count."

Elaina looked puzzled. Harald nodded.

"Said I sounded like your mother. So do you."

The next time he joined the column it was next to Leonora.

"Bright girl 'Laina had."

"Kara? Yes. Only reason my Elaina hasn't gotten herself killed yet."

"Rode south with Anne three across. Knew I'd see. Knew I saw."

She closed her eyes. He leaned over, put one arm around her waist; she let her head rest a moment on his shoulder as they rode. He spoke softly.

"Would be proud of her."

They rode together, saying nothing. After a while he fell out of the column, trotted back to the King.

Two days later they reached the long valley that led to

Eston and the royal castle. Anne and the wounded, with a small escort of the King's guard, took the turn. The rest continued north, moving slowly to let the horses graze. When they reached Stephen's hill another army was camped below it—the rest of the levy of the two border provinces. The combined force moved north, spread out on a ten mile front, waited.

Early morning. The King, bored and curious, followed Harald and Egil out of camp. They reined in on a low hill, both facing west. The morning sun caught the peaks above the high pass, struck sparks. He had almost come up with them when Harald wheeled the mare, spoke.

"What's your count?"

"Four thousand from the provinces. My people . . . the Maril, Andrew's guard, almost balance our losses—twelve hundred. Four hundred crossbows and pikes."

"'Nora has twelve hundred and change. Egil takes the cats out today, make sure no surprises. The rest move tomorrow."

The next day the army moved north and east to a ridge a day's ride south of the river. From time to time a scout arrived, spoke to Harald, went off again. Late that afternoon he shifted the whole force half a mile west. The Order set up pavises along the crest of the ridge, crossbowmen to their right where it rose to a small hill. The cavalry made camp on the next ridge back, cats at the bottom of the slope between. A little before dark scouts came in to report the Imperial army encamped some three miles north.

"Have a count?"

"Banners of three legions, about as many lights. Cavalry, not a lot, ten cacades, maybe less."

"Commander's banner?"

"Stripes, red and gold."

"You're sure?"

The cat nodded.

"May get you back to your wife in one piece. Me too."

The King gave Harald a puzzled look.

"You know who the commander is?"

"Who he isn't. Second Prince must be on the outs again; Artos is his man. Best they have. Got the army back across the river after Fox Valley."

"Not good enough to keep you from beating him."

"Battle started, junior legion commander. Before dark, highest rank officer left. Morning, we surrounded the earthworks—nobody there but a few wounded too bad to move. Trail of bodies north—but he got most of them home. Good man. Hope he's safe in bed, farther the better."

That night the men ate their fill. The next morning they formed up. The ridge top was archers—Order center and left, crossbows on the right. Harald and the King were at the right end of the line; someone had set up an extra pavise for them. Partway down the slope behind them, the royal guard waited to protect the right flank—or the King. The main body of heavy cavalry, under Stephen's command, was massed along the lower slope of the next ridge south, sheltered from arrows, positioned to charge down that, up the battle ridge, and over. North was another long ridge, another beyond it.

A dozen cats came over the ridge to the north, riding hard for the right end of Harald's line. Behind them, a mass of Imperial light cavalry. Seeing the line of archers along the crest of the next ridge they slowed, spread out, stopped well out of arrowshot; from their center a rider back over the ridge.

On the far ridge more men. Three bodies of infantry— a tight block in the center, looser formations at each side. Cavalry on the flanks. As they moved down the slope the cavalry in front of them split, moved. By the time they came to a stop halfway down the slope, there were only two bodies of cavalry, one covering the right flank, one the left. Over the ridge more infantry, behind them a small cluster of mounted men, banners. Harald turned to the King.

"See the center, tight formation? Ninth legion on the right, twenty-second left, sixth between. A thousand men each—three thousand Imperial heavies. Either side light infantry—Bashkai by the look of them. Fast, fierce. Not fond of taking orders. Medium cavalry, some light for scouting. The crowd farther back is archers—Norlander, mostly. Behind that, commander, staff, messengers."

The infantry began to move downhill, drums beating time. From the top of the battle ridge, arrows. The legions' shields came up. The Bashkai on the right were pulling ahead of the legions; trumpets. They slowed, stopped, moved forward again.

"They're coming at a walk—why?"

"Fair way to go, still at long range. Big shields; arrows don't do much to a formed legion. Have to break them first. Bashkai'll suffer some, worse if they arrive by themselves."

The legions had reached the bottom, started up the long slope towards the archers. Behind them their own archers formed up. A few fell, most got pavises set up, took position behind them, started shooting uphill. An arrow buried itself in the dirt a few feet in front of the pavise sheltering Harald and the King. The crossbows shot back, range lengthened by the advantage in height.

Harald signaled to Egil. The cats moved out to the right, came over the ridge, down, shooting as they rode, pouring arrows into the flank of the light infantry on the Imperial left. Harald watched the Imperial cavalry, massed well out of range of his archers. It didn't move.

"Harald!"

He turned. The King was pointing east, beyond the cats.

The newcomers were nomads, moving at a trot, heading for the rear of the cats. Behind them a banner—blue bear on gold—a cluster of more heavily armed riders. Already cats were falling. Harald stood up, called something, signaled.

The King went down the back slope at a run, yelling to his guard. The column of heavy horse formed, moved out, the King at its head. The nomads saw them coming, wheeled, scattered east. Trumpet calls. The guard slowed, came back. A few arrows followed them. The cats were already back behind the ridge. Egil nodded to the King as he came by, went back to bandaging a wounded arm.

By the time the King got back to where Harald still watched the battle, the legions were halfway up the slope, still formed, a few bodies marking their path. The Bashkai left and right of them had lost more but were still coming steadily. Harald called something down to Egil, readjusted the shield on his left arm, drew an arrow from the quiver

at his belt, aimed high, released. Again. Watching, James
saw that the arrows were short; Harald was drawing the
point behind the bow, using the shield now covering his
wrist to guide it. Dismounted cats were forming up along
the ridge, shooting at a high angle. The legions kept coming.

In the Imperial command group on the far slope, something was happening. A horse ran wild. The group was
moving back, farther up the slope.

Harald sheathed his bow, looked along the ridge. The
legions were a little more than sixty yards from the line of
archers. He signaled; somewhere a horn call, whistles.
The Ladies, abandoning their pavises, turned and ran
down the back slope of the ridge towards the massed
cavalry. The crossbowmen were moving back as well. The
army was retreating. He turned to the King.

"Cavalry to get ready to charge."

"Charge? The legions aren't broken. You said . . ."

"Do it."

The King spoke to the trumpeter downhill; the trumpet
call rang out, was echoed. The lower slope of the ridge to
the south came alive, men mounting, lances.

The King felt Harald's hand on his shoulder, turned,
looked. Behind the Imperial army, a line of mounted men
came over the ridge, started down. A second line. A third.

Downslope of them, where the command group had
been, was a tangle of bodies.

"Hrolf's back."

The King stepped clear of the pavise to see better.
Harald pulled him back.

"They still have archers. Not much longer."

On the Imperial left their cavalry, attacked from

behind, men falling, fled east out of the battle. The riders on the right wheeled, charged into a storm of arrows, made it halfway to the advancing cats before what were left broke and fled.

The front line of cats was moving down the slope faster and faster, lances lowered. Behind them the second and third lines, shooting as they came. Too far to see arrows, but the Imperial archers were chaos. The line of lancers hit what was left of them, went through, shifted to bows, poured arrows at short range into the rear of the Imperial infantry. The second and third line, halfway down the slope, shifted targets. Under the rain of arrows the light infantry broke formation, ran for the ridge. In the center, shrill trumpet calls. Three legions, precise as on the drill field, reversed in place, each man facing about, raised a shield wall against the rain of arrows. Long spears, passed forward to what was now the second rank, coming down to face the cats. Another trumpet call; the legions moved forward over their own dead.

The King never saw the signal for the charge, but he heard the thunder as five thousand heavy cavalry came over the ridge. Left and right they smashed through what was left of the Imperial light infantry. The center, lances down, horses at a gallop, hit the rear of the legions.

Still the Imperial center did not break. What had been the middle of the formation, now the rear, reversed again, started pushing back. Trumpet calls, shouts; Stephen pulled his men back uphill, beyond javelin range. What was left of three legions reformed in a rough square, perhaps as many as a thousand men still standing.

Everything slowed. The Imperial heavies were a triple

line of shields, front rank kneeling. On the ridge above them archers were again forming up, interspersed with blocks of heavy cavalry. On the opposite slope the cats had for the moment stopped shooting. Harald and the King, mounted, picked their way through the bodies that littered the slope.

Harald stopped just out of javelin range from the Imperial line, held up his empty hands, waited. In a few minutes the line opened enough to pass an Imperial officer. He held one arm up, hand empty; the other dangled useless by his side. Harald dismounted. After a short conversation he mounted again, rode back to the King.

"They surrender on terms. Wounded go home, wagons for the ones who need it. The rest camp our side the river, personal weapons only, until the Emperor pays head money. Could finish them, but it would cost. This way's better."

The King looked around the field.

"Yes."

Harald rode back to the Imperial officer.

By sunset, dead sorted from living and each other, wounded dealt with, men could rest. The surviving Imperials made camp in the flat between the two ridges. Egil, having seized the Imperial supply train while his father was negotiating the surrender, contributed tents and bedding. Just before dark, he came back with two more wagons—one loaded with food, one with barrels of beer.

The legionaries thanked him profusely. One of the surviving Bashkai muttered something in his own language. Egil looked down at him from the wagon, grinned.

"I think this fellow is afraid I've poisoned the beer. Just to prove I haven't . . ." He filled a mug, drained it. One of the legionaries fed him the next line.

"Maybe you poisoned a different barrel."

"Wouldn't want you to think that. Only eight barrels. I can manage."

On the ridge, Harald's decade, Hrolf, around a fire toasting sausages. A figure moving through the Kingdom camp towards them, stopping along the way.

"James. Join us."

The King came up to the fire, held out his hands.

"I have two questions."

Harald looked at him.

"The first is where the hell did you find firewood out on the plains? There's not a tree for miles."

"Your folk broke a lot of lances this morning."

"Second question. Are you the luckiest man alive?"

"Anyone else ask that question, answer's easy. Leonora, then Gerda, yes. But considering what's waiting back at your castle . . ."

"If Hrolf had showed up half an hour later, we'd be dead. Half an hour earlier, a lot of Imperials would still be alive. Birds can't find an army on the march—besides, you didn't have any. How did you do it?"

Harald looked at Hrolf.

"Told you."

Hrolf stood up, looked around, nodded. Harald spoke again.

"North peak, thousand feet or so above the high pass, there's a ledge. Couple of friends with good eyes, lot of warm clothes. Sheet of bronze so wide, polished like a mirror. Weather's good, they can see right across the plain. Man, maybe not, but an army's big. Sunlight off that bronze, be surprised how far you can see it. Got me to one side of the Imperial army, Hrolf the other. After that scouts."

"The Imperials had scouts too. One or two men I understand, but how did they manage to overlook eighteen hundred?"

"Light cavalry see a few cats, don't go looking for what's behind them, not if they want to come back."

"They saw cats. Whose did they think they were?"

"Mine. No reason my scouts have to be the same side of them as my army. Sometimes aren't. Egil had lunch with Hrolf day before yesterday."

Harald handed the King a sausage, stuck another on the point of the javelin. The sausage finished, the King rose, thanked Harald for the use of his fire, headed back towards his own camp. Harald watched him go. When he turned back to the fire Hrolf met his eye, nodded.

BOOK III:
Caralla's War

Fortune to see the foe first

News

Much is lost by the late sleeper
Wealth is won by the swift.

A servant in the royal livery.

"His Majesty bids Her Majesty, the Lady Commander, to Council."

Anne carefully lifted the squirming bundle from her lap, kissed it, handed it to Elen.

"Be good."

She stood up, went to the door, through it. Leonora, behind her, turned.

"You too."

The door closed. Elaina got up from the floor, went over to Elen, started making faces at the baby.

In the council room, Anne took her seat beside her husband, Leonora at the far end of the long table next to Egil. Of twelve provincial lords, four were present themselves, four more in the person of officer or heir. Stephen spoke.

"Your Majesty. Brand being occupied about urgent affairs, I speak for his province as well as mine."

Anne glanced sidelong at James, doing his best to look as if he believed in the urgent affairs; under the table her hand found his. Her father was speaking.

"My brother has been ill all winter. His son is east with the Maril, learning his trade. I speak for fen and vale."

The other lords remained silent; finally the King spoke.

"Gentles, I called Council to profit by the presence of so many guests. My best news you all know. I have a daughter, my lady wife is well."

Estfen looked as if he would say something, didn't.

"Our borders are quiet. Word from the Empire has His Majesty ailing, the succession in doubt, the princes gathering supporters, shifting troops—Second Prince to the western province, where he's governor. Trouble there should be peace here. Yet . . ." He turned to Stephen.

"You all know the ford where the North Road crosses Borderflood. They are building something on their side. Men, wagons, timber. Not a large army, but more troops than common. Perhaps a fort."

The King looked around the room. It was Egil who spoke.

"So far as the Empire, our word the same as yours. Maybe they fear you will attack them?"

The King looked startled.

"A fort commanding the ford would make it harder for us to take advantage of civil war their side of the border." It was Estfen who spoke, Stephen who responded.

"A month before Harald can bring his host over the Northgate. So they build now."

"If they expect a civil war, wouldn't they have more urgent things to do—each side gathering forces?" That was the Queen. For a moment nobody responded. Finally the Lady Commander spoke.

"I distrust all accounts of Imperial politics. Believe the Old Man's failing when we have word of his funeral—from at least three witnesses. But it's early in the year for an invasion. Soldiers need to eat. Horses too. Bad time of the year to ford Borderflood."

The Council fell silent. When it became clear that nobody had more to add, talk turned to other subjects.

Anne leaned over, whispered to the King:

"I think our daughter has more need of me than our lords."

She went out. A few minutes later, the door opened again.

"Mother. Rider from Caralla, urgent."

Leonora glanced at the King; he nodded.

"Bring her in."

Splashed with mud, swaying with weariness, leaning on Elaina's arm. The Lady looked across the room at Leonora.

"Caralla. A bridge. Building."

"The Lady Caralla sends word that the Empire is bridging the Borderflood where the North Road crosses it?"

She nodded. Leonora spoke to her daughter.

"You were right to bring this to Council. Take care of her, get her to bed. You and Kara ready to ride in the morning." She turned back to the King.

"We have our answer."

Stephen was the first to break the silence.

"I ride in the morning too. Can you send a courier to Brand with messages?"

The King nodded, thought a moment.

"Brand and Stephen, with what help the Lady Commander can provide, can observe the enemy, perhaps harass the crossing. But if they come in force we will need more."

"Our host, the royal forces, half the provinces—that's as much as we can feed this early in the year." That was Leonora. "Messengers out tomorrow morning. By my counsel, the kingdom host to assemble on the plain west of here, near the North road. Garrisons to your northern keeps. Our host to North Province, with levies of North and River."

The King looked soberly around the room.

"I have seen few battles, ordered none. The Lady Commander has been at the business thirty years and more. Saving your counsel, I am minded to take hers."

There was a long silence. The King spoke again.

"Then be it so. Birds to the far south and east, riders elsewhere. Have you other counsel to give us before you ride North, Lady?"

Leonora looked at him, thought a moment, spoke.

"By your leave I stay here, ride with your host when it assembles. I know what the next weeks will be and my bones are too old for it. Caralla will command in the North."

Egil stood up.

"By Your Majesty's leave?"

"Of course; you must be elsewhere?"

"In Eston."

Egil went out. The King looked curious, said nothing; Leonora took pity on him.

"There are always a few cats staying the winter. Eston taverns are open late."

James thought a moment.

"Speaking of cats, should we send a bird to Harald with the news? The pass is closed, but still . . . This may mean they are moving against him as well."

"Yes."

Four days later Stephen reached his hold, spent a busy day, then headed north and east. Caralla, accompanied by most of her octave, her sister and Kara, met his party on the road half a day south of the river. Stephen's men pitched a tent, posted sentries, the Ladies a wider ring of scouts. Inside the tent, Stephen and Caralla.

"You know that Mother has given the field command to me?"

"Nothing's forever. I ache after a day's riding; 'Nora's ten years older. Maybe more. Besides, King means well, took lessons from the best—but a few weeks doesn't make a general. I'll be happier knowing she's there."

"Brand will follow you; it's us."

Stephen nodded.

"What do you have?"

"Two hundred and fifty odd—four tataves. Mother sent word out, should be close to a thousand in a week. The rest longer. You?"

"My levy is six hundred, Brand's five. But I have to get my people safe into the hills before the Imperials show up and start killing them. Hard to do if the able-bodied men are all off fighting."

"If you have most of them, how long will it take?"

"Clear the path I think they take south. Get folk farther out up to the hills with enough food to keep them alive. Help garrison Markholt, Grayholt, get them set to stand siege . . . I can do most of it in a week, but more time would help. Started already."

"You think they'll siege the holds?"

"Siege or storm. Don't you?"

She nodded.

"Early spring, food's a problem for everyone. Worse problem for them—they have to get it south to the army, keep getting it. Can't leave garrisons sitting on their supply lines."

She thought for a minute.

"We have a day, maybe more, before they cross; been doing our best to slow the bridge. The legions are camped half a day's march north of the river, hoping we won't see them. Send me a hundred heavies, more when you can. I think I can buy you a week, with luck two."

A mile north, Elaina watched Kara emerge from the tangle of brush and small trees that marked a creek bed. Closer, what she was holding was a rabbit.

"I still don't understand how you do that."

"Why I didn't take you yesterday."

"That wasn't rabbits."

"You hunt rabbits, don't catch them. Imperials, they catch you. Like you better in one piece. I caught it, you skin it."

She retrieved the cloak from her tethered horse, wrapped herself up in it, went to sleep.

Now You See It . . .

**Hew wood in wind-time,
in fine weather sail, . . .**

Gavin, sitting his horse while the columns formed up, turned to his second.

"Archers this side of the river. Sixth across, fifty yards in, field entrench."

Kyro saluted, rode over to the officer commanding the archers.

"Orders. Your people along the north bank. Sixth is crossing, Commander wants them covered just in case."

"High time."

While the archers took positions along the river bank, Kyro rode back to the sixth legion's banner, its commander standing beside it.

"Commander's orders. Your boys over the bridge, fifty yards, then start digging. Archers cover from this side."

"It's only two hours past noon—we could make camp ten miles in."

Kyro met the officer's eyes, shrugged, rode back, saluted Gavin.

"Orders delivered."

Three hours later, with the sixth across, spread out, dug in, the archers started to cross, interspersed with units of the seventh legion, shields up to protect both. A messenger, returning by small boat, reported a few wounded, no deaths, from archers at the top of the ridge.

It was an hour before dark when Gavin, accompanied by the commander of his heavy cavalry, rode up to the ridge, seized by the legions a half hour earlier.

"If you want the next ridge, my boys can get there a lot faster than the turtles got here."

Gavin stood silent a moment, looking south down the slope. The trampled grass was the only sign of enemies. He shook his head.

"Council, my tent, after dinner."

In the tent, servants passed goblets of wine to the commanders of the two legions, the two cavalry commanders, Kyro. When all had been served, the commander spoke.

"Two hours back, Ivor offered to ride over to the next ridge and take it. Might be he could. Might be we'd be fighting the rest of the campaign without him and his boys. Some of you think I'm taking things too slow. I've seen one of Harald's battles—one too many—my left arm still aches when it's cold. Studied the others. There's a lot to be said for being careful."

Ivor looked up, surprised. "I thought the Valeslord was on the far side of the mountains keeping Artos awake. Wasn't that half the point of moving so early, before the pass is open?"

"The pass is closed, but that's not to say which side he's on. The wife of the Karls' king, Harald's ally, was brought to bed a few weeks back. He might have stayed the winter to welcome it. I wouldn't spend winter in the mountains if I had a choice.

"I hope he's Artos's problem. Anyone hear what Artos said when he got the news, last time we crossed south?"

Kyro nodded, hesitated, spoke.

"He said Harald was a sorcerer. His special trick is making armies disappear."

"Not this one. We're all the army His Highness has, pretty near, and I plan to bring it back to him. Hope to bring news we hold the Karls' border holds, but I'm not taking chances. The first step is to assume Harald Haraldsson might be out there somewhere, planning to include us in one of his magic tricks. Council dismissed; see you in the morning."

Two miles south Caralla was holding her own council. In the fading light she could still see the horses of her scouts, tethered just below the top of the next ridge north.

"Ladies, Captain. Nobody killed on either side today, far as we know. Empire spent a day getting from the north shore of the river to the first ridge south. That pace, they get to Markholt by midsummer.

"Killing people isn't our job, not this week, odds ten to one against. Buy time for Stephen to get his people safe, the King to call up levies, reinforce his holds. Buy it cheap. Look dangerous, stay out of trouble. Lots of almost battles. Questions?"

Stephen's captain was the first to speak.

"Your archers can set up on a ridge top, harass the enemy, outrange their archers at the bottom, run when the legions get close. What you did today. We're lancers—province archers are heading for the holds. We hit them, they can hit us. What are we good for?"

"Part you did today, riding around the far slope of that ridge over there making tracks. They'll know we have heavies, maybe a lot. Make them cautious.

"One of these days their commander might get impatient, call our bluff. We run, they want to catch us, have to use light cavalry. Get far enough from the legions and their Belkhani heavies, we smash them. Commander slows down again. Drill it tomorrow morning, waiting for Imperials to show up."

She looked around the circle. Kara, by invitation, was sitting on a stone between two of the captains.

"Kara. Some here came in after your report. Tell us again what you saw north of the river."

"Two legions, sixth and seventh, looked like full strength. Belkhani heavies, maybe a thousand. Leatherbacks, more, two thousand at a guess. I don't know where from, not Westkin. Lots of transport—I counted twenty wagons. Mules. More still coming in, wagons and men. The commander's flag looks like a gameboard, blue and gold."

"Archers? Lights?" That was Stephen's captain.

"Not in camp."

One of the Order captains cut in. "The archers are camped by the river. A thousand easy, maybe twice that."

Caralla spoke slowly. "Not enough."

"Speaking for myself, rather fewer than more." That was Stephen's man.

"Last time, eight or nine thousand—and they thought

they were coming into a civil war, Andrew's people on their side. This time six or seven. They know we don't have cats—wish to hell I did. Still seems light."

Kara spoke. "The day I watched, two or three cacades came in, two wagons."

One of the Ladies looked up.

"The flag is Gavin. He's the First Prince's man. Sixth used to be his."

Downslope, voices. She recognized one of them, was on her feet when Egil arrived. He stopped, looked at Caralla, sketched the Imperial salute.

"Egil Haraldsson reporting in, Commander."

"Idiot. I don't suppose you brought any friends?"

"Every cat in Eston—two decades. Made enemies of a lot of tavern keepers."

"Just what I needed. Consider yourself scout commander for Hrolf's army."

"Uncle's here with an army?"

"You're it. Two decades. Enough for Father to siege a castle with. Scouts do their job, nobody has to see the rest of the army. Or not. Borrow an octave or two if you need them."

The next morning Elaina watched, hidden behind brush, as the Imperial army moved out. First the legions, forming up outside their camp, moving most of the way down the slope south, holding. Behind on either side, massed cavalry. A dozen riders moved forward ahead of the legions, rode at a gallop for the ridge where she was hidden. Elaina put the whistle to her mouth, waited.

They were more than halfway up the slope, a hundred yards or so from the ridge, when she blew, dropped the whistle, put arrow to string. Beside her Kara loosed. Along the ridge the rest of three octaves were shooting steadily. Two of the cavalrymen fell, a third was thrown by his wounded horse. The rest wheeled, rode back out of range, back to their army.

Now the legions were moving again, down the slope, up towards the ridge. Behind them archers were forming up. Kara shot high, over the heads of the advancing heavies. The archers below were shooting back, mostly short. Cavalry moved to the bottom of the slope, formed up, more waited above, just below the ridge the legions had camped on. Elaina blew again, two short blasts, repeated. The two Ladies slithered backwards, came to their feet, ran down to where their horses waited, mounted. Just downslope the rest of their tatave and all of another were waiting, mounted, lances in hand. Elaina rode over to the senior captain.

"Heavies are formed up at the bottom, legions halfway, archers behind them. More heavies still by the camp."

More whistles blew. The two tataves rode south down the slope, up the next, to where the rest of their sisters were setting up pavises. Behind them two thousand heavy infantry moved slowly uphill towards an empty ridge.

Gavin, watching, turned to Kyro.

"Twenty to one it's a bluff. If they're going to make a fight, they'll wait until we're deeper in. We can use the practice."

As the legions approached the ridge, trumpets sounded. In the front rank, shields and javelins. In the second, the long spears came down. At a half run they hit the ridge, stopped there. A rider came back to the command group, sitting its horses downhill from the legionary camp.

"Sir. Ladies, a hundred or so, riding for the next ridge. Looks like shields on top, a fair number. Sixth wants to know what next."

"Tell him to do it again."

While the messenger rode back, the rest of the army started forward; by the time the legions had taken the second ridge, cavalry and supply wagons were on the first.

"Commander wants to know if we take the next one?"

"No. Wait for the rest of us, throw up field fortifications. Eat."

The rider saluted, rode back.

It took more than an hour to shift the army, including the supply wagons, one ridge south to where the legions had been busily throwing up a rectangular earthwork. Once arrived, Gavin stationed half his archers inside the fortification with orders to keep their heads down, sent the legions south against the Order's archers. The cavalry remained in reserve on the southern slope of the ridge. When the legions reached the bottom they stopped to let the remaining archers take up position behind them.

Caralla, on the southern ridge, signaled; the Ladies started shooting, aiming over the legions for the Imperial archers. The legions started forward; they shifted their target. On the northern ridge, Gavin spoke to the commander of the light cavalry.

"Half a dozen scouts north to the ridge we just came from; tell them to send back word if they see anything. Two more squads east and west."

Ivor got the commander's attention.

"Sir, turtles can take the ridge, but soon as they get close, off the archers go. Turn me loose, over that ridge in a few minutes, ride them down if they try to run. Aren't more than a few hundred of them."

"A sensible plan if all we are facing are a few hundred Ladies. Risky if they have backup. The Karls field eight times your force in heavy lancers. I can't see over that ridge; can you?"

"A lot of those lancers are at the other end of the kingdom."

"It doesn't take all of them. You'll get your chance. Today, tomorrow, maybe next day. Just now, you're here in case those scouts find something that isn't grass."

Ivor looked skeptical, said nothing.

Kyro responded.

"What can they find? The enemy's south of us."

"That's what we thought last time I came this way. This time, scouts."

"Last time it was an army of cats. There shouldn't be any cats this side of the mountain, not till the pass opens."

"Shouldn't be."

He walked his horse up to the top of the ridge, looked north, pointed.

"Then again . . . ."

Six scouts had ridden north; five were coming back at a gallop. Straining his eyes, Kyro could just make out mounted figures on the top of the far ridge.

"Ivor."

"Sir?"

"I want your men in line facing uphill, far enough back from the ridge so they can't be seen from the far side. Lances ready. If we get very lucky I may have a use for them."

Gavin dismounted, walked over to the gateway of the earthworks, called in.

"Gavros! Keep your men down. If you see enemy riders don't shoot till I give the order. Anyone shoots early, I'll hang him."

The first of the scouts was back, reporting to his officer; Gavin joined them.

"Tell the Commander."

"Cats, sir. Top of the ridge. Took out Tomos, rest of us ran for it."

"How many?"

"Didn't have time to count, sir. Twenty or thirty, maybe more."

"What was behind them?"

"Don't know, sir. Top of the ridge, didn't seem friendly to visitors."

More scouts rode up, dismounted; one had an arrow in him. None had seen over the ridge. Gavin turned to their commander.

"Form up behind Ivor. Wait my signal."

Both cavalry commanders went off; the scouts helped their wounded comrade into the fortification. Kyro looked down at his commander.

"You're setting a trap. They get close, archers open up on them from cover, heavies break them, lights catch what's left."

Gavin smiled.

An hour later, southern ridge taken, trap unsprung, cats invisible save for three or four watching from the far ridge, a single rider came into camp from the west.

"All of the others, sir; I'm it. Don't know how many there were. We figured five of us could handle one cat. Must have been more in ambush."

"How far west of here did you run into them?"

The scout turned, saw the commander, saluted.

"Three, four miles, sir. We were chasing one of their scouts, trying to see what was behind. He stopped running, started shooting, so we charged. Must have been more in cover."

Gavin turned to Kyro.

"Still think I'm being too careful?"

"No, sir."

Another hour. Gavin, mounted, unmoving. A rider came over the far ridge, stopped, rode west. The enemy scouts on the ridge followed him.

"Damn."

Kyro looked at Gavin; Gavin watched the ridge, said nothing more. A long wait.

"Gods. They're coming."

Gavin shook his head.

Kyro looked again at the ridge to the north. The men pouring over it were on foot. Block formation in the center, irregular masses on each side.

"Ours?"

"Tenth legion and friends. The other jaw of my trap. Maybe next time. At least they're bringing the rest of the supplies."

Caralla woke up to voices in the distance, rolled out of her hammock, was on her feet by the time Egil rode up.

"Evening. Your Ladies are awake."

"How far off did they spot you?"

"Over the first ridge all right, two miles west of here,

avoiding our friends. This ridge, half a mile west, got challenged."

"Your half of the battle?"

"Another legion, lots of Bashkai, wagons, came in early afternoon. Uncle's army is north and west of them. Killed four scouts, drove one back. Your half?"

"As usual. Last I saw, before we ran, their cavalry was formed up just this side of the ridge facing your way. Archers at the bottom—but I don't think they were all there."

"Two legions march out of the camp, archers march in, stay down. Uncle attacks. Archers shoot, cavalry charges, third legion comes in from behind. Nice fellow. Good thing Uncle didn't fall for it. Next?"

"Something new. Be careful; you're all the cats I have. Not that many brothers either. One more day, maybe two, before he calls our bluff. I'm for bed."

The next day the Ladies again formed up on the ridge south of the Imperial camp. Again two legions came down the ridge, up, archers behind. Again Gavin was disappointed; the cavalry army that might or might not be hiding behind a screen of cats failed to appear in his rear. Nobody got close enough to his field fortifications for the hidden archers—or the hidden legion—to deal with.

Early the next morning Egil rode into camp, this time from the east, accompanied by most of his force.

"Cavalry coming. Sweeping east to get behind you."

"Araina, Kila, sisters off the ridge, back. Everyone mounted, ready to move. 'Laina, Kara, tell Stephen's people, Brand's, break camp fast, we're moving out."

She turned back to Egil.

"How many, how soon?"

"Less than an hour if they use the backside of the next ridge. A thousand Belkhani, two thousand odd leatherbacks somewhere."

Ivor brought his column to a halt on the far side of the ridge, waited for his captains to come up.

"Enemy should be a mile ahead, two ridges north—maybe some on the ridge between. At a gallop, back side so they can't see us. On my signal wheel, charge north. The turtle boys are coming south. Karls between us. Leatherbacks behind to chase what we miss. Clean up and the damn army can stop crawling.

"The Karls might have heavies with the archers. A few, we ignore. Lots, we hit them. Watch my signal. Questions?"

"Cats? Fast as we are and have bows."

"Last three days we've seen maybe thirty cats. My guess, the rest are on the other side of the mountains keeping Artos awake. The commander isn't so sure. If the Karls magic two thousand cats out of the grass, run for the legions. No more questions? We move."

They moved. Ten minutes later he looked right—a plume of smoke a mile or two to the north marked the legion camp. He signaled the troops, wheeled right, started up the slope. Someone yelled "Behind us." For a moment he thought it was the enemy—but they wouldn't be yelling in Belkhani. He turned.

On the ridge behind, a scattering of mounted men. One of his own was down. An arrow missed. Cats. Ivor fought for calm, won, counted. Fifteen men. A diversion. He signaled again, yelled. The Belkhani charged north, over the ridge and down.

Below him empty grass, down and up. With luck, the enemy were one ridge farther north, about to run from the legions. He signaled again. A thousand lancers plunged down the slope.

They were halfway there when troops started coming over the ridge—Bashkai lights, then the solid formation of the legions. The trap was empty. Ivor signaled, called to his trumpeter. The line came to a stop. Another call and they were moving again, back the way they had come. The cats might still be there.

They were. The Belkhani charged. An arrow glanced off Ivor's breast plate. Another past his cheek. Fifteen men— were they all shooting at him? He came over the ridge. Streaming down the other side were hundreds of riders.

Again calm won over panic—the fleeing riders were light cavalry, not cats. Hard to catch, easy to kill. He yelled to his men, plunged after them. Down the slope, up the next, over the ridge, down, the enemy opening the distance.

Coming up the next ridge, arrows again—a lot of arrows. Horses and archers at the top of the ridge. He looked left and right—line getting ragged. But this was the finish.

When he got to the ridge, there was nobody there—the enemy archers, again mounted, were in full flight down the slope. He slowed, stopped, yelled at the men streaming past. Where was his second? A few of his Belkhani saw him, slowed, stopped. Most did not. He turned, looked back down the slope they had come up. Dotted with bodies of men and horses.

"Anyone have a horn? Blow the damn recall, loud."

The call rang out. Some of the figures moving up the far slope slowed, turned. Some did not.

Noise behind him—horns, hooves. Leatherbacks—his own light cavalry—surged up around the clump of heavies.

"Where the hell are the Karls—killed them all already?"

Ivor pointed.

"Running south, half my men after them. They open the range, stop on a ridge top, shoot us, run again. Fast."

"So are we. How many?"

"Maybe five hundred."

The two officers looked at each other. Ivor shook his head.

"Commander won't be happy if you get cut up too."

"Damn happy if the enemy get smashed. Odds of four to one."

Ivor hesitated, looked back where the smoke plume still marked the location of the legion's camp, forward at where the track of trampled grass left by the retreating archers and their pursuers slanted up the opposite slope.

"They're cutting west."

"You think Gavin was right after all?"

"Cats they would have used—besides, the pass is closed. But the Karls have more heavy cavalry than anything else. Maybe that's what the cats were hiding. Could come over one of those ridges into an unpleasant surprise."

The light cavalry commander turned to his second.

"Two squads over the ridge. If they don't see anything dangerous, we follow. Hold at the next ridge, repeat."

Ivor had the last word. "If you see my boys, send them back."

. . . Now You Don't.

**A flying arrow, an ebbing tide,
Are never safe: let no man trust them.**

The next morning, as the legions broke camp, Gavin summed up the situation for his officers.

"We know they have Ladies, maybe five hundred. Scouts saw a couple of hundred heavies before our lights broke off yesterday. Maybe thirty cats. If they had a lot of cats, Ivor and his boys would be pushing up grass—as it was, the damn Ladies cost us fifty men, more horses. They might have had a lot of heavies waiting farther back, been baiting a trap." He turned to the scout commander.

"Last time you saw them, their main body was south and west of us. How far?"

"About five miles at sunset. My boys get too close, cats drive them off, but at least they aren't coming this way."

Gavin thought a moment.

"The castle we're here to take is south and east, in the hills, maybe twenty miles from here. One long day's march if we didn't have the damn wagons. Say two days. If we can get there before they do, if there isn't much of a garrison . . . We'll have to take it fast if their main army is loose behind us—no supplies from home. If they cut over to defend it—they can move faster than we can—makes the castle harder to take, but then their field force is bottled up, we can take our time. Comments?"

Silence for a moment; the Belkhani commander broke it.

"Leatherbacks out ahead of us. We might lose a few scouts but at least there won't be any surprises."

Kyro looked at Ivor in surprise, said nothing. Gavin nodded. "Yes."

An hour later, scouts at the top of the next ridge, legions beginning to move out, heavy cavalry flanking them, the commander and his second watching from below the abandoned camp.

"Looks like someone's got another magic trick."

Kyro looked at his commander curiously.

"Ever seen a cautious Belkhani before?"

Kyro thought a moment, shook his head.

With two legions and the light infantry at the top of the next ridge, Gavin sent the wagons to join them, then the third legion and the Belkhani. He repeated the maneuver at the next ridge, heading south and east. By noon the force had covered three miles. The next ridge was defended, abandoned as the legions approached. Three days and two minor skirmishes later, the sixth legion pitched camp in sight of Markholt. The next morning, Gavin called council.

"Sixth, what did your boys see?"

"Lot of horses ahead of us—mud thirty yards wide. Their rear was still going into the castle when we made camp. Nothing but Ladies, far as we could see—the track that cut south five miles back might be the Karl heavies. Hell of a lot of archers behind those walls."

"More mouths—we aren't the only ones short of supplies this time of year. With the Order locked in the castle and the Karl heavies south of us, the northern plains should be ours for a while. Siege. Legion engineers can go to work—there's lots of timber—make life interesting for the Karls."

Ivor caught his commander's eye. "What do you want me and Bertrand and our boys to do while the turtles are sieging?"

"Watch our back. I'm leaving one legion camped on the road in, just to play safe. Bertrand's boys patrolling the plains five or ten miles out to let us know if the Karls turn up with an army, threaten us or our supplies. Your boys are backup, in case it's a small army. If it's a big army, fall back on the legions. In a day or two, escort empty wagons home, full wagons back—four hundred lights, two hundred heavies should do it."

By late afternoon all three legions were dug in—the sixth west of the castle, the seventh northwest, the tenth blocking the road in. That left the south, under the looming shoulder of the mountain, for the Bashkai. They were still making camp, setting up tents, starting cooking fires.

"How does anyone find anything?"

Gavin looked up and down the colorful chaos. "Slowly. Tent banners give rank, clan. Look long enough . . ."

"What if someone attacks them?"

"Ant nest. But mostly they run forward, not back. Ever see a Bashkai without his weapons?"

"In the bath?"

"Ever see a Bashkai in a bath?"

Kyro thought a moment, shook his head.

"What the hell . . . ?"

Gavin was pointing at an arrow quivering in the ground. Voices were yelling. Someone ran past. Someone else staggered, fell clutching his belly, an arrow. Gavin reached down, grabbed the shield the Baskhai had dropped, looked around for the enemy. Beside him Kyro yelped. The feathered end of the arrow sticking out of his shoulder pointed up. Gavin looked up, around. Many of the Bashkai had shields raised, mostly against the castle. He saw one of them stagger, fall. That wasn't it—too far. He turned, looked up to where the lower slope of the mountain rose almost vertically from the edge of the camp, pointed, yelled. One of the Bashkai saw, called out something in his own language, raised his shield against the arrows sleeting down from above. Where the slope above flattened out, Gavin could see figures outlined in black against the eastern sky.

Gavin recognized the banner on a tent. "Arkhal! Out here, shield, get your damn people into cover in the woods."

There was no answer. He stepped to the tent door, looked in. The blue carpet bristled with arrows. So did the man lying on it.

"Back to the trees! Back to the trees!"

Someone else had figured it out. Voices yelling in Bashkai, men pointing up at the mountain, more running for the shelter of the forest behind them. Most made it.

Gavin's tent, a single lamp—outside dark. The commander, the legion commanders, the Hetman of the Bashkai, a bloody bandage on his arm, a ferocious scowl. Gavin spoke first.

"Karls got a hell of a lot of archers up on that hilltop without us any the wiser. Any guesses how?"

He looked at the commander of the sixth. The officer thought a moment before responding.

"We saw them go into the castle last night before dark. They could have come back out again after; the castle wasn't surrounded. South along the bottom of the hill, into the forest somewhere, up. Stayed back out of sight."

Gavin turned to the Hetman, spoke slowly.

"Do you know how many men you lost yet?"

"Too many. Morning climb mountain, chop archer women, feed black birds."

The tent door opened. Kyro came in, shoulder neatly bandaged, spoke:

"Might not be a bad idea, sir. I wouldn't fight Baskhai in the woods. Not with a bow."

Sitting by a fire, less than a mile away as the crow flies, Caralla expressed much the same opinion.

"If all my Ladies could move like Kara and fight like you, what's left of the Bashkai would be a fair fight. I don't like fair fights. The first three tataves are moving already, the rest follow. I'm leaving you four octaves. Kill anyone, that's fine, but your job is to scare them, make them move slow. Lose any of your Ladies, very unhappy with you. Get yourself killed, very unhappy with Kara."

Elaina thought a moment.

"The last week on a smaller scale? Where it's clear, ambush, one flight, run?"

"And don't take chances. Think about fighting in the woods against a thousand Karas. It's not like the legions."

The next morning, the edge of the woods, watching the bare shoulder where they had spent a day and part of two nights. Noises the other side. Kara nocked an arrow, Elaina lifted her whistle, waited.

Out of the woods a line of big shields. Elaina blew, nocked, released.

Kara's voice was urgent. "It's legionaries. Bashkai move faster. Out of here."

Elaina hesitated only a moment, lifted the whistle again, two short blasts. Turned back towards the path. A nightmare face ahead of her, streaked red and yellow. She thrust left-handed at the face with her bow, snatched right for the dagger at her belt, stepped in. The Bashkai blocked the bow with the axe in his right hand, grunted. She stepped back, he threw, she knocked the axe aside with the bow. Both hands over his belly, scarlet, he took a slow step forward, buckled.

"Run."

She started forwards. Another, farther ahead. She threw the bow like a javelin, stepped sideways. He turned to block it, looked down in surprise at the feathers sprouting from his side. Her sword was out, struck, past. Another, no space to let Kara shoot. The arm came down, the axe spun. Elaina stepped forward into it, felt the shock of the haft on her left shoulder, struck with the sword. He stepped back clear of the blow, in, long knife in his left hand, right reaching for another axe. She thrust, felt the shock run up her arm, pulled the sword free.

"Run."

She ran, found the path, along it. Shouting behind. She yelled.

"'Laina and Kara!"

Out of the woods into the small clearing, through. At the far side, turned. Kara came out of the woods at a run, through the clearing. Two Bashkai after her. Arrows sleeted from the woods, they dropped. Yells.

"Here."

She turned. Kara handed her her bow. More Baskhai, more arrows. Elaina put the whistle to her mouth, two short blasts, waited a moment to let the others get to the path. Kara loosed blind across the clearing into the woods, Elaina imitated her. They turned, ran.

Two hours later they came out of the tree line. On the slope above them, thirty or forty Ladies were sitting around fires cooking dinner. Elaina spotted Caralla at one fire, yelled.

"Get out; they're coming."

"Shut up and have dinner, sister."

Elaina's mouth fell open. Kara caught her by the sleeve, spoke quietly.

"Do what she says."

Five minutes later, as Elaina was trying to choke down a bit of bread, the Bashkai burst out of the woods, charged uphill yelling.

"Down."

The Ladies at the fire went to their faces; Elaina heard the hiss of arrows over them. A lot of arrows. When she looked back, most of the Bashkai were down, the last few vanishing back into the woods. The slope uphill was alive with archers. Caralla's voice.

"The real camp, the horses, another mile. How many did you lose?"

Elaina glanced around, where the Ladies were standing up, dusting themselves off. She counted again.

"Nobody."

"Congratulations. You get to do it again."

A week after the attack on the Bashkai camp, Gavin was watching the trebuchets come into action. He liked trebuchets, counterweighted monsters throwing rocks a man could barely lift from safely out of arrow shot of the target. The Karls had smaller engines up on the walls, but rough log walls shielded his teams from most of what they could throw. He turned to Kyro.

"They're slow, building them is a pain, but they're safe—and with enough time and rocks no wall can stand against them. Including that one. Any word of the supply train yet?"

"Any day now. What are we short of?"

"Beer. Three of the damn barrels had leaks."

Kyro gave his commander a quizzical look.

"Didn't say where the leaks came from."

"Commander!"

Gavin turned. It took him a moment to recognize the figure.

"Where the hell have you been?"

"Four days through the mountains with the Hetman and his people, two days more getting back. Didn't Hanno get here?"

Gavin shook his head.

"Damn. Fastest runner I had."

"What did you lose, what did you kill, where is the enemy?"

"Didn't lose anyone, sir, saving Hanno if they got him. Couple of scratches. Hetman lost people. Didn't get any of the enemy that I know of, sir—they kept running."

"Where are they?"

"They came out of the woods two days north of here, sir. Last I saw of them. They had horses, we didn't."

"Gods. Where are the Bashkai, chasing them over the plains?"

"No sir. Hetman doesn't like plains—too easy to shoot people. Coming back through the woods along the base of the hills. Longer, should be here soon."

Gavin looked at Kyros, said the obvious.

"Whole damn Order between us and the bridge. Guess we do without beer for a while."

The trebuchet's weight came down, the long arm up, the sling whipping above. Four hundred yards away they heard the crack of the rock hitting the castle wall. Gavin went over to talk to the engineers. Enough time might be a problem.

Fifteen miles north, Caralla was arguing with two of her captains.

"How do you propose we carry them—slung under the horses' bellies?"

"Hide a few barrels in a gully, send the rest with the wagons up into the hills."

"And spend the next week tied to your beer. No. Sisters can drink some now, fill up water bottles for later, but the barrels go with the wagons. Mound for 'Riana, mound for the three beggars that earned it. Horses too if there were time—I wouldn't have charged us. Rest of the bodies the Imperials can take care of when they find them. Wagons up to Stephen's people in the hills, Lyra on the litter. We've been here too long already."

Kara, in the ring of Ladies listening to the argument, said something to Elaina, Elaina spoke.

"We could take one barrel in a litter, dinner, breakfast tomorrow."

"Do it. The two of you—your idea. One barrel."

A week later, Gavin called his officers to council.

"The stone throwers are doing fine, but they aren't bringing down the wall today or tomorrow. If they did, better hope the Karls have lots of food, because we don't. Two supply trains taken that we know of and I'm not counting on a third. Time to go home. Bring back all of the legions, most of the cavalry, some of the Bashkai—not what we hoped, but a hell of a lot better than last time. Comments?"

"Bertrand and I could take our boys north, bring the next supply train back with us."

"Might not be one. Might not get back. Karls have had three weeks and more. Might be six or seven thousand heavies out there, two thousand lights. Your boys are good but I don't like those odds."

He looked around; nobody said anything.

"Break camp, move out, three hours. Engineers spend what time they have throwing lots of little stones over the wall, see if we can hurt someone. Tenth and sixth lead with Bashkai, seventh guards the rear. Archers, wagons, wounded in between. Leatherbacks scout all directions— including behind us once we're clear of the woods. Rest of the cavalry on both sides. Both of you remember they have more cavalry than we do, so don't chase. Bertrand, a report from your scouts before we move."

Three hours later the Sixth Legion formed up beside the seventh, outside the latter's camp. Trumpets blew, drums beat. The army was going home.

A day and a half later, forty miles north, sixty feet higher, Marcus was staring south across the river when he heard boots coming up the narrow ladder.

"Consider yourself relieved. Anything out there?"

"Seventy-three million five hundred and ninety-seven thousand four hundred and seventeen blades of grass. One hundred and thirty-three ant hills. Twenty poor bastards under cover at the far end of the bridge. Six leatherbacks watering their horses at the river and thinking up excuses for not scouting. From what I've heard the last few days, can't say I blame them. No armies—ours or theirs."

"What's raising dust at the top of the ridge?"

"Don't know—maybe one of the scouts is scouting."

The two men, crowded into the top of the fort's single observation tower, watched.

"It's a wagon. Coming fast. Like someone's chasing it."

Marcus lifted the horn to his lips, sounded the alarm. The single wagon was coming down the slope towards the bridge. On the ridge above, one of the escorting leatherbacks clutched at something, fell off his horse. The rest of the troop followed the wagon down. Now the ridge was black with riders. More of the leatherbacks were falling. The wagon rumbled onto the bridge, stopped. The guards at the south end were behind their earthworks, crossbows ready. On the ridge, riders had been replaced by figures on foot. It was too far to see arrows, but Marcus had no doubt why the guards were under cover; the Karl archers had demonstrated before their ability to reach the south end of the bridgehead from the nearest point of the ridge. He looked down at the wagon. The driver was gone; a head bobbed in the river. Marcus hoped the man could swim. The leatherbacks were all down, their bodies spotting the slope. Below him, archers lined the fort's wall.

"What the hell. Look at that. Damn wagon's burning."

The plume of smoke rose into the air; in the fading daylight, Marcus thought he could even see a tongue of flame. In the fort below, men were yelling. The gate opened, a couple of legionaries with buckets ran for the bridge. Neither of them made it across. In front of the gate a group formed up—eight men with shields, a turtle formation four wide and two deep, behind them four with buckets—and moved onto the bridge into the rain of arrows. Smoke from the burning wagon—and the planks under it—blew back up the slope where the dead leatherbacks were coming to life, running for the ridge.

By full dark they had the fire out. The Order archers, with nothing to aim at, stopped shooting.

"Hard to say how much damage till morning, sir. Maybe eight, ten feet of planking gone. Whatever was in that wagon burned fierce."

The garrison commander thought a moment before putting the next question.

"What about the beams? Harder to replace."

"Doubt the fire got that far. "

"We'll have to send a boat in the morning to check from underneath. Anyone know how much spare planking we have?"

An officer with a gray beard spoke from the back of the room. "Not much."

"Send a messenger to the Prince's man in that village up north, get people to work. The Karls may have more tricks—a couple of spare beams would be nice too. By the look of that wagon, size of that army, I don't think Gavin's been getting his beans and beer lately. Might be coming home in a hurry."

He looked around the room; the officers were silent.

"Two jobs. Patch that bridge. Protect it—against five or ten times our number of Karls. How?"

There was a brief pause; the commander of the garrison's archer company broke it.

"From the walls, my men can reach almost halfway to the ridge, the engines a little farther. We have a hundred archers, a dozen engines. If the Karls try to storm the bridge, take it apart, use it for firewood, we can make things pretty unhealthy for them."

The graybearded officer spoke from the back: "They might be willing to give up a little of their beauty sleep. How do you hit them in the dark?"

"Half moon tonight, waxing."

The commander shook his head.

"We can't count on the moon—all it takes is one cloudy

night. Besides, they could wait until it was down. Get the engines sighted in now, spear throwers at the far end of the bridge, stone throwers a little farther—no point smashing the bridge ourselves. Stack a couple of big piles of straw south of the bridgehead; if the troops on the far side can't fire them, you can use fire arrows. Enough light to shoot at an army."

The older officer spoke again.

"When we repair the end of the bridge, leave planks loose, tie them in place. Take them up at night. Eight foot gap. If they get to the end of the bridge all they can hack up will be the ends of the beams. If it's dark, some of them might find out the hard way."

The commander looked around. One of the legionary officers spoke.

"We have twenty men on the far side of the bridge. Dangerous but useful. Have them build up the earthworks in front. Behind too. If Belio's boys are shooting blind . . ."

"Messenger north tomorrow morning. Boat under the bridge to check the damage. Belio sees to getting the engines sighted in. When he's done, we send out tortoises, engineers, to start fixing the damaged bit. If there aren't enough planks to do all of it, half width, space out planks if we have to. Once that's done, send loads of straw across for bonfires. Orders to the troops the other side to build up earthworks in front, behind, best they can manage— they may need them. See to tying shields to one of the boats so we can get people across that way if we can't use the bridge. Word up and down the river to send more boats just in case. What have I forgotten?"

⚜ ⚜ ⚜

The answer was drifting downstream through the night. Egil put his question in a whisper.

"How do you stop one of these things?"

"Pole. Anchor. Run into a bridge."

"My pole's a quarter mile upstream; hadn't let go I'd be there too. Happen to see His Excellency Lord Stephen again, tell him to send two men next time. "

"You said you knew how to swim."

"Held onto the damn pole I'd have proved it. Doesn't mean I can steer a raft."

"Don't worry. A bridge is hard to miss."

He was right. An hour later the garrison commander woke up to horns, someone pounding on his door.

"Are they attacking?"

"The bridge is burning."

From the ramparts he could see the whole scene. The middle section of the bridge was a mass of flames. Men were running out the gate, shields up, buckets instead of swords. One of them was down. An arrow struck the rampart.

"That wasn't from the ridge; they've come downhill in the dark."

"Damn little we can do about it." He yelled down. "Gate is in range of their archers. Shields up when you come out."

He turned to the officer next to him.

"Time to rewrite my dispatches. We're going to need a lot more planks."

"Damn."

Kyro turned in the saddle to look at his commander.

The bridge, its center a scorched ruin, was not what they had been hoping to see over the final ridge. Four days of half rations, harassment by archers, the continual threat of thousands of heavy cavalry, and now this.

Gavin sat his horse for a few minutes, looking down at the bridge, the river, the fort on the other side, then turned to his second.

"The legions on the ridge—full field fortifications. Cavalry, Bashkai on the flat by the river. Archers in the legion camp. At least the terrain is on our side—not counting that damn river. I'm going down there to talk to the idiots responsible. Tell Ivor to give me a squad for escort. A banner, too—I'd rather not be shot by my own people. Suggestions?"

"If they can't patch the bridge, can we ford it? What everyone did before."

"Not this time of year they didn't—look how high the river is. We might swim it with ropes to help, but we'll lose people, horses. Not to mention leaving most of our gear behind. We might get across on boats. Eight thousand men, three thousand horses, hell of a lot of boats. And the Karls won't be sitting on their hands. Not so bad if we weren't short of food."

The first good news was that the men guarding the bridge didn't shoot him. The second was a boat. On the far side the garrison commander was waiting.

"My boys are hungry. What do you have and how do we get it to them?"

"We've been accumulating supplies, waiting for more wagons. Seven or eight loads. The boat you came in, one more, are all we have. I sent riders upstream, downstream, but no more boats so far. The bridge needs one section of long beams, a lot of planks. I sent a rider to the Prince's town up north; no word back."

"Two boats aren't much, but better than nothing. Supplies over, wounded back. Start with a couple of barrels of beer. How long ago did you send the rider?"

"Two days. Should have been back today at the latest."

"Send again. With an escort; this isn't the only ford. The same thing up and down river for boats. Let me get a look at the bridge."

Two miles south, Caralla rode into the royal camp, ignored a dozen banners, found the pennon she was looking for. As she dismounted, her mother came out of one of the larger tents. Caralla turned to her.

"Three killed, twenty-four injured, four badly."

"Supplies?"

"Five days for the Ladies—resupply courtesy of our friends. Even brought us beer. Horses have grain for two days; we're grazing them now."

"And I already have your estimate of their losses. Doubt your father could have done better."

That silenced Caralla. Her sister's arrival provided a change of subject.

"Couldn't have done it without Egil. Kara too. 'Laina took half a tatave, brought them all back. She'll do."

"If she doesn't get herself killed first."

"Mother! I didn't even get wounded."

"Better than last time. Learn to be careful; you're good, but I've buried better. Don't have a lot of daughters. Council in the tent yonder."

Before following her, Caralla turned to Elaina.

"Get Father talking sometime—his trip this side the mountains during the troubles."

"Bergthora told me the part she saw, when the Wolves almost killed him. Said she had never seen anyone fight like that."

"When things go wrong. Mostly he makes sure they don't. That's the part you need to learn."

The next afternoon yells, men pointing south. Down the slope a line of wagons, heavy cavalry as escort. Elaina recognized the banner, turned to Caralla.

"What's Stephen bringing?"

"Something someone left behind."

Three of the wagons stopped in the camp to unload supplies. The rest continued over the ridge, down the other side, up; they came to a stop just below the top of the ridge that separated the camps of the two armies. The riders dismounted, started unloading. Two hours later the pile of lumber was gone; where it had been stood two trebuchets, just downhill from the archers on the ridge.

Elaina turned to her sister.

"Monsters. Where did Stephen get siege engines?"

"From a siege. Small engines get disassembled for the parts. Trebuchets are mostly wood, heavy to carry. They didn't get around to burning all of it."

The engines assembled, Caralla rode over to talk to Stephen.

"Brother says you damn near got him drowned."

Stephen looked up. "Did it work?"

"Whole middle section out."

"And Egil got a bath. Don't see what you're complaining about."

The next morning, Gavin woke to voices near the tent. When he came out, Kyro and a cluster of legionaries were staring at the opposite ridge.

"Archers still there?"

"Yes. Something new. At the west end—look."

The flagpole was almost a mile west of the enemy position. As Gavin watched, a flag ran up it, blew out in the wind—red. It dipped, came up again, down. A minute later it was followed by a pale blue flag; that one dipped twice. Then red again.

"Who the hell are they signaling to?"

Ten minutes later, the pattern was clear—two different flags, varying numbers of dips once the flag was up. Gavin shook his head, looked up and down the enemy position— nothing. Hoofbeats.

It was Ivor.

"Splashes. In the river. I think they're throwing at the bridge. Don't know where the engines are, how they're aiming them."

Gavin watched the flagpole a moment longer, turned, stood watching the river. A minute later he saw the splash, a little upstream from the bridge. A minute later another, downstream. He turned back to his officers.

"They must have trebuchets just the other side of the ridge—any farther they'd be out of range. Someone in cover farther west on this ridge, beyond our lines. He signals where the splash is, flags relay. Get Bertrand, the

Hetman, tell the legion commanders to start their men forming up, then come here."

The three legion commanders showed up first.

"There are trebuchets just the other side of that ridge, trying to smash the bridge we plan to go home on. You're going to take them. Karls aren't fools; they have to know we're coming. Might be six or seven thousand heavies waiting for us; do it by the book. Lights to guard the flanks. Get close to the ridge, long spears down."

He turned to Ivor.

"The Karls have someone watching the fall of the rocks, signaling. Has to be on this ridge to see the river. The flagpole on the next ridge relays. Take five hundred heavies in case of trouble, down the ridge, catch the observer if you can, take out the flag pole. Circle back, maybe block their retreat if we break them. My guess is their army is south of here waiting for us to come after the trebuchets, but be careful. The rest of your boys, Bertrand, can make sure Karls don't get anyone behind us. Archers on the ridge till we need them somewhere."

Imperial discipline brought order fast. Three legions formed, down and south towards the next ridge, its archers, the hidden engines. Ivor's column went west at a gallop. The rest of the cavalry, heavy and light, formed up in two bodies, one west of the camp with its right flank on the river, one east with its left flank on the river, the supply wagons and the bridgehead protected between them.

One of Ivor's men yelled, pointed. A figure had broken from cover, was running down the slope towards the flag pole on the next ridge, the men around it. Ivor slanted left, led his column down the slope, up. Five hundred

heavies against four Karls—five counting the runner—
and a flagpole. It looked to be a one-sided battle.

A mile east the legions were moving up the slope.
Gavin, his horse abandoned as too good a target, was with
them. The rain of arrows from the ridge slowed, stopped.
The legions broke into a trot, long spears coming down as
they reached the ridge, came over it. Below them the
trebuchets, abandoned, a mass of mounted archers—
Gavin guessed a thousand or more—fleeing south.
Something odd about the engines. One of the horses was
dragging something—a long pole. The throwing arm. The
legions came over the ridge, down. Men swarmed around
the trebuchets, taking them apart under the orders of the
legion engineers, loading the pieces on men's backs. Some
way to replace the missing arms . . .

Over the ridge behind them a rider, yelling. Face and
leather armor splotched with blood.

"Karl heavies. Behind us. Thousands."

Gavin shouted orders. The legions reversed in place,
started back up to the ridge, reached it.

The next ridge, where the legions had been camped,
was spotted with bodies, the space between the two
ridges a confusion of mounted men and archers fleeing
south towards the legions. Gavin saw a runner stumble
and fall. One of the Belkhani angled across, up to where
Gavin was standing by his banner. His lance was gone,
shield broken.

"Where's Ivor?"

"Gods know. Behind the ridge, thousands of them. We
were coming up the slope."

The man turned, pointed.

"Smashed us, came along the ridge, smashed the archers. Their archers up there now."

"What happened on the other side of the ridge?"

The man shrugged.

"Wasn't looking that way."

More orders. The legions moved north, up to the final ridge, broken troops rallying behind them. Beyond was the slope, the river, the space between scattered with the bodies of men and horses. Gavin thought he could see heads in the water, horses too.

At the bridgehead a knot of men in the water, some swinging axes, some with shields raised against archers on the fortress wall. Gavin turned, spotted the Hetman, yelled, pointed. The Baskhai streamed down the slope.

From the west along the river a rider, low to the horse's back, more horses behind. The men at the bridgehead mounted, rode east. As Gavin watched, the south end of the bridge, cut from its anchors to the shore, swung in the current, broke free.

Gavin took a long breath, looked around. His legions at least were still safe. The Bashkai. Some archers, some cavalry, had rallied to the legions, some no doubt had made it across the river. Defeat, not catastrophe. In the long run, it was the legions that mattered.

He looked again. Between him and the river, where the wagons of supplies had stood, the slope was empty.

Turnabout

Early shall he rise who rules few servants,
And set to work at once:
Much is lost by the late sleeper,
Wealth is won by the swift.

It was almost noon when Caralla, having made a complete circle around the legions, led her half of the host back into camp. Her mother met her.

"It worked. Stephen smashed the cavalry, archers, we took the ridge, shot up what was left both sides of it, kept going. Egil and his friends cut the bridge free, 'Laina got them away."

"Wagons?"

"Stephen's bringing them. Emperor's beer with dinner."

"Resupply first. Kingdom can tie itself to wagons; we don't."

Caralla nodded.

Later that afternoon, while the royal army was celebrating its victory—despite the disappointingly small amount of beer—Egil drew his sister aside.

"I plan to cross tonight, next ford west, make trouble. Need two or three 'taves of Ladies who can swim, get a horse across."

"I'll pass the word. Your camp?"

"Three hours before dusk. Gets us to the ford by dark."

Caralla walked off. Egil turned to a familiar voice.

"Kara and I can swim; she's crossed twice the past month. Knows the other side. We could bring friends."

"Do it. My camp, three hours before dusk."

Farther north, Gavin was solving such problems as he could.

"We have two boats. Wounded over, firewood back."

"Yes sir."

Gavin heard the puzzlement, answered it.

"Karls took our beans and beer, left a lot of dead horses. Better than starving.

"Tonio—can your boys get those trebuchets working?"

"Not with what we have. Lots of wood, but too short."

"What about rafts?"

"Rafts?"

"Lots of wood. Can you make a couple of rafts, ropes from one bank to the other, move stuff?"

"Should work."

"Do it. I'm getting tired of this side of the river."

There was a brief lull. Kyro looked up from the tablets where he was trying to keep track of what was left of the army.

"If it works, we're home."

Gavin shook his head. "We still have to eat. A garrison of two hundred doesn't have supplies for five thousand.

There should be more wagons coming in but I don't know how many—we've drained this province already. Only supplies I know about for sure . . . The Hetman. Send someone for him."

In the Kingdom's encampment as the sun set, commanders gathered in the King's tent. Stephen summed up the situation.

"Three legions, light infantry, not much else left. The bridge is a mess. Couple of boats. Their supplies are in our camp. If I were Gavin I'd face the facts, abandon everything heavy, run ropes across the river, swim what I could. They'll still have a hungry time of it their side of the river—especially after Egil's finished. Our job's done."

The King spoke.

"You don't think it's worth trying to smash what's left?"

"All respect, Majesty, no. They still have teeth. We might do it, but it would cost. Emperor can find men easier than we can."

A brief pause. Stephen spoke again.

"Feeding an army's expensive. My advice, send the southern provinces home—this army isn't invading again any time soon. Leave me Brand, the Order, my people. Enough to keep Gavin from getting bored, deal with any more boats fool enough to come downstream in daylight. I've already sent a few of my extras off. Yosef's boy, the one Harald's fond of, been taking care of the horses for their company, asked leave to go after the battle. Missing his father, maybe."

Caralla in her hammock, eyes closed, a whistle. Dream?

She opened her eyes. Again. Out, rubbing her eyes. Downslope the noise of men moving. In the faint light of early morning, a dark mass. She put her own whistle to her lips, blew the alarm, shouted:

"Enemy Attack! Up! Out!"

Under the hammock and its cover her swordbelt, bow, quiver, boots; this near the front she slept in mail.

"Form on me. Slow them."

The rough line of Ladies formed, moved up to the ridge, poured arrows down, withdrew as the legionaries came closer. Back to where the horses were tethered, no time for a saddle. Around her, sisters were finding their mounts. Further back voices, yells. The royal camp was a confusion of men armoring, mounting, tripping over tent ropes. Stephen's voice carried over all:

"Armor, weapons, horse, and out. Forget the tents. Form up on the ridge behind."

The legions moved forward, through the lines of hammocks, into the undefended camp, slashing ropes and canvas to bring down tents. At the far side of the camp they stopped, shields raised against the arrows from the far ridge where a chaos of archers, cavalry, dismounted men putting on armor, was gradually taking order.

Leonora turned to James, buckling on arm harness, sleeping robe showing above his breastplate.

"Things some people will do for a good meal."

The King gave her a puzzled expression. She pointed downhill. The legions were withdrawing. So were the wagons.

"Ours and theirs; only fair." The wagons, what remained of the supplies of two armies, gradually vanished over the ridge.

Once the royal camp was restored to something near normal, the King called council in his tent.

"Tonight's dinner is in Gavin's camp—do we try to fetch it back?"

Leonora looked at Stephen, hesitated a moment, spoke.

"No. They'll expect that, be ready. What Stephen said still holds. My people have supplies for two weeks, his are in their own territory, can manage somehow. Everyone else spreads out, goes home."

Stephen nodded, looked around the circle of lords.

"Make sure your captains remember these are our people—buy, don't take. I have a long memory."

By the time Egil returned, the encampment below the ridge had shrunk drastically. Stephen and Caralla were standing by a mound on the ridge—four lances, pennons flying. The column of riders, tired horses, came to a stop. Caralla answered the unspoken question.

"Early morning yesterday. Bashkai got our pickets; one lasted long enough to give the alarm. People made it out but Gavin has the wagons."

"He'll need them. Two wagon trains—one supplies, one timber. Burned both—and a bridge. Took all the boats we could find back across, sunk them on our side of the river. All safe back—eleven cats, two octaves of Ladies, one boy. Some sacks of beans, courtesy of our friends."

Stephen looked up, startled. "What boy?"

"'Laina's friend from Forest Keep. He said he had your leave to go."

"He did. I thought he was going home." Stephen

walked down the line of riders, stopped by the smallest. Caralla turned to Egil.

"Couldn't you see how young he was?"

"Said he had leave from Stephen. 'Laina, Kara brought him. A little trouble in the river—none the other side. Useful."

"The boy's fourteen, fifteen at most."

"How old was Father when he ran away to Conor's people?"

"That's Father. Hen's a child."

"Don't stay children. Good shot, calm. Wouldn't care to go against the three of them. Hen, Kara don't get you at range, your baby sister deals with the problem. Dangerous lady."

"Ever seen Mother?"

"Hand-to-hand?" Egil shook his head.

"You're good. I'm good. Should be—trained enough. Mother, 'Laina, it's like a dance. Why Mother worries, more than she ever did about me. I know I can die. 'Laina, moving, it feels perfect. Still be killed."

BOOK IV:
Harald's War

He who journeys to mountain and firth
Needs food and fodder.

Salt Water

Never was colt on lighter lead

"You forgot your armor."

Hrolf closed the door behind him—there were still patches of snow in the fields around Haraldholt and the wind was cold.

"I need armor?"

"Helm at least. My grandson's got a new toy."

Hrolf walked over to the bench on the other side of the fire, sat down, waited.

"'Bjorn sweet-talked Niall's lady friend into showing him how to build a baby rock thrower. Cousins on the ropes. Damn near brained me this morning."

Asbjorn spoke from the floor beside his grandfather's chair.

"Not even close. Want to come see, Uncle?"

"Use snowballs. Less dangerous."

"They come apart."

As the day darkened, the hall filled—one end Asbjorn and his cousins playing an elaborate game of their own

247

invention, the other end parents, grandparents, assorted relatives. Niall's voice rose above the general racket.

"He says it's forty feet long and twenty wide, all blue and gold with green fish."

Harald abandoned the attempt to make sense of what his grandchildren were doing and came over to the adult end of the fire.

"What is forty feet long and twenty wide, blue and gold with green fish?"

"The Prince's swimming pool, Father. Donal saw it."

"What was Donal doing in the Western Capital?"

"The Oasis, on his way back from visiting Bear clan— after a girl there."

"The Second Prince has a swimming pool at the Oasis? What do they put in it, sand?"

"Filling it with water for the Prince's visit."

"If they haven't filled it yet, how come there are fish? And how did they get them there?" The voice was Asbjorn from beside his grandfather's chair.

The game at the far end of the hall came to an abrupt end, its leader having defected; the players drifted back to the fire and their elders' conversation.

"The fish are tile work. Not just painted—Donal says they stand out a little from the wall. The whole thing is lined with colored tiles. Gold for the Empire, blue for the Prince's banner. Green for fish and seaweed. I want to see it."

"When was Donal there, how full was the pool, and how are they filling it?"

Niall stopped a moment to think.

"Saw him two days ago, down vale. Just come in, maybe six days from the Oasis? A couple of feet of water in the pool when he saw it. Filling it with the extra from the spring, their wells. And he saw a bunch of water wagons come in."

The door to the kitchen—a separate structure built onto the end of the hall—opened. Asbjorn led his cousins into it, back with steaming bowls, pitchers of beer, platters piled with bread. The inhabitants of Haraldholt settled down to the serious business of dinner.

Children off to bed, some of the adults as well, Harald drew his youngest son aside.

"Where is Donal now?"

"My guess, still guesting down vale. Foxes should be coming east in a week or so, no point his going west and back again. Invited him to come home; said he might. You think this is more than a swimming pool."

"Yes. Tomorrow, down to Valholt. Ask 'Liana which of the sisters knows rock throwers best. Both of them up here tomorrow; I'll explain. You head down vale, talk to Donal, bring him back with you."

The next morning, after Niall had set out, Harald found Asbjorn.

"Show me your new toy—from the right side, this time."

Four days later, when Niall came back with his foster brother, Harald and Asbjorn took them into the back pasture. Asbjorn's trebuchet stood four feet at the pivot, nearly ten with the throwing arm vertical.

"I call her Little Bird."

"Biggest bird I ever saw."

"Black Bird's bigger."

Harald's engine was nearly twice the size, its pivot well above even Donal's head.

Asbjorn demonstrated. The arm down, a rock in the sling attached to the end. Four of Harald's grandchildren caught hold of the ropes at the other end of the arm. At Asbjorn's command they pulled together. Their end went down, the long end of the arm up, the rock down range. Under Asbjorn's delighted instruction, the adults, joined by Hrolf, tried to duplicate the performance with the larger machine. The first rock went straight up; everyone scattered as it came down. By the fifth, they were going consistently in the right direction. Harald called a brief halt to stake out the target—a rectangle on the ground forty feet long by twenty wide—and specify rules. The rest of the day was spent throwing rocks.

In the kitchen, Gerda looked up from the fire.

"When did you take over the children's job?"

"Forfeit. They beat us fair and square."

Harald picked up the platter of bread, carried it out to his grandson.

The next morning, he called together Niall, Donal, and Aliana.

"One more day practicing, another packing. Then pick up Bergthora at Valholt—need at least one person who knows what she's doing, as 'Bjorn showed us yesterday. Donal to recruit clan brothers—at the eastern end of Fox range by then. Other three to the mine to load horses. Meet at the Northflood crossing. More practice there with the clan brothers—plenty of rocks, splashes to tell you where they're going."

He reached over the arm of his chair, caught firm hold of his grandson's tunic.

"And since you insist on coming to councils you are not

invited to, I have an errand for you too. Message to Jonholt, top of Greenvale."

Asbjorn looked up, calculation in his eyes.

"I'll go now; where is it?"

An hour later, his grandson having vanished over a path better suited to a mountain goat, Harald found the other two, with several new recruits, throwing rocks.

"Take her apart, pack."

"I thought we had two more days."

"Pack this morning, out this afternoon. Time 'Bjorn gets back, long gone. Know a better way of keeping him from going with you, tell me. Do your practicing full team, river to throw into."

Three hours later Black Bird, disassembled and divided between two pack horses, was riding down vale—with Niall, Donal, and Aliana to keep her company.

Andros looked carefully around the deserted square, lit only by the lanterns of the legionary guards, took three quiet steps sideways towards the other guard, spoke from the side of his mouth in a hoarse whisper.

"What'd you do?"

"Last out this morning. You?"

"Captain said shield wasn't shiny. Getting awful picky. You'd almost think . . ."

"Buddy of mine, someone told him chest of gold in the pool; need an excuse for guards."

"Afraid someone will put a killer fish in, bite His Highness."

"How'd they get something that big?"

"Put in a baby. By the time they get the damn pool filled . . . what's that?"

"Drum? Tearing?"

"Behind us."

The two guards turned to face the covered pool. A second sound of ripping cloth. One of them reached back for his lantern, held it up.

"Idiots laced the cover too tight—it's splitting."

Something struck the center of the canvas cover, making it billow out. Another ripping sound. The guards stared, frozen. Again.

"Get the officer; I'll stay."

By the time the officer of the watch arrived, the canvas cover was in tatters. He stared wide eyed at the splash as something fell into the pool. Another. Another.

"Attacking us, sir. Engines. Sound the alarm? Sir."

Fifty yards the other side of the wall that guarded the fortified oasis, the Lady Bergthora spoke in a low voice to her team.

"Pull."

The five men tugged down on the harness attached to the short end of the throwing arm. The long end came up, the sling flung its ten-pound load high.

"Up."

Harness up, arm down, another lump in the sling.

"Pull."

From the gate around the corner of the wall, voices. Someone was raising a lantern on a pole to illuminate the space beyond the gate. More voices, yells from the wall:

"Arrows. 'Ware arrows."

The lantern went out. Voices, running feet. Along the wall figures moving.

The piles on either side of the trebuchet were gone. Black Bird's team, white as ghosts, looked around. Bergthora brushed salt off her tunic, the men, bare to the waist, off their skin. Donal put two fingers in his mouth, whistled. By the time the engine was reduced to a pile of pieces the horses had arrived to be loaded. A few minutes later the rest of the clan brothers, already mounted, joined them.

"Front gate tight; must think we're an army."

"Time to go."

They went.

Three days later, sixty miles north, a column of tired riders cautiously approached the cluster of tents around a well, men, horses. From the lead rider's lance a fox pennon. Donal's uncle, as senior member of the party, spoke for all.

> "No feud, No foe
> Friendship
> Grace ask
> of guest peace."

A graybeard, bear clan tattoo on his chest, came forward:

> "No ill done to,
> No ill doing,
> Our water drink, our well draw
> Three nights, three days."

He handed the lead rider a horn cup. Donal took a sip of the water, passed it to his uncle. Niall, at the end of the line, emptied the cup, rode forward to return it.

The formalities over, the Fox clan riders dismounted, saw to their horses. Their hosts eyed the string of unloaded pack horses, politely said nothing about the blood-stained cloth wrapping the arm of one of their guests.

Around the fire that night, conversation drifted gradually towards their presence far north of their own territory. Donal muttered something about more guards than they expected; his uncle glared at him, cut into the conversation:

"An unprofitable trip, save for the pleasure of guesting with you. Maybe better luck later. Any problems, foreigners, Ravens, not your folk. Eagle territory anyway."

The next morning they set off again, headed for another well a day's travel south and west. Once out of sight of their hosts, Donal and Niall moved forward until they were riding beside Maelsach. The older man turned to Niall.

"Too much last night?"

"Kept offering; guest's duty to drink. Talk too. I did. Wagons full of Empire's gold—or something else worth six hands of Ravens to guard. They wanted to know more, told them if there'd been fewer guards I'd know more. Only thing I'm sure they were carrying was arrows. Lot of guards for a caravan of arrows.

"Didn't see my brother." He turned to look at Donal.

"Better than drinking. Pretty lady asks questions, what can I do? Didn't know for sure what they were carrying. Had our guesses. Take more men than we had to find out."

Kiron

To ask well, to answer rightly,
Are the marks of a wise man.

The guards at the door came to attention, spear butts
striking the stone floor precisely together. Slender, medium
height, scarred face—the visitor came into the governor's
office, dropped to one knee.

"Highness."

"Commander. Your news?"

"This morning a rider came in. Raven clan—from the
supply train that set out four days ago. He says the wagons
were attacked by raiders—Eagles. Taken, the guards
killed or driven off."

"How big was the escort?"

"Twenty riders, a dozen crossbows. He says the attackers
were two or three times their number."

"Why would they be raiding a supply caravan? Is there
any word of famine on the plains?"

The commander shook his head.

"We're sending the wagons with big escorts. Maybe

they thought they were carrying something more valuable than food for your troops, water for your pool."

"We can't have them raiding our supplies; what do we do?"

The commander glanced at the young man standing behind the Prince's shoulder. The Prince answered the unspoken question.

"You can speak openly."

"The Eagles' oasis is a long day's march west of here. The Second has been too long in camp. With Your Highness's leave, I find any Eagles in town and send them back to their chiefs with a message. The men responsible for the raid to be delivered up to us, the supplies, wagons, horses returned, blood money for the dead, hostages against future behavior."

"Will they do it?"

"No. Before dawn tomorrow, the Second, a few hundred light infantry, mostly archers, all the Ravens we can find. We reach Eagle Oasis before dusk, demand an immediate answer. They refuse. We take the oasis."

"What do they do?"

"They can't stay around in force because there's not enough water. They might try to take it back then and there—get killed. Might meet our terms. If not—land with water is scarce. We settle the oasis with our people, maybe Ravens too. Eagles move west, try to take someone else's territory or find a clan with spare land willing to have them as clients. Your Highness's province is a day wider. The clans don't raid us again. All over before the main campaign starts—and the troops get a little exercise."

"Do it. Before you go, I have a favor to ask. I would like

my son Kiron to join your staff. You may find him useful;
he will surely find what he learns useful later."

The commander looked curiously at the young man,
nodded. "Of course."

The Prince motioned his son forward.

"Kiron, Commander Artos. You will obey him."

The young man bowed, saluted. His father turned back
to the commander.

"I'm sending Giorgios with him. He finds peace boring."

"Like old times, Highness; sure you don't want to come
along?"

The Prince shook his head.

"I would only get in the way. Besides, I have my own
war to fight here. I hope my son will learn from the two of
you as I did."

The commander turned to the Prince's son.

"You have your equipment?"

"Yes sir. Giorgios told me what I would need."

"He'll know the house I'm using for staff. Meet with me
half an hour before dinner. The legions dine early."

When Kiron arrived at the house he was shown up to
the commander's office; Giorgios remained behind to
gossip with the door guards. Artos was alone. He
motioned Kiron to a seat.

"What do you know of the planned campaign?"

"A surprise attack on the Vales to seize their northern-
most valley and the river that comes out of it—more if
possible. The Oasis as supply base and staging area."

"What do other people think we are doing?"

"Some think His Majesty is failing and the army is to
fight my uncle. I've heard a few say that you plan to ally

with some of the clans, move against the others, expand the province into the plains. There's some talk about moving south into the Vales, but not much. I heard one legion officer say their chief is the trickiest bastard alive."

"He is. Not chief—Harald's title is Senior Paramount. Worth remembering. What do you say?"

"As little as I can. Talk about horses, women."

"Good. Spreading rumors is a useful tactic, but doing it badly is worse than not doing it. What do you think?"

"Giorgios says the problem isn't finding troops but supplying them—that there isn't a lot of water between the Oasis and the river. I thought, if you had a way of doing it, you might get there before the Vales have time to raise an army."

"Yes. If everything goes right, they find out we're coming when we get there. Against someone else, there's a good chance it would work. Fooling Harald isn't impossible, but I'm not counting on it. What do you know about the pool at the Oasis?"

"Father's swimming pool? I've heard people talking. Seemed like an awful waste of money and effort to be doing . . . Oh."

"When the army reaches the Oasis, your father's swimming pool will have the water it needs to refill and continue south. If we are very lucky, Harald either hasn't heard about it or hasn't figured out what it is. If we aren't very lucky, the river we need to reach will be defended by several thousand cataphracts, under the best general alive."

"I thought you . . ."

"If I thought that, I would lose. Harald has spent the past twenty-five years defeating every army sent south, most of them bigger than his. Remember that. If it makes us too scared, we give up before we start. If it doesn't make us scared enough, most of us don't get back. I plan to break his record, but it isn't going to be easy."

"It isn't fair. You have Harald to deal with; Gavin doesn't."

"I have the fox to deal with, he has the vixen—the Lady Commander's been helping Harald win battles longer than you've been alive."

Dinner, with Artos, a dozen members of his staff, the commanders of the second legion and the light infantry that would accompany them, was mostly spent on plans for the morning's advance on the Eagle clan oasis. Kiron said as little as he courteously could. When the others left, the commander motioned for him to stay.

"What do you think about tomorrow's plans?"

"Father says the nomads are the best light cavalry you can get."

"They are. I recruit them when I can—half Raven clan is taking your father's gold at the moment."

"So why is everyone so sure we can beat them tomorrow?"

"Good question. Always ask it.

"First rule: If nobody makes any mistakes, infantry can beat cavalry but can't catch it. Remember that; it's important."

"We have the best infantry; why don't we always win?"

"One reason is that we make mistakes. The other is that soldiers have to eat and drink—if they didn't, we'd rule the world by now."

Kiron looked puzzled. The commander gave him a moment to think before he went on.

"Infantry controls any place but not every place. As long as the enemy has the cavalry, everywhere we aren't is theirs. That includes all the places supplies have to cross to get to our army. Try to hold the whole supply line, get too thin, they concentrate, break you.

"Eagle clan can't hold their oasis against a legion—and without the oasis they don't have the supplies to hang around and make trouble. Once they're gone, we leave a few lights—more of them than we can use for the main campaign anyway—and settlers. If some of the settlers are Ravens, their clan brothers will keep an eye on things— we don't even have to pay them.

"Fighting Harald is going to be harder, but once we have the river, better yet the vale it comes out of, the hardest part of the supply problem is solved. And he has the same problem if he tries to move north and cut our lines—horses drink a lot more water than men. If we can get a foothold and keep it, we'll settle the vale, raise crops, herds. See you in the morning—early."

Visit to the Vales

**The man who stands at a strange threshold,
Should be cautious before he cross it . . .**

A trumpet blew. The gate of the Oasis swung wide; Artos rode through it. After him long lines of dusty legionaries, a column of crossbowmen, a lot of wagons, a second legion. The garrison commander met him, drew him into the cool of the guardroom by the gate.

"You came anyway? We don't have much water."

The commander looked puzzled.

"What about the pool?"

Konstantin looked in turn puzzled, worried, frightened.

"You didn't get my message?"

Artos shook his head.

"I sent it off as soon as it happened—been waiting for an answer telling me what to do."

"As soon as what happened?"

The garrison commander hesitated a moment, spoke:

"Weeks ago. A night attack. While we were guarding the gate someone lobbed a lot of chunks of salt over the wall into the pool. Got out what we could, but nobody's going far on that water. I sent a messenger to you the same day. Since then we've kept the cistern filled, all the barrels we have—but . . ."

The commander went to the door of the room, started yelling out names, then sat down at the table and started writing messages. Over the next few minutes the room filled with staff officers.

"We have a problem. Some unfriendly people dumped a lot of salt over the wall into the tank we were planning to use for drinking water. Not wanting us to lose any sleep, they also took out the messenger Konstantin here sent to tell us about it. Thoughtful folk.

"First step is word to the cavalry to turn back, hold at base until there's water enough to get them where we're going. Giorgios, go find a courier, four Ravens for escort. Here's the message, but have him check with me before he leaves.

"Next is a water census to figure out how bad a hole we're in. Lagio, that's your job. Konstantin can find one of his people who knows what they have.

"Kiron, you're with Lagio. Your job is to see how much of the water in the pool we can use. If all that's in it is salt, we can dilute with regular water for the men—a little salt in the water isn't a problem. Figure out how many parts of good water it takes to one part of what's in the pool to get something nobody will mind."

"Should I check what the horses will drink too, sir?"

"Salt in water makes horses drink more—loses us more than it saves. Men have more sense.

"Fintal. Since they're expecting us, we need more

scouts. Talk to your Ravens about the trip south; see if you have enough riders to screen us. Send a few out today, just to check."

Half an hour later the courier, with escort, rode north, a troop of Ravens south. By dark errands were run, tenting up; the army settled down to enjoy the brief hospitality of the Oasis.

The others having retired, the commander turned to Kiron.

"Tell me what happened, what we should do now."

Kiron paused for thought before answering.

"Harald figured out the pool, sent some of his cats to dump a lot of salt into it; I don't know how."

"More likely nomads; he has friends in the clans. Cats have a salt mine near the bottom of Mainvale; they sell it east and west. By what Konstantin says, I'm guessing a traction trebuchet—little rock thrower. Set it up outside the wall, five or six men pulling on ropes, dump a lot of salt."

Kiron thought a moment before he continued. "After they left here, his people went farther north, ambushed the messenger so you wouldn't know about the water. Did they put Eagle clan up to raiding our wagons too?"

"If so, it's the first part of Harald's plan that didn't work—it cost us a few men and wagons, but let us push the border west. What now?"

"Twenty-five hundred infantry, a hundred Ravens. Counting the horses, well over two thousand gallons of water a day—three thousand counting horses pulling wagons with water and supply. I don't see how you can do it. We could leave part of the army here, but not much;

the Oasis doesn't have enough water. Going back doesn't solve the problem either—we still need water to get there. It looks bad; I think I'm missing something."

"Between here and the river isn't no water, just not enough. Ravens can sweep wide, use wells too far west for the army. A few more tricks; you'll see. Suppose I get the army to the Northflood; what next?"

"That takes care of water, assuming Harald can't stop you from getting to it. He'll have an army by now. We still need food. Without cavalry as escort, how do we get supply wagons back and forth? Even if he can't supply an army on our side of the river, he can raid. Use the Ravens as escorts?"

"Not enough—and we need them for scouts. I'm not planning to leave our cavalry out of the campaign forever. Think about how I get them to the river once I'm there. See you in the morning."

A hundred miles to the south, the Northflood poured deep and fast out of Newvale, spread out, flowed west. Along the south bank men were digging earthworks. The plain north of the river was scattered with horses, herds of sheep. South of the river orderly rows of small tents, a short line of covered hammocks, farther west a Fox clan encampment—the host of the Northvales and friends.

"Donal."

He looked up, saw his foster father looking north across the river.

"Get mounted. We have guests." Harald whistled; the gray mare stopped grazing and trotted over.

The two men rode their horses through the ford. On the far bank, the first knot of riders had grown—easily

forty Westkin. Their leader raised an empty hand to
Harald.

> "Foreigners our fields fell upon
> Force too fell.
> Our foes, your foes.
> Women, weak children to friends west
> Warriors willing
> War to wage.
> A fool fights alone.
> Foe of my foe
> Friend."

Harald paused a moment, gave answer.

> "Fell to foes
> Faith to my folk
> First our fields guard.
> Fortune favors, foe falls
> For his freedom
> Far fields of friends
> a fair price."

The Eagle chief drew an arrow from his quiver, jabbed
himself above the heart, smeared the drop of blood over
the point, handed the arrow to Harald.

> "Faith I fail
> Against friend's foe
> This finds me."

Harald took the arrow, carefully wrapped the point in a scrap of cloth, slid it into his bow case.

> "Bow and bolt
> Bend and death's bearer
> Gold banner's bane."

Without dismounting the two men embraced, then set to dealing with details of their alliance. Eagle clan made camp a safe distance from the Fox encampment, left a few men north of the river to deal with further arrivals; Harald set in train preparations for a feast.

Two days south of the Oasis, the Imperial army—two legions, five hundred crossbowmen, sixteen wagons—drew to a halt. To their right, the western plains, slightly rolling, low grass, farther west patches of sand merging to desert. Left, the mountains, rising out of the plains in an irregular line of low cliffs. At the base of one of them, two men.

"Make camp here. Lagio, a squad to our friends over there. Take down the stone wall they're standing in front of. If nothing has gone wrong, there are ten barrels of water behind it. Take the water, use it; leave the barrels. We'll need them again. Kiron, go with him."

Disassembling the dry stone wall exposed a row of barrels against the cliff face, a trickle of water down it, a tent, a small fire. The two legionaries in charge helped Lagio transfer the contents to smaller containers; men lugged them out to where the legion's camp was going up.

Later, sitting around a fire outside the staff tent, the commander explained:

"There are streams up in the mountains that come over the edge and vanish—not enough water to make a river. We have four collection points; this is the first. Just a trickle, but they've been filling those barrels for two weeks. Tomorrow morning the wall goes back up; makes it less likely rumors get to our friends south. Kiron here did his sums, worked out by the time we got to Northflood we would all be dead. This, some wells I know about, are what he left out. No baths till we get to the river, but if nothing goes wrong, we make it."

For the next two days, nothing went wrong.

The end of the fourth day, tents going up. Kiron saw some of the legionaries pointing west. Horsemen. Quite a lot of horsemen. Nomads. He turned to Giorgios.

"Ours?"

"Scouts. All of them."

Fintal walked out to talk with the Ravens, came back to the commander.

"They need water. Eagles are holding the wells."

"Can't they drive them off—how many are there?"

"Five or ten at each well. Our boys can drive them off all right—did, twice. No water."

One of the staff officers cut in.

"They poisoned the water?"

Fintal looked shocked.

"Drank it. Good well gives maybe fifty, hundred gallons a day. Ten men, their horses—never gets full."

The commander held up his hand for silence, thought a moment.

"How many wells west of the road, next fifteen miles?"

"Three near, two farther."

"Say we give them water now. They take those wells. Nomads can carry a day's water. A well supplies ten horses and men, take it with twenty, leave half. The other half take all the water, take the next well. Hold a day, then shift everyone a day's ride farther south, in range of Northflood, join us there. We'll be pretty thirsty, them too, ought to all make it. The extra scouts stay with us."

"Think it works; I'll check with Finnvar. Can I tell him they can have water from our wagons for men and horses now? Some of them need it pretty bad."

"Yes. We'll be on half water ration next two days. Officers walk—easier on the horses. Tomorrow we start at dawn."

Late afternoon, two days later, the river in sight, its far bank lined with earthworks. Artos halted the army well out of bowshot.

"Pass word to watch the horses; they can smell water." He turned to Kiron, walking beside him.

"They've fortified the ford. If we have to fight for the water, might as well do it where they can get shot too."

Staff, senior officers of the legions, gathered around the commander while the soldiers stood resting, staring at the river—and the enemy. Plans made, trumpet calls, the army surged into motion, slanting west. On the other side of the river riders streamed west as well, dismounted, set up pavises; others led horses back out of range.

A quarter mile from the ford, just out of range of the far bank, the army halted, reformed. A double line of

legionaries with shields, behind them crossbows, forward
at a trot. A hundred yards from the river they stopped,
front line on their knees, back standing, a solid wall of
shields nearly six feet high, crossbows behind.

While the front line traded bolts for arrows, a second
double line advanced behind them, took up position. The
men they sheltered were armed not with bows but shovels.
By nightfall their work was done, the legions—and their
wagons—sheltered behind walls of earth. From their
camp they could see the river, smell it. The commander
being busy, Kiron put the question to Giorgios.

"What do we do? Fetch water at night, hope they don't
see us, hear us, start shooting?"

"That's one answer. He'll have a better one."

On the other side of the river, Knute, watching the
Imperial encampment as the light faded, put the same
question to Harald.

"The men can sneak down at night with shields, with
any luck manage to get a drink; the moon won't rise till
near dawn. But how the hell do they plan to water the
horses?"

"Asking the wrong man. Artos knew we'd be here.
Didn't have an answer, wouldn't have come."

Dawn showed it—a trench from the river to the
Imperial camp.

Return Visit

Wealth is won by the swift

By noon, the pattern was clear. The trench provided the camp with water. From the camp, a long earthen wall was rising, slanting away from the river towards the road.

"How does he get his men to the ford?"

Harald turned to answer Niall's question.

"If he's in a hurry, he marches them there at night, pushes across night or early morning. Risky. More likely, another wall east, archers, engines opposite the ford, covering fire for a push across. We do what damage we can, if need be fall back—main force south, couple of cacades up into Newvale to hold the neck of the vale. Make sure everything worth eating gets uphill first—started already. Speaking of which . . ."

Harald turned to cut a chunk of mutton. Before taking a bite, he turned back to Niall.

"My question is where Artos got water to bring that many men after you dealt with His Highness's pool. Also," he spoke in a louder voice, "when is that idiot boy going to show himself?"

"Where the hell . . . ?"

"That stand of grass; figured he'd get hungry one of these days."

Asbjorn ignored both his uncle's surprise and his grandfather's lack of surprise.

"And I have two answers." Asbjorn looked at Harald, waited.

"What's the other?"

"Streams come down off the mountains, go over the edge of the cliff. Donal thinks they help feed the wells. Imperials have a couple of men under the trickle, lots of barrels, rock wall to hide them. Heard them talking; they never looked up. They figured the barrels would be full by the time the army came by. I spotted two streams, might be more. Thought you'd want to know."

"Yes. Show me where."

Asbjorn drew a roll of thin leather from the wallet slung over his shoulder. Unrolled, it was a carefully drawn map. Harald spent a minute looking at it, following his grandson's explanation, spoke:

"Arinbjorn Hrolfsson's camped off that way with his cacade—see the pennon from here. Find him, bring him. Work for both of you."

The boy helped himself to a chunk of mutton, a slab of bread, took a bite from each, set off in search of his cousin. Niall turned to his father.

"I thought you planned to keep 'Bjorn home."

"How—tie him up? Lower slopes north of here the safest place I could think of. Legions don't climb if they can help it; not even Westkin ride up cliffs. Artos doesn't have any Bashkai. Wildcats, bear, fall off and break his neck. Can do that at home too. Hasn't yet. Besides, things I wanted to know. Took a couple of friends. Boy's no fool."

When Asbjorn returned he was accompanied by Arinbjorn.

"Uncle. Little 'Bjorn says you want me."

"You and your boys have been looking bored. Need thirty men used to mountains, no horses. Easy part involves keeping an eye on our friends over the river. Hard part keeping my grandson from breaking his neck. He's your guide."

After a week of watching men dig, Kiron was getting bored.

"Looks like the sand garden at the summer palace before the gardener had smoothed it out again. Only we didn't have a river to play with."

Giorgios, stretched out in the shade of the earth wall, opened his eyes.

"It's the legions' best weapon."

"The shovel? Slow."

"But sure. Can't put an arrow through two feet of dirt. Not even a bolt from a siege bow. Have to go up against two or three thousand archers, might as well get cover close as we can first."

"I thought we were in a hurry."

"In a hurry, we would be on the other bank by now. Some of us. Commander's waiting for something. My guess, cavalry. While we wait, we dig." Giorgios pointed out over the growing earthworks.

A staff runner: "The Commander sent me to fetch you, sir."

Kiron and Giorgios followed him to where the road

bent around a spur of rock. Beyond, out of sight from the river, a dozen wagons, horses. The commander turned, spoke to the runner.

"Tell Second to start sending his boys, small groups. He knows."

Then to Kiron: "What am I doing?"

Kiron looked at the wagons curiously.

"Water barrels. Part of getting the cavalry here? Two weeks to base, then the cavalry has to come back. Besides, not enough wagons."

"The cavalry left base yesterday, if everything went right. They have wagons with them for the first part, water caches, like we had. Due to meet these thirty miles this side of the Oasis—enough water to get them the rest of the way."

"You're sending part of the Second as escort?"

"Four hundred men, some archers. Fifty Ravens for the first day. Past that, they should be safe, but I'm not taking chances—gods know how much of Eagle clan Harald has, and they may have tricks, know water holes I don't. Giorgios says you're bored. Eight days to get the cavalry here, escort and wagons back. Then we move."

"You need cavalry to force the ford?"

"I could do it today, assuming no surprises. I need cavalry to protect our supply lines after we cross, make the enemy keep together. Besides, once they arrive we have to move—nothing this side of the river for the horses to eat."

Kiron looked curiously at the commander.

"You haven't been a farmer. Harald grazed horses and sheep on this side of the river till we came. The grass is eaten all the way down. We could graze our horses farther

west, but there might be fords and they'll know where.
Too far from the legions gets risky. Once the cavalry
comes, we push across."

Night time, four miles west of the ford. Harald peeled
off his war coat, spoke to the men around him.

"Supplies on the rafts, armor, anything might sink you
or the horse."

The first raft loaded, he called across the river. The
rope leading into the dark went taut. Men pushed the raft
into the stream; it drifted down and across.

"By decades, when your gear is loaded. Anyone can't
swim, ride a raft."

He led the mare into the water.

"Now we wait for the horse boys to show up. Tomorrow
if we're lucky. Keep your archers with the wagons while
my people dig—less likely to get in the way."

"Lot of work—haven't seen an enemy since we left the
river."

"Always a first time. Matter of fact . . . those ours or
theirs?"

The captain commanding the escort started shouting
orders; the legionaries traded shovels for shields and
javelins, formed up in a line two deep. The archers took
position behind the shield wall, strung their crossbows.

"Ravens went home three days ago; besides, we don't
have that many. This is it. Wish they'd given us another
two hours."

More orders bent the line into a long rectangle, two
shields deep on the outside and ends, one on the long side

towards the wagons and, just beyond, the cliff edge. Behind the shields, crossbowmen. At the center of the formation, surrounding the standard, the reserves. The nomads charged, released a cloud of arrows, split left and right and streamed away. Most of the arrows fell short. One crossbowman shot back.

"Not without orders; till they get closer they're bluffing."

A second charge, this time a little closer. Closer still. The third time the force wheeled right, rode out of range, stopped. Started to move.

It was Kalios's first battle. On one knee in the front rank, shield up, javelin ready, two more clutched in his shield hand. Voices behind him; he knew enough not to turn.

"This may be it. Don't throw till they're in range."

From his left a torrent of riders, some shooting, others flat to the far sides of their horses. Still out of javelin range.

"Archers, at will."

Click of trigger, twang of bowstring behind him. More. Arrows poured from the riders; one glanced from his helm, two hit the shield. Behind him someone cried out. In front, the nomads a continuous stream, half hidden in their own dust.

A panicked voice: "Behind us. Archers on the cliff." A rattle of orders, men shifting position. Kalios held, facing the horsemen, waiting orders, hoping someone was covering his back. The riders kept coming, shooting. The last horse passed, a last few bolts flew after it.

"Gods."

The lancers came out of the dust straight at the line of infantry. As time froze he saw a bolt glance off the chest

armor of one of the horses. Kalios drew back his arm to
throw. A lance point—shield up to block. Something hit
the shield, hard enough to knock him over. Arms and legs
in, shield over. Thunder of hooves.

Kalios came to his feet, felt a sharp pain, looked down;
an arrow. Looked up. Hundreds of nomads, sitting their
horses just out of javelin range; he raised his shield against
their arrows. Turned his head left, right.

Where the legionary line had been was a ruin of dead
and wounded, mostly theirs, a few enemy lancers, horses.

A desperate trumpet call. What had been the center, a
cluster of men around the legion's standard, long spears, a
few archers, the space around them empty save for bodies. Kalios limped back to join them, went to one knee in
the front rank. The javelin he was still clutching was broken; he dropped it, drew his sword, waited.

The nomads had stopped shooting; the lancers—cats—
reformed, sitting their horses some distance off. One rode
forward, empty right hand raised.

"Don't shoot; it's a parley. Anyone speak their jabber?"

The rider stopped just beyond javelin range, called out
in Tengu.

"Willing to offer you terms; send someone out."

From behind Kalios, the captain's voice.

"Terms hell. Try again, this time we do some of the
killing."

The rider hesitated, lowered his hand, pointed.

"Long way home."

Kalios followed the pointing finger. The cliff. Between
it and the remnants of the escort, the road was bare. The
wagons—food, water, gear—were gone.

⳥ ⳥ ⳥

Andros was enjoying the quiet. Also the leisure of guarding the gate while much of the Oasis garrison was busy cleaning up. A thousand men, twelve hundred horses packed in and around a small fort for a night made a considerable mess. Now they were gone, south towards the river, the army, the enemy.

Above his head, someone was yelling. Out the gate, in the distance, a cloud of dust. Cavalry coming back?

By the time they were close enough to recognize, half the small garrison was by the gate staring out, the other half on the wall. Forty or fifty legionaries, marching in something well short of their usual rigid order, two pairs carrying stretchers. One wagon.

"Something's gone wrong."

As they came near, more shouts from the wall. A second cloud of dust, moving faster. Mounted men. A lot of mounted men.

"Cavalry's back."

Bugle calls, orders. The crowd inside the gate thinned out, vanished, as men went for weapons, manned the wall.

"What's the commander worried about?"

From above, someone answered him.

"Nomads. Not sure they're ours. A lot of them."

By the time the tired legionaries reached the gate, the uncertainty had gone; the cavalry was shooting at them. One of the men fell, lay still.

"Get that damn wagon clear; we need the gate closed."

Instead the lead legionaries attacked the gate guards. Men behind pulled bows and quivers out of the stretchers, started shooting at archers on the wall. The front rank of the pursuing cavalry split, nomads circling the wall, pouring in arrows. Behind them a long column of cats through the gate at a trot. The defenders, surprised, outnumbered ten to one, caught between archers inside and outside the wall, surrendered or died. In a few minutes it was over.

Konstantin felt hands on his body, a stab of pain. He opened his eyes. He was lying on his back in one of the bunk houses; someone was leaning over him.

"Arrow's out. Lie still. Don't want to start the bleeding again."

"Who. What . . ."

"Surprise attack; Oasis is ours now. Artos won't be happy. Don't worry; we don't eat prisoners."

"You're speaking Tengu."

"Wake up to someone pulling arrows out of me, helps if they speak something I understand. Here."

The commander drank down the water, closed his eyes a moment, opened them.

"Artos won't be happy with me. How'd you get here?"

"Rode."

"Water?"

"Artos sent water wagons north to meet his cavalry. We used them instead. He took Eagle clan oasis, now we've taken his. When the war is over we can trade, everyone goes home. Fair man, won't blame you. Rest."

The next time the commander woke it was almost dark. Noise of wagon wheels on stone pavement, voices. The door opened. By the light through it he could see that the bunk room held half a dozen wounded. The man coming through was medium height, broad. Lamellar armor.

"Awake again? Water wagons just came in. Between them and what you have, shouldn't die of thirst any time soon. Might even get your cavalry home alive, with luck."

"I don't understand."

"Cavalry you sent south this morning. We dodged them coming north. Wagons did too, not so easy. Artos sent troops with his wagons, folk we borrowed armor from to get through your gate. About now the cavalry is meeting what's left of them. Three days to the river—they don't have the water, not even close. One day back here. Ravens might scatter, head west. Run into some friends of mine if they do. Rest of the cavalry should show up here late tomorrow. Thirsty. My problem, theirs, not yours any more."

"You're Harald."

"And you're Commander Konstantin. Easier for me; we don't use rank badges. You guested my foster son two months back, spoke well of your hospitality. Impressed by your pool, too. Told me all about it."

"And you . . ."

"Green fish, nothing like that around here, sounded like something belongs in salt water. My boys, clan brothers, couple of Ladies, dropped by one night to deliver."

Horse Fair

**He starts to stink who outstays his welcome
In another's hall**

When the Imperial cavalry got back to the Oasis they found the gate shut. After a few arrows from the walls, one of the riders noticed that what was flying above was no longer the gold banner of the Empire. They withdrew out of range to consider the matter.

The gate opened. A man on foot came out, right hand raised and empty, waited. More deliberation before a cavalry officer dismounted, came to meet him.

"'Fore you and your friends try to get this place back, come in and look around. Six hundred cats, two hundred Westkin. Bows, behind walls. Water. Rather not kill horses if I don't have to. Or men."

When he got back to the cavalry, the rest of the command group gathered around him.

"Not a chance. They have near as many men as we have, maybe more. Mostly cats. We could make a grand charge and die gloriously, but it'll be outside the walls. We can't siege; they have water, we don't."

"We could send a courier back to base for help."

"By the time he got there we'd mostly be dead. Same thing the other direction."

There was a long pause before someone asked the obvious question.

"What terms are they offering?"

"They get horses, armor, gear. We swear not to fight outside the Empire or against Harald or his allies till we're ransomed—leave a few officers as hostages. We get wagons, water—enough to get us home on foot. One horse for a courier to base to tell them to send supplies and more water to meet us."

"Once we give them everything and march north, what's to keep them from coming after? At least now we have armor."

"Die from an arrow in the ribs, die of thirst, not much difference. Besides, it's Harald."

One of the other officers spoke:

"Buddy of mine was in the army he smashed east of the mountains two, three years ago. They surrendered on terms. He got home alive. I say yes."

They set off the next morning, a long column of men on foot, two wagons. The last were scarcely out of sight when the first group of nomads arrived and set up camp—half a dozen riders, Bear clan pennon. Harald went out to meet them, exchange courtesies. By noon, they had been joined by parties from three other clans, each with its own small camp outside the walls.

Konstantin, shaky but on his feet, watched from the wall, tried to make sense of what he was seeing. Nomads on foot were wandering through the herd of captured horses, looking at them, occasionally leading one away from the water troughs to join a small herd next to one of the camps.

"What's going on?"

The cat who had helped him up the stairs looked blank. Konstantin tried again, this time, slowly and carefully, in the speech of the plains.

"What are they doing?"

The cat grinned: "Biggest horse market plains ever saw."

As the day passed, more buyers appeared. Over one camp Konstantin noticed a Raven pennon. Later, having accepted Harald's invitation to join him for the evening meal, he asked about it.

"I thought the Ravens were on our side."

"Far as I know they are. Doesn't keep them from buying; can always fight us tomorrow. Emperor's gold as good as anyone else's."

He reached into his pouch, looked at the gold coin in his palm.

"Better. His face on a coin, full weight. Best money I know."

By the next morning the captured horses and their buyers were gone. Where they had been, most of Harald's army—four cacades of cats, a hundred or so nomads, a dozen hostages—formed up outside the gate. Before he left, Harald took a minute to say good-bye to Konstantin.

"Enjoyed your hospitality, stay any longer get a bit thirsty." He gestured at the swimming pool, partly refilled during the past weeks, now again almost empty.

"Leaving one cacade to hold the place. Four or five

speak Tengu, most everyone some plainstalk; you and your people, ones that didn't go home with the cavalry, be all right. Rest of us back south to see what Artos has been up to. Wife's brother, friends, keeping an eye on him, but you never know. Time you've healed, fighting all over, everyone home. Come visit; promise I won't shoot you. Top of Mainvale. Wife brews the best beer in the vales."

Three days later, Harald would have settled for the worst. Better yet, water. The wagons, sent south the night before they left, carried one day's water, the hidden barrels, left behind for the final dash to the Oasis, a second. What had accumulated in the collection points along the cliff since they came north made a scant third. Thirsty men, thirsty horses.

Niall called back from the head of the column, angled right off the road. The sun down, they kept going; the full moon gave light enough to see the broad trail of tracks marking the route they had followed coming north. Harald moved up the column, talking quietly with the men.

"Think this is bad; ever hear Conor's story, his trip south?"

No one had.

"Well dry. Waterhole dry. Filled a cup from his skin, time he had it to his lips cup was dry too."

"How'd he make it back alive?"

"Drank straight from the water skin. Skin empty, started to rain. Rained so hard, riverbed flooded, washed him back to the foot of Mainvale. His story, not mine. Night we captured a wagon loaded with wine barrels."

One of the hostages looked blank; Harald repeated the story in Tengu.

Past midnight Niall stopped, pointed. Harald signaled the weary column to a halt.

A wooden pole slanting up from the ground marked the buried cache. Harald took one of the water skins, filled his bowl.

"Little farther, lady mine, all the water you want."

The mare emptied the bowl; he filled it again. Again.

By the time the moon went down they were in sight of the river, by dawn across it.

So was Artos.

Ends and Beginnings

The generous and bold have the best lives

It was almost noon before the exhausted riders, having made a wide circle around the Imperial encampment south of the river, rejoined the main army. Half an hour later most of four cacades were asleep on the grass. Hrolf helped Harald unsaddle the mare, rub her down.

"Two days back. Either he got word or figured the cavalry weren't coming. Started before dawn. We lit the bonfires. Must have been filling in the ford somehow where we dug it out—men across in formation. Most of them—rock throwers opened things up a little, we did some damage. Had to pull back.

"Bad part is Newvale. Still don't know how he did it, but by the time the fight started he had men in the mouth of the lower vale, our side the river. Couldn't get our people past. Has the ford, mouth of the vale. Herds probably all made it to the upper vale—boys have been shifting them for weeks, ever since he got here. Lower vale to upper isn't easy. Nothing but boys, women, old men to stop him, though."

⊕ ⊕ ⊕

Artos, most of the way up the lower vale with what was left of the second legion, would no doubt have found the news encouraging. From where he stood he could see the steep slope, almost a cliff, that joined the lower vale—pastureland between steep cliffs, on one side the river—with the upper.

"That's where dinner went."

He pointed at the path that zigzagged up the slope. The top portion was choked with stones. Giorgios, standing on Kiron's other side, responded:

"Drove the sheep up, shut the door behind them. We get to open it."

The commander looked at Kiron, waited.

"We send a turtle up to clear the path?"

"One way. They probably have more stones at the top— hard to hold a shield up over your head when someone drops a boulder on it."

"You brought all the archers. Sweep the top edge of the slope above the path to keep them back. They can still try rolling boulders, but it will be harder, and they'll be blind."

"Helps. We have stone throwers too; captured four yesterday. The boys have been practicing. What are we fighting?"

Kiron stopped a moment to think.

"There were two archers in the cliff across the river. They stopped shooting when the crossbows showed up. If they had a lot, you'd think they would have kept it up— they had cover, high ground. Other than them, we haven't seen a soul. Where are the cats?"

"Out on the plain. Bellio's company paid to keep them that way—four men drowned, crossing above the ford night of the attack. I'm betting Harald had all his people at the river to stop us, planned for some of them to fall back up Newvale after we crossed. If I'm wrong, we have a problem. If I'm right, there should be enough herds, stored food, even this early in the year, to feed us for a while."

From the ledge high up on the south cliff, the scene spread out below—legionaries busy in the lower vale, elders in the upper, steep slope, blocked path between them. Neither group could see the other; the three boys, peering over and between their wall of piled rocks, could see both.

"Your Gran, his friends, they have the roof up. Oddest house I ever saw."

"Said if they had any sense the crossbows would shoot high, drop bolts on their heads. Roof should stop them. Don't need back or sides, wall in front gets in the way. Low roof instead. What are those things?"

"What things? I can't see from here."

Kolskegg scrambled backwards and to one side; Asbjorn took his place.

"See? A little out from the slope—like giant birds. Some sort of engine?"

"Rock throwers; bet they captured them when they crossed the river. Hope your Gran built his roof solid. More than bolts falling on it. Turtle's forming up."

Twenty men, a shell of shields, moving to the bottom of the winding path, up it. Thorvald, the older of the two brothers, spoke.

"Ready, 'Skeg? Almost there."

"Ready. Say when."

"Now."

Kolskegg lifted the flag above their wall, waved it.

"Nothing happening. They don't see me."

He stood up, waved it wildly.

Rocks bounced down the slope; one hit the middle of the formation. Bolts flew back to answer them, rocks from the captured engines. The turtle moved on, leaving two bodies behind.

"Get down, idiot."

"Oh." Kolskgg looked at the bolt sticking through his arm, sat down.

Asbjorn scrambled back.

"Hold still; I have to break off the end, pull it out."

He bound the wound tightly with one of the lengths of cloth from his belt. The other two watched admiringly.

"Don't carry bandages, have to tear up my clothes, another battle when I get home. Grandfather told me. Says he'd rather fight the Emperor any day. What's happening?"

"Turtle's gotten to where the path is blocked, clearing it. We're supposed to signal. Three, one, three, one."

"I'll do it."

Asbjorn took the flag that Kolskgg had dropped, waved it. Bolts flew above him, bounced off the cliff face.

"Why you don't stand up."

"More turtles. They're carrying something."

Asbjorn put down the flag, scrambled back to his place by the wall.

"Ladders. First group clearing the path, other two up the slope either side from the clear part lower down. Hope your Gran thought of that one."

More rocks were bouncing down the slope, aimed at the men clearing the path. Most missed, some didn't. The turtle, a little smaller, crept forward.

"Our turn. Hope it works."

Thorvald moved back from the wall, took a round rock from a pile, put it carefully next to a peg driven into a crack in the cliff, gave it a gentle push. The rock rolled down the cliff face out of their sight, gathering speed, reappeared as a puff of dust on the slope just below the second turtle.

"Close but you missed. They're putting up ladders."

The fourth rock; one of the men at the base of the near ladder crumpled, rolled down the slope, hit the bottom, lay still. More rocks; a second hit. Now both ladders had men on them. Farther up the path, what was left of the first formation was still doggedly moving forwards, clearing rocks, rolling them down.

"Rock throwers have stopped; afraid of hitting their own men."

A figure crawled from under the low roof, out of sight of the attackers. Shield held over his head, long pole in the other hand, he limped across the upper slope. Shield down, pole against the end of the ladder. Another man came out to join him. One of them fell; the other kept pushing. The ladder end slid sideways across the face of the slope, down, shedding bodies as it fell.

"They haven't spotted the other one. Let me by."

Asbjorn, bow out, quiver beside him, kneeling at the end of the wall, looked down at the remaining ladder, the men near its top. He drew, tucking his head under his right arm, right hand at the back of his neck, shot almost straight down. Four arrows, two men hit, before someone below noticed him and bolts started flying up. He leaned back into cover.

"Aunt Cara taught me the trick; lets you shoot down from a rampart without leaning over. Never been on a rampart, but this is close. If you wave the flag again, will they think it means anything?"

"Nope. One signal for starting up, one for getting to the blocked part."

"Do it, other end of the ledge. Distraction. Stay down—don't need to get shot again."

Kolskegg waved the flag; bolts rattled off the cliff behind him. Asbjorn snapped off two fast shots, back into cover.

"Wish big 'Bjorn and his people were back; dozen of us up here it would be easy."

"Dozen cats wouldn't fit here; tight enough for three of us."

"Can't be the only ledge."

"Only one we can get to in the dark. Hard to climb with people shooting at you."

Thorvald's voice from behind him. "My last rock; are they still climbing?"

"One ladder. Turtle's down to six men."

"Use this one." Asbjorn pulled a rock from the wall, rolled it back to Thorvald. A moment later they saw it bounce down the slope, barely missing the ladder.

Trumpet calls from below. What was left of the lead formation stopped clearing rocks, started back down the path. The man halfway up the remaining ladder looked down, abruptly reversed direction. Two more rocks bounced down the slope from the men above; both missed. The attack was over.

ⵠ ⵠ ⵠ

Kiron stepped back from the stretcher party, looked away from what they were carrying, turned to Giorgios.

"Why did he stop?"

"Wasn't going to make it. Turtle runs out of men before it gets to the top of the path. Could send another one up, but things were getting pretty crowded, bodies, rocks coming down. One ladder was down, the other getting men picked off from the cliff. Getting two or three men to the top isn't going to do it."

"So what now?"

"Cleared a good deal of the path; doubt they have the manpower to fill it up again with bolts flying around their ears. We'll build more ladders, maybe some long enough to get all the way up from the bottom. More rocks for our throwers. Patch the wounded best we can. If nothing changes, should take it tomorrow."

"Who's the Commander talking with?"

"Has a horse; probably word from Niko. Hope nothing's gone wrong."

When they reached Artos he was standing still, eyes closed. He opened them, saw Kiron.

"Harald wants a parley."

"Why?"

"One way to find out. Second can get ready for the next attack without me. Come along; he's worth meeting."

Before dark they reached the encampment by the ford; the commander of the fifth legion met them.

"There's a tent at the halfway point, out of range of both sides. He's waiting; two men with him."

"Giorgios, Kiron, gives us even numbers."

Niko hesitated, spoke:

"Sure you want . . . ? I could lend you Konstin."

Artos shook his head.

"No need. Not Harald's kind of trick."

"What do you think . . . ?"

"Tell you when I get back."

The three men rode out to the tent—a roof, no walls—where Harald was waiting. At the sight of the man sitting behind him, the commander's eyes widened.

Harald stood up.

"News for you. Brought Danio along to tell it."

The cavalry officer hesitated, looked down, up.

"We surrendered. I'm one of the hostages."

"Everyone?"

"Ravens cut out west; don't know if they made it. Everyone else."

"Tell him where you surrendered; it's the important part."

"The Oasis. Outside."

He looked up at the commander.

"They were inside. With the water."

"You're holding the Oasis?"

"Took it a week ago. Get your whole army there you can have it back; my men have orders to leave if anything big shows up. Don't see how you'll do it. I've got more than half your water wagons, all the collection points along the cliff edge. Prince knows by now; sent a courier to tell him your cavalry would be walking home, needed food, water. How long for him to put together an army—when most everything he has this end of the province is here—supply train, get them to the Oasis, take the Oasis, get supplies to

you? Doubt he can do it—damn sure he can't do it before
you run out of food."

The commander remained silent.

"Lower vale, nothing to eat but grass. We're still holding the upper vale; I'm guessing you tried today, didn't
make it. Might tomorrow, might not. Get through in force,
they torch the grain stores. Flocks have been leaving since
you took the ford, goat paths up into the mountains. Start
early tomorrow, everything goes well, might get a good
dinner for your boys from what's left. Not two weeks
worth. Don't believe me, welcome to send someone up
vale and look—flag of peace, one of mine to keep him
company.

· "One thing more. Pass is open, word got here today.
Gavin's back his side of the river. Lost a lot of his cavalry,
Bashkai, got the legions safe home. Can't prove it, but it's
true."

The commander's voice was calm.

"Your proposal?"

"You get your oasis back, Eagles get theirs. Other than
that, same terms I gave Danio here. We keep the gear,
everything but personal stuff. Make sure your boys get
home—maybe a little thin, but alive. Ransom is two gold
emperors a man. Till it's paid, they can't fight outside the
Empire, can't fight me or my allies inside. Officers as
hostages till we get the gold. Looking forward to your
company. Hardest I've had to work since Talinn died.
What—twelve years back?"

"Thirteen. I accept your terms on behalf of His
Highness. Me, legion commanders, company commanders
as hostages; enough officers left to get the men home."

He stood up. So did Kiron.

"I have a different proposal. One hostage. Me."

"You're sure?"

"Father needs you. Needs the rest. He sent me along for an education. Can't ask him, but I know the answer."

Artos nodded. Kiron turned to Harald.

"I am Kiron son of Iskander son of Alkiron. I offer myself as hostage for my father's men."

Harald looked at him carefully, turned to Knute.

"Fetch Donal."

Turned back to Artos. "Not that I don't trust you—but there was that swimming pool."

"His Highness's idea."

"Get back, give him my best wishes. Don't blame Konstantin—ten times his numbers and a trick. Lost a lot of his men, got hurt himself, getting better. Escort too. Had to kill a lot of them; rest would have kept fighting if I hadn't grabbed their water. Good men."

The two felt silent. Kiron watched both, wondered what the next few weeks would be like. Not dull.

The silence was broken by Donal's arrival. He dismounted, walked over to Kiron, looked at him carefully, spoke.

"Yes. Prince's eldest son. Won three silvers off him."

Kiron looked back at him.

"I didn't think the horse . . ."

"Guesting with us, education, first rule: Don't bet with Westkin. Second rule: Especially on horses."

A Guest

Better gear than good sense
A traveler cannot carry

"Camp here, Mainvale tomorrow. Beds the night after."

"How do cats make camp? I'm used to traveling with wagons, tents."

Niall grinned. "I'll show you. Gets me even with Egil."

Kiron looked puzzled. Niall got out tent cloths, lance sections, stakes and went to work. When he was done, Kiron kneeled down to look into the tent.

"Not much room."

"Two people, bedding. Infantry can afford wagons; we can't. Too slow."

"Who's Egil and how does showing me how a tent goes up . . . ?"

"My big brother. Couple of years back, after Father captured King James, Egil got to show him how we put up a tent. I figure the grandson of an emperor is about even with a king."

"You captured the king of the Karls? I thought you were allies."

"So did we. Your grandfather bribed one of the King's kinsmen to give him bad advice. Ended up taking 'Nora prisoner, trying to get control of the Order. Father got her out, took James prisoner, talked sense into him. Now we're allies again."

Kiron still looked puzzled.

"Who is 'Nora, what does she have to do with the Order, why did your father go to war with his allies to rescue her . . . ?

Niall stopped a moment to think.

"Forgot—you're a foreigner. Leonora is the Lady Commander of the Order. Also the mother of my big sister. Egil's big sister too—Cara's the oldest. She found the castle they were holding 'Nora in, she and Father got 'Nora out, all three of them went after James. I wasn't there, heard about it later."

"I thought you people, the Karls, a man only had one wife."

"Mostly. Father and 'Nora were before Father married Mother. Still friends, though. Family. Is it true your grandfather has dozens of wives?"

"Of course not. Just three, and the senior only gave him daughters."

"My brother Donal said there was a whole women's palace in the Western Capital."

"That isn't just for the wives—concubines too."

"Sounds like fun. Job you're planning for?"

"I don't have to be Emperor for that."

"What do you have to do, your part of the world, end up with a palace full of beautiful women?"

"Stay alive. Grandfather had four brothers. None of them managed."

Knute cut into the conversation. "Could stay here. Lots of beautiful ladies—whole holds full. Ask Niall. Safer, too. He started with three brothers, still has two—back to three counting Donal."

Kiron looked puzzled, changed the subject. "Both of you speak Tengu, Harald as well as I do. I thought I wouldn't be able to talk to anyone."

Knute answered. "Two years caravan guard, Imperial traders. Some vales folk speak it, mostly learned the same way, more don't. Want to talk to ladies, got a new language to learn."

"That sounds like a good reason."

By lunch time, bored with language lessons, they switched back to Tengu.

"Ever hunt in the mountains?"

"Near the summer palace. It's south of the low pass—mountains, but not as big as yours."

"With a bow?"

Kiron nodded.

"You'll like our mountains. Rabbits, goats. Climbing fun too. May take a few days to get used to it."

"What do you mean?"

"Harder to breathe high up. Not bad at Haraldholt, but you're used to the plains. Over the high pass everyone has trouble, even us—and we're the highest hold in the Vales."

Before dark the riders reached the Silverthread, turned up it into Mainvale. At the first farmstead Niall rode ahead, returned shortly.

"Dinner, beds in the hayloft."

The next day was spent riding, at times walking, as the

vale narrowed and grew steeper. Where they stopped for lunch its sides were linked by a wall of weathered stone twice the height of a man, a narrow gap for the stream, the road beside it. Kiron looked at it curiously; Niall answered the unspoken question.

"Two hundred years ago, to keep Westkin from the upper vale, back when that's where the people were. Oldest wall in the vales."

"It isn't all old. See."

"That's one of the bits Father talked folk into patching when he heard about His Highness's swimming pool."

It was almost dark when they reached Haraldholt. Niall led the other two to the stable, where they unsaddled and rubbed down the horses with the assistance—loosely speaking—of half a dozen younger members of the household. As they came out of the stable a woman met them, a bundle of cloth over her arm. She looked inquiringly at Niall. He spoke slowly in Tengu.

"Mother, this is Kiron, the Second Prince's son. Father sent him to guest with us for a while. Kiron, my mother— Gerda Bergthordottir."

"Be welcome." Gerda nodded to a grandchild, who stepped forward; the plate held a chunk of bread, a small bowl. She reached into the bowl, sprinkled the bread with salt, offered it to Kiron. He took the bread, ate it.

"My thanks for your hospitality, noble lady."

Gerda returned his smile, handed the bundle of cloth to Niall.

"All three of you—I can at least send Knute back home clean."

"Yes, Mother."

Niall led the other two through the woods to a small house. For a moment Kiron thought it was on fire, then realized it was steam.

"Hot spring. Reason they settled here, first folk over the pass."

The next day Niall spent introducing Kiron to the hold and its occupants. The day after he found his guest a long-bow and they went hunting. Three hours and a lot of scrambling later, they were on their way home with two rabbits and a bird.

"That's a lot of work for lunch. Wouldn't a mountain goat be better?"

"Less fun. More food. Aren't any this close."

"I might at least be able to hit the thing."

"Just need practice. Strange bow."

Kiron looked skeptical.

"You're mine."

Kiron looked up, startled; a moment before there had been no one there. The youth had a bow in one hand, the other pointed at them.

"Fair enough." Niall handed over their catch. "You get to clean them."

He turned to Kiron.

"The bandit who has just ambushed us is my nephew Asbjorn; it's his favorite game. 'Bjorn, this is Kiron, guesting with us a while."

Kiron spoke slowly in the vales tongue. "Honor defeated so valiant a hunter by."

Asbjorn looked at his uncle: "*He* noticed."

Kiron watched as Asbjorn, booty in hand, vanished downhill. Niall spoke in a puzzled tone:

"Noticed what?"

"What language he was speaking. He knew who I was. How young do they go for caravan guards?"

"Not that young; learned from Father. Tells a story in our tongue, mixes in Tengu, Llashi. Been doing it since 'Bjorn was little. For us too."

"He wasn't one of the ones I met yesterday, was he?"

"Arrived last night, across from Newvale. Boy climbs like a goat. Pretty good at stalking, too. Caught Father once—above himself for a week. Till Father caught him."

"And?"

"Took a mountain goat off him—had spent two days hunting it."

Over the next weeks, Kiron learned what he could of both hunting and stalking, including one fruitless afternoon under cover watching the path they thought Asbjorn would come home on. Evenings were spent learning the language, trying to make sense of the busy chaos around him. One evening, as he sat watching the children play, he heard a footstep, looked up. Gerda was watching him. She spoke slowly in her own tongue.

"I hope my son is taking proper care of you."

"Yes. Not boring. Different."

"The language. Is it a problem?"

"Hard. Learning. Slowly."

"You are doing very well." This time she spoke in heavily accented Tengu. "Better than I would so short time."

He switched with relief to his own language.

"Your speech is a little like Alteng—what the common people speak in our province. When I was little my nurse sang me songs in the Old Speech."

"You find it different here. Different how?"

"Less orderly."

"Vales less orderly than Kingdom. Kingdom than Empire. Like it that way." She smiled at him, held up a hand for silence, listened a moment, went off to deal with a quarrel between two of her grandchildren.

Kiron was still considering the difference between Haraldholt and his own childhood at breakfast the next morning when Niall sat down across the table from him, spoke hesitantly.

"I'm going down vale. Probably back tonight. Be all right, won't you?"

Kiron nodded. "I can practice my archery, language. Plenty to do. I could go hunting, but I'm afraid the rabbits and your nephew are both too much for me."

"Could go with him. Couldn't ambush you then. Lot of climbing, though. It's Aliana. My Lady, the one Knute teased about. Valholt Ladies should be back today—got word last night. Want to be there to meet her. Too long."

By early afternoon, having concluded that hunting with Asbjorn, although not dull, was too strenuous for an old man of twenty, Kiron made his way back to the hall in search of food and drink. The room was empty save for a lady in a chair by the fire, eyes closed. The boots by her chair were splashed with dried mud, the brown tunic almost black with dust. Kiron went into the kitchen, came back with a pitcher, mugs. Sat down, searched for words.

She opened her eyes. He spoke. "Beer. Weary from travel seem you."

She blinked, looked at him curiously, accepted the mug, drank.

"Weary indeed—left Cloud's Eye yesterday morning. That's good."

"Pool of hot water, for traveler."

"Plan to soak when I'm done sitting. Might take a while. What do you speak when you're at home?"

"Tengu. Know you any?"

She nodded.

"I'll never believe Knute again."

"Because?"

"He told me that if I wished to speak to beautiful ladies in the Vales I must learn his tongue."

"Mostly. I'm just visiting."

"In what fortunate land do you make your home?"

"Kaerlia. Other side of the pass I just came over. Is Harald back?"

Kiron shook his head.

"Do you know where he is?"

"At the Northflood ford three weeks ago. Figuring with Artos how to get our army home."

She looked at him curiously, hesitated a moment: "What happened? Did Harald beat him?"

"More or less. Why I'm here."

"Word the invasion was ended, nothing more. What happened?"

"Artos forced the Northflood, got halfway up Newvale. While he was doing it, Harald made it all the way to the Oasis, took it, forced our cavalry to surrender, came back. The Commander couldn't fight without supplies, cavalry. Surrendered on terms."

"How did—I can ask him. Must have been quite a campaign. Our side of the mountains tame by comparison."

"Harald told us Gavin got back across the river with his legions. Do you know what happened?"

"Some of it."

"Was there a battle? A siege? How did the Karls drive him back?"

"You're from the Empire. How much do you know of Imperial politics?"

"Some. What does that . . . ?"

"You know Gavin's the First Prince's man?"

Kiron nodded.

"His legions didn't get home, Second Prince's did, bad news for him, his patron. Made him too careful. You understand all that?"

"Yes."

"Attack supposed to be a surprise, almost was. Could have pushed straight to Markholt—damn little to stop him. Order, part of the border provinces, pretended to be a trap. Gavin stayed out of it for fifty miles—more than a week. By the time he started the siege his supplies were half gone, our levies coming in. Too careful—can't play safe in war. He should have known Harald was the other side of the mountains."

"Maybe he did. Artos said . . ."

The lady looked at him curiously.

"He said he had the fox to deal with, Gavin the vixen. He meant the Lady Commander. You know about her?"

She nodded. He thought he caught the shadow of a smile.

"Order got behind him, cut off supplies. Stay, try to take Markholt, starve. Went home instead."

"So he got the whole army back. Better than we did."

"He lost half the cavalry, Bashkai, maybe more. Fighting by Markholt. Fighting at the bridge."

"You're sure? Father says the farther you get from a battle, the more people were killed."

"Wise man. Yes."

"You talked to someone who was there?"

She nodded, rose.

"So have you. Think I can make it to the bathhouse now."

She went out. He thought about it.

That night, half asleep in the shut bed, he heard horses, people. Niall back? The next morning, wondering if it had been a dream, he followed the smell of bread baking across the courtyard to the side door of the hall.

Seated at the table was Harald, the lady beside him. Kiron tried to keep his face blank as his host rose to his feet.

"Kiron, my daughter Caralla, back from chasing your uncle's army back across the river. Cara, our guest, the Most Noble Kiron. Here learning bad habits from your brother and nephew; His Highness may never forgive me."

Kiron bowed, tried to keep from blushing. Caralla nodded, smiled.

"We met yesterday. Honors about even."

"The noble lady is as generous as she is . . . valiant."

Niall came late to breakfast. The Lady with him— young, pretty, shy—was introduced to Kiron and Caralla as Aliana. She used one hand to eat, one to hold Niall's, spent most of breakfast watching the older Lady.

Afterwards Niall suggested archery. While he was setting up the butts, Kiron, having determined that this Lady, at least, spoke no Tengu, took the opportunity to practice the vales tongue.

"Niall sister, Lady, know you?"

"Lady Caralla? Her first trip over the pass since I came west. I've heard of her. Everyone has."

"She your fellowship is?"

Aliana looked at him curiously, decided the question was real.

"She's the daughter of the Lady Commander. And Harald. And a famous captain. Two years ago she and Harald rescued her mother, captured the King, ended the troubles."

"I told you all about it weeks ago."

Kiron turned to Niall, switched languages with relief.

"Did you? You told me about someone called Nora being rescued."

"And my sister Cara helping. You were more interested in how many wives people had."

"Cara is Caralla?"

"And 'Nora is Leonora and 'Bjorn is Asbjorn unless its big 'Bjorn—Arinbjorn—and 'Liana is Aliana. Don't you have short names, for friends?"

"Kiron is my short name for friends. The long one has my father's name and his father's name and his father's and grandfather's too if someone is being really formal and wants to prove how learned he is, and a bunch of titles that don't mean anything. I can starve to death being introduced."

Aliana was stringing her bow; Niall imitated her. His first arrow missed the piece of branch stuck into the face of the target by almost a foot.

"And I can starve to death shooting that badly."

Later they went hunting. By the time lengthening shadows signaled time to turn back, Niall's archery had improved. So had Kiron's.

"I think I was lucky."

"Rabbit wasn't."

"Stop a minute; I want to keep it."

Kiron stopped by a small brook, filled his game bag with clumps of moss, twigs, a few small rocks, carefully stained the bottom with blood from the dead rabbit.

"Ask your lady to carry the game, stay behind us. She's harder to see than you are."

When the three hunters came into the kitchen, Asbjorn was sitting at a table, looking with disgust at the contents of the captured bag.

A Trading Expedition

Seldom do the silent
Speak foolishly

"Grandfather. Hall. You come."

Kiron lowered his bow, turned. The words were Tengu, the accent reasonably good, the speaker about seven. He replied, slowly, in the same language.

"I will come now. Thank you."

Harald was sitting at one end of the hall, his daughter beside him. On the table a small wooden cage. Nearer, Kiron could see a gray pigeon inside, fast asleep.

"From a friend of yours."

The paper was as thin as gold foil.

"Isk held Santio. Self to cover G.B. K. knows pig. A."

Kiron thought a moment.

"You sent the bird back with Artos?"

"For emergencies. Two weeks ride from here."

"Father's being held in the summer palace; that must mean Grandfather . . ."

"Is moving against him. Probably both of them. Wonder what the plan was if the attacks worked."

"He can't. Not unless he plans to bring out one of his bastards."

"Doesn't want to cut the princes' heads off, just make clear who's Emperor. Lock them up while he's busy, out if they ask nicely enough. Might buy him ten years—maybe all he's got anyway."

"I don't think Father . . ."

"Was planning to give him ten years. Neither was your uncle. Been playing them against each other for years; they decided to change the game. So did he."

"But why . . . ?"

"Send to me? Enemy's enemy is friend—for a while. Know what pig he's talking about?"

"That part is easy. The Commander's gone to cover in the Golden Boar. It's a big tavern in the capital, regular warren. Legionaries, twenty-year men, not many officers. Giorgios took me there twice. The manager is a friend of his."

Caralla looked up.

"Go as traders, find Artos, give him a hand?"

Harald nodded.

"You've never been to the Western Capital. Worth seeing."

He turned to Kiron.

"Can you tell Cara where the Golden Boar is, how she can get in touch with the Commander, maybe your friend's friend?"

Kiron thought a moment.

"He won't trust a stranger—especially not a woman. I'll go. If I have your leave. Give my word to come back."

"Up to you; your father's paid most of the ransom, good for the rest, may need you. Always welcome."

Two days later, they were on the road. As the line of loaded horses and mules moved up to the pass, Caralla went over details.

"First question is who is what. Mostly by age and language. Tengu is your birth tongue—can you tell where I'm from?"

"You don't talk like a highborn, but most people don't. If I heard you on the street I wouldn't think twice."

"What about Gudmund?"

"He sounds more foreign. A lot of people from the provinces learn Tengu second. Like that."

"What about you? Can you talk so you fit in with us?"

"Speaking highborn in the wrong place is stupid. In a tavern, I talk like Giorgios, or close. Easy."

"Remember to do it. Gudmund is the trader; I'm his wife. You don't look like us so you're my sister's boy. Rest of Gudmund's decade gives us five guards, four drivers. Poor traders—no servants. Guards are easy—cats. Erik is Gudmund's second and speaks some Tengu, so he can be guard captain. The rest, decide who's what for yourselves. Problems?"

One of the younger cats spoke.

"Suppose I'm a driver. Not from the Vales, what am I? Don't speak much Tengu."

"Good question. We want drivers from somewhere edge of beyond, nobody recognizes what they look like, how they talk. Kiron?"

"Northeast, beyond Belkhan? Lots of hill tribes."

"What do they call themselves?"

"Damned if I know."

Caralla thought a moment. "Drivers are Vlathi.

Somewhere past Belkhan. Can't meet any others—aren't any. Need a language, Plains talk, Fox dialect, hope nobody knows it. Mostly, don't talk if anyone can hear. Drivers out of armor tonight. Tomorrow, we're a trading caravan, Vales to Western Capital, wool."

The second night, at Cloud's Eye, they met a westbound caravan. Gudmund—renamed Gudion—paid a brief visit, exchanged news, returned to share with wife, nephew, chief guard.

"Grain, beans, everything high. Long wait at the ferry. More than the usual griping. Sounds like he's started moving. Supplies, shipping. No word on troops."

"Send word to Harald?"

Caralla shook her head.

"He'll hear from the caravan. What he expects."

Kiron looked curious, said nothing. She explained.

"Princes went after barbarians, got beat. Maybe glorious Emperor will show how, earn triumph himself. Not to repeat, Nevvy—traders safer out of politics. Lot of beans, grain, for an army, less for us. River down, may ford instead. Save wait, save ferry fee."

Two days later, the last hour of light brought them past hostel, campground, caravans, to make camp a mile up the north road. The next morning Kiron woke early. Caralla and Gudmund—Gudion and Karia, mother's sister and her husband—asleep at the other side of the tent. He rolled out of the low bed to the ground, stood up, went out. Stopped. There was a familiar figure bent over the fire pit.

"What are you doing here?"

"Starting the fire. Want to help, fetch some dead wood.

Should have been done last night. Need someone can look farther than a warm bed."

"Where did you come from?"

"Haraldholt, like the rest of you. Couple of miles behind through the pass. Cut north above the hostel through the woods—'Liana made me a map. Hope Niall marries her. Nice to have an aunt who doesn't try to order me around."

Caralla came out of the tent behind Kiron. "Lot of good it ever did. Does Father know you're here?"

"Does Grandfather know which side of the mountains the sun comes up?"

"Meaning you didn't tell him."

"Gerda would have said I couldn't, made Grandfather pretend to try to stop me. Easier this way." Asbjorn turned back to the fire, blew gently. Kiron went off in search of firewood.

Three weeks and several hundred miles later, Asbjorn spoke in a hushed tone.

"Now that's a river."

"East and west branches join at Sarga, eighty miles upstream. If a raindrop falls in the mountains, east range or west, this is where it goes. Right by the golden wall."

Kiron pointed downstream, where the low sun of late afternoon lit up the capital's river wall.

"Going to tell me it's made of gold?"

"If I thought you would believe it. It's yellow stone from quarries southwest of here. The summer palace is built into the hole in the mountain that wall came out of."

"It's high."

"Ten times a man's height. All the way around the city."

"Have to siege it. How wide's the river?"

"Hundred yards, maybe more."

"Easy for bows, big rock throwers. One camp up stream, one down, no boats get by. Lot of people inside the wall—wait till they get hungry. Take a big army though."

"Took Konstantin the Great twenty legions, a two-year siege. A hundred years ago, nearly. Now it's ours."

"When you children finish sieging the Western Capital you might help the men set up the tents, stake out the animals. Too far to make the south gate tonight."

"Yes, Mother." Asbjorn almost sounded as if he meant it.

By twilight the work was done, the little caravan quiet. In the trader's tent, Caralla spoke quietly to Kiron.

"In tonight, try to find the Commander. Tell him we're here to help if he wants us to. City's hard to miss—can you find your way back in the dark?"

"I think so. If not I can wait till dawn."

"Something goes wrong, we might try sending someone after you. Can you tell us how to find the Golden Boar, get word to your friends?"

"It's in the barracks quarter—no barracks any more since they expanded the keep, but it's still popular with the legions. South gate is closed at dark but the little gate next to it is open all night, always a trickle in and out. Follow the road north till it joins the road of triumphs—built so a legion can march down it ten men across. Keep going north past two arches, then the barracks road goes left—maybe half as wide, still big. Red paving stones if there's enough light to see. Ends in a big square, statues,

arches. It gets messy after that—west of the square you're
in a tangle, used to be barracks, not too safe at night. Best
go around. You might want to ask someone. The Boar is
the biggest tavern in the quarter; everyone knows it. Niko
runs it, friend of Giorgios."

Caralla put down the stylus, read back the directions,
folded the tablet. Kiron looked once around the tent,
pulled his cloak around him, picked up lantern and firebox, went out into the night.

Asbjorn was waiting; they moved off into the dark,
spoke in whispers.

"It isn't like hunting in the mountains. I know the city,
you don't."

"Why you have to go—besides, he doesn't know me. No
reason you can't have someone to watch your back. Night
before last you were talking about how dangerous parts of
the city get after dark. Your friend isn't hidden as well as
he thinks he is, might be watchers. Wear my hair like the
boys we saw last week—nobody worries about kids.
Servant to carry your lantern."

Three hours later it occurred to Kiron that he might
have to follow his own advice—if he could find someone
to ask. The narrow street past the south wall of the massive
building that had once lodged a legion bent left instead of
right. Whatever the streets, he knew the general direction
of the Boar, cut right down something even narrower. An
open space, bounded by blank walls. Footsteps behind
them.

The larger held a heavy staff; the light from the lantern
glanced from the iron-bound end. The smaller, a few steps
back, had something in his right hand.

"No trouble, no blood. Give us what you've got, see dawn. Or not."

The servant carrying the lantern dropped it with a clank, backed off, vanished into the shadows. The man with the staff spoke without turning.

"Don't bother. Time he finds help around here, we're long gone."

Trust looked an even worse gamble than fighting; Kiron's hand slid under his cloak, reached the dagger hilt next his purse. "Yes sir. No trouble."

The smaller man jerked his head up and back, as if to look at something above him, collapsed with an odd gurgling noise. The other stepped back from Kiron, half turned. The figure standing where his companion had stood stepped forward, caught the staff left-handed, pulled as its owner pushed. The man grunted, buckled, fell to the ground, lay still. Asbjorn picked the lantern back up; it was still burning.

"Told you it wasn't safe alone. Best out before someone else shows up."

He leaned over one of the bodies, carefully wiped his dagger blade, sheathed it.

The second time Kiron guessed right; five minutes more brought them to a door, a gold pig crudely painted above.

Inside was a tangle of rooms, smell of smoke, sweat, beer. They got lost twice before Kiron found his way to the central hall, sat down at one of the tables. Asbjorn squatted beside him.

"Beer a tenth bit, dinner two for you, one for the boy."

"Beer now, dinner later. Can you take a message to Niko?"

The woman looked at Kiron. "Who from?"

"Friend of a friend."

"Name? Niko's busy this time of night."

"Friend of his friend Giorgios."

"Friend of Giorgios. Right." She moved off, leaving a pitcher and one mug behind her. Kiron filled, drained, refilled, passed the mug down. Asbjorn took it without looking, continued to watch the room.

Half an hour later, a big man, gray, limping a little, made his round of the tables, stopping at some to exchange a few words. When he reached theirs he looked down at Kiron.

"Thena said a friend of Giorgios. Look familiar."

"I'm looking for another friend of Giorgios. Very old friend. I heard he was staying here. Quietly."

"What do I tell the friend of your friend who might be staying here, supposing I see him?"

"Tell him the boy who knows the pig is home, looking for him."

"The boy who knows the pig. Come to the right place." Niko drifted off, stopped at two more tables, vanished through a door.

It was almost dawn before they got back to the camp. While they were talking with the cat on guard, Caralla joined them. Kiron spoke softly:

"He wouldn't let me see the Commander. Either he isn't really there or he's afraid someone might be spying on him—or me. But Niko took a note, brought one back. He'll meet us at a place I know from hunting, a couple of miles from the walls. Half an hour after dark."

✠ ✠ ✠

Moonlight in the clearing, three figures. Artos stood still trying to make them out. One stepped forward:

"Commander. The Lady Caralla ni Leonor, her companion Gudmund Ottarson."

He nodded, remained silent, looking curiously at the two strangers. The tall Lady spoke.

"Came about a bird; Father thought you could maybe use a hand. The Most Noble wanted to come along; brought him."

"Kind of you. Hand with what?"

"His father might want to be somewhere other than where he is at the moment."

A figure stepped out of the shadows, spoke to Caralla in the vales tongue, too quickly for Artos to follow. A boy. No. The Lady turned back to him.

"Any friends following you?"

Artos shook his head.

"Then not friends. Two. We'll deal with it."

She turned back to the young man, said something. He vanished into the trees.

"What sort of help?"

"Father thought finding safe people might be a problem; the Old Man's no fool. Not a problem for us. Brought a decade of cats, my nephew, the Most Noble. You want him out, see what we can do."

"May I take council with the Most Noble?"

The Lady nodded. "Quarter hour do it? We don't plan to be here much longer than that."

He nodded. The Lady and her companion stepped out of the clearing, vanished. Artos moved to the center; Kiron joined him. The two spoke quietly.

"The Lady?"

"Daughter of Harald and the Lady Commander, Order captain. Harald said she drove Gavin back across the river; I think he meant it."

"How did they get here?"

"Small caravan, some cats guards, some drivers. Quiet trip."

"Do you trust them?"

Kiron hesitated. "Haraldholt was strange—more like visiting a big family than prisoner in an enemy hold. Some day, peace, Father doesn't need me a while, I'll go back. He's clever, might have fooled me, but I talked with the children, watched them. Good people. Wouldn't help us if he didn't think it helped him, but I think you can trust him. Them."

"Emperor is moving in force against the Karls. Harald knows or guesses. If we can get your father free, west of the low pass where our people are, one more thing for the Emperor to worry about. The more things he has to worry about, happier Harald is."

"Do we do it?"

"For His Highness to decide. I have someone in the palace. For now, we go with them."

Without Taking Leave

Two wooden stakes on the plain,
On them I hung my clothes:
They looked well born,
I a nobody.

Artos spoke quietly. "Sure the cloth could be seen from the palace?"

Asbjorn nodded.

"Tallest tree, near the top, branch on the palace side."

"She should be coming soon. Best just me."

"Yes." Asbjorn, Caralla, Hedin faded back into the trees, leaving Artos alone in the open space by the road. West in the faint moonlight loomed the palace wall, the greater bulk of the cliff behind. He waited.

It was almost half an hour before he saw the figure approaching. As she drew near he spoke in a low whisper. "Janel."

She started, said nothing, stopped in the road next to where he stood.

"Tosi?"

"Yes. How is he?"

"Well. Not counting the headache I'm out finding herbs for. What is it?"

"Chance to get him out if he wants. I need to talk to him."

"Message do?"

"Talk would be better. Can he get to the lower orchard? Bit of wall there—guard posts don't cover the bottom. We can settle what we're going to do, messages later on when and where."

"I can get him there. He might be alone, might not."

"Tomorrow evening, a little after dark. Outside the arrow slit by the big tree. Tell him to whistle 'cherry tree' if he's there, it's safe. If he wants me to run for it, drop something that makes a loud noise, curse."

"Yes. 'Cherry tree' to talk, drop and curse to run."

They were both silent a moment. He reached out, gave her a brief hug.

"Find your herbs. Luck."

A rattle of stones, loud voices. The Prince looked up from his book. The guard by the gate was staring up at the cliff behind the palace. A moment later a second guard appeared, spoke to him quickly. The first guard turned.

"Someone on the rocks behind the palace; up to something. Your Highness should stay here, other side of things, safe enough." He went out the gate; Iskander heard the bolt slide, got up. After a few minutes wandering about restlessly in the fading light he picked up his chair, carried it over to the outer wall, set it down where he could rest his back against the gnarled trunk of an old apple tree, returned to his book. In a little while he began to whistle softly.

From the wall two sharp clicks, one, two more. He

stopped whistling, looked around. The gate was still closed, the orchard empty.

"Yes?"

"Your boy's back. Fellow he was staying with sent some friends. We think we can get you out if you want to go."

"Maybe. How goes it in the city?"

"A couple of men followed me from the Boar. Safer west of the pass with people we trust. He's moving, twelve legions, cross the bridge, south for Eston. Gives us time. In a few weeks we can have more at this end of things than he does. Work from there."

"What's our friend want in exchange?"

"Nothing. Fight on his hands, maybe he figures this helps a little. Doesn't cost him much. Your boy likes him, trusts him—might be a reason to favor you."

"Everyone does—one reason he keeps beating us. Can he do it again?"

"Twelve legions, cavalry, lights. Early harvest is in, enough supplies. Emperor commanding—won't make stupid mistakes. Anyone else, take a miracle. I would have staked my life he couldn't get an army to the Oasis. Have to bet, bet on Harald."

Iskander thought for a long minute.

"Harald wins, Emperor weak—safer out of his hands. Emperor wins, I can still bargain myself back here. Maybe. Looks like I have to bet. Do it. Let me . . ."

At the sound of the gate opening—he must have missed the bolt—Iskander stood up. The book fell with a thud onto the stone paving.

"Damn. Lost my place. Can you help with the chair? It's getting cold out."

⊹ ⊹ ⊹

"Beautiful things. Surely some of the highborn ladies would want . . ."

"Not this late, miss. Gate closed, two of us to keep it that way."

"It isn't really dark yet. Perhaps one of the highborn could come down and see?"

"They don't buy from peddlers at the front door, miss, not like your ma or mine. Real highborn ladies in golden chairs with maids to fan them, musicians."

He raised the lantern. Not young but not bad looking if you liked them tall. He thought a moment.

"I can't get you in tonight, but come back in the morning, some of the serving ladies might buy. I could tell them, maybe get you in then if any of the highborn say so. What sort of pretties do you have?" The other guard caught the glance, stepped back to the inside of the gate.

Two steps brought them out of his line of sight, into shadow. The guard cupped her cheek with one hand; she closed her eyes, leaned back for the kiss. Something struck him hard on the back of the head; Caralla caught him as he fell.

A few minutes later the second guard saw his comrade come back into sight, still talking quietly with the woman, one arm around her. A familiar voice from the shadow of the tree in the inner court.

"His Highness is still sick; they asked me to try to find some herb the physician wants. Can you help with a lantern?"

The guard let go of the woman, picked up his lantern, stepped back through the gate. Its light showed a figure wrapped in a cloak. He nodded, escorted her through the gate, handed her the lantern, turned back to the woman still standing by the wall.

It was half an hour before it occurred to the second guard that there might be something wrong, other than someone else having all the luck.

A mile east, where the road from the gate crossed the main road running north to the low pass, south to the ford, a brief conference.

The Prince had dropped the borrowed cloak, was pulling off the robe while he spoke.

"Do you know if Janel got out all right?"

Kiron handed his father a spare tunic.

"'Bjorn was supposed to meet her outside the back gate; they should be here soon."

"The Commander?"

"Should be back with Cara any minute."

"The Lady the Commander was pretending to be distracted by?"

Artos stepped into the light of the lantern, the Lady behind him.

"Had jobs I liked less."

"Father, this is the Lady Caralla. Harald's daughter."

She stopped glaring at Artos, turned to the Prince.

"Luck, half an hour. Might be less. Spare horses for you, yours. Commander says north. We're going south."

She turned to Kiron. "Be careful. All over, come visit."

BOOK V:
The Emperor's War

Eat at morn,
None knows what evening brings;
Luck is ill to lose

Opening Moves

Better brave heart than bright blade

"What do we know? Lord Stephen first."

Stephen nodded to the King, looked around the small council room. In addition to the King and two of his captains, it held Brand of River Province and the lord of Westval, come with the King. At the far end of the table Leonora, Harald standing beside her.

"They've been rebuilding the bridge, with most of a legion this side of the river to protect it. Troops are assembling on their side. There are probably more farther back, out of sight. I won't risk men scouting there—too many troops, especially Bashkai. But we can see loaded boats on the river, word of mouth has a lot of stuff on the roads." He stopped, looked at the Lady Commander.

"I won't risk scouts across the river either. But we have friends. Rumor says a big army assembling, the Emperor out to do Gavin's job right."

Harald spoke:

"Word three weeks ago. Emperor moved against the

princes. Second Prince locked up in the summer palace. Don't know about his brother."

The King looked puzzled. "You think it's connected?"

"Emperor's old, sons ambitious. Second Prince is clever, has Artos, support in the West, some in the legions. First Prince not quite as clever, richer, kin through his mother to half the highborn in the eastern capital. Old Man's been playing them off against each other past five years, more. They got tired of it.

"This spring, a gamble. One invasion wins, one loses, loser backs the winner against the Emperor. Emperor's been trying for twenty years, hasn't beat us yet. One of the princes does it, legions may decide they've been backing the wrong man.

"Emperor's old, not stupid. Don't know what he planned if they pulled it off—maybe offer whichever was weaker the succession in exchange for support. I think he expected what happened. They attacked early spring, food tight, each prince used his own people. We beat them. First harvest is in now, Emperor can move in force. Pulls it off, does what they couldn't, wins twice—beats us, beats them. Peaceful old age. Much to be said for it."

"So you think this is an invasion in force?"

Harald nodded. "Why I'm here. Crossed east with two cacades—what I could raise fast. Hrolf, Egil, Donal, a few other friends later with more. Empire will move south with everything they can raise and feed—eight legions at least, probably more. Can't match us in cavalry, but close as they can manage."

"You"—the King's glance encompassed both Harald

and the Lady beside him—"have been fighting him for twenty years. What will he do? What should we do?"

Harald looked at Leonora, back to the King.

"Emperor makes mistakes—but not the same mistake twice. Army bigger than ours, slower. Wants to show up the princes, can't use Artos even if he could find him, which with luck he can't. Emperor will command, knows his own limits. Simple strategy, overwhelming force, as little maneuver as he can manage.

"Could imitate Gavin, go for the northern holds. Takes them, can't feed that army forever, goes home. Eventually we take them back. Doesn't just want to do better than the princes, wants to finally beat us. He needs a target we can't move, have to defend."

The room was silent. Finally the King spoke.

"Eston."

"Eston and the royal castle. Army with supply train, a week and a half from the border. Straight down the road, siege both of them. Takes them, holds the mouth of Eston valley with two legions, one more for the city, rest of the army goes home, picks up the northern holds on the way. Had his army, his generals, fighting me and 'Nora, what I'd do."

"Can you stop him?"

"Maybe. Best guess, a couple of weeks before they move. You and I head south, get city, castle ready to hold, maybe set up a few surprises. Stephen, 'Nora, most of my boys stay here, keep an eye on things."

Leonora broke in.

"Caralla crossed west a month ago, no word since. Things start moving, she should take the field force, leave me free to hold against one of the sieges."

"Off with a few friends to deal with something. All went well, back before trouble starts."

Outside Stephen's council chamber, a ring of boys and young men, some armored in hardened leather. In the empty space in the middle two more, fighting with wooden swords. The smaller blocked a series of hard blows, stepped back, tripped. A moment later he was on his back, the other's point to his throat.

"I yield." He looked up at Mikel, one of the oldest of the boys, more or less in charge. "What should I have done?"

"Not tripped." That brought a laugh from some of the others. From behind them a voice.

"One answer, others. May I?"

Broad, medium height, graying hair. He reached out a hand. The boy handed him the sword. The Lady following him took a matching weapon from one of the bystanders.

"By your leave?" Nobody objecting, the two stepped into the middle of the circle. The attack came at half speed, three blows. The Lady retreated, tripped over an invisible obstacle, fell to her back, sword up. As the point came at her throat her left hand slapped the flat of the blade aside, her sword swung one-handed. The two froze, the man's sword pointing at the ground, the Lady's edge against his right side.

Mikel called out over the sudden silence. "Easy enough moving slow like that."

The man glanced at the Lady. This time the blows came as fast as when the boys were fighting, the result the same.

"Any faster, need armor." Harald handed the sword back to Hen, turned to go.

"Show us more."

He turned back, looked at the faces—most eager—reached out for the sword.

Mikel felt a hand on his shoulder.

"Know folk would pay good silver to watch those two at practice."

He turned, recognized Stephen, behind him the King, both watching the two figures in the ring.

"My lord." He stopped, hesitated.

"Yes." He turned back to watch.

Later, Harald met Leonora emerging from the bath house, hair dripping.

"Fun; should do it more often."

She nodded. Hen joined them.

"That was wonderful. Father says you're riding south to the city. Can I come? I could help with the horses."

"Up to Yosef. Doesn't need you, glad of the company. Friend I'd like you to meet."

The next morning they were on the road—Harald, James, Hen and a decade of cats.

By the end of the second day Hen had lost his awe of the King, discovered a subject of common interest. The next morning they fell to the back of the line of horsemen to discuss it out of his earshot. Hen was halfway through the fight by Willow Creek when the King's horse shied to one side.

Hen shouted "'Ware ambush," wheeled his horse, charged at the men coming out of the forest edge. The King's horse bolted down the road. By the time he had it back under control everything was over. Most of the cats, mounted, were clustered around Hen. A moment later two more came out of the woods.

"Ran."

"Too late to catch them now. Knute, help James with the horse—arrow in the left rump. Hen?"

"Is the King all right?"

"King's fine. His horse has an arrow in it. What about you?"

Hen looked down.

"Oh."

One arrow was standing out of his side, a second in his left shoulder.

"Let me get you down. Gently, lady mine."

The gray mare stepped daintily sideways, next to Hen's gelding. Harald lifted the boy out of the saddle, handed him down to one of the two on foot, then dismounted.

"Was I right? You said—about archers. I knew, but . . ."

"But they didn't. You were right. Why they ran." As he spoke, Harald was reaching into his saddlebag. A moment later he was kneeling by the boy.

Half an hour later the arrows were out, Hen still, eyes closed, breathing. Harald looked up. Knute gestured at the two horses, the litter between them.

"Safe to move?"

"Think so—rib stopped it. Inn's not that far."

Harald listened a moment to the noise of voices in the street outside, poured a last dipper of warm water over himself, climbed out of the wooden tub, dumped in his discarded clothing, stretched. A few minutes of stirring got rid of most of the river mud. He wrung out tunic and drawers, hung them over the back of the bench, pulled on dry clothes, went out into the inn courtyard, damp garments over one arm.

Waiting for him were two familiar faces. He looked at one, spoke to the other.

"What are you doing here? Should have him back to Forest Keep by now."

Knute shrugged. "Not my kid; said he wanted to come south."

Harald turned to Hen, waited.

"James . . . His Majesty . . . said to visit. Never seen the city, almost there. Besides, you had a friend you wanted me to meet. Keep's boring."

"Dying is worse. Let me see."

He led the boy back into the privacy of the bath house, helped him pull off his tunic, looked over the wounds in side and shoulder.

"Not bad, should still take it easy."

"I walked the horse all the way—Knute said."

"All the way home too. Dinner, good night's rest here; I'm too old to go scrambling over rocks. Tomorrow visit your friend James, couple of ladies. Head back, stop by some friends of mine, take care of an errand, back north. Walking."

A day and a half later, rested and fed, they rode out of the King's castle headed west, Hen quieter than usual. After a while he spoke.

"It felt like home."

"Save a man's life, womenfolk are apt to appreciate you."

"Didn't."

"He had sense enough to wear mail—not like some I could mention. Arrow can still go through it."

"Elen was nice." He looked down a moment. "Like Mother when I was little."

"Good lady. No children of her own."

"The little girl was sweet."

Knute snorted. "Visits the most beautiful lady in the kingdom, all he notices is the baby."

"Is she?" Hen looked frankly curious; Harald answered.

"Beautiful. Brave. More sense than most. Better than James deserves—anyone else I can think of. Pretty baby too—takes after her mother." They rode on in comfortable silence.

By late afternoon they had left the river valley, following a path that climbed north. On their right a small river, sometimes near, sometimes out of sight. At last Harald stopped, motioned Knute back, rode forward with Hen beside him. On their right the forest fell back, plowed land, meadow. A small house, a barn, a young man pulling weeds. He looked up. Harald called out:

"How's the fishing?"

Before he was finished the gray mare was in motion. So was Jon. He absentmindedly fed her a handful of weeds, looked up at her rider. Harald slid off the horse; Jon hugged him, head against the taller man's shoulder.

"Too long. Brought a friend. About your age."

Jon looked up, Hen down.

The next morning, Harald, Hen and Knute went with Jon and his mother to help a neighbor, some miles farther up the little valley, put a new roof on his barn. A dozen families were there already. When the work was done, the householder thanked the visitors for their help. One of the other men asked about news.

"War. Imperial army coming south."

"I heard the King drove them back this spring."

"Bigger army this time. King thinks it's headed for Eston. Don't expect they'll forage this high, but might want to get women, herds, up hill a bit, hide things."

There was a long silence. One of the men broke it.

"How sure are you?"

"Emperor hasn't told me his plans. King thinks they're coming this way. So do I."

"The King told you?"

"Knew I was coming up here, thought I should warn you, maybe see what could be done."

The man looked skeptical. One of the others moved to the front, looked carefully at Harald.

"Thought I'd seen you before. Last time was Fox Valley. Good advice then—least, we won the battle."

Harald looked at him carefully. "With big Henry, royal spears?"

The man nodded.

" 'Ware archers!"

The shout was from Knute, the arrow still quivering in the ground a few yards from where Harald stood. The next few seconds were chaos as farmers scattered, Knute ran for his horse, Harald whistled for his. Both men had bows out and arrows nocked by the time the two boys came around the side of the barn into sight, Hen with a bow in his good hand, Jon a quiver of arrows.

"Anyone see an arrow?"

Harald pointed, spoke to Jon.

"Shooting at your friends is bad manners."

"It wasn't him; I did it. Sorry."

Harald looked in puzzlement at Hen, his wounded arm still strapped to his side, the bow in the other.

"How . . . Oh."

"Jon told me how you shot two Wolves with a broken arm. Never thought it would go all the way over the barn."

Back at Stephen's hold, the first person Harald looked for was Yosef. He found him camped with the province levy.

"Where's Hen?"

"Got himself hurt protecting the King from an ambush on the way south—did the right thing, did it fast, wasn't wearing mail. Not bad, started to heal, riding was opening it again. Left him with friends in the hills above Eston valley. Don't expect Imperials will get that far, can move farther up if they do. Anne would have been happy to take him, figured this was safer. Friend his age to keep him out of trouble. Good kid."

"Never managed with us or 'Bjorn. Think you can do better with other people's kids?"

Harald turned to the familiar voice, hugged his daughter, held her out at arm's length.

"Iskander didn't decide to keep you for his harem after all? Thought I had it all arranged."

"Iskander behaved very well. Ever gives you any trouble, threaten to spread the story of how he escaped from the summer palace dressed as a woman. Artos, on the other hand . . ."

"More your type anyway. Everyone safe?"

"Including your grandson."

"Figured that was where he was off to. Make himself useful?"

Caralla hesitated a moment, looked around. Again.

"Probably saved Kiron's life in the capital. Helpful getting Iskander out. Don't tell him I said so. More later, too; you'll hear when we go up hill."

When they got to Council—the King was already back—"more" turned out to be a detailed account, in writing, of the Imperial army.

"Stalked one of the officers, held his feet to the fire till he told?"

Caralla shook her head.

"Into their camp to beg, do tumbling tricks. Left me a note—said he'd rejoin us this side the ford. Did. Got a handful of coppers and two silvers."

"Twelve legions, Emperor commanding. Fifty cacades heavy cavalry, forty mixed, no Westkin, another thirty of archers, Bashkai, odds and ends. That's it?" Harald looked up from the paper.

Caralla nodded.

Five days later a scout brought more news. The Imperial army had crossed the river.

"You counted ten banners?"

Kara nodded. The King looked puzzled.

"I thought there were twelve legions."

Harald answered: "Were. Question is who's missing."

He turned to Kara.

"See the First—Sunburst Gold on red?"

She shook her head.

"Thought so. Bet the other's Fourteenth or Fifteenth. Banner's . . ."

She interrupted: "Fourteenth isn't there. Rest fit 'Bjorn's list."

Harald nodded.

"Got the news. Wants to be sure, gets back to the Western Capital, someone to open the door."

"What news?" This time it was Stephen.

"Few weeks back, Second Prince got out of where the Old Man put him. Must have made it home. First is Emperor's old legion; headed for the capital. Fourteenth is out of the east, no ties to the princes. Put it in the pass, make sure Artos and Iskander don't come visiting."

He nodded at Caralla.

"Next ten won't be so easy."

Valley and Plains

Be not over wary, but wary enough

Two weeks later the Emperor's tent was pitched at the forest's edge within sight of the royal castle. Its owner sat silent, watching the legions make camp. Only when all the commanders had arrived did he speak.

"The first question is where are the Karls and their allies? Vija?"

The scout commander bowed, thought a moment. "Coming south, their army was growing, maybe levies coming in. Five thousand heavies, it could have been more. Two, three hundred cats. A thousand of the damn mounted archers.

"A lot of them fell back up the valley—too narrow to count numbers. The King's banner went the same way. Nobody is left outside the walls so they must all be inside—castle or city.

"I have a better count of what was left on the plain—we had room to see them. A few hundred heavies, a few hundred cats, more Order. Not much of an army—our cavalry pushed, they fell back."

"Garth?"

"I left the camp at the valley mouth yesterday morning. Legion commanders there say all they've seen are a few cats. Cavalry want to deal with them, catch any levies still coming in."

A tall man sitting in the rear of the tent looked up, spoke:

"The King is in the castle—you can see his flag from here. The provinces won't be happy to assemble, go into battle, without him. Lords aren't all the best of friends."

"Anyone else?" Nobody responded; the Emperor summed up.

"Our best guess is that Harald has a few hundred cats, a few hundred heavies, a thousand mounted archers out on the plain. The King in the castle and whoever's commanding in the city have four or five thousand dismounted cavalry between them, a thousand Order archers, maybe more. It won't be easy, but we should be able to deal with them."

The tall man spoke again:

"Eston has a few hundred trained crossbowmen, more archers, lots of militia—numbers, not much armor or training. The mayor and the city guard captain in command. Castle garrison—James is young, doesn't know much, but he might listen to his captains." He fell silent. The Emperor nodded, continued:

"We have two sieges to run. Third, you're senior, in charge of this one. Twentieth, the city is your problem—take a look at cutting their water. Both of you report to me, messages daily if I'm at the other siege.

"Garth, you and Vija start back today for the valley

mouth. If I had time I'd talk to Justin myself, but it's a day's ride and more. Here's what I want you to tell him:

"Our best guess is that Harald doesn't have much of an army out on the plain—a few hundred cats, less than a thousand heavies, a few more coming in if our friend is wrong about the provinces. Maybe a thousand mounted archers, probably less.

"There are a lot more cats on the far side of the mountains. That's why Vija has scouts halfway across the plain. We might lose a few, but leatherbacks outrun cats. My guess is the Vales fought a hard campaign their side of the mountains this spring, sent Harald and a few hundred men, and that's probably it. If he asks for more and they don't come there's not a damn thing he can do about it.

"My best guess is he isn't getting much more. Best guess, our cavalry outnumber him four to one, maybe more. When the cavalry commanders hear that, they might decide it's their chance for glory.

"Justin's senior in the western force. He's a day's ride from here; I can't hold his hand. Tell him from me, our best guess is still a guess—in twenty years we've made a lot of wrong guesses. If he smashes the Karl cavalry out on the plains, we still have to win here. If he loses our cavalry trying, we have a problem. Not a good time to take chances, not a good commander to take them against. If he has to fight, he should use cavalry and legions both—if our guesses are wrong Harald might have more cavalry than we do. Questions?"

Garth thought a moment. "Your Majesty's best guess is that Harald has only a small army but Justin is not to risk his force on that or let the cavalry commanders risk theirs. If it comes to a fight, he is to use both his legions and the cavalry together."

"Correct. Go tell him."

"I know you can ride and shoot. If I point out that you don't have a war coat you'll borrow a lamella each off two hundred cats to make one with—and one of them will get an arrow through the hole."

Asbjorn looked at his grandfather with suspicion.

"But you are not trained to fight as part of a decade; learning in the middle of a battle can get other people killed. Besides, putting you in the line would be a waste— more useful doing other things."

"Such as?"

"Playing beggar boy in the Imperial camp and bringing me a count of what I was fighting. And no, I don't need you to do that again just now; I know what they have. Scouting still to be done, some of it on foot. Messages to carry. Maybe help steal some horses in a day or two.

"Speaking of which, I have to find an uncle of yours." Harald gave Asbjorn a brief hug, set off through the encampment.

Halfway to where he had left the mare, he saw Stephen, stopped a moment to talk.

"Off to find some friends, back tomorrow. One thing like you to deal with—message to Ragnar, hills north of Eston valley, last little valley east—Knute knows where. Fourth steading up from the main road. Can't find Ragnar, find Jon, his mother, first steading up; they can pass it on. Tell Ragnar to signal our friends east of him—

he knows—shut the gates. Rest of it as we planned. Have someone can get over the hills? Eston valley's crowded just now."

"I can find someone to send. Ragnar in the fourth steading up Red Rock Creek. Tell him to signal east."

Harald nodded. Almost as soon as Harald was out of sight, Stephen noticed another familiar face, stopped a moment.

"Lord Stephen? Grandfather doesn't want me in the line, said I could carry messages. Don't suppose . . . ?"

"Stephen sent him off yesterday with my message. Asbjorn, Hen, Jon, all in one little valley in sight of an enemy army. We have a problem."

Caralla considered the matter briefly.

"So does the Emperor."

"There is that. Good boys. Not exactly cautious."

She looked at her father, responded more to tone than words.

"Might be something I can do."

Mischief

**Brand kindles brand till they burn out,
Flame is quickened by flame:**

Tonio looked up, sniffed.

"I smell smoke."

His partner kept his eyes on the forest edge.

"Of course you smell smoke; what do you think the army cooks over?"

"This smells different. Leaves, like the meadow at home in the fall. Look."

The other guard followed his finger. The plume was rising from somewhere past the near ridge above them, pouring lazily down the slope into the valley.

"It is odd. Think the Karls are trying to fire the forest?"

"Just one fire. I'll go tell Marko, see if he wants us to do something."

Ten minutes later, half a squad of legionaries was moving warily up the slope through the woods. Nobody. Over the ridge a small clearing, a bonfire mostly burned out.

Tonio felt something strike his shield, yelled out.

"Archers. Shields up."

More arrows from the woods beyond. One of the legionaries was kneeling behind his shield, a feathered shaft sticking out of his leg. The squad commander signaled the rest forward.

By the time they rejoined the wounded man, the fire had mostly burned out. Tonio poked at it curiously while two of the others improvised a stretcher.

"I think Your Majesty should see this."

Tonio, eyes down, urged forward, held up his blistered hands.

"Tell His Majesty what happened."

The legionary hesitated, spoke:

"It was the Karls, sir. Majesty. They had a bonfire upslope. Smelled funny. Officer took half a squad of us up to see. Two or three of them shot at us, ran away—one man hurt."

"Did you have anything particular to do with the bonfire? Put your hands in the smoke, did you?"

"No sir. Just poked it with my sword, make sure it was out, try to see what was in it."

"And you then wiped off your sword blade, as a good soldier would."

"Yes sir."

The Emperor turned to the physician. "Anyone else?"

"Not like that. But two soldiers, one the wounded man from his squad, had skin blisters, said they itched. After I saw Tonio . . ."

"Yes. There might be more—look into it. Not much we can do now. Next time . . ."

He turned to one of the other officers in the tent.

"Karol. You said your savages wanted to get into the fun, kill someone."

"Everyone still all right?"

The other two boys held out their hands; Asbjorn looked them over carefully.

"Good. Poison weed doesn't do much to me, some people touch it, scratching all over for weeks. Careful not to touch, washed after, still a risk."

"Do we do it again?" That was Hen.

Asbjorn thought a moment.

"Cleared out the big patch Jon knew about. Getting that much again a lot of work. This time we do it without the weed."

"What good does that do? Oh."

"Know where the enemy is going to be, half the battle."

Their preparations took most of the day. When they were done, all three went swimming, then Asbjorn and Hen went upstream, Jon into the woods. When they met again at the empty house—Jon's mother and the farm animals were with a neighbor ten miles farther up the little valley—there were trout from the stream to clean and cook, two rabbits from Jon's snares.

Hen pointed at the biggest trout.

"I got that one. It really works. You just have to stay very still, everything but the fingers."

Jon looked up from cleaning his rabbits.

"Harald told me. Didn't ever show me though. Said he couldn't do it left-handed."

"Tomorrow, after the ambush. All three of us can go—if I can't make it work, 'Bjorn'll show you."

Asbjorn held up a hand for silence, looked around, shook his head, went back to grilling fish over the fire.

In the middle of the night Hen woke up. Smell of straw, animals. The barn door closing. Asbjorn's head appeared as he climbed up to the loft.

"What is it?"

"Nothing. Just scouting to be sure. Thought I saw something earlier, maybe not. Go to sleep—lots to do tomorrow."

The first legionary came out of the woods into the edge of the clearing, shield up. More. The line moved cautiously forward, shifting right to avoid the blowing smoke. One man stumbled, cursed, fell forward. Arrows out of the woods; he jerked, lay still. The others kept coming, more cautiously still. A sound of cracking branches, two of the remaining four waist deep into a pit. One of them screamed, reached down, lowering his shield; more arrows.

Asbjorn saw a flicker of something off to the right, drew, released, yelled.

"Run."

He loosed a second arrow blind, followed his own order, cursing silently at the sound of the other two crashing through the woods ahead of him. No time to look back, skin crawling. Sunlight ahead. Through the small meadow. At the far side he turned, nocked, waited, sounds moving away, trying to remember.

Three figures out of the woods at the far side, running. Painted faces, hide shields. He loosed, heard the arrow strike the shield, aimed lower, loosed. No time; he snatched for his dagger.

One of the Bashkai dropped his axe, clutched at an arrow sprouting from his throat, stumbled, fell. The other two retreated back into the cover of the trees; 'Bjorn saw that one of them had an arrow in his leg.

"Run."

A stranger's voice. Glanced to one side. Mail, his own size, tunic gold brown. Another beyond. Longbows.

"More coming. Run now, talk later."

He saw them again clearly when all three came into the field below the house. Ladies of the Order, bow, quiver, sword. The one in the lead jumped the low stone wall, took cover behind it; a moment later she was joined by Asbjorn and the other.

The first Lady turned to look back at the house, Jon and Hen staring wide-eyed. He had heard women compared to flowers; this one reminded him of a sword blade. Something familiar. Who? She called out in a low voice: "Hen. Form up with us; they may still be coming."

Both boys picked up their bows, joined the three at the wall.

Half an hour later, the second Lady lowered her bow, turned to Asbjorn.

"Want to check out the woods on the far side. Can you cover—stay behind, shoot anyone tries to kill me?"

He nodded. She came over the wall, a weaving run to the forest edge; he followed.

By the time they got back, the other three were sitting talking, Jon still watching the woods. The slender Lady stood up as they arrived; so did Hen.

"'Bjorn, this is Elaina; 'Laina, Asbjorn."

"And my sister's Kara. Caralla said she was afraid her crazy nephew would get Hen and his friend into trouble, asked me to come keep an eye on things."

Hen looked up, spoke in a tone of honest astonishment.

"She sent you to keep us out of trouble?"

Kara glared at him; Elaina grinned.

"Actually, she said that if Kara had kept me alive for the past four years, Asbjorn should be easy. She and Mother worry too much."

Asbjorn stopped watching her, turned to Kara.

"It was you in the woods last night?"

She nodded.

"Hammocks in the forest, wanted to scout things out a bit."

Jon spoke. "You can have Mother's bed if you want it; Hen and 'Bjorn are in the barn."

Kara shook her head.

"Woods are safer. Harder to find."

High Tide

**The halt can manage a horse,
the handless a flock,
The deaf be a doughty fighter,
To be blind is better than to burn on a pyre:
There is nothing the dead can do.**

A room, a bed, a cradle. Two women arguing.

"Please, my lady."

"It won't work."

"You could disguise yourself as a servant. A boy. They don't even know you're here. None of our people would tell."

Anne looked at her affectionately, bent over the cradle, reached down. The baby found what she was looking for, fell silent again.

"I haven't looked like a boy since I was thirteen, and certainly not at the moment. And you're forgetting Andrew. We don't know if any of his people are inside the castle—Captain Henry and the Lady Commander have been watching. But there are surely people of his, maybe

Andrew himself, with the Emperor, and they know what I look like."

"There must be some way. Hide in the dungeons maybe. His Majesty, Harald' would say the same."

"James might. Harald would expect me to meet His Imperial Majesty at the door of my chamber, greet him politely, and advise him to get out of my kingdom before my husband and his allies show up."

She stopped a moment, thought.

"Or perhaps to be feminine and incompetent. Flirt with my guards. Wait until we're on the road north, steal a horse, ride west. If the Imperials take the castle they'll go through all of it, including the dungeons—looking for loot if nothing else.

"Better yet, do my best to see they don't take the castle. Men fight for things they can see. My daughter and I are going down now; you come too. Maybe Henry will try flirting with you again. You could do worse. Harald thinks well of him."

Three flights above them, the open roof, a view over the ramparts.

"More engines than yesterday—must have brought them up from the Eston siege. Archers too. They're going to try."

The Lady Commander fell silent, turned, started down the tower stairs; the castle captain took one more look over the scene, followed her. Arrived in the courtyard, both started giving orders.

With the front wall of his tent raised, the Emperor could see one side of the castle, the gate, both siege towers,

the movable shed that would shelter the ram. Archers on
the other side as well, but here where the slope up was
gentlest was where the attack would come. Was coming.
Pushed by hundreds of men, two siege towers crept
towards the dirt ramps that led to the walls. As they came
within arrowshot, a trumpet rang out. Too far to see, but
he knew the besieging archers were pouring arrows at the
top of the rampart, every arrow slot.

Now the ram was in jerky motion as the men inside the
shed lifted it, ran forward, dropped it. Almost to the moat,
where the lifted drawbridge had been replaced by masses
of earth and rock.

The ram and its shed had stopped moving. More trumpet
calls, men running back to the cover of the earthworks,
runners from the command group. Something was wrong.

In the castle courtyard, inside the gate, thirty rock
throwers, each with a team of five men pulling, one Lady
loading and aiming. A whistle. Over the sudden silence,
the voice of the Lady Commander.

"We got their ram. Engines against the wall, clear the
courtyard, start shifting."

The commander of the third legion heard a familiar
voice, looked up. "Majesty."

"What happened to the ram?"

"Rocks. Lots of rocks. Karls must have a bunch of
throwers inside the castle at ground level, where archers,
bolt throwers can't reach them."

"Can't we . . . ?" The Emperor saw where the commander was pointing.

"I've ordered the engineers to start throwing over the wall at the courtyard behind the gate. Little engines don't have much range; I doubt they could have reached the ram from anywhere else. Slow—but a sling full of rocks does a lot of damage. Wouldn't want to be in that courtyard just now. I'm keeping the turtles back, just in case—rocks might go short. We'll stop throwing before they go in—job should be done by then."

On the top of the siege tower, trying to keep his footing as it jolted forwards, it occurred to Gerin that this was an honor he could have lived without. At least nobody was shooting at him; the archers on the castle wall had either been killed or, more likely, decided there were safer places to be. For himself, he could think of a lot of places safer than the top of a siege tower, first onto the wall.

Looking back, he could see the turtles, masses of legionaries roofed with shields, beginning to move forward. The other tower had stuck, men heaving on it. The castle wall was getting closer, the captain yelling for the men to form up and move. The wooden wall that had been sheltering them swung down, became the bridge across the remaining gap, its far end resting on the castle wall. Shield up, in line, forward. This was it.

As he came onto the wall, something struck his shield hard. Another. He could see the head of a crossbow bolt sticking through. Something glanced off the armor of his lower leg. The keep was at the other end of the castle— where the hell were they shooting from?

A glance between the shields gave the answer. Under

his feet, the stone of the castle wall. In front, fifteen feet of nothing. On the far side of the gap, a wooden wall, hanging in the air. Maybe the Karls really were sorcerers after all. A second look. The enemy archers were on a platform resting on a rough scaffolding of logs. At least one siege bow. An arrow glanced off his helm. The man beside him was down. Gerin dropped to his knees for better protection. Behind him the captain was yelling something. Stopped.

A wooden box on wheels, ladder crowded with men, shields on their backs. At ground level the tower's back was open, more men crowded behind, shields over their heads. Something struck it a hard blow, a giant's spear through the front wall, massive iron head, tree trunk for a shaft. A second blow, a third, as the ram smashed a splintered hole in the front of the tower. Through it something dark that hit the wooden floor, broke, showered burning coals.

"One more day, Majesty. Two at most. We know their tricks now. If we throw enough rocks, they can't use the little engines against the ram and the turtles. Finish another tower. Fill in more of the moat—they won't know where we're coming. If it doesn't work, we can always use ladders."

"How long will it take to fill in the moat all along this side? Assume you can borrow any men and gear you need from the other legions."

The commander thought a moment.

"Tomorrow to fill in. While they do it, I'll have a few hundred men carrying loads of rocks up from the river bed to the engines. Retrieve the ram and the shed tonight. Rebuild them tomorrow. Finish another tower. Get more big engines up from the city—start disassembling this evening, bring them up next morning, a day to reassemble and get the aim. By day after tomorrow we'll have two towers—maybe three. The ram and its shed. Enough big engines to shower rocks into the courtyard, anywhere they might set up throwers. We already have the bolt throwers and archers from the city; I can use one of their legions and my two for the attack, two others in reserve."

"Do it."

In the castle courtyard a dozen stone throwers, each protected by a slanted roof of heavy beams, beside each a pile of rocks. Leonora, standing with her back against the castle wall, turned to the Lady beside her.

"Need more, but we don't have enough timber. Next time, remind me to cut down a forest first."

"If there is a next. Lot of legionaries out there."

"Fewer by the time they get here."

On the rampart, someone raised a red flag, swung it twice. Leonora raised her hand for attention:

"Thirty-second warning. Start throwing on the signal, watch your observer on the wall. First section red, second blue, third yellow. Lose your observer, use someone else's. When I blow withdraw, do it—if they get archers on the wall, court's a deathtrap."

She hesitated, watching the red observer on the wall. The flag went up, down.

"Start throwing."

⌘ ⌘ ⌘

From the top of the keep Henry could see part of the courtyard, most of the space outside the walls. Two siege towers—they had built a second to replace the one burned in the first attack. The ram moving towards the gate. Between the towers and at either side were the turtles, each two hundred men, shields over their heads. More turtles coming against the far side of the castle, where the slope was too steep for towers. Fifteen—three legions. Almost six times what he had inside the walls, easily another legion formed up out of range of the walls in front of the big siege engines.

The ram reached the gate, hidden from him by the castle wall, swung once, twice—he could hear the blows. On the wall above the gate two big rocks, a dozen men straining on levers to move them. One went, then the other. He heard them hit the ram roof, smash through it.

The towers were close to the wall, the turtles, their path a trail of bodies where stones had broken through the roof of shields or arrows found holes, mostly out of his sight. As the towers reached the wall, so did ladders, between them, on either side. The castle guards were fighting with the legionaries from the towers, helped by arrows from the keep and the courtyard below. He saw one man catch hold of the top of a ladder, shove—guard, ladder, its invisible load of legionaries swung away from the wall, down. Another guard was using a pole arm to push a ladder sideways.

On either side of the towers his men were still fighting, but between them the wall was held by the enemy, legionaries pouring out of the towers, up the ladders between, shields raised against arrows raining from the keep. A few steps across the roof put him in sight of the back wall of the castle—no siege towers, but ladders, legionaries fighting with guards, pushing them back by weight of numbers, a few starting down the stairs into the courtyard. He lifted the horn to his lips, blew, looked around once more, headed for the stairs down.

Leonora already had her whistle raised when she heard the signal. Three sharp blasts. Again. The surviving crews abandoned their engines, ran for the ramp that led up to the open door of the keep, joined by archers fleeing positions in the wall. Leonora picked up her spear, prepared to follow them.

Around the corner of the keep legionaries, the first heading for the ramp and the door—brave man. Leonora crossed the courtyard at a run, drove her spear through his side just below the ribs, kicked the falling body free, spun to face the men coming after him. Two, shields raised, advancing slowly together, the man on the right a little ahead. She glanced down and, as the shield twitched to follow, drove her spear blade into his throat. As the other turned to face her she swung the spear's butt to the side of his head.

A familiar voice. "On your left."

She stepped sideways into the shelter of Henry's shield, lowered her spear to waist height. Of the next two legionaries, one hesitated, one didn't. Henry's sword came down, the shield up to block it, Leonora's spear under the shield.

The two backed up the ramp into the keep. Behind them the door swung shut.

The feast hall had become a field hospital, wounded on

the tables or pallets on the floor, in one corner a pile of bodies. Anne leaned over a guard, a goblet in one hand, the other steadying his head. Her daughter, in Elen's arms, watched fascinated as another man, one arm bandaged to his side, made his remaining hand a spider crawling across him, stopping to wave its feet at the baby.

"Beautiful little girl—mine are bigger now."

"Best baby in the world."

Anne heard something, looked up. The Lady Commander and the captain.

"They have the walls?"

Henry nodded. She glanced around the hall.

"We've bought Harald and James two weeks; let's hope it's enough. Any more looks expensive. Besides, the cistern's only half full—water for two days, maybe three, if they don't storm first."

"Your Majesty gives me leave . . . ?"

Anne looked at Leonora, back to Henry.

"To surrender. Get the best terms you can, spend as long as you can getting them."

"Walls are ours, Majesty. Karls still hold the keep, but they're willing to talk."

"Offer them the usual terms—their wounded treated like ours. If the army goes home, anyone too hurt to walk stays here, the rest go with us; they can ransom them back when it's over. Before they surrender, make it clear to your boys that none of the prisoners gets mistreated—man or Lady. The Order's the weakest third, most at risk. If we can break them out of the alliance, the next war will be easier. That's for your ears.

"For your boys, you might remind them the war isn't over yet. Harald's somewhere between us and home with an army. If things go wrong, some of them may be his prisoners next week—it wouldn't be the first time.

"If you don't think that's enough, tell them the first man who mistreats a prisoner hangs."

"I spoke to one of my people, Majesty. He never saw the King, doesn't think he was there. The guard was being commanded by one of the captains, the Order by their own people. It looks like the banner went one way, King the other. Out on the plains with Harald."

The Emperor turned back to the senior legion commander.

"We searched the place top to bottom, Majesty, every male prisoner. He could be hiding somewhere, I suppose, but I don't know where."

There was a brief pause. The Emperor spoke again:

"At least we have his wife and daughter. We'll take them home with us, see what he offers to get them back. If she stays with us a while she might get used to civilized living, persuade her husband to be a bit less unfriendly. Is she likely to be any trouble?"

The commander shook his head.

"Not her, Majesty. Biddable enough, friendly once she saw we were going to treat her proper. Have to keep a close eye on our boys, though. On the good side, I expect he'll be eager to get her back—I would be. What do we do next?"

"Eston."

Twenty miles west, where Eston Valley opened into the

central plain, the legions had built a fortified camp to guard the valley mouth—square earthwork, gate in each side, observation tower of crude lumber, tents for two thousand legionaries, three hundred archers. Between camp and forest edge the cavalry had their lines—space for nearly nine thousand men, more than nine thousand horses.

Justin looked around the command tent, spoke to Anton, the senior of the cavalry commanders.

"How many did you lose?"

"Almost two hundred head. Karls must have come through the forest after dark, cut tethers, spooked the horses. Their friends west of here grabbed them, left."

"What were your guards doing?"

"There's more than a mile of forest on one side, plains on the other. Takes a lot of people to cover all of it at night—only took a few getting through. My horsemen aren't much good in the woods anyway."

The scout commander looked up, spoke:

"We need Bashkai. A few hundred of them wandering around the forest, no damn horse thieves coming through alive."

"The whole army only has six hundred—His Majesty has them covering the main body. Lot more woods in there." Justin gestured at the mouth of the long valley.

"If we can't guard the forest side, we should move farther out. Besides, the horses have grazed down most of the grass between here and the forest."

Justin looked around the circle of faces, thought a moment, spoke:

"Vija, Garth, you were at council with His Majesty. He thinks the force out there is small but doesn't want us to take chances. He didn't order us to stay in camp. Is that right?

Both men nodded.

"Vija, what do your scouts tell you?"

"No word from the central plains for the last couple of days. Scouts near in say the enemy body is nine or ten miles south, not far from the woods. They can't get close enough to count numbers. We need horse archers, nomads. Somebody mounted who can shoot back."

"If you need nomads, ask Artos. Need Bashkai, ask Gavin. Recruit two thousand savages, only a thousand come home, makes it hard next time. There's not a whole lot we can do about it. Better to think about what we do have. More cavalry than the Karls. Two legions. Here's my idea; what's wrong with it?"

Up and Out! Up and Out!

Red hair on the pillow beside him. James smiled, knew he looked foolish, didn't care, leaned over to kiss his bride.

Up and Out! Up and Out!

He tried to fit the trumpet calls into the dream, failed, opened his eyes, rolled out of bed into the morning cool. The tent was still scattered with camp chairs; Council had gone late.

"Majesty."

"I'm awake; what is it?"

The guard captain came through the tent door; James wondered if he slept in armor.

"Order scouts. There's cavalry moving our way. Stephen is ordering tents down, wagons loaded and out, men ready to ride. Half an hour, not much more."

⊕ ⊕ ⊕

By the time the Imperial cavalry came in sight, the royal army had formed up in a long double line, right crossing the road to the forest beyond, reserves behind. Horn calls rang out on the Imperial side; the advancing force slowed, stopped. On their right, almost out of sight, sunlight caught ripples on the Caldbeck, the river that carried the mountain streams north to Borderflood.

Anton turned to Vija. "Your count?"

The scout commander took one more look, thought a moment.

"More than His Majesty thought, fewer than he feared. Five thousand or so heavies, maybe a thousand lights—mounted archers. Haven't seen any cats, aside from a couple of scouts west of us—I expect the rest are off making life hard for my boys."

"And we have almost nine thousand, more than half of them heavies."

"Looks like they can count too."

The royal army was moving, retreating south along the forest edge. Anton watched for a moment, signaled the trumpeter, turned back.

"I think we have them."

Half an hour later, James turned to the captain riding beside him.

"Other than exercising their horses, what are they doing—trying to chase us a hundred miles south?"

"Don't know. I thought they'd use the fast cavalry to get around, try to force us to battle. Their right wing is pushed a little ahead of the main body, but not much. Something . . ."

As they came over the next low rise and started down the answer became suddenly clear. Less than two miles south of them the river swung in a long bend towards the forest then away. At the narrowest point, from the trees to the river, a solid line of spears, behind them the banners of two legions.

Half a mile the other side of the royal army, Anton gave the scout commander beside him a fierce grin, turned to his trumpeter.

And Turn

**A bear's play, a breaking wave, one night's ice
Are never safe—let no man trust them.**

Behind them, someone was yelling. Anton hesitated, turned in the saddle. A scout, forcing his way through the ranks of heavy cavalry towards his commander.

"Cats, sir. Behind us. Thousands and thousands of them."

"Vija. See what the hell it is. If the Karls start shifting west to get across the river we charge; as long as they don't we can afford to wait."

The scout commander pushed his way back. In the rear ranks he could see men pointing backwards, hear the rising clamor. He spent most of a minute looking before turning, moving again through the lines to the commander's side.

"What is it? There can't be thousands and thousands of cats—whole damn host is only two thousand. Your boys supposed to be watching for them."

"The whole damn host is here—west and north of us, moving this way. They brought some friends."

Anton gave him a puzzled look. "More Karl heavies?"

Vija shook his head.

"Nomads decided to come after all. Two or three thousand of them. The numbers don't look so good any more."

Anton looked south. The Karl cavalry in battle formation facing him was beginning to move, heavies center and right, lights on the left. One last order to his trumpeter. He lifted his lance from its socket, swung it down as the notes of the charge rang out. In the middle of the enemy line he recognized the banner of the Karl king, aimed his horse for it. Faster and faster.

Center and left met center and right, five thousand heavy cavalry on each side at the charge, a tangle of men and horses. On the royal left the Order, outnumbered four to one, wheeled, fled south and west. Trumpet calls on the Imperial right called back pursuit, swung the lighter forces to fall on the royal center from behind. The Order swung round in turn, dissolved into a line of archers on foot shooting into the rear of the enveloping force.

James, lance shattered, pulled out his sword, pushed forward. A big man, beard sticking out under his visor, struck two-handed; the blow drove the King's shield back into his face. He backed his horse, saw his guard captain catch a second blow on his shield, strike back. Something hit his shoulder with numbing force. He wheeled the horse, the next mace blow on his shield, return blow blocked. Forward against the enemy, tried to get in a second blow. More around him, a pain in his side, his own guard coming up on his right. Another blow on the armor. The bearded man again. He tried to raise his shield, half made it, felt the blow on shield and helm. The two-handed sword again. Slow as a dream, the sword drifted up. James tried to raise his shield, knew he would never make it in time. Red hair on the pillow.

⚜ ⚜ ⚜

Anton, shield raised against a Karl sword, felt a sharp pain in his back, another in his leg. Struck, blocked, struck. Something was wrong with his arm. He looked down. An arrow point sticking out of it. The Karl had pulled back; Anton turned in his saddle. Fifty yards behind him a solid line of mounted archers, pouring arrows into the rear of his dissolving line. Filled with fury, light as air, he wheeled his horse, charged them.

Harald lowered his bow, turned to Donal beside him.

"Thought so; they're digging."

He pointed beyond the ruin of the battlefield. A mile farther south, where the advancing line of the Imperial legions had been, a shorter line—a wall of freshly dug dirt.

Justin leaned on his shovel, wiped the sweat from his eyes, wondered when the last time was a senior legion commander had helped move dirt. All things considered, more digging and less commanding looked like a good idea.

"Sir. Karl to talk to you."

At the front entrance he stopped, looked back. The wall was up to four feet; with luck the enemy couldn't see the rear rampart, where men were still working furiously. He didn't know how many the Karls had out there, but with a legion and a half to hold them he needed all the help he could get.

"Want an escort, sir?" He shook his head, walked through the gateway.

The man waiting for him was a cat, dismounted, one hand on his horse's neck. Not young. Should have brought a translator. But surely the man they sent would speak at least some Tengu.

The cat said something to his horse, looked up, gave the commander a friendly nod.

"Figure your boys could use a rest. Must have been up all night getting here."

Justin said nothing, waited.

"Field ours. Lot of wounded out there, both sides. Truce till dark, free to bandage them there, carry here, we don't interfere, your people don't get in our way doing the same. Lend you some horses to help. Wounded prisoners who can ride we keep, can't ride, give us their word not to fight, yours. Too badly hurt, village west of here, you don't try to get them back. After sunset no promises either way. Agreed?"

Justin thought a moment, searched for hidden traps, failed to find any.

"Very generous. I'm the senior commander, can accept for our side. You have authority for yours?"

"His Majesty isn't in shape to agree to things just now. Leaves me."

He reached out a hand, Justin took it.

Three hours later, Harald plunged arms, face, into a pool at the forest edge. As the ripples died his reflection looked back. A little less like a butcher. He straightened, sore muscles complaining, whistled. The mare trotted over. Blood, his or other people's, was nothing new.

Riding back to the field, he noticed a body of cavalry, dismounted, disarmed. A smaller number of cats were guarding them, one talking with one of his prisoners.

"Hedin. Friends of yours?"

"One of them—three years ago."

"Interested in another try—starting now?"

"Empire might have hostages."

"I don't speak Belkhani. Put it to them, welcome to come over to our side, any that can without getting kin killed, reasonable terms, let me know. Can't promise them help afterwards, do what we can—no province I'd rather see out of the Empire. Fight for us, at least get back horses, arms, can go home when it's done."

He took one more look at the prisoners—three hundred men, most of them still on their feet—rode back to the battlefield.

Just before dark, he spoke with Justin again, this time on the field where tired legionaries were carrying away a last few men too badly wounded to walk.

"I don't suppose you want to extend the truce till morning?"

Harald responded with a friendly smile, shook his head.

"Emperor decides to go home, leave me and my friends alone, sleep all you like. Not just now. Sun sets, hope you don't get killed, do my best to see you do."

By the time the camp came in sight, gold flag flying as bravely as when they set out, Justin was stumbling with exhaustion. He called a halt to dress ranks; however tired, he would come home in good order. The ragged mass of cavalry, horses, wounded, was past his power to deal with. At least the legions were still unbroken.

The gate was closed; half a legion made only a skeleton garrison, but the junior commander should at least be able to find sentries who could see. Now it was opening. Behind him he heard a scout, something about the cavalry behind them. Justin didn't bother to turn around; without looking he could feel the weight of the army that had followed them all day, never attacked. Soon it would lift. Harald had been unwilling, even against exhausted men, to risk storming last night's camp, unwilling to attack in the open in daylight. Two legions, behind walls, would be safe. He could sleep. The morning, the report to the Emperor, what followed . . . For now, sleep was enough.

The gates swung closed. The ramparts were black with heads. Under the rain of arrows the front ranks, eyes on the ground, shields on their shoulders, melted. Justin turned. Arrows from the other side as well, cats finally closing. Archers in front, archers behind. The trumpeter next to him was staring at his horn, frozen in panic. Justin snatched it from his hand, raised it. Square, what was the call for form square? Something struck him in the throat. He tried to breathe. Out of the corner of his eye the banner staff coming down, reached out to catch it, stumbled, fell.

Justin tried to close his eyes against that final picture, his legion's banner, falling, around it a chaos of dead and dying. Close—his eyes were closed. He forced them open.

A low cot in a tent full of bodies. One moved, another moaned—wounded men. He tried to form words, say something. One arm bound to his body; he lifted the other. His neck was wrapped in bandages. He closed his eyes. This time behind them was dark.

He woke to someone lifting his head, water dripping into his mouth.

"Swallow. Know it hurts but need to drink. Arrow through the neck, missed the artery. Out now."

He opened his mouth, swallowed. The voice was right. Swallowed again, again. Sank back into the familiar dark. Sleep.

Half a Loaf

**Rash to count fortune your friend
At a stranger's door.**

Something was wrong. By the river downhill from the tent, a rising clamor, coming closer. Voice of the guard outside:

"Council, soldier. His Majesty . . ."

"Send him in."

The soldier was out of armor, bare to the waist, half a dozen waterbags slung over his shoulder. He saw the Emperor, saluted.

"Majesty, it's the river. It's dry."

The man looked down at himself, flushed.

"Pardon, Majesty. I thought . . ."

"Pardoned. You were right. The river has stopped flowing completely?"

"Yes, Majesty. There's still water in some of the pools."

The Emperor looked around, thought a moment.

"Twelfth, you aren't doing anything just now. The Karls are damming the river somewhere above Eston. Your job is to find the dam, take it, break it.

"It could be a trick, with an ambush somewhere up slope. Watch for it. Harald's a tricky bastard.

"Gerd, you're in charge of supplies—as of now, that includes water in pools in the riverbed. Fill every barrel we have, guard what's left, don't let some idiot wash in it. All up and down the valley, till you get to where the next river comes in.

"There are big storage tanks in the castle. Empty our barrels into them, send the wagons west, refill at that stream that comes down from the hills, bring the barrels back full. The siege may last a while yet, we could get thirsty."

The Emperor spent the next afternoon inspecting the siege, accompanied by the senior of the three legion commanders conducting it. Eston was ringed by earthworks, behind them archers. Farther back, siege engines, slowly pounding at the city wall.

"I suppose mining is hopeless?"

The commander shook his head.

"Like the castle—the whole thing is built on rock. You can see how the river bent around it. We'll use archers and engines to clear the walls, breach if we're lucky, rams, mostly for the gate, siege towers. The river's shallow—if it fills up again, men on that side can wade it when we go in. They'll still need ladders to get up to the wall—you can see it's almost a cliff—then over it. It isn't going to be easy. Wish I knew how many soldiers were inside."

"Not as many as we thought."

"Your Majesty has someone . . . ?"

The Emperor shook his head, started back to his tent, the commander beside him.

"The garrison of the castle was only five, six hundred—and the King wasn't there. I'm guessing it's the same story here. The last few days we were coming south the army ahead of us was getting smaller, not bigger. It was down to a thousand or so by the time we turned east. Five hundred south of us in the open, where we could count them, five hundred up the valley ahead of us where we couldn't.

"We figured that was the whole army, most of it retreating behind walls. The real army was assembling out on the plains with Harald to lead it. I hope Justin is being careful."

The Emperor stopped. The commander had turned his head, was listening to something. A moment later he heard it too—a dull roar from the direction of the river. It faded. For a moment he thought he could he could hear the noise of running water, then it was drowned out by distant voices.

"Twelfth did it. "

An officer was hurrying up from the river; the Emperor sat down on his chair in the tent, gestured to one of the servants, looked up as the man came into the tent.

"The river's back. You don't look happy."

"No, Majesty."

"Any idiots camped in the riverbed got washed away, we're better off without them."

"Yes, Majesty."

"Don't just stand there, tell me what's wrong."

"Bodies, Majesty. A lot of bodies. Twelfth legion."

"What killed them?" Even as he spoke the Emperor was pushing himself out of his chair, reaching for his stick; the slope down to the river could be tricky.

"I don't know, Majesty."

When he got to the river he saw the legionary physician leaning over one of the bodies that had been pulled from the water. The Emperor waited impatiently until he had finished.

"What happened?"

"Not a battle. Battering, but the river could have done it. They drowned. The crest was man high down here—I saw it. Worse farther up."

It was past dark when one of the survivors reached camp.

"Half the legion, Majesty."

"Sit down before you fall down—someone get him a chair. What happened?"

"Nine, ten miles up river from the city. Narrow valley, wall across the choke point, archers on the wall, canyon spread out a bit lower down, not too steep. Commander put two hundred men on each side up above to make sure nobody ambushed us. I was on the right. The rest of the legion went up the valley to take the wall, tight formation, shields up."

"The wall was the dam and they broke it."

The man nodded.

"Wave of water twice my height. We saved some, washed up one side or the other."

"How many left alive?"

"Four hundred of us out of it, Majesty. Junio thinks maybe fifty more, one side or the other."

"Junio is the surviving captain?"

"Senior captain left, Majesty. He sent me to tell you what happened. We took the dam, what's left of it, camped next to it, dug in. He wants orders."

"Find a bed somewhere, get a good night's sleep. I'll send someone in the morning; you can show him the way."

The Emperor looked around the tent. One of the officers spoke up.

"Majesty, the last word from Justin got here five days back, left him six."

"Have you sent to ask how he's doing?"

"Three days ago, Majesty. They haven't come back."

The Emperor closed his eyes, listened to the silence, opened them. Three days, and only getting worried now. Young men, mostly. If Artos . . . That choice was made; too late to change it. Loyal to his prince—to the boy's credit. For a moment he could almost see Talinn sitting in his place in Council, his lord's right hand, calm, quiet, solid as rock. Dead. Too many years. It was his war now. He pulled his mind back.

"Fifth is camped farthest down the valley. Move the whole legion west. Assume the Karls have the camp. If we're wrong, the boys get some exercise. If right, have them build earthworks across the valley mouth, start siege operations against the camp, send word back for help. Claudio, you brought the bad news, you deal with it. As soon as you know, send word.

"Karol. You have better forest scouts than theirs—use them. Your boys go west on both sides of the valley. Have them send back word about what's happening on the plain."

Tent empty, he could stretch out on the cot, close his eyes, think. Justin was gone—he knew it in his bones. If all else failed he could cut his losses, abandon the siege, force the valley mouth, take the army home—with the Queen of Kaerlia in his train and the royal castle burning behind him. Nothing in the Kingdom, nothing in the Vales, could hold a field fortification against eight legions.

Two days later, the Emperor called his commanders to council.

"We're lifting the siege, going home."

He spoke into the silence.

"Word came back from the encampment west—most of you have heard it by now. Fifth legion got there. The Karls pulled out when they saw us coming—left four hundred of our wounded behind.

"Justin's alive. He took an arrow in the throat and isn't talking yet, so he used a stylus and tablet. Harald has the host of the Vales, half the Order, two or three thousand nomads, five thousand Karl heavies. They won two battles—seven days ago, the cavalry, next day, the legions.

"Most of you saw the river—dry again. I figure the Karls had another dam farther upstream, closed it last night. There's a smaller river, Karls call it Red Rock, that joins this one five miles west of here. We just got word— it's dry too. The big river out in the plain runs north to the Borderflood. It's time to follow it. Empty the castle, add what supplies are left to ours, burn it, start west in the morning."

"Majesty?"

"Claudio?"

"Eston river runs east and north, no telling how far. The small one comes down from the hills north of us. All we've seen there are a few archers, scouts. Why not push up Red Rock valley, stay out of the river bed this time, break the dam?"

The Emperor thought a moment before he answered.

"Someone in those hills has been trying to annoy us—nothing big, ambushes, throwing rocks down at the camp. Pin pricks. I've been wondering why.

"Harald's had six days since the last battle. Cats are used to mountains, Karls know the paths—these are their hills.

"Staying is too big a risk. We're low on food and water, no cavalry left to cover our supply lines, and Harald is out there somewhere with ten thousand men. He hasn't run out of tricks in twenty years.

"Time to go home."

The Way Home

Some are valiant
Though they stain no sword

Standing at one side of the road, his squad at his back, it occurred to Garo that while guarding prisoners was less exciting than storming a castle, it had its compensations—especially when half of them were women. However strict the Old Man's orders, they couldn't stop a soldier from looking. Some were worth looking at.

They came by single file, hands bound in front of them, roped together in groups of sixty, each separated by a squad of ten legionaries. One of the Ladies, tall, eyes alert in a scarred face, caught his eye. Fifty by the face, forty by the dark hair, thirty by the smooth stride.

"Captain Garo."

It was a legionary runner. Garo raised his hand.

"Message from the commander, sir. Karls coming up from the south—lots of them. He wants the prisoners off the road the other side, out of the way if there's a fight. Sent a guide—courtesy of His Majesty's pet Karl.

Doesn't speak anything civilized, but he'll show you where
to go."

The young man gestured to the still younger man following him, pointed to the captain.

"Captain Garo. Commands prisoners. Lead him."

The guide looked at Garo, said something. Garo shook
his head. The runner spoke again, slowly and loudly.

"Show. Lead."

The guide set off for the head of the column at a trot;
Garo followed. Half a mile farther west, where the road
ran over a dry riverbed, the guide pointed right.

Two hours later, the riverbed out of sight, the path winding
uphill through thick forest. A figure stepped out of the
woods, sword raised, struck twice. Leonora stepped clear of
the cut rope, stretched out her bound hands; a third stroke
and they were free. She turned to the Lady behind her.

"Keep moving; guards suspect anything, they may start
killing people. Move as slow as you can. Get a battle song
going, loud—we need the noise. 'Laina, cut 'Thora free,
give her your knife. 'Thora, free everyone ahead of you,
swords for some of them pretty soon."

Elaina obeyed orders, then turned to her mother.
"Ambush ahead, two archers, far side of clearing to the
right, any minute now."

As she spoke, Elaina handed Leonora the sword she
was carrying, drew her own. Her mother glanced down at
the blade, up.

"Good. Follow me."

At the head of the column the guide said something to
Garo, pointed. On the right the woods had fallen back,
exposing a few small buildings and a stone wall.

"What the . . . !"

At the legionary's shout, Garo turned back. The guide was gone. One of the guards pointed at the woods to the left.

"Want me to go after him?"

Garo shook his head, shrugged the shield down from his shoulder.

"May be the least of our problems."

Another shout.

"Arrows. 'Ware arrows. On the right."

Garo looked right as he slid his shield arm through the straps. Archers behind the wall. One of the legionaries behind him grunted. An arrow glanced off Garo's helmet.

"Second half after them, first half watch the prisoners."

His shield raised against the archers, Garo looked back along the path. The man at the head of the rope had seen the archers and stopped, more prisoners piling up behind him.

"Form line; they may try something."

Someone was past the knot of prisoners, running straight at the guards—the tall Lady of indefinite age. This time she had a sword.

The nearest guard thrust at Leonora. She slapped the blade aside, twisted past to the left, struck back-handed at the exposed neck. Three more in line, a fourth behind them, one down, more chasing after the archers. On her left forest; she circled right instead. The fourth man, the captain, said something to the other three and came after her, shield up—behind him his men were advancing on the prisoners. 'Laina's problem.

❖ ❖ ❖

The tall woman moved with frightening grace, but Garo had armor and shield and she didn't. A blow straight down at his helm. He blocked with his shield, stepped forward swinging low. Her leg wasn't there, the sword a line of fire down his forearm. He stepped back, felt his grip loosening. Back again, stumbled over a body, shield swinging up as he fell.

Elaina faced a line of three guards, the prisoners behind her. As the legionaries moved forward, the one on the right thrust at her. She struck the sword down, stepped in, drove her point up where the armor opened under the arm, stepped back. The second guard swung; she blocked with her blade, struck him in the face with the butt, backed again. Leonora, behind the guards, stepped over Garo's body, struck twice.

The next minute was chaos, freed prisoners sharing out swords, daggers, javelins from the six bodies, fading back into the forest. As the second squad came past the bend, Leonora stepped between them and the prisoners, sword raised, Elaina at her side, behind them a dozen Ladies, each with a javelin, more, armed with swords, coming out of the woods on the legionaries' flank.

"Touch a sword and you die. First squad did." She nodded at the pile of bodies.

Leonora was overseeing the distribution of weapons, setting guards for the prisoners, when two figures came out of the woods on the far side of the farm. She waved. When they reached her Leonora handed Kara the sword.

"You keep it as sharp as she did. What happened to the men chasing you?"

"Two still out there somewhere. Getting dark, thought Hen and I would be more use back here."

"Yes. Get some rest—later tonight I'll want you out watching for visitors. Nicely planned rescue, but don't count on things going that smoothly next time."

"'Bjorn's idea. Just followed orders.

"Speaking of which, better tell the sisters not to throw javelins at him."

Kara pointed down the road. The figure, coming at a trot, was dressed as a legionary runner save for bow and scabbard at one side, quiver at the other. He slowed, approached with both hands raised and empty.

"Not a problem—boy can catch them out of the air. I've seen him do it."

"Didn't get hurt?"

"Not till his grandmother found out they had points."

When Asbjorn reached the two Ladies, Leonora caught him in her arms, gave him a long hug.

"Thanks—couldn't have stood another week of legion cooking. Now report."

"Commander asleep—most of an hour before someone showed up looking for his prisoners. I left the body out of sight—another hour, maybe more, till they notice he's gone, find it. Won't be here tonight—legions think night time is for sleeping. Maybe tomorrow."

"What about Bashkai?"

"Might be a few this end as scouts. Most of them went west two days back."

"Even a few could be dangerous, especially at night.

Get some rest now; you and Kara go out in a couple of hours, just in case."

He nodded, looked up at her.

"Makes you look more like 'Laina."

"While Henry argued with them about surrender terms. Figured someone might be looking for a tall Lady with gray hair. Couldn't do much about being tall."

Elen, the baby in her arms, walked over to Anne, glanced around, spoke in a whisper.

"It's hopeless. They won't let the mare off lead, cavalry rider on each side, you should have . . ."

Anne shook her head.

"I want your opinion on something in the packs."

Elen gave her a puzzled look. Anne walked over to the nearer packhorse, fumbled in one of the saddlebags, pulled out a long strip of green cloth.

"Do you think it goes with my coloring? As a sash, maybe?"

She wrapped the cloth around her waist, straightened, looked at the other woman.

"Would this one be better? Not with a dress this dark. Trim for something lighter, maybe gold—a complement to His Majesty."

The second strip was dark blue. She hung it around her neck, ends falling forwards over her breasts and down.

"Little 'Laina looks like she's starting to wake up; let me hold her a minute."

"She's sound asleep. Quietest baby I ever knew." For a moment the two women's heads were together as they leaned over the sleeping baby. Anne picked her up, took a few slow steps, stopped between the nervous stallion and a tall fir tree. Elen moved in the other direction, looked up as if she had heard something, reached the edge of the clearing, screamed.

As the guards turned to the noise, Anne cut the tether rope, slashed the rump of the stallion, took two steps sideways into the cover of the fir tree's thick boughs. The horse bolted. She slid the little knife back into the concealed sheath, bound the blue cloth crosswise over her daughter, around her own waist, back up, tied the ends at the back of her neck, started to climb.

Twenty feet up she stopped to catch her breath. Little Elaina slept quietly, her head between her mother's breasts. Below Anne heard angry voices, farther off yelling, hoofbeats fading into the distance, more. Elen's voice.

"I saw a snake, a big one—of course I yelled. I have no idea where my lady is, and if I did I wouldn't tell—you or His Majesty."

Another voice, this time in Tengu, slow enough for her to follow.

"Don't waste your time; we know where the Karl queen is. On the plain, as far west as she can get, on your damn stallion that you told her was the fastest horse in the army. Better hope you were wrong." He moved off. Anne hugged her daughter, listened. The young officer was speaking again.

"That horse isn't safe for most men, let alone a lady carrying a baby. Hope we don't find them both lying out there someplace."

"Half Estfen is pasture; my lady rode before she could walk. If you can handle him with two hands she can manage with one."

The two moved off, still talking. Branch by branch, with infinite care, up. Finally a wide fork. Anne settled her back against the trunk, legs around the branch, unwrapped the green cloth from her waist, wrapped it tight around waist and tree. Closed her eyes.

Twice during the night the baby woke, nursed, fell back to sleep. In the morning Anne made faces to keep her daughter quiet while the men below broke camp and, with increasing difficulty, for most of an hour after they had left. With the world's best baby reaching the limits of her patience, Anne climbed down, changed her daughter under the sheltering boughs of the fir tree—the green wool might not be as smooth as linen, but it was better than nothing—and set off south. A slow hour through the forest with no sign of stray legionaries, then back to the road.

Late that afternoon she stopped to nurse the baby, rest her legs, and explain to her daughter the one clear advantage of her original plan.

"Not a problem for you, love—you've got your beast of burden. But it's a long way, you aren't as little as you used to be, and I can't eat grass."

The sound of horses; she looked up. Coming north along the road. Too late to hide, too many to fight. Anne came to her feet, the baby in her arms, stood watching the approaching riders.

The smallest slid off her horse, took the baby from her mother's arms, lifted it into the air, kissed it on the stomach, was rewarded with gurgles.

"My namesake behaving herself?"

Anne nodded, blinked away tears.

"Like a lamb. Stayed quiet when it mattered. Are you scouting for Harald? You know your mother's a prisoner? They took Esthold, captured the garrison."

Elaina shook her head.

"Not any more she isn't. We haven't seen Harald and the army for weeks—came north hoping to steal a couple of horses."

"Is there something wrong with the ones you have?"

"Horses with people on them—two ladies and the world's best baby."

"You were planning to steal us out from the middle of the Imperial army?"

One of the riders spoke—young, bow, quiver, no armor, a stranger but something . . .

"Managed 'Laina's mother and three hundred of her friends. You're Anne?"

Elaina cut in.

"Your Majesty, this is our friend Asbjorn. 'Bjorn, Her Majesty of Kaerlia."

Anne responded with a friendly nod and a curious look.

"You rescued the Lady Commander and the rest of the prisoners? How? Where are they?"

"Legionaries are good soldiers—obey orders. Don't always check on where the order came from. Second time would have been harder. Aunt 'Nora and her friends should be back in Eston by now, sitting down to dinner a day late. Speaking of which, might consider the matter of food."

"'Bjorn!"

Kara, pointing north up the road. A moment later the others heard it too—at least one horse. Elaina handed the baby back to its mother, reached for her sword, moved past Anne; Asbjorn nocked an arrow.

A slight figure on a horse. Elaina let her sword slide back into its sheath.

"My lady. You're safe. Both of you. What happened to the stallion?"

"No idea; we weren't on him. Spent the night up a tree—little one as quiet as a mouse. In the morning you went north, we went south."

"Up there all night? I thought . . ."

"So did they. How did you get away?"

Elen dismounted, leaned over to kiss the baby.

"His Imperial Majesty sent me with a message. He says when the war's over, you're invited to guest with him in the Capital. Brought little 'Laina's linen, too."

She reached into the saddlebag. Asbjorn, hands again empty, turned to Jon and Hen.

"Set up camp out of sight of the road. We'll see what we can find for dinner, back when we find it."

He dismounted, said something to his horse—Anne caught tone but not words. Kara joined him. The two vanished into the woods. Anne looked after him, turned back to Elaina.

"Interesting friend you have. He reminds me of someone I know."

"His grandson. Parents died when 'Bjorn was a baby, Harald and Gerda raised him. Mother told me. Don't worry about dinner—only person I've ever seen Kara willing to hunt with."

Passing Through

**Triumph to some
Treasure to others.**

Some legions added something new every campaign; the Fourteenth was content with its red flame on a gold field. Marko remembered, two years back, one of his men asking with a straight face if it was true that after the Sixth brought in cats to protect their grain stores they had added a mouse to their banner to commemorate the victory. The riot that followed nearly wrecked the Boar.

Nobody but the First in the capital now, nobody else but him and his boys this end of the Empire. Not counting the legions on the other side of the low pass. The Emperor hadn't quite said so, but he figured they were why he was sitting on this side. Dangerous times.

A rider on the lower slopes, heading this way. Farther down, twenty or thirty more. South and east, smoke still rising. Maybe he would find out why. The legion commander stood up, brushed himself off, climbed down from the low observation platform, set off for the gateway of the camp to wait for the first rider and whatever news he brought.

"They drive off horses, cattle, burn what they can't steal. Thousands of them. Pania, garrison ran for their lives. Burned it."

"What about . . . Oh."

"Just you and the legion in the capital. Nothing else but city guards, a few locals. Everyone else down south fighting the barbarians."

"Commander. More visitors."

Marko turned, looked out the gate. They were sitting their horses a little out of range of the camp wall. Armor, leather by the look of it, brightly decorated. Bows, quivers. One rode a little forward, hands up, empty, palms out.

"Anyone here speak plains jabber?"

One of the men by the gate raised his head.

"I know a little, sir. Not much."

"Leave your weapons here."

The commander unbuckled his own sword belt, leaned the weapon against the wall, stepped out of the gate.

The leader of the nomads, brighter armor than the rest, stylized fox head tattooed on his forehead, greeted the commander in fluent Tengu.

"Me and my friends have a problem. So do you."

The commander looked curiously at him, said nothing.

"Our problem is getting home. You and yours are in the pass, more of you the other side."

"That's your problem, what's ours?"

"Us. Have to eat. The longer we stay this side of the pass, the less left behind when we go home." He gestured at the smoke still rising from the general direction of Pania. "Don't know if we can force the pass, damn sure you can't catch us on the level."

The commander thought a moment, looking out, down, where the plain funneled up to the pass.

"We both have a problem. What's your solution?"

"You get out of the way, we come through. Talk to your people on the other side of the pass first."

Two days later, Marko was wondering if his choices were right. The officer Artos had sent had agreed to the proposal—both forces to draw back, each watched from the top of the pass by a few of the other's men. The nomads free to come through the pass, out onto the western plains. Marko wondered if Artos planned to keep his side of the bargain with the nomads. Perhaps. Artos had to live with the plains as neighbors.

Marko didn't. From where he stood he could just see his men under cover, ready to come down on the nomad column where the road narrowed. Five hundred in ambush, five hundred more ready to move out of the camp, fall on the rear of the enemy. With Artos he would keep his agreement, but barbarians who burned an Imperial city were another matter.

"Commander."

The man sounded worried. From the top of the tower Marko could see why—a mass of men and beasts spread out across the valley floor. Too far to count heads, but after twenty years he had a fair idea how long, how wide, a column of a thousand cavalry should be. A thousand nomads he could manage, two thousand if the gods gave him luck. Five thousand were a problem for someone else to deal with. Maybe Artos. He started back down the stairs, yelling for a runner.

Sitting his horse a little below the top of the pass, Kiron looked west across the plains—at the limit of his vision a patch of green, again held by Eagle clan. Turning the other way, the first of the nomads coming through the pass.

One rode down to him. The leather armor was bright with elaborate designs. No tattoo—not a war chief. Bow one side, quiver the other, hand raised, empty. Time to see if they had a language in common. Not nomads—Westkin.

"Name Kiron. Speak for commander, Governor. Know you Valestalk, Tengu?"

"Getting better, but I still speak your language better than you speak mine."

A long pause.

"Niall?"

"In the flesh. Got bored with rabbits."

"This is your army?"

Niall shook his head.

"My brother Donal is war leader for Fox Clan at the moment, four hundred clan brothers. Eagle, Bear, half this end of the plains sent someone along for the ride. Some day you try to get a couple thousand Westkin, fourteen clans, all moving in the same direction. Make running the Empire feel like a vacation."

"And you came along to . . ."

"Just now, to sell some horses. Thought your father might be interested; heard he was a few short. Cavalry mounts. Trained. Even have the right brand."

"How many horses—trained cavalry mounts with the Imperial brand—are you prepared to sell us? Assuming we can agree on a price."

Niall looked at him, considered.

"Sure you want to know?"

Kiron nodded.

"Four thousand. Don't expect you'll want all of them. Give you a good price, though. Market, this end of the plains, not what it used to be."

It occurred to Kiron that raising and supplying an army off the resources of a mountain farm presented difficulties to which Harald, being Harald, found his own unique answers. This one had a certain wild logic to it.

Last Act

**For these things give thanks at nightfall:
The day gone, a guttered torch,
A sword tested, the troth of a maid,
Ice crossed, ale drunk**

The Emperor reached the top of the ridge, looked north. It was true. The bridge was there, unharmed. Beyond it the fort, gold flag flying. This time of year the army could ford if it had to, but getting the supply wagons across might have been a problem.

By late afternoon the legions were dug in on three sides of a square, the river the fourth, the wagons rumbling across the bridge into the safety of the fort. In the meadow south of the bridge the archers were forming up. Last would be the legions, the wall of men and dirt and spears that protected the rest. They had seen nothing but scouts as they came north, mostly cats; without cavalry they were marching blind. Somewhere south of him was an army.

News from the Empire, most especially the western end of it, was what he wanted now, but until the last wagon got off the bridge nothing was coming the other way. The officer he had sent ahead of the wagons had brought back only a report of enemy scouts on the south bank two days earlier. Should be a boat—odd that there wasn't—but he could wait. Getting the supplies to safety came first. He was good at waiting.

"Majesty!"

He looked up. The wagons were off the bridge, the last almost through the gate. The archers had started across. Something was wrong. The columns were shredding, men running away from the bridgehead, most of them south up the ridge. On the bridge itself, where there should have been a column six men wide crossing at a fast walk, a tangled mob.

He looked again. The north end of the bridge was gone, in its place a twenty foot gap. He thought he could see heads in the water.

Something caught his eye. The gold flag was coming down. As he watched, another rose, broke out in the wind. Darker gold, almost brown, a green circle. The banner of the Order. The gate swung shut.

An hour later, as he watched the fourth wall of the square go up south of the river, men with shovels working behind a wall of shields, the Emperor noticed a cluster of figures on the other side of the river, carrying something. A boat. One man turned to face the river, held up empty hands, palms out.

"Let them come. We can always kill them later."

Two men in the boat. One limped, the other, gray beard, one arm tightly bandaged to his side, stepped forward, saluted.

"Commander." He looked again, went clumsily to his knees. "Majesty."

"Get up—this is an army, not a court. Who are you, what the hell happened?"

"Under-captain Katelo, Majesty. Commander's dead. Almost two weeks back—dawn. We had a garrison of a hundred and fifty. Don't know how many the Karls had, but a lot more than that. Cavalry. Archers. Must have crossed at the next ford upstream."

"What do they have holding the fort now?"

"A couple of thousand archers, Majesty, mostly Order Ladies. Some crossbows came in two, three days ago. They have some heavy cavalry too. Our engines—four big bolt throwers, four little. I saw some stone throwers. Must have brought them—little ones."

"What else should I know?"

"The ford, Majesty. They spent most of a week digging it out, planting stakes. Two days ago a pack train came up from the south, over the bridge. Loaded with caltrops. Lady Commander was with them. She brought me along to watch her scatter them."

"Majesty." It was the other man. The Emperor turned to listen.

"Nomads, Majesty. Seen some two, three years back, scouting for us. This time there were thousands."

"Where are they?"

"Heading for the pass home. Karls sent me out with a couple of cats as escort, one day north, one west, one south, then back again. I didn't see any bodies; think they let the people run north. The nomads stole what they could—food, beasts—burnt what they couldn't carry.

Lady Commander says a sweep forty miles wide, here to the mountains. Her people have been foraging further east. She says if anyone plans to send a message to the capital, bird better carry provisions."

The Emperor looked around the familiar faces. This was the last time.

"Karls hold the fort, dug out the ford, planted stakes and caltrops in it. Harald is on the next ridge south, two thousand cats, a lot of Karl heavies. We have eight legions less losses, four thousand light infantry, maybe half archers, no cavalry worth mentioning. Food for maybe two days."

The commander of the Third legion was the first to break the silence: "Majesty. Karls got our supply wagons by tricking us, their men pretending they were ours. The only people who have seen the garrison, the work they did on the ford, are the ones they sent us."

"Good question. Three men in the Eighth, one in the Twelfth, know Katelo. Harald offered to let us send someone across, see for ourselves. I sent Claudio."

"Other fords, Majesty? There's one fourteen, fifteen miles downstream. Not as good as this one, but this late in the year we should be able to get men across."

"The Order is mounted archers. We send a big force west, they follow. It's a lot harder to wade neck deep when there are people shooting at you. If we stay on the back side of the ridge out of their sight, Harald sees us. He's got to have signals set up with the fort.

"Somehow we do it. We pray for clouds over the moon, march all night, cross at dawn. The Order doesn't make it to the lower ford in time, or do and we force it. You're the Lady Commander. All cavalry—can go home any time you like. What do you do first?"

He looked around his commanders. One face after another. Justin put it in a harsh whisper: "Burn our supplies."

The Emperor nodded. "March tonight, cross at dawn, march tomorrow, take the fort back—with no engines, no heavy gear. Eleven thousand exhausted men, less than a day's food. Country cleaned out. Nothing to feed an army this side of the capital."

"They accepted? It's over?"

Harald looked back at his daughter, nodded.

"By now it's signed and sealed, probably on the way here. Legions surrender. Leave their gear, keep personal stuff. Cross the bridge in small groups, get ten days' food, go. Officers and banners stay till the ransom is paid—two gold pieces a man."

"The Emperor?" She was looking at something over his shoulder.

"Emperor gets to go home." He turned.

One rider coming up the slope. Harald and Caralla stood watching. By the time he had reached the top and dismounted, the others had joined them.

The Emperor came forward. His gilded armor was splashed with mud and he limped a little, catching himself once with his stick. He looked at Harald with fierce falcon eyes.

"Won, have you? The best general alive, I'll give you that."

Harald stood there, Caralla on his right, Stephen on his

left, the three boys and Elaina standing wide eyed by Caralla. The Emperor handed him the scroll.

"Beat me, but that doesn't end it. My clever son waiting in the West with his pet general. It's their game now. Your lady friend, where was she?"

"The Lady Leonora commanded the defense of the Royal castle."

"Easier work than riding around with her damned lady archers. She won't be in the field again. One less. You're not young either."

"No."

"A few years. Time for them to build back what you wrecked here. You'll be older.

"The Commander. Artos. Sitting by the fire on your cold mountain, Harald Haraldsson, while he rides south. Think your little king can take him, do you? Your little king you kept where you could hold his hand and your lady friend his castle for him? You won't be there. She won't. He will."

He fell silent a moment, glancing about. Hen looked up at him.

"You there, boy. Remember. When you're full grown and I'm maybe buried. You'll see the Gold Banner flying where your king's banner flies today. I lost the battle, but dead or alive I'll win the war. Remember."

He struck Hen hard on the shin with his stick.

"Remember."

Hen stood like a statue, looking up at him. The Emperor looked round once more, turned, walked back to his horse.

Hen stood silent. After a moment Elaina spoke.

"What a fierce old man."

"Three brothers on his way to the throne. The Old Emperor's death was—very convenient."

Jon spoke. "He's wrong. Our king's brave as can be."

Hen looked up.

"Courage loses as many battles as it wins. Harald told me that, winter he guested with us."

Caralla turned to Harald.

"Is he right then?"

"By the time he gets home he will have thought again. Two loyal legions in the West, one of them in the Western Capital. Lots more east and south of here in the old provinces along the coast. Enough, perhaps, to stand against his son. He has played the game longer than any man alive."

"So the Prince will lose?"

"No fool either, and time on his side. Make peace, fight, not fight, play for power. Six months ago the Emperor's game, although the princes didn't know. This past month, we changed that."

Stephen turned from watching the Emperor riding back to his own lines.

"Because he doesn't have an army any more?"

"It isn't just the army. Legion he best trusts is in the capital. A man who wastes legions and lets foreign troops ravage his countryside. How many will support his last few years? It isn't a war they're fighting with each other."

"Then he's right. Ten years, fifteen at the most, an army bigger than ours, a competent Emperor, a more than competent general. Hard enough with the balance the other way." Caralla spoke in a hushed voice.

"His other mistake he was looking right at. Never saw."

"What do you mean?"

He put one hand on Caralla's mailed shoulder.

"Commander comes south, it isn't the King he'll have to face, Daughter."

> Cattle die, kindred die,
> Every man is mortal:
> But the good name never dies
> Of one who has done well.

Glossary

Alteng: Language of what are now the western provinces of the Empire.

Belkhani: People from the province of Belkhan, recruited by the Empire as heavy cavalry.

Bashkai: Forest dwellers recruited by the Empire as light infantry.

Cacade: Ten decades.

Caltrop: Four pointed metal object, designed so that one point is always pointing up to injure a man or horse that steps on it.

Captain: Middle level officer.

Cat: (Cataphract) Heavy horse archer/lancer.

Commander (1): High ranking officer commanding a legion or unit of comparable size, a fortification, or an army. (Empire)

Commander (2), The: Artos

Decade: Unit of ten.

Helper: Male associate of the Order. Typically farmer on Order land.
Hetman: Commander of Bashkai.

Highborn (1): Noble. (Empire)

Highborn (2): Dialect of Tengu used by nobles.

Ilash: Plains nomads in their own language ("people").

Karl: Inhabitant of the kingdom of Kaerlia (Imperial slang).

Lady: Adult member of the Order.

Lady Commander: Commanding officer of the Order.

Lashi: Plains language.

Leatherback: Slang for light cavalry (leather armor). (Empire)

Maril: Neighbors of Kaerlia to the southeast. Mercenary heavy cavalry.

Monster: Slang for (big) counterweighted trebuchet.

Most Noble: Member of the Imperial family.

Nightbell: Hallucinogenic mushroom.

Octave: Unit of eight.

Order, the: A female military order, self-ruling, now mostly in Kaerlia.

Paramount: Top level of the Vales legal hierarchy. A lawman must be associated with a paramount, a landowner with a lawman, in order to connect to the legal system. The associations are voluntary in both directions. Each paramount is associated with a specific vale for historical reasons.

Pavise: Large shield for an archer, supported by a prop.

Rock thrower: Traction trebuchet.

Senior Paramount: The Mainvale paramount.

Siege bow: Very heavy crossbow, slow rate of fire.

Sister (1): Any Lady of the Order.

Sister (2): Within the Order, close comrade.

Tatave: Eight octaves. (Order)

Tengu: Imperial language.

Turtle (1): Infantry formation with a roof of shields. (Empire)

Turtle (2): (slang) Legionary. (Empire)

Twenty-year man: Retired legionary.

Westkin: Plains nomad. (Vales)

Wolf: Member of the Royal Messengers (Wolf's head badge). (Kaerlia)

MORE ...
ERIC FLINT